W9-COJ-994

SCARS AND STRIPES FOREVER

Claudia Turner

ISBN: 1492346306
ISBN 13: 9781492346302
Library of Congress Control Number: 2013916329
CreateSpace Independent Publishing Platform
North Charleston, South Carolina

To tiny dancer, as we count the headlights on the highway

Acknowledgements

Sometime during 1989, my postdoctoral advisor, Eric, loaned me a book called, *Mafia Kingfish: Carlos Marcello and the Assassination of John F. Kennedy* by John H. Davis. I was hooked and continued to read voraciously, transitioning from an "Oswald did it" mindset to one more skeptical. So thank you Eric for making me the conspiracy "nut" that I remain today.

My reading led me to admire and respect the many researchers and witnesses who have dedicated their livelihoods and, in some cases, their lives, to bringing the truth about the Kennedy assassination to light. I hope that I have done them justice by presenting the results of their courage and conviction in a way that inspires people to demand the truth behind what happened that day in Dallas.

As a rookie in the world of fiction, I am grateful for the assistance of those who helped bring this story to fruition. I thank the instructors at Grub Street in Boston, notably, Cam, Grace, and Becky, who helped me appreciate the craft of writing. While there, I was also fortunate to meet many talented fellow students and would like to call out my writing group, Brenda, Elizabeth, Alyssa and Lisa, who provided valuable input that helped shape this work. Rowan at Grub Street enabled me to enlist the expertise of award-winning and best-selling novelist, Ben Winters, who provided excellent guidance through his review and critique of the manuscript.

I value the assistance of my Create Space team for getting this book published. You made a complicated process manageable, and your professionalism is unsurpassed.

To my family and friends, who endured my incessant talk about the book without rolling their eyes, thank you. Your confidence in, and caring for me were instrumental to its completion and mean more than you'll ever know. Specifically, I want to thank the following: Cyndy, for your help with scene-setting, numerous reviews and vigorous support of my dreams; Sandy and Gail, for your meticulous proof-reading, humor, and words of encouragement; Jen, for lending your artistic eye; Judith, for the reality check. Bruce, thanks for sharing your experience which helped bring some credibility to the story. Betsy, your timing could not have been better. I was despairing over whether the story would ever see the printed page and your enthusiastic response kept me going.

Last, but far from least, I want to express my sincere gratitude to my sweetie, Luanne, who patiently read and provided insightful comments on almost every iteration of this work and, most importantly, never stopped believing in me. I love you.

Prologue

By the time he heard about the fire, the first responders and curiosity seekers had long since departed. Still, he raced home only to find his life's work reduced to ashes. He staggered into what was left of his office, kicking away the charred remains of books and papers.

Upon hearing the grinding of gravel, he looked up and saw a Hummer enter the drive. A hulking man climbed from the car and padded, panther-like, toward the wreckage, carrying a large cardboard box. His demeanor was as black as his suit.

"So you're the one who called me?"

Absorbing the enormity of the destruction, the stranger nodded and handed him the parcel. He took the box and saw his name, Robbie O'Toole, penned neatly by her hand.

The stranger quick-marched back to his Hummer as though on a mission. Before climbing in, he turned and finally spoke. "She went through hell to get that to you."

Alone again, Robbie placed the box on the ground, pulled out a pocket knife, and slit the packing tape with an angry swipe. The first thing he saw was a cassette that sat on top of papers, film reels, and flash drives.

He carried the box to his car, retrieved his reporter's tape recorder from under the seat, and placed the cassette inside. He reached for his hip flask and gulped a healthy swig of the anesthetic, feeling it both soothe and burn his throat. "Here's to you, Kat." He took one more swallow and hit "play," wincing at the sound of her voice, which seemed unusually fragile.

"Hi Robbie. I guess I petted one too many bears. I want to explain everything, but don't have much time. I hope the contents of this box help you find your truth. For what it's worth, I would have said yes." There was a pause. Then, in a bolder voice, she continued, "It all began about a month ago when Ben Douglas called me to his office."

CHAPTER ONE

"I've got a job for you, Hastings. Get over here. Now."

I hadn't heard from Ben in months and he picks four o'clock on a Friday afternoon to contact me about another one of his "jobs." I logged off, filed some papers in my desk drawer, and locked it, thinking about Pam and Trevor's party and hoping that whatever gofer assignment Ben had in mind didn't destroy the weekend. Pam had promised a surprise.

I pushed the paper-clip holder to the back of my desk, straightened my chair, and adjusted the frame of my Intelligence Commendation until it was perfectly straight. Although a year had passed since I'd received the medal, referred to as a jockstrap award within the Company, I still could not resist reading its words:

> *For the performance of commendable service that exceeded normal duties and contributed significantly to the mission of the Central Intelligence Agency, this Commendation is issued to Katharine Hastings in recognition of her meritorious service to her country in the fight against international terrorism.*

It was the most satisfying achievement in my thirty years with the Agency. When I received it, I thought that maybe Ben's frivolous assignments would end. I was wrong.

In need of some fresh air, I decided to go outside and cross the grounds to Ben's office. I donned my blue pea coat and pulled a wool cap over what my father had dubbed my Katharine Hepburn red hair. Supposedly, I was named for her. I walked downstairs to the lobby, pushed open the wide doors of the original headquarters building, or OHB, where I worked, and glanced at the façade. Even though the name, "The George Bush Center of Intelligence," now adorned the building, old-timers like Ben and me still referred to the site as Langley.

I cut across the courtyard to the new headquarters building, or NHB, which consisted of two six-story towers of glass and steel built into the hillside behind the OHB. The transition between the old and new CIA was mirrored in the contrasting architecture of the two buildings. I loved the skylights, sweeping arches, and open spaces of the NHB and welcomed the opportunity to leave my rabbit warren in the OHB behind.

I pressed the elevator button for Ben's floor. As the deputy chief of clandestine operations division, he enjoyed a corner office at the end of the hall. I walked slowly and quietly by closed office doors, hoping that Ben had something of substance for me this time. Raising my hand to knock, I paused, knuckles in midair, and took a deep breath. "Never tip your hand," my father would say. "Be ready for anything."

Ben beckoned me into his spacious office. I faced the back of his head as he sat in his leather-bound chair, gazing through broad windows to a spectacular view of the OHB and the campus beyond, not making any effort to greet me. That wasn't unusual. He could be as cold, hard, and secretive as the file cabinets that flanked him. My 201 file, which contained all of my training and operational experience, sat opened on his massive mahogany desk. I took a chair on the other side.

"What's up?"

"How much do you know about the Kennedy assassination?" he asked, still facing the window.

I stared at the back of his grizzled head, wondering why he'd dragged me up here to ask me about a long-ago event. Despite the many books, various "confessions," and thousands of previously classified documents that were now in the public domain, I knew very little. I was about to say as much when he abruptly swiveled around to face me.

"Since the fiftieth anniversary, we've been under considerable pressure to provide more information. I've been reviewing documents being prepared for public release." He meant redacted. "I came across this one." Ben waved a piece of paper that he had been holding in front of me. "It refers to a room here at Langley that was set up in the late fifties by the Op-40 guys." Bending toward me, his ball-bearing eyes blazing, Ben snapped, "I want you to find it and tell me what's inside."

My hands sprang up with palms facing out. "Wait a minute. Who's Op-40?"

"They were a wild bunch. Cuba, South America—assassinations, coups, invasions—nasty stuff." He pulled out a 1964 floor plan and spread it on the desk between us, pushing my 201 file aside. Ben circled an area in the depths of the OHB, a place I had never been—not surprising given that the OHB had over a million square feet of office space. "Funny thing is," he continued, "I come across a memo mentioning a room and, suddenly, renovations are ordered right here." He pointed to the circled area. "Supposedly this floor was 'flooded out' during the last hurricane, and they need to 'renovate.'" He raised two fingers on both hands in mock quotation marks. "Bullshit. Damn building's been here for more than fifty years and never flooded."

I swallowed the bile rising in my throat, caused by yet another lame assignment. "So let me get this straight. You think there *might* be a room that *may* contain something of *potential* importance which *may* be lost due to some trumped up reason for renovating the area?" A sigh of frustration escaped my throat. "If this room contained something incriminating, wouldn't it have been destroyed by now?"

He shot me a look that was equal parts irritation and reluctance. When he finally spoke, it was with a detached and bitter voice. "Back then, the Red Scare gave rogue agents carte blanche to do whatever they damn well pleased while presidents and Congress looked the other way; people more powerful than them were pulling the strings. These agents knew that if they hid something, no one would touch it. Now most of them are gone, that is, except your father."

My father is Henry Hastings, known inside the Agency as H2. I joined the Company against his wishes; however, he made sure that I reported to Ben, a man he trained. Women operatives were rare in the seventies, which may have been the reason I was fast-tracked through the Agency's equivalent of basic training, including: self-defense,

3

evasive measures, encryption, and firearms. But just as my career began to take off, Father intervened again, arranging my transfer to the terrorism analysis department. No daughter of his would sully her hands with the dark deeds of clandestine ops. So instead of traveling the world stalking the bad guys, I monitored their activity from the confines of my cubicle. The mother of all domestic terrorist attacks, 9/11, necessitated the invention of the TIDE database, compiled by sixteen different US intelligence agencies. My job was to find the needle in the haystack of more than five hundred thousand known and suspected terrorists who are listed in this database and avoid a second 9/11.

And now, all I could think of were the hours of work awaiting me. "Isn't there someone else who can do this? I'm up to my eyeballs."

"It can wait." He skimmed his close-cropped hair and added, "I need someone who has a low profile. If this room is for real, and if there's something in there concerning Kennedy's assassination, I want to know about it. The last thing we need is another leak. The conspiracy nuts would have a field day."

"Don't you think if there was something to the conspiracy, we'd know it by now? Besides, you have plenty of other *low-profile* people." Even I could hear the brittleness in my voice.

He clutched the edge of his desk, whitening his fingers. Although always intense, this reaction came as a surprise. Maybe there was more to this than I thought. "You're H2's daughter—he's a legend around here. No one would dare hurt you. You'll be retiring soon and will disappear. You're meticulous. I need meticulous." He released the desk and sat back. The color returned to his fingers, but drained from his face. "And I trust you."

His neck was as taut as the tie that bound it and now, so was my spine. So he wouldn't notice my apprehension, I looked off into the distance, somewhere beyond Ben, his broad desk, his diplomas and awards, his golf trophies, through the window past the vast parking lot to the pewter sky of McLean, Virginia. "What do you mean, 'no one would hurt me'?"

"It means, just find the damn room and tell me what's in it." He pulled out a piece of paper and thrust it at me. "Here's a schedule. You have an expanded security clearance and can go anywhere in Langley.

A computer guy named Wheeler has overridden the security system. No one can follow your movements around the campus on these days, so stick to it. Start Monday."

He meant Greg Wheeler, a man who joined the Company when I did. We'd attended the same orientation class and remained friends ever since. I attended the weddings of his children and always took time to see the latest picture of his grandchildren. I liked his quirkiness. Like a true child of the sixties, Greg gave his gadgets pet names, like "The Led Zeppelin," a special bullet that disintegrated on impact, making it impossible to trace, or "The Strawberry Alarm Clock," which had a home surveillance device hidden inside. He'd wear a short-sleeved shirt with khakis and sneakers in the middle of winter. An unruly lock of hair flopped over his forehead, making him look like a little kid going gray. But Greg was always there to listen or provide pep talks and that made him the closest thing to a real friend I had at Langley.

While I examined the list of dates on the paper and mentally tried to dovetail them with my current workload, Ben added, "One more thing, only you and I know about this project. You're not to tell anyone, especially your father."

"My father?"

Ben rubbed his upper lip and looked away, "H2 still has considerable influence here at the Company. I can't let him interfere."

I willed him to meet my eyes, but when he did, he said something peculiar. "One more thing. Don't try to put any pieces together—just inventory. Got it?"

"Hold on." I jumped out of my chair. "If I *do* find this room, and if there *is* something in it, you're telling me *not* to analyze it? Analysis is what I do. I don't get it."

"Dammit, Hastings. Do you have to question everything?" The veins in his neck bulged like cables. When he spoke again, it was in a far more temperate voice. "Kat," he had never called me by my nickname before, "I don't know where this could lead. You may see things that few people have. Sure, most of the players are dead, but there are those who may go to great lengths to learn what you may learn, either to expose the truth or bury it deeper. RYBAT, got it?" Hearing the word RYBAT, a CIA code word for highly confidential, made the hairs on my neck spring to attention. "If anyone asks you what you're up to, just tell them you're... you're...I don't know, tell them you're assessing flood damage." Then he snorted.

"Got it." Keeping something from my father was not a problem. We hardly spoke to each other. But I didn't understand Ben's anxiety. Maybe this assignment *was* different, but I didn't want to get my hopes up. I had known Ben for too long.

"I'm going out of town. I want a full report when I get back next week. Punch these numbers into your phone. Call me if anything goes wrong."

Then his phone rang. "Douglas," he answered. A scowl marred his face. With a backward wave he motioned me to leave, but on my way out I heard him say, "Yeah, I'm still on board, but it's too soon. No guarantees."

I left and descended in the elevator, walking briskly through the atrium, passing various sculptures, including a piece dedicated to William Stephenson, the man they called Intrepid. All were inspirational in their own way; all underscored the value of the Agency and its people. Seeing the images added a little more spring to my step, and even though my career was nowhere near as daring as I had once hoped, a good feeling warmed me every time I saw them. They made me proud of my work. But at fifty-nine and with thirty years' service, I wanted to accept the silver retirement medallion without regrets and yet, I still held out some desperate hope for one last hurrah before calling it quits.

Although glad that I could still go to Pam and Trevor's party, my thoughts soon gave way to the assignment and then to the Kennedy assassination. I remembered it vividly. Right after we returned from recess, our principal lumbered into our fourth-grade classroom and whispered something to our teacher. Her face blanched. Her shoulders bowed. In a strained voice, she told us to go home. I sprinted the entire way, ecstatic to be released from school on such a sunny, crisp fall day and hoping for an early kickball game with the kids on my block. I tore open the door of our house and yelled "I'm home" and ran to the kitchen for a snack, rummaging through the fridge and then the cookie jar. While stuffing Oreos into my mouth, it occurred to me that my mother hadn't come to greet me, so I searched the house for her. A heap of dirty clothes lay on the laundry-room floor. The Hoover Upright, still plugged into the wall, stood in the middle of the living room. The bedrooms were empty. I heard a sound from the den and ran toward it.

I found her sitting on the edge of the green sofa that we'd bought from Sears during their Veteran's Day sale two weeks before. Her shoulders heaved with ghastly sobs, causing the tattered Kleenex in her hand to shake like a flag of surrender. With eyes swollen and red, she stared at Walter Cronkite's grim face plastered on the black-and-white TV, her hand covering her mouth.

"What's wrong, Mom?" I wrapped my arms around her. She hugged me so hard I thought I would break.

"They killed him. They killed the president. I wish your father was home. I'm worried about him."

But my father was never at home when it mattered—not for my first day of school, my prom, or my graduation and he barely made it in time to escort me down the aisle at my wedding. When he was home, he wasn't—not emotionally anyway. His face was a mask and what lurked behind, one didn't want to know, but I did know one thing. When he returned from that trip in November of 1963, his luggage bore a tag that read, "Dallas."

CHAPTER TWO

I threw my keys on the table in the foyer of my Shirlington Village apartment in Arlington, Virginia, where I had lived for almost twenty years—long enough to see restaurants come and go, the construction of the two-story grocery store, make casual friends at bars like The Bungalow, and frequent The Curious Grape, my personal favorite. Scout, my ninety-pound lab-rottie mix, bounded toward me. Two years before, I found Scout in an animal shelter. The many times I came home exasperated by the day's events and was welcomed by him, leash in mouth and prancing like Nureyev, I wondered who'd rescued whom.

While Scout inhaled his dinner, I removed my tailored, wool pantsuit and hung it next to others like it in the closet. I tossed my silk blouse into the dry-cleaning bag to drop off with the concierge and returned my silver necklace and earrings to their spot in the jewelry box. Ben said I was meticulous; some might call it OCD. Early stages of arthritis gnarled my fingers, so I wore no rings. That excuse allowed me to deny the real reason; there was no special person in my life.

Once upon a time, there had been a special person—Robbie O'Toole. Robbie asked me to marry him, even asked for my father's approval, but H2 forbade it. Back then, that meant something. Today, we would have married anyway. I never forgave myself; nor did Robbie—especially when I settled for Nate, a pilot who flew with numerous flight attendants, literally and figuratively. Our marriage lasted five years—five years too long. I sighed as I realized that the only marriage that did last was that to my job, and now I was contemplating a divorce from it as well.

Thankfully, my other joints still worked well enough for an evening run. I threw on jogging clothes, stepped into a pair of Asics, and pulled my hair into a ponytail, drawing it through the hole in back of an Orioles baseball cap. Within minutes, Scout and I were out the door and on the main street of Shirlington, passing restaurants of every ethnicity as we ran toward the river. The late fall air had an invigorating effect as Scout ensured a brisk pace. He knew my routine.

The first mile was always a chore. My breathing was not yet rhythmic; my steps clunky, not fluid. But sometime during the second mile, I entered the zone, where thoughts about the day's events swirled randomly. My new assignment seemed trivial, except that Ben's intensity suggested otherwise. Then I wondered about the snippet of the conversation I'd overheard. What did Ben mean that he was on board, but that it was too soon? He was to return in a week and expected my report then. Was there a connection? Ben was fairly high up in clandestine services, but I had little knowledge of his department, even though once I had been one of them.

Finally, my thoughts meandered to the upcoming party, a mini-reunion of sorts. What was the surprise Pam mentioned? Could it be Robbie? He moved to California after we split. I heard he married, so I gave up any notion of reconnecting, not that he would consider it. We didn't part on the best of terms. I forced the thought from my mind. I didn't want to entertain false hopes. Instead, I focused on how fun it might be to see some old college chums. At the very least, it would certainly beat another weekend spent home alone, reading mystery novels.

By the time we returned, I was ready for a steamy shower and a hearty dinner. It had been a good run, and I felt both spent and revived as we entered the elevator and rode to my floor. When the door slid open, I slogged down the corridor to my apartment and pulled out my key. It was then that I noticed the door was partially open. I was sure that I had locked it.

I could feel a tingling sensation at the nape of my neck as I cautiously peered inside, letting Scout free to run ahead of me. My heart pounded faster than it had while jogging. My apartment was quiet except for Scout's panting and jumping about near the pantry, anxious for his usual post-run treat. Had he done otherwise, I would know someone was still inside.

Regardless, I removed a stun gun from the utility drawer in the foyer and slowly entered, checking the living room, kitchenette, both baths, and the guest bedroom. Every muscle tensed. I watched for any movement, listened for any sound. I pushed hard on my bedroom door, slamming it into the wall behind in case someone stood behind it, waiting to pounce. There was no one, nothing except for a single yellow rose resting on a pillow at the head of my bed. A note was attached that read:

Enter the vault and you will die. Rest in Peace.

Ben's room *must* exist, and it meant something to someone.

The wine I drank was less for enjoyment and more to calm myself after finding the intruder's note. I had no idea how he got in. The lock wasn't forced. I checked with the concierge; he'd seen no one, nor did he give anyone elevator access. I felt violated and vulnerable, enough to swish and swirl the wine like mouthwash. I tasted hints of cherry, currant, and was it, chocolate? Tomorrow, I'd get a second dead bolt. I couldn't call the police. They'd ask too many questions—not a good thing in my line of work.

After jamming a chair under the doorknob and ensuring the door was locked, I wrapped myself in a comfy robe and sat back in my recliner with my laptop open. I Googled "Op-40." Numerous links appeared; the one I clicked on revealed that Operation 40 was created by Eisenhower, headed by his vice-president, Nixon, and included high-ranking members of the CIA, NSA, Defense, and anti-Castro Cubans. They organized, equipped, and trained Cuban refugees to use interrogation, torture, assassination, and guerilla warfare in their attempts to overthrow Castro. When that didn't work, Op-40 created Brigade 2056, consisting of fifteen hundred CIA-trained Cuban exiles who fought in the Bay of Pigs invasion. Several more names popped out—David Atlee Phillips, David Morales, Frank Sturgis and E. Howard Hunt, all names dropped by my father over the years.

The more I read, the more I drank, and then I remembered an August Saturday drenched in humidity. My family arrived at a party to welcome Mr. Morales and Mr. Phillips home from Mexico City. My sisters ran to the group of teenagers who were talking about the Beatles going to India and the hippies to San Francisco. I strolled to the far lawn, partially hidden by some azaleas, and saw my father with some men. I ducked behind an ancient oak and listened, unable to hear what they were saying until one of the men got angry and yelled something like, "Get Liddy or Sturgis or Hunt for your break-in. I'm done." The others told him to keep it down. The cabal disbanded, but my father stayed behind with Mr. Phillips. His face was like concrete, his eyes dark, and his brow creased. Something was wrong.

But it was 1968; all sorts of things were wrong. Martin Luther King was killed in April and Bobby Kennedy was killed in June. Rioters burned cities and draft cards burned on campuses. Dr. Spock, whose guidance shaped my entire generation, was jailed for protesting the Vietnam War where more than half a million American soldiers now fought, many against their will. We all wore tie-dye shirts, bell bottoms, wide belts, and long hair and claimed that we were nonconformists.

I remained at my watch until my father and Mr. Phillips returned to the party, socializing as though nothing had happened. I hadn't thought of that incident until Watergate exploded on the front page of every newspaper in the country, but I didn't say a word. It was a family rule: don't ask and definitely, don't tell.

I logged off, unable to stop the questions bombarding my brain. Who had been in my apartment? Ben said my assignment was confidential, but obviously someone knew about it. How did they know my routine? Were they just trying to scare me? If so, why? Why didn't they confront me in person? If they did confront me, would I be in danger? What kind of information might I find? How could it be so damaging? And what the hell was I getting into?

It was time to pay my friend, Greg Wheeler, a visit. In addition to a computer expertise that enabled him to fool the security system so I could search for Ben's room undetected, his genius enabled him to create the latest in technical tradecraft used by agents in the field. It had been ages since I'd been in the field. I hardly knew how to play the game anymore. Not only did I need to learn the rules, I needed new equipment. Next time, I'd be ready.

CHAPTER THREE

I called Ben the next morning and told him about the rose and its accompanying warning. He was clearly agitated, as evidenced by a series of rapid-fire questions concerning time, place, and content of the message. He assured me that he had taken every precaution to keep the assignment RYBAT, but would look into it and make some further arrangements. He asked if I wanted off the assignment. I said no.

It took most of the day to find and install a second dead-bolt lock, but now that it was in place, I could focus on Pam and Trevor's party, a temporary distraction from my home invasion. Pam was an old friend from the University of Virginia that I'd run into in Georgetown a month ago. We promised to stay in touch and, true to her word, she called and invited me to a dinner party at her house. "You'll have a great time," she said. "Some of our classmates from the Stone Age will be there." Pam was right. I needed to get out more. It would be good to see some friends from my past and perhaps meet some new ones.

I obsessed over what to wear, tossing numerous outfits on the bed before settling on a pair of black, slightly flared wool slacks, short black boots, and a white silk blouse—basic, dressy enough, but not too much. I pulled my hair back, let it down, and pulled it back again before finally leaving it fall to my shoulders. I was going to go with a gold necklace and gold hoop earrings, but at the last minute selected a necklace with large, chunky gray, black, and white stones. A routine that normally took a few minutes took much longer and made me realize that I was eager, but also more than a little nervous—maybe even anxious. Revisiting my past could be a mixed blessing.

I rushed downstairs and to my car, a British racing-green BMW convertible. I pressed the remote ignition and smirked when I remembered my father's words. "In the city, you don't want to be fumbling with keys if someone is waiting to mug you." I zoomed off, hoping that DC's infamous traffic would cut me a break and I'd make it by seven o'clock—just in time for drinks before dinner.

Pam and Trevor lived in Old Town Alexandria. Their 1800s townhouse sat on a narrow street of tightly packed, brick homes. I walked up three marble steps to a flagstone stoop and rang the doorbell next to the weathered oak door. Shifting from one foot to the other, I turned to survey the panorama of Lee Street Park and the river beyond. Pam and Trevor must be doing well to afford this view.

Pam, flushed from hostessing, welcomed me inside. *The Big Chill* soundtrack played in the background. I stood in the grand foyer, awed by the large palms, ornate urns, and brass light fixtures. I gazed up at the ten-foot ceilings, down at the wide-plank, heart-of-pine floors, and then at the intricate molding that caressed each doorway. She called Trevor in for greetings.

"I'm so glad you could make it. You remember Trevor," she said. I hadn't seen Trevor since their wedding. The years had treated him well— tall, trim, and tanned with streaks of gray in his dark, wavy hair. Were it not for the Georgetown University crew-neck sweater with the Hoya logo, Trevor would pass for landed gentry, not a city denizen. Pam, a petite, fair-skinned, sandy-haired, rugged beauty, fit well within his arm that gently enveloped her waist. She was wearing a UVA sweater and UVA earrings.

"Nice to see you again, Trev. Thanks for the invite. Your home is beautiful!"

His genial smile melted my anxiety and dissolved the concerns now preoccupying me. He offered to get me a drink and left to retrieve a glass of Zinfandel.

Pam pulled me into a living room that looked like a museum. Maybe its formality caused guests to congregate elsewhere; I could hear their voices from other rooms. In a conspiratorial voice she said, "I'll be right back." She winked at me and was gone. I looked around the room and admired the Tabriz Oriental rug and the majestic red-blue-and-gold chintz curtains. Mint-condition antiques, including: rosewood-inlaid end tables, embroidered ottomans, Tiffany lamps, and a humpback sofa, surrounded me. It was like stepping back in time to a nineteenth-century parlor.

Trevor returned with the wine. We made small talk, mostly about the house and his job as a history professor at Georgetown, piquing my attention when he mentioned his specialty, the Cold War era. I was about to probe that further, but Pam returned with a man in tow. I would have recognized him anywhere. Robbie O'Toole. His curly hair now looked more like granite than coal, but his eyes were just as blue and his smile just as electric, eliciting long-dormant sparks I hadn't felt since—well, since I last saw him. But there was a scar—an ugly, red, jagged slash from his ear to his chin.

In an instant, I remembered Robbie's painful puns, his taste in food, movies, and music. I remembered his encouraging words, and his willingness to challenge the very institutions that my father worshipped. He was five feet ten inches of pure kinetic energy, and his crusades left me both invigorated and exhausted, like the time I missed my eight-o'clock class because of his all-night anti-war protest. Then there was the weekend we spent repairing houses in the slums of Richmond. My arms were stiff for days.

My father called Robbie a troublemaker, saying that I deserved better. Just thinking about it made me angry, both at my father for his narrow-mindedness and for my own weakness. Life with Robbie would have been so different from my sham marriage with Nate, a man of whom my father approved. Now here was Robbie, thirty-five years later, with the same crooked smile, the same mischievous glint in his eye, but also that profane scar.

"I'll be damned. Kat Hastings. How's it goin'?" His voice transported me back to a time of carefree runs through the woods and picnics on the quad, before life's stones found their mark. We stared at each other until it became awkward. Pam yanked Trevor's arm and told him they had to talk to Beau, another ghost from my past.

"It's so good to see you. I don't know where to begin," I paused, hoping that the warmth of my face didn't mean I was blushing. "How long has it been?" I asked, even though I knew exactly how long it had been to the day, maybe even the hour.

"Let's see, when did you dump me for Nate?" His voice, though light, threw me.

"Not my best decision," I said, shaking my head and looking down. "It didn't last." He asked me what happened. All I could say was, "Different priorities, I guess." I wasn't ready to give him the satisfaction of knowing that Nate was a philanderer, just as Robbie warned me he'd be. Eager to change the topic, I asked, "So what do you do?"

"Let's see, after UVA, I went to Columbia for journalism and then took a job as a reporter in San Francisco. I moved back East a few months ago. I freelance now. It's kind of liberating not having to produce a column every day, and I can write about the things that interest me." He gestured with strong, workman-like hands. I couldn't help notice that he wore no rings. "How about you?"

"I, um, work for the State Department. It's a desk job—research, analysis. Not very exciting." I was hoping that he wouldn't delve further. Technically, it wasn't a lie since my department did report up through State.

"Always daddy's little girl." That stung and he sensed it. His face softened. "Sorry. I guess old feelings die hard. Is he still alive?"

"Yes, but my mother passed a couple of years ago," I answered quietly, subdued by the memory. "I don't go home much anymore. It's too hard with my mother gone and my father...," I attempted a smile, "well, he's...he's still the same."

"Sorry to hear it." He said it more as a joke than with any bitterness. In a kinder voice he continued, "My parents are both gone. It's just my brother, sister, and me now. Gives you a whole different perspective. The torch has been passed, and we're the senior generation now. Scary thought, isn't it? If we're going to do something with our lives, it's now or never."

"But you have done something with your life," I said. He just nodded, unconvinced. We shifted to neutral topics like family, friends, and where we lived while avoiding the elephant squatting between us. It was going well, that is, until my next words tumbled out before I could catch them. "I heard that you were married."

"My wife died." He traced his scar. His pain seemed fresh. For the first time, I noticed the years etched in his face.

"I'm sorry," was all I could manage.

We stood in an awkward silence until he eventually smiled. "Nice place, huh?"

"They must be paying faculty well these days," I said, trying to restore goodwill. "I guess I'm in the wrong business." I hated this small talk. We had never been superficial with each other. Without thinking, I gently placed a finger on his scar and asked, "How did this happen?" He pushed my hand away. His smile vanished, and the room swiftly became cold and dark. He didn't answer. I'd asked too much too soon.

Thankfully, Pam announced that dinner was being served, so we joined the others in the dining room. I took a seat at one end and was relieved when Robbie sat next to me. Pam was on the other side. Throughout the salad, pecan-encrusted salmon, new potatoes, and green beans almondine, Robbie and I reminisced about days gone by. It never failed. I'd take a forkful of food and he'd have me laughing so hard, I was afraid I'd choke. Occasionally Pam would chime in but, otherwise, it felt as if we were the only two people at the table. Somehow the years vanished and I felt young again.

At one point, I looked up and saw another college boyfriend, Beau, staring at me from the other end of the table. Beau and I dated early in my freshman year. He took me to nice restaurants, for rides in his bright red sports car, or we'd hang out at his apartment. He was the only freshman I knew that enjoyed such a luxurious life. Back then, my head was easily turned, and Beau was considered quite the catch. Not only was he rich and drop-dead handsome, he was a good guy who was well liked. I felt badly for leading him on and when I met Robbie, I knew I had to break it off. I went to Beau's apartment, hoping to end it gently. He became angry and told me to get the hell out. I walked the mile back to my dorm alone on a frigid winter's night. The next day, he stopped by my dorm to apologize. No matter how many roses he sent, or how many times he called or came to see me, I never dated him again. He finally gave up.

Now, here we were after all those years. When he caught my eye, he gave me a mock salute and smiled, revealing teeth as white and perfect as the ivories on a grand piano. He was always a great storyteller, and his thick southern accent added texture to his words. He could charm the habit off a nun. The only problem was, he just wasn't Robbie. But then again, there were no guarantees that things with Robbie would work out. I returned Beau's smile and thought it might be fun to catch up with him as well. He winked, and my heart skipped a beat. Surely, he wasn't single after all these years.

"Well, all good things must come to an end," Robbie said.

"Huh?" I asked, abruptly turning back to Robbie. "What do you mean?"

"I gotta go. There's this guy I've been wanting to talk to. The only time he can meet with me is tonight." He saw my disappointment and added, "The life of a reporter, I'm afraid."

"That's too bad. I mean, after all this time. There's so much more to talk about."

"I know. It's been great to see you."

"Really? I thought you would hate me after...well, you know."

"I don't hate you." He chuckled lightly. "Ancient history." He stood to leave. "See me out?"

I followed him as he said good-night to Pam and Trevor, and thanked them for the evening. We reached the door and he pulled his coat off a hook in the hallway. He stood for a moment, as if debating his next words.

"There's this place in Georgetown where these two guys perform. They're really good. They play songs from the old days; you know, the ones we used to sing. If you're not busy, I was wondering if you might want to go see 'em sometime. Maybe we could have dinner first or something."

"I'd like that," I said and before I realized it, blurted out, "How about next Saturday?"

An instant smile broke upon his face. "Okay, sure. Yeah, I think next Saturday would work. I'll call you just to be sure."

"Um, how about coming to my place for dinner first?" I stammered, stunned by my impetuous offer.

"You sure it's no trouble?" he asked, as he wrapped a scarf around his neck.

I shook my head. He took my address and phone number and gave me a gentle kiss on the cheek before vanishing into the night. I closed the door and rested against it with eyes closed and a light-headed feeling clouding my brain. Had this really happened? Things never went this well for me.

Quickly, I reined myself in. Nothing really had happened. We were just going to a bar to listen to music. Nothing more. He had an entire life after me, a life with a woman he married, and then she died. He had a scar that he wouldn't discuss and grew distant when asked about it. I couldn't assume that he was the man I once loved.

I returned to the party and found that the group had left the dining room. A few guests enjoyed after-dinner drinks in the den, but with Robbie's departure, I felt a void. I wished I could have left with him. Pam rushed over, her eyes sparkling with curiosity. "You two seemed to hit it off."

"I'm so glad you invited me. Seeing Robbie was..." I couldn't even find a word to describe it. "I haven't felt this way in a very long time." A little flame of hope began to thaw the frost inside. I bent toward her ear and whispered, "Is he seeing anyone?" She told me that she didn't think so, but asked if we were going to see each other again.

"Next weekend."

"Way to go, girl." She gave me a squeeze and smiled broadly.

"I'm still in shock. I just hope I'm not trying to live in the past."

"There you go, overanalyzing everything. Just have fun." She poked me in the ribs. "It's not like you have men beating down your door, you workaholic."

"Yeah, you're right. Tonight was fun. We talked so easily, like we'd seen each other yesterday, not thirty-five years ago."

"Has it really been that long? I think I need another drink. I'll get you one, too."

Once Pam left, I looked across the room and saw Trevor and Beau talking. Maybe I could ask Trevor about the Cold War and salvage something from the remainder of the evening, but first, I would have to disengage him from their animated conversation. They noticed me looking at them and ceased. Beau flicked his manicured finger across his brow in another mock salute.

"Well, if it isn't Kat Hastings. I'm amazed that you're here alone." Beau smiled warmly. "I figured you'd have a man on each arm."

"Hardly," I replied. "Too much work, too little fun."

"I could help you, that is, unless O'Toole has beat me to it once again. Where is the devil?"

"He just left. Had an interview or something."

"And left you alone? What an idiot, putting work before a beautiful woman." He laughed lightly. I could feel the blush on my face. He moved a bit closer. "Can I get you a drink?"

"I was just about to ask Kat the same thing," Trevor jumped in.

"No thanks," I answered. "Pam's got it covered. But Trevor, I was wondering whether you might tell me a bit more about how you got interested in the Cold War sometime." Trevor seemed bewildered by my request, but quickly recovered and said he'd be delighted.

"I've heard this all before. So if you'll excuse me, I will freshen my drink. Great to see you, Kat." Beau walked away, but not without one last salute. It seemed so out of place for a man of his bearing.

"How about now?" Trevor asked. I nodded. "Come into my sanctuary. We can talk more easily there."

His sanctuary was a study with hundreds of books on shelves surrounding an antique oak desk with a small brass lamp that illuminated Santayana's familiar quote, appropriate for Trevor's profession. *Those who cannot remember the past are condemned to repeat it.* A pipe sat in an ashtray, and the rich, sweet scent of tobacco suggested Trevor had had a few recent puffs.

"This is where I come to escape," Trevor smiled. "How did I get interested in the Cold War? Hmm, I guess because I lived it. I'm a little older than you and Pam. Yes, those were fun times; probably what landed me in Nam."

"You were there?" I knew a few guys who had been to Vietnam, but most didn't bring it up. Trevor seemed all too willing to talk about it.

"Thanks to LBJ and his cronies. He told the joint chiefs of staff, 'You can have your damn war, just get me reelected.' They did, and I landed smack-dab in the middle of the Tet Offensive." Trevor grunted. "We should have listened to Ike. He tried to warn us about the damned military-industrial complex."

A little drink and a lot of professor was evidently the right combination. Although afraid that he would launch into an all-out lecture, I asked, "What do you mean?"

"Once we dropped the bomb, the world's paranoia rose to an all-time high. In the US, this translated into approving the National Security Act of 1947, which basically launched the Cold War."

Trevor looked at me as if gauging my level of interest. With hopes that he might touch on the link between Kennedy and Op-40, I begged him to continue. Even so, my gaze wandered to the various titles of the books lining the shelves. Pam must have the patience of a saint. All I heard was "blah, blah, blah" until he said, "It led to the formation of various agencies, including the Office of the Secretary of Defense, the Joint Chiefs of Staff, *and* the CIA."

Now he had my attention. "You say it like it's a bad thing," I responded, a little too defensively.

"That act gave the CIA the power to do anything and not be held accountable—propaganda, sabotage, demolition, subversive actions, you name it. It didn't matter if it was South America, Africa, Cuba, or Vietnam."

It was time to take the plunge. In my most nonchalant voice, I asked, "Funny, you should mention Cuba. Do you know anything about Op-40?"

Almost imperceptivity, Trevor's face hardened. "What makes you ask about them?"

I shrugged and mumbled something about a show on the History Channel, but knew he didn't buy it. "They had something to do with the

Bay of Pigs, didn't they? Didn't Kennedy take heat for that?" I hoped that I wasn't tipping my hand.

Trevor nodded. "Kennedy was blamed for withdrawing the expected air support. The entire brigade was either killed or captured and tortured mercilessly. After that, Kennedy lost the backing of the military and intelligence organizations and won the unmitigated hate of the anti-Castro Cubans." Trevor's voice was now clipped and stiff.

"Kennedy got the Russians to pull their missiles out of Cuba. That must have placated his generals." I was in too deep, no sense stopping now. Trevor picked up an autographed baseball from his desk and began palming it like Sandy Koufax, but did not take his eyes off of me. He seemed edgy. I didn't understand why. People discussed history all the time.

"Kennedy had lost control of his government. His own State Department was leaking information to the intelligence community, so he communicated with Khrushchev secretly. He told Khrushchev that he was concerned about a military coup in the US and that to avoid a nuclear war, Russia had to remove their missiles from Cuba. In return, Kennedy promised to take our missiles out of Turkey and Italy."

"Wait a second. Kennedy was worried about a coup? Here, in the US?" I stared at him with eyes like saucers.

"Kennedy's policy was seen as appeasement by some people. In their eyes, that made him a traitor. He had to go." Trevor continued to study me. We had gone beyond superficial repartee and both knew it, but I had to get to the crux of the matter.

"So you think they killed him because of Cuba?" I asked, knowing that we were treading on shaky ground now. Trevor put the ball down and began playing with his pipe. He was dying to light it.

"It wasn't just Cuba. Things inside the States were also a mess. JFK came down hard on industry, challenging pricing policies and preventing our corporations from exploiting the resources of third-world nations. He took control of defense contracts and used them to improve his chances in the next election. Racial issues sprang up all over the place. Malcolm X and Martin Luther King were hitting their stride, and Kennedy was pushing for integration." Trevor's bravado prevented him from stopping, but his fidgeting lingered.

"So the military rejected Kennedy's foreign policy and resented his taking over defense contracts; big business scorned his economic policy; white America felt threatened by his stand on racial matters. Who do *you* think killed him?" As soon as I asked it, I realized that I'd overstepped my bounds—especially when Trevor jammed his pipe between his lips, lit it, and took several puffs.

"What I think is that I'd better stop before I fall off my soapbox. I tend to ramble a bit." I could see his pipe quiver on his lips. "Hope you don't mind. Pam hates it when I smoke this thing." He forced a laugh and puffed some more.

I still didn't understand his uneasiness but answered, "No, it reminds me of my father. He enjoyed a pipe now and then." I resumed my survey of his library, turning away from his slightly arched eyebrows.

Trevor dropped the pipe back in the ashtray. "Funny how you and Pam should run into each other after all these years of living in the same area. She's been bursting at the seams all week, wanting to tell you that Rob was coming. Her and her damned schemes. She told me that you and Rob were an item in college."

I nodded, but said little else on the subject. Instead, we reminisced about the old days. He told me about when he and Pam first met and the lengths he took to woo her into marriage. A few of the anecdotes were funny enough to dispel the awkwardness created by my questions. We looked up as Pam teetered in, clutching Beau's arm and feigning irritation. "Hey, you two. We were wondering where you ran off to. Everyone's gone home, but Beau wanted to say good-night."

Beau's eyes sparkled beneath trimmed eyebrows. He moved closer. His aftershave, though pleasant, was still strong.

"Have you been boring Kat with your historical soliloquies, dear?" A wine-laced giggle escaped Pam's lips.

"Hardly. I could listen to Trevor all night," I said. "What time is it?" I looked at my watch and saw that it was almost midnight. "I'm so sorry. I really should go. Thanks so much for tonight. It was fun. Let's do it again, okay?"

"Of coursh!" she slurred. "Beau shuggested that we all go to dinner shome night."

"That sounds like fun," I said, smiling in Beau's direction. "Beau and I never got a chance to talk." I brushed his arm. "But it's late. You and Trevor really outdid yourselves tonight. What a great party. I'll see myself out." I began edging my way out of the study.

"I'll come with you," Beau interjected as he jumped to my side. "Good-night, Pam, Trev. Thanks." He flicked his fingers against his brow once more. I left the room with Beau at my heels.

"Can I give you a ride?" he asked.

"It's nice of you to offer, but I have my car."

A shadow briefly appeared on his face, but he tailed me to the door and gave me a quick peck on the cheek. "Can I call you?"

"I'd like that." This time, I took his arm and squeezed it lightly.

He walked me to my car and sprang to his. As I pulled away from the curb, he was right behind me in his black Mercedes. He followed me all the way home and flicked his salute one last time before zooming off as I turned into my parking garage. I thought to myself, how considerate of him. Would Robbie have done the same?

CHAPTER FOUR

As I lay in bed, random thoughts swirled in my head—someone had been in my apartment and threatened me, Ben's reaction to the incident, my new assignment, would I find anything, and seeing Robbie and Beau after so many years. My runaway train of thought derailed any possibility of sleep.

Robbie and Beau were so different. Robbie wasn't dashing, but seemed comfortable in his own skin. He wasn't tall, just a few inches more than me. He was fit; he must still run. His curly Irish hair still had a mind of its own. He was obviously still passionate about his work. Why else would he leave a party for an interview on a Saturday night? Thinking about him was at once joyful and painful. How had I let him go? And for who—Nate? I was an idiot.

Beau could have been a model for a Brooks Brothers catalogue with his blue shirt, sports jacket, khakis, and loafers. Tall, trim, with Tom Cruise looks, he somehow managed a tan in November. Beau didn't leave the party for a story. *He* offered to drive me home and followed me to make sure that I made it. Still, I couldn't assume that either Beau or Robbie was the same man that I knew in college.

Next morning, in an effort to clean my mental house, I ran seven miles along the banks of the Potomac, with Fleetwood Mac blaring on my iPod and Scout leading the way. When I returned, I called Pam to thank her and tell her how much I'd enjoyed the evening. She said that Trevor had some important meeting and asked if I could come for lunch to help her eat some of the leftovers from the party.

When I arrived, she answered the door, complaining of a headache and saying something about how much easier it was to party in college.

As she pulled Tupperware containers from the fridge and nuked them, I had an opportunity to grill her. "How often do you get together with Robbie?" About once a month. "Does he ever mention my name?" Occasionally. "How did he get the scar?" It was this last question that yielded the most intriguing answer.

"He doesn't talk about it much," she answered. "But he was working on a story out in California—something to do with illegal immigrants and organized crime." She paused, as though debating how much to tell me. After setting a couple of plates on the table, she added, "He and Chloe were in the car. The brakes failed and they crashed into a tree. She was killed on impact; Rob was cut up, but otherwise okay. That was several years ago."

I put my glass of iced tea down and gasped, "Poor Robbie. No wonder he got so quiet when I asked him about his scar." I thought a bit before asking the next question. "Were they, uh, happy together?"

Pam brought two serving dishes over and answered, "He loved her a lot. They were married for about ten years. It's probably why he's still single."

I asked her if she had ever met Robbie's wife, and she nodded. "Chloe was nice—just what Rob needed; supportive, kind, patient about his exploits. After you two broke up, he was a mess. He threw himself into his work and didn't seem to care about the dangerous people he was pissing off. She was the first one who was able to reach him; you know, get inside his head and understand him. When he lost her, he changed. Became more distant."

I took a bite of salmon and realized that it pained me to hear that Robbie loved someone else, but what could I expect? I had my chance and blew it. Not wanting to talk about Chloe further, I asked, "Did Robbie ever finish the story?"

"Knowing him, I'd say yes, but he doesn't really tell me what he's working on. It's why he moved here. He told Trev he had to come east until things cooled off. We invited Rob and Beau to dinner, and Beau offered to let Rob live at his place."

My forkful of food came to a sudden stop on the way to my mouth. "Robbie lives with Beau?"

"Not *with* him." She rolled her eyes. "Beau lives in some big-ass mansion. Rob lives in a small carriage house on the grounds. It's kind of cute. Trev and I visited him when he moved in."

"I remember that Beau seemed well-off when we were in college. Family money?" I asked.

"I guess that's one way of putting it." Her eyes had a gossip-columnist glint.

"Okay, I'll bite. What is it?"

Like a kid who couldn't keep a secret, Pam's words gushed forth. "What I heard is that his mother had an affair with some rich oil guy down in Texas. This guy had a family and a wife that could take him to the cleaners, so he paid Beau's mom hush money—enough to provide Beau a pretty cushy life."

"How did you find this out?" I asked, totally engrossed.

"Beau told Trevor one night after they had thrown a few back. You won't say anything, will you?"

"Of course not," I reassured her. "But it certainly explains why he's in a mansion, wearing Guccis."

"Actually, it doesn't," she responded thoughtfully. "The cash flow ended when Beau graduated and the tycoon died. Whatever Beau has now, he's earned on his own. And good for him. He deserves it. The guy is a prince."

"It's nice of him to rent Robbie a place. That's for sure," I said, musing about the two of them before adding, "but they're polar opposites."

"Don't know how much they see of each other, really. Beau usually goes south in the winter and Rob, well, he's always running around. Still a mover and shaker—just like in college." Pam rose and took the dishes to the sink before adding, "You may have a problem on your hands. What if both Rob and Beau are interested in you?"

I laughed at the thought. "Robbie was friendly, but I'm sure he hasn't forgiven me for what happened between us. As for Beau, I don't know. I'm sure he's not hurting for female companionship."

"No, but he did change his plans when he heard you were coming." Then, more shrewdly, Pam added, "Besides, I know for a fact that he likes you. Always has."

I grinned. Robbie and Beau—not a bad cure for a workaholic.

CHAPTER FIVE

Armed with my expanded security clearance, laptop, and a lunch that I had made early that morning, I entered the OHB and then walked toward the rear of the building. Checking the ancient floor plan, I found a single elevator shaft noted and walked toward it, acknowledging that part of me was a little curious after all. When I reached the spot, I saw no elevator buttons, only a door that looked like every other door in Langley—metallic gray, windowless, and shut, except there was no handle to pull, only a raised groove to scan a security badge, which I did. The door disappeared into the wall and after a moment's pause to ensure that no one was around, I stepped inside and began my descent into the bowels of the OHB. Cables groaned, gears ground, and the car lurched unevenly as I rode to the bottom floor. The air inside was stale; the space was half the size of a modern elevator. I couldn't help but wonder who last rode this elevator, when and why.

The door opened to a dark, cool corridor. I pulled my iPhone from my computer case and pressed the "Over 40" app for a flashlight. It illuminated the tiled wall of a hallway. As I stepped out of the elevator, motion sensors activated lights in the ceiling. I looked both ways and then down at the floor plan. If Ben was right, I needed to go left. With the exception of the lonely echo of my footsteps, it was eerily silent, too silent. Occasionally I stopped to listen. Water dripped somewhere. There was an occasional hum, but no human sound. Surely in a place as big as Langley, someone had to be here.

I looked up to the ceiling. There were no surveillance cameras. I thought that was odd and wondered if this part of Langley was still in use. The entire floor seemed vacant, like a government ghost town. Part of me wanted to slow down; the other part wanted to run. I stiffened each time the lights flashed on as I entered a new hallway, then another and another. By the time I reached the designated area, I was drenched with sweat and yet, was shivering. There was no hint of any flood damage, but at least now I could begin my search.

The first door I opened revealed an office with weary furniture slumped across a linoleum floor, its tiles curled up like the toes of a corpse. The walls were the color of bandages. Generic notices were buried in mounds of boxes stacked on one side. I pulled open barren desk drawers. Nothing here suggested that this was the room, nor were the next twenty. I felt frustration at the seeming folly of the assignment; I had better things to do. But there was something else, a curious blend of disappointment mixed with a mounting dread as I opened door after door, only to find one benign room after another. Peeking inside each one, I wondered if I would recognize Ben's room if I saw it. Perhaps I was passing through too quickly. Although Ben warned that finding this room and its contents might place me in danger, the only danger I faced so far was terminal boredom.

By noon, I had searched the entire corridor in vain, opening doors, scanning rooms, and shutting doors, wondering where I should go next. I stared at the floor plan. I had covered the area Ben circled. The corridor ended in a T, with two long hallways extending in opposite directions. I was torn between continuing Ben's wild-goose chase and returning to tell him I had found nothing. Leaning against a wall, I released a sigh of exasperation and slid to the floor. I removed the ham-and-cheese sandwich from my computer case and scarfed it down. During the last few bites, I decided to keep going. I had nothing to lose but time. Better that than endure a sermon for not being thorough.

Never having been one to successfully navigate the cornfield mazes of my youth, I tossed the empty lunch bag in the hallway as a marker and resumed my search. Turning left, I found more offices, with an occasional conference room interspersed—all cloned government-issue tombs, relics from the CIA's distant past.

By midafternoon, the only things I discovered were more dusty desktops, cobwebbed corners, and outdated memos. I marked off the parts of the floor plan I had covered, for my benefit as well as for my anticipated meeting with Ben. Retracing my path, I passed my lunch bag with wilting enthusiasm and entered the next wing of the T. About a dozen doors later, I pushed open the door of yet another conference room, fully expecting to pull it shut as I had the others. But upon flipping the switch, my hand rose reflexively to my gaping mouth.

This room was unlike any of the others. It was large and immaculate. There was no dust, no papers, and no stacked boxes. OHB was built in the late fifties, and the traditional furniture in this room was reminiscent of the era. A U-shaped cherrywood table, punctuated by now-forbidden ashtrays, faced a large screen mounted on the wall opposite the door; smaller screens abutted it. Twenty large, leather-bound, brass-tacked wing chairs surrounded the table. A podium stood off to one side of the main screen. At one time, the room's electronics were probably state-of-the-art; now they seemed obsolete. Except for the screens, the grayish-white porous walls were bare—no maps, no CIA internal bulletins, and no pictures.

I stood briefly by each chair before placing my computer case on the table. I couldn't help but wonder who had sat in these chairs: my father? Mr. Phillips? Mr. Morales? Mr. Dulles? I sat in one and spun in a circle, taking the entire room in. With each turn, I pondered what kind of history was made here—maybe Cuban-missile-crisis briefings, planning the Bay of Pigs invasion, or U2 spying over Russia. This had to be Ben's room. It had its own aura, something that woke a sixth sense.

I rose and circled the room repeatedly, looking underneath each chair, beneath the table, behind the screens. With each revolution, I strained to see something I might have missed. But there was not a single artifact—nothing but the ghosts of the Cold War who now haunted me. They would reveal no secrets. If any souvenirs of the assassination had been here, they had been removed. Ben would be disappointed, but no more than I was. I wanted this to be the room, chock-full of evidence, and I wanted to be the one to find it. I couldn't bring myself to leave. I felt my father's spirit pulling me into a chair, where I viewed the floor plan once more. There was no place left to go.

A knock on the door startled me. I looked up to see a tall man with a shaved head and wearing a black suit glaring at me. No one was supposed to know that I was here. Given the catacomb hallways I had traipsed through, his appearance could not be by chance. He was looking for me, or maybe he watched the room to protect it from people like me finding it. The thought made me stand abruptly, knotting my hands into fists.

"Who are you?" I asked. With effort, I kept my voice steady.

"Jermaine Biggs," he answered brusquely. His name seemed appropriate, given the way his frame strained the shoulder seams of his coat—indicative of many discretionary hours spent at the gym. "And you?"

"I'm Agent Katharine Hastings. I work for Ben Douglas," I said, hoping that Ben's name would provide some needed gravitas. "What are you doing here?"

"Ben asked me to stand watch while you're looking around. He doesn't want anyone bothering you." He looked me up and down as though appraising me, not in a sexual way but more as though he was buying a car. Was I fast enough? Would I last? It made me bristle.

"I was told that no one knew about my assignment. Do you have some ID?"

He pulled his wallet from his coat and flashed a badge at me. It seemed legit. His ID number, his picture, and name were above the CIA seal and a bar code ran up the side. It looked just like mine. Maybe Jermaine Biggs was part of the arrangements Ben made after I told him about the rose on my pillow. "So what are you supposed to be doing while I'm here?"

"I've set up a desk by the elevator. If you run into any trouble, just let me know. By the way, cell phones don't work here, so you won't be able to call me. Here." He handed me a beeper. "Use this if you need to reach me."

"I've looked through the entire floor and I haven't found anything, so I'm calling it a day. It looks like you came down here for nothing."

Not wanting to be in this remote area with a strange man, I gathered my belongings and walked toward the door. He closed the door and followed behind. As we approached the T, I asked, "Did you see a lunch bag here? I left it as a marker to find my way back."

"No one's been down here, ma'am. I would have seen them. Maybe you picked it up and forgot about it." Either Jermaine was lying or someone else *had* been in this part of the building. Neither possibility was comforting, which tripped a silent alarm inside me. Ben must have given him my schedule, but said nothing to me. Jermaine said, "ma'am." That suggested military, and although the CIA and the military worked hand in hand, it seemed odd that he just appeared with no warning and dismissed my missing lunch bag so easily.

We walked through the hollow hallways in silence until we reached the elevator, where a desk now sat outside, with several magazines on top. Jermaine took a seat while I ran my card through the scanner next to the elevator.

"You're not leaving?" I asked. "I told you, I'm done."

"I've been assigned here for the day, ma'am. Just following orders."

Thoughts bounced around in my head as I entered the elevator and began my ascent. Perhaps Jermaine's presence rattled me enough to quit too soon. I'd found the room, I was sure of it, but there was nothing there. I had scoured every inch of it. But wait. I hadn't seen any controls for the lights, the projectors, or the screens. There had to be some sort of panel, maybe in the podium. I had looked it over, but maybe I'd missed something. I had to go back.

I hit the button in the elevator and returned to the bottom floor. Jermaine was still sitting there, flipping through an issue of *Sports Illustrated*. He looked up as I exited, showing no reaction.

"I just thought of something. I'm going back to the room."

He nodded casually. "I'll be here."

It was time to learn a little more about him. "Just out of curiosity, were you in the military?"

"Got back from Iraq four years ago. Been here ever since."

"Who do you work for now?"

"My dad once told me that the problem with the government is that you're never sure who you really work for. Let's just say I work for you, Agent Hastings." He smiled perfunctorily. "Let me know when you're ready to leave, ma'am. I mean, for real this time." He smiled briefly and returned to his reading. Evidently, our conversation was over.

I turned abruptly and stomped away, waiting until I was down the hall before consulting the floor plan on which I had marked the room's location. Many corridors later, I stood outside the room and gazed down the hallway, looking at the slate-gray doors lining either side. There had to be at least forty: twenty on the right and twenty on the left, all evenly spaced—except for the door to Ben's conference room and the next one which appeared to have an extra ten feet between them.

I entered the conference room and gazed at the wall to my right. If there was a secret chamber, it would have to be between that wall and the next room. But I had been over every inch of the wall and noticed nothing, only the creases of soundproofed panels, suggesting that highly sensitive discussions were held here.

I walked to the podium and took out my iPhone to illuminate deep inside it. Against the back wall of the recess, I saw a panel of electronic controls and read the labels over various buttons: Lights, Projection, Temperature, Telecom, and pressed them all. Other than illuminating the room, turning on the projector, and hearing the drone of an air conditioner, nothing unexpected happened. Seeing no additional controls, I ran my fingers along the sides of the recess. Opposite the buttons I'd already pressed, I felt a tiny latch and pulled it, revealing two small buttons with no labels. I pressed the first one and heard a grinding sound. I looked in the direction of the noise and saw a door slide into the right-hand wall, exposing an entrance.

Tremors of excitement or trepidation palsied my fingers as I hit the second button and saw lights brighten the entry. I sprang to the opening and peered inside an eight-by-ten-foot vault with floor-to-ceiling shelves lining its perimeter and spanning its width; all piled high with canisters, files, and boxes of varying shapes and sizes. I looked at the floor plan. There was no indication that this space even existed, a secret kept from those who keep secrets.

I had found it. My heart was racing. I wanted to scream in triumph and tear into the vault. I wanted to call Ben and tell him the news. It took every ounce of self-discipline to stop and think. If this room was a secret, if someone was warning me to stay out, and if someone was assigned to protect me, I had to proceed carefully. I jumped to the door of the conference room and checked the hallway. No one was there. I pulled the door shut and rummaged in my computer case for something I could use as a doorstop to prevent someone from getting in. Anything I saw in the vault would be for my eyes only. I found a mouse pad, bent it in two, and jammed it into the space between the door and the floor. It fit snugly and I pushed it until it would go no farther. I tried the door. It would work until I came up with something better.

Practically on tiptoe, I entered the musty, cluttered vault. There was so much here. Some of the boxes were labeled, so I left to retrieve my laptop. Once back in the vault, I booted up and created an Excel spreadsheet. The first box was marked "Oswald." I began to type. "Oswald—family information"; "Oswald—military service"; "Oswald—residences"; "Oswald—jobs held." I noted that some of the boxes were dated 1958 and realized that Oswald was on the CIA's radar well before 1963. Either the CIA knew that Oswald was a problem and didn't intervene in time, or maybe Oswald was a CIA contact. Ben's anxiety was starting to make sense.

Why wasn't this information in the National Archives, instead of some secret vault? If it was still hidden, that meant the Warren Commission probably never saw it. I tried to convince myself that maybe once Ruby shot Oswald, the information was no longer needed, so it was left here, but my gut disagreed. I needed to get inside these boxes, but it might be a bad idea to start pulling them off the shelf and disturbing things. I needed to get some gloves now. Maybe Greg had some.

I dashed to the podium and closed the vault. After pulling my wedge from the door of the conference room, I maneuvered through the hallways back to the elevator and saw Jermaine at his desk, now reading *Men's Fitness*. I told myself to remain calm. I didn't want him to notice my newfound fervor. He wasn't even startled when I greeted him.

"I forgot a few things. I'll be back, but you really don't need to stay. I'll be fine."

"I'm here as long as you are," he said, barely looking up from his reading.

"I see." He wasn't going to budge. I didn't have time to argue, so I let it pass. "Just so you know, it could be a long day."

"I imagine that you'll need several long days, since they're going to rehab that whole area in a couple of weeks. They'll be getting rid of all those old desks, painting the walls—the whole works."

His words sounded an alarm. A couple of weeks? As I stepped into the elevator, I couldn't help but think of the amount of material in the vault. I would never get it all inventoried in time—not if I stuck to Ben's schedule.

Greg's workshop was on the other side of OHB from my office. I cut across the Memorial Garden, passing "The Bubble," our pet name for the auditorium, and the statue of Nathan Hale, the first American spy who died serving his country. The cool air hurried my steps, but not as much as my need to get back to the vault.

Greg was in, but was sitting at his desk with his feet propped up on some computer boxes and talking on the phone. A pen dangled from his mouth, and he was squeezing some sort of rubber ball in time to Janis Joplin screaming about another piece of her heart. His face brightened at seeing me. He sat up, waved me inside, and held up a finger indicating he'd just be a minute. I strolled around the room, which was lined with steel cabinetry and counter tops. There were few windows, so fluorescent lights glared harshly upon a variety of electronics as well as baseball hats, odd-looking pens, and sunglasses sitting on various counters. There were even some fake-fingernail sets and shirt buttons.

I jumped when I heard him say, "Great to see you! What brings you to my neck of the woods?"

"Well, I was in the neighborhood, and you're always telling me to stop by, so I thought I would." I hugged him lightly. "How's the family?"

"Great. Another grandchild on the way."

"That will make what, seven?" I asked.

"Good memory. We're hoping for a girl. We've cornered the market on boys." He laughed.

"It looks like you've been busy. What is all this stuff?"

He beamed with pride. "Most of these things..." he began, pointing at the electronics, "...are scramblers for cell phones, computers, security cameras, you know—in case you don't want someone to know what you're saying, what you're working on, or where you've been, but some of the other things are, ah, more creative."

"You mean, like the fingernails?" I asked, pointing in their direction.

"I call them 'Black Magic Woman.' You scratch someone with one of these and they won't bother you anymore. They're loaded with ultra-pure sarin, stabilized with tributylamine, and can kill a person in a minute if you scratch hard enough." He snapped his fingers; I flinched. "Five hundred times more potent than cyanide."

"What about the baseball hats?" I picked one up and looked it over.

He took it from my hand. "These aren't just any baseball hats. They're equipped with a tiny camera and recording device." He put it on and flicked the bill. "Go ahead, say something."

"Okay," I began, trying to think of what to say. "Sorry I haven't been here sooner to see you. I have a big project, lots of papers to review and file. I feel like I'm chained to my desk."

He took off the hat, pressed a button, and instantly my words were repeated. Seeing that I was impressed, he moved to the items that I thought were pens. "You say you have a lot of paperwork? These might help. You can run these across a page and they will scan everything, word for word."

"Really? They would be handy. Are they hard to use? I'm the slowest typist in the world." I picked one up and looked at it. "How do you download the information after you scan it?"

He picked one of the pen-sized implements up and demonstrated how the scanner worked, explaining that they were faster and more accurate than the ones that were available commercially. "They'll even translate to or from a foreign language." Then his eyes widened. "But if you're really a slow typist, you might want one of these." He opened a drawer and pulled out a metallic device the size of a matchbox as well as a small, button-sized object with a small clip on its back. "I call it 'The Talking Head.' Just plug this part into the port on your computer like this," he connected the device into his computer, "and clip this microphone onto your collar. It's wireless and works anywhere." He clipped the mike onto my shirt. "Okay, talk."

"Hmm, let's see. Coming here is like going to a Brookstone for spies. Could I borrow some of this stuff for my work?" I laughed. Sure enough, as I spoke them, the words appeared on his screen, with the word "laughter" at the end.

"Nice, huh? You don't even have to speak the punctuation, like the publicly available speech-recognition software, and there's nowhere near the same number of typos. I worked with some of the linguists at Microsoft, and we came up with a program that does it all for you."

"I'm impressed. I don't know how you come up with this stuff." I scanned the room for other gadgets. There were so many. Then, turning back to Greg, I asked, "This may sound silly, but do you know where I can get some gloves? I'm working in this dusty area, and I, um, don't want to get dirty."

"The only gloves I have are pretty special, but I don't mind loaning them to you." He went to a drawer and pulled out what looked like ordinary plastic gloves.

"What makes them special?" I asked, as I picked them up and looked them over.

"Let me show you." He took one of the gloves from me, put it on, and grazed a dusty surface by the window. His fingerprint left no indentation.

I blinked my eyes and my jaw went slack. "How did you do that?"

"They have two layers. The outside layer is made of a highly reactive polymer that automatically blends with whatever is left on the surface—dust, dirt, blood. If you had a magnifying glass, you'd be able to see a finger impression, but the naked eye can't. The inside layer is made of an inert material to protect your hands." He pulled off the glove. "Neat, huh?"

"I'll say. You're amazing." I meant it. "I'd love to see your other stuff. Could I come back again?"

"Anytime." He brushed the unruly forelock from his eyes. "There's lots I could show you. What's this project of yours?"

"Oh, just another one of Ben's crazy requests. Not my real job. I just want to get it over with." I grinned, attempting to be blasé about it. "Ben said you arranged for me to move around Langley unnoticed. Did he tell you anything else?"

"I didn't ask, but I'm guessing it's Internal Affairs. Be careful. People get all squirrely about that kind of thing."

"No, just inventory," I replied in the most casual voice I could manage. "You really don't mind if I take these?"

He gave me a questioning look, but answered, "No, not at all. Do you want to try the scanner or the voice-activated software? I might even have a suit you could wear to keep from getting dirty. It's made of burn-resistant material, but you could use it to keep clean."

"Don't need the suit, but the other stuff would be great. Thanks. You're going to save me tons of work."

He placed the software devices into a box and handed the other items to me. I stuffed the scanner and gloves into my pocket and took the box. I hugged him lightly as he held the door open for me and said, "Stop by anytime, but you might want to call first. This room is locked when I'm not around. You know, security and all." His chest puffed just a bit.

"I can see why. Thanks again. You're a lifesaver." I ran out of the room, not believing my luck. With Greg's help, I could make a dent in the vault's contents before the renovations began.

I practically sprinted back to the vault, passing Jermaine, who waved nonchalantly, but I could feel his eyes on my back. I scanned my badge by the door of the conference room, switched on the lights, dashed to the podium, and pressed the button that opened the vault. Now that I had found it and was ready to unearth its secrets, I didn't want anyone to know what I was up to. I checked the hallway before pulling the door shut and cramming my mouse pad underneath.

I was finally ready to begin. I pulled on the gloves, booted up, opened an Excel spreadsheet, and plugged the voice-recognition software into my computer. "Testing, testing." The words instantly appeared on my screen. I was in business.

CHAPTER SIX

I hauled down a box and looked inside at dozens of files. The first was labeled, "Hosty Notes." I said the title out loud and the computer displayed my words. Then I logged in "Fritz Interview of Oswald, November 22–23, 1963." A chill jerked my shoulders as I realized that this must have been after the assassination, before Ruby shot Oswald. My curiosity begged me to read, but I promised Ben: no analysis, just inventory. Reluctantly I continued, logging in "Witness Compromise Campaign," "Media Contacts," and "Death List." After robotically voicing all of them onto the spreadsheet, I snuck a peak at the last one and saw more than a hundred names listed. Some were eyewitnesses. Some were reporters. Had these been arranged? The implication was too jarring. I quickly closed the folder, remembering my promise to Ben.

The work was now going much more quickly—at least until I came across the next box and three files that were labeled "Oswald 1," "Oswald 2," and "Oswald 3." Unable to distinguish these from the previous entries, I glimpsed inside.

The "Oswald 1" file contained more than a hundred pictures of Oswald at various points in his life—as a child, a teenager, in the military, with Marina, protesting for the Fair Play for Cuba Committee—nothing unusual here. Then I opened "Oswald 2." There was a picture of a man who bore little resemblance to Oswald. He was heavyset, like an ex-football player, and balding, with a round face. I learned that "Saul" behaved in a disruptive manner so that employees at the Cuban and Soviet embassies in Mexico City would remember him. The impostor's requests for entry into Cuba were denied, so he returned as "Oswald" to the United States. At the bottom, there was a handwritten note that read, "Tapes must be destroyed as impostor is heard speaking rudimentary Russian; Oswald is fluent." The initials at the bottom—H2—shot through me like a Magnum. My father wrote this.

I dropped the file as numbness consumed me. This was exactly the finding that I had dreaded. Ever since that Friday long ago, my father's luggage tag gnawed at me, and now I was holding the proof of his complicity. He helped cover up a murder that changed the course of American history. I slumped against a wall, burying my face in my hands and began breathing one deep breath after another.

For my entire life, I had viewed my father as a hero. Distant, yes, but a distance I forgave because of his work. Now I was overcome with shame. Part of me wanted to run screaming from the vault; the other part lusted to learn everything I could. My chest heaved with increasingly rapid breaths. My eyes widened as I surveyed the contents of the vault. My ears strained to hear phantom sounds. Inventory be damned; I freed the scanner from my pocket, turned it on, and opened the next file, "Oswald 3."

I ran the scanner across each page. Although Oswald 3 differed markedly from Oswald 2, he bore an uncanny resemblance to the real Oswald—slight of build with thinning, light-brown hair. They shared a similar military background, complete with comparable assignments, including Atsugi, but like Oswald 2, this Oswald was trying to make an impression, behaving badly at firing ranges and car dealers. He was also in Dealey Plaza on November twenty-second.

With each scanned page, it was becoming clear that the real Oswald was set up. Still, something didn't fit. I cross-checked with the first file. The real Oswald was working at the book depository when Oswald 2 made a scene at the embassy. The real Oswald couldn't drive a car. Why would a decoy make a scene at a car dealership by driving way too fast in a demo car? Oswald was supposedly in Mexico City during the firing-range incident. Whoever had worked to create these fake Oswalds had screwed up. My father did not screw up—ever.

As the consequences of what I was seeing sank in, I made a pivotal decision. I couldn't let the contents of this room remain hidden, or perhaps be destroyed, without documenting them somehow. I had the scanner to copy files, but there was physical evidence here as well. Next time, I'd bring a camera and a very large bag. History deserved it.

Knowing that an uncomfortable dog was waiting at home, I pried myself from the vault at seven p.m. I could have stayed all night. Reluctantly I closed up, pulled on my coat, and secured the room before exiting. Still at his post, Jermaine wished me a good-night as I passed. I could only hope that he wouldn't go back to the room and examine it for himself. As I walked through the lobby of the OHB, I glanced up at the inscription on the wall. "And ye shall know the truth and the truth shall set you free." Knowing what I now did, the irony of Dulles ordering that inscription was profound. I was learning the truth, but it sure wasn't setting me free.

I enjoyed the invigorating half-mile walk to catch the 23 bus to Shirlington. Thankfully, it arrived within a few minutes, and I found a seat next to a kid plugged into his iPod. The forty-five-minute ride allowed me some time to reflect on Ben, Robbie, Beau, and my father— four men who influenced my every thought and action.

Wants and needs—that's what it was all about. I wanted to do a good job for Ben, and needed to analyze. I wanted to know more about my father's involvement in the conspiracy, and needed to hear his explanation for his actions. I wanted to remediate my past with Robbie, and maybe Beau, and needed to know if I had any chance with either of them. Then there was the vault. I wanted to know its secrets and needed more time. But as Mick Jagger said, "You can't always get what you want, but if you try sometimes, you just might find you get what you need."

Once home, I took care of Scout's wants and needs. As we embarked on our nightly run, I pondered some of the things I saw while in the vault, like Oswald's time at Atsugi. As we turned onto the path along the park, my mind began to wander.

The eighteen-year-old, known as Ozzie, lay on his cot in barracks number five, his hands folded under his head. He stared at the ceiling, sweat dampening his forehead. Had it really been just a year since he'd joined the Marines? He thought about home. This was the first time he'd been out of the States. It was good to get away from his mother, but he felt alone. The other marines lived on the east side of the base, leaving him surrounded by members of the Air Force's U-2 spy-plane detachment. He hated their practical jokes, but his size and naiveté made retaliation impossible.

Still, he enjoyed his new assignment to MACS-1, where he could work at the aviation electronics center. Unfortunately, he didn't have the security clearance for the U-2 spying program, and he had heard some rumblings about some sort of mind-control experiments which sounded interesting. Even so, Ozzie felt as if he was part of something big. He liked that—a lot. If he played his cards right, better things would follow.

He looked up at the clock. Time to get to work. He pulled on his fatigues and crossed the twelve-hundred-acre facility, noticing the farmland and forest on all sides. New Orleans was on the other side of the world, and that was just fine. He was on leave the coming weekend and thought about what he might do. Maybe he'd hop on the Odakyu electric railroad for the twenty-mile ride to Tokyo. It would be good to get away from the jerks in the air force, but still he'd be alone, always alone.

I shook my head and my reverie ended. I could see how Oswald's stint at Atsugi would make it easy for people like my father to paint him as a communist. All they had to do was claim that Oswald had defected to Russia to reveal secrets about the U-2 spy program. It didn't matter that he wasn't cleared for that kind of information. It made for a good story.

Then I remembered scanning a statement from a guy named Bullock who knew Ozzie at Atsugi. When Bullock was shown the picture of the man that Jack Ruby killed on November 24th he said, "It looks nothing like him. That's not the man I knew." Was Oswald 3 the man that Bullock knew at Atsugi and not the real Oswald?

Scout and I made the turn for home and minutes later entered the apartment, where we were greeted by the incessant nagging of the phone.

"Hey Kat, it's Beau. I was wondering if you're free this Saturday."

"Hi. Great to hear from you." I started twirling the drawstring of my running tights. "I'm really glad you called but, uh, unfortunately, I already have plans."

"Break them." He laughed, but I think he was serious.

"How about some other time?" I asked.

"It's Rob, isn't it?" There was the slightest hint of irritation in his voice.

"We're just going to a bar to hear some music. No big deal." I was hoping that it would be a big deal, but would never admit it. "You could come with us if you'd like."

"Uh, no thanks. Three's a crowd."

"Please call again. I mean it."

"Sure." An awkward silence ensued before he added, "Well, maybe I'll see you around."

I hung up, thinking that I should have proposed another date, but then again, I had led Beau on when we were in college and didn't want a repeat performance. Didn't it figure? I go for years without any significant dates, and now, two incredibly attractive men were in my life. Somewhere, the fates were laughing.

To take my mind off my new conundrum, I began reading the files I had scanned about Permindex, short for Permanent Industrial Expositions. Permindex was allegedly behind an assassination attempt on Charles de Gaulle. The Italian government expelled Permindex in 1962 after learning it was a front for CIA espionage activities. The Permindex board of directors included known businessmen, organized-crime figures, government officials, and media moguls. I could see them all, seated around a big table at some posh European hotel, plotting the overthrow of governments and the assassination of world leaders. Did a board member, possibly a mobster, or maybe even Clay Shaw, leave a Permindex meeting with a mandate to make November 22nd JFK's last day?

I shrugged my shoulders several times in a futile attempt to loosen the tension. Fake Oswalds, a deceitful father, an institutionalized conspiracy; Ben's demeanor now made sense, and his discomfort was now mine as well.

CHAPTER SEVEN

Overnight, I suffered bizarre dreams of Mafia hit men driving Kennedy's limo or Lyndon Johnson hoisting drinks in a bar with Jack Ruby and Oswald, pointing at me as I walked in the door. Thankfully, Tuesday was a normal workday and passed without incident. I managed to make a dent in the files that buried my desk, but could not avoid my preoccupation with the vault. I was dying to go back, but had to wait one more day thanks to Ben's schedule. By the time Wednesday morning dawned, I was manic.

After a brief jog with Scout, I showered, dressed, and was at my desk by seven to check e-mails and voice mails. Very few colleagues were around, but I made certain to greet them so they would notice my presence before I left for the vault. Today would be different. Ben would get his inventory, but I wanted some insurance for myself. In addition to the scanner, I brought a flashlight, camera, and satchel. I descended into the depths of the OHB and, as expected, Jermaine was at his post.

"Good morning," I said. He looked up and barely nodded. "It's going to be a long day, so if you need to leave..."

"I'll leave when you call it a day, not before."

"You really don't have to," I replied. Despite his claims that he was there for me, I found his presence unsettling. I preferred to work anonymously.

"Ben ordered me to be here when you're here. Take as long as you need."

"Humph," I grunted as I walked away. Once in the vault, I began my inventory. After entering each item or file onto my spreadsheet, I photographed physical evidence and scanned each document. I came upon a bullet inside an envelope labeled, "Autopsy." It must have fallen out during the procedure. Was it from the Mannlicher-Carcano rifle?

Then I opened a box and found more documents containing testimonies from fifty-eight people. If they were here in the vault, the Warren Commission or the HSCA probably hadn't seen them. I read a few and immediately realized why. None supported the lone-gunman theory. In fact, all testified to more shots, more gunmen, and none of them described individuals that looked like Oswald.

Moving to the next shelf, I noticed some film reels. The first was labeled "Beverly Oliver—looking toward grassy knoll," supplied by Regis Kennedy, FBI. Another had no name, but was labeled, "Grassy Knoll," supplied by Oscar Roe, Dallas police department. Perhaps these were hidden because they showed additional assassins behind the wooden fence. I entered the titles, threw the reels in my satchel, and kept moving.

I came to a list of fingerprints, including one lifted from the sixth floor of the book depository and identified as that of Malcolm Wallace. I'd check him out later.

I walked to the next aisle and hit my knee on a purple trunk with the name, "Nagell" written on top. Inside were photos and film reels labeled, "Oswald, Angel, and Arcacha." Damn. Oswald must have trained with the Op-40 Cuban refugees. I began to shake. Those camps were run by the CIA. No way was Oswald pro-Cuban; he was one of us.

Then I found another box with more film reels. One was labeled "Pitzer." His name had been on the death list. I trembled.

With each entry, the weight on my shoulders grew. I slumped against the cinder blocks of the back wall and closed my eyes. My breaths were no longer involuntary but deliberate and necessary. My arms fell to my sides. That was when I felt it. My fingers inched along a panel with several buttons. I removed the flashlight from my case and directed it toward them. I pressed the first button and the door to the vault closed. Claustrophobic as I was, I quickly pressed it again to open the door. I hit a second button, but there was no similar response; only a hum of white noise. When I pressed the third button, I heard a whoosh from the back of the vault right above my head. I looked up and saw a square opening in the previously solid wall. I aimed the flashlight into the alcove and peered inside.

A large, cylindrical, stainless-steel container sat between some other items. The light was so poor that I had to pull it out for a better look. Liquid inside the canister made it heavier than I expected. I pulled and twisted the lid, until finally it opened. The stench of formalin assaulted my nose, making my head jerk back and away. Once the odor dissipated, I looked inside and shuddered upon seeing something I shouldn't have. It couldn't be. I swallowed hard, forcing the reflux back into my throat.

I felt cold and lifeless. It seemed as though my skin was crawling off my neck. My arms moved as though they belonged to someone else as I raised the camera and clicked, hoping the pictures weren't blurred by my erratic tremors. Once done, I quickly screwed the lid back on tightly, returned the canister to its original spot, and pressed the button to close the panel. I staggered back to the computer as if I were walking a tightrope, afraid to fall. I spoke a single word onto the spreadsheet. "Brain."

Weak, numb, and nauseated, I packed my things, closed the vault, and fled the room. It was eight p.m. I didn't want to see anyone. I wanted to go somewhere far away, somewhere where no one could find me or threaten me, somewhere where I could curl up into a cocoon and try to pretend that I'd seen none of this. Unfortunately, I had to pass Jermaine on my way out.

"Long day, ma'am. It's about time you went home." Still dazed by my discoveries, I didn't respond. He stared at me. "Are you okay?" he asked. I must have looked awful because he was no longer aloof, but instead, seemed genuinely concerned.

"I'm fine," I lied. "It has been a long day, but I'm making progress." The thought of coming back here again was more than distressing. "Could I ask you a favor?"

"Sure, what?"

"Would you call me a cab? I need to get home, and the buses don't run as often this late."

He stood and walked from behind his desk to face me. "Are you sure you're okay?" I didn't answer. He gathered his belongings and pulled his coat off the back of his chair. "I'll walk you to the cab stand. It's outside the grounds."

"That's okay. I can make it on my own." I still didn't trust him. Wouldn't Ben have told me if he'd assigned someone to watch out for me?

"Negative. I'm coming with you." His voice was stern. He rose quickly and pulled on his jacket.

I argued some more, but to no avail. It was clear that Jermaine was determined to accompany me. Maybe I could learn more about him. We navigated the labyrinth of hallways and soon were outside of the OHB, walking toward the gate to find a cab. It was brisk outside, but a pleasing change from the stale, suffocating vault. I had difficulty matching Jermaine's stride. A light mist thickened the air, blurring the streetlights and muffling the sounds of traffic.

"Let me walk near the street." Jermaine said it like an order, more than a suggestion. He didn't strike me as the chivalrous type, and given our minimal interactions, I looked at him, confused. He must have sensed it and added, "A car pulled out when we left the building, and it's been following us real slow. Just look straight ahead. Don't let on that we've seen them. Pretend we're having a conversation. Laugh like I said something funny."

I did as he suggested, but removed my iPhone and discretely took a picture, hoping to catch the license plate. If it was a government car, maybe I could determine who signed it out. Jermaine kept walking.

"They're just watching us right now. I don't think they'd do anything here, but someone sure is interested in you. Drop something on the ground. Take a long time picking it up. Let's see what they do."

I took some coins from my pocket, pretended to fumble with them, and let them fall. We bent down to retrieve them and I snuck a look. "It's a black sedan with two men inside." We continued to stay low as the car revved, passed us, and drove away.

"Tonight's your lucky night. Forget the cab. I'm taking you home." I stared at him, wondering how he could stay so calm, but relieved that one of us was.

"Thanks, but that won't be necessary. I'll take a cab." I saw no wisdom in accepting a ride with someone I hardly knew.

"Negative, ma'am. People are following you, and I've been ordered to keep you safe."

"I don't even know who you are or why you're here. I'm not getting in your car."

"I told you that Ben Douglas ordered me to protect you." Outwardly, he maintained his poise, but I could sense that he was getting testier by the minute.

"Ben would have told me."

"He didn't have a chance, and he couldn't risk sending you a message. Your line is not secure."

"Who else knows about me besides you and Ben?"

"Ben told me that your assignment is RYBAT, so I assumed that no one else knows. Obviously, someone does."

He used Ben's word. That was reassuring. Perhaps seeing the brain dulled any residual reason; I agreed to the ride. We turned back into the wind, which was now hurling stinging drops of rain, forcing me to duck my head. While walking to Jermaine's car, it became clear that decades of deceit *were* still relevant to someone, but I couldn't figure out why. Most of the country didn't believe Oswald had acted alone. What was the big deal? I'd ask Ben when he returned, which would not be soon enough.

I climbed into Jermaine's dark-brown Hummer H1 and embraced its warmth. "Somehow, I didn't picture you as a Hummer owner."

He laughed, the first time I'd seen an unfettered emotion from him. "Reminds me of my days in the service. Yes sir, they were good times, even if it was hotter than hell in Iraq. Makes Virginia seem like the North Pole."

"Good times, really? I can't imagine being shot at being all that enjoyable."

"Me and my buddies got real close. We'd do anything for each other—even that reporter who saved my life."

"A reporter? Saved you?" I found it hard to imagine. Jermaine seemed so capable, so strong. "How?"

"He was embedded in our unit. He took the hit, not me. IED took off both his legs."

I winced. "Is he okay now? I mean, did he live?"

"Yep, but I'm not sure how much of a life he has now. I hear from him occasionally." Jermaine pulled onto the highway, passing cars easily.

"Did it ever bother you that no weapons of mass destruction were found?"

"A little," he answered. "Never was sure why we were there, but the government's been good to me. They paid for my education and I got a good job, so it all works out." He took the next exit and maneuvered the Hummer through the twists, turns, and stoplights with ease, apparently familiar with the convoluted traffic patterns and unpredictable driving behaviors inside the beltway.

A few minutes later, he pulled into the circular drive in front of my building, hopped out of his seat, ran to the passenger side of the Hummer, and opened my door. "Do you want me to take you to your apartment?"

"I'll be fine. Thanks for the ride."

"If anyone bothers you again, just call me."

I stepped from the car, surveyed the driveway for any suspicious activity, and turned to Jermaine. "Guess I'll see you next week. Have a Happy Thanksgiving."

"You be careful now, you hear?" he smiled before returning to his vehicle and driving away. His manner was completely different; he seemed friendly and protective. I waved good-bye and entered the building thinking that maybe, just maybe, I *could* trust him. I punched the elevator button and rode to the sixth floor, briefly pondering the coincidence—Oswald purportedly shot from the sixth floor of the Texas school book depository. Jeez, I was obsessing.

I spent the evening downloading photos and the spreadsheet to a flash drive, reviewing everything with persistent disbelief. Then I began to read the files I had scanned and found statements from the physicians and attendants at both Parkland Hospital and Bethesda. All of the doctors described the back head wound as "the size of a baseball," that "a portion of his cerebellum was falling out," that the wound was in the "occipital-parietal area"—the side and back of Kennedy's head.

Paul O'Connell, a Bethesda lab technician, even drew a picture of the damaged skull with comments like "brain completely blown out" and "the wound on the right side of the skull was huge, but not big enough to remove the brain without tearing the organ apart." How had they kept this secret? I had my answer when I read the following: "You are reminded that you are under verbal orders of the Surgeon General, US Navy, to discuss with no one the events connected with official duties on the evening of 22 November – 23 November 1963...an infraction of these orders makes you liable to court-martial proceedings." They muzzled those performing the autopsy.

Then came the statement from Floyd Riebe, a medical photographer at Bethesda. When shown the official autopsy photographs he said, "The two pictures you showed me are not what I saw that night." When shown the X rays, he said, "It's being phonied someplace. It's make-believe."

Of course it was.

I continued reading, feeling resentment festering inside, causing a gangrenous decay of everything I ever thought and believed, only to be accelerated by what I read next. Lieutenant Commander William Bruce Pitzer, a photographer present at Kennedy's autopsy, was found shot to death, with a thirty-eight-caliber revolver lying at his side. The navy ruled his death a suicide; his family never bought it. His slides and films from the autopsy were never found.

Now, *I* had them in my satchel.

When I reached a link concerning the missing brain, I had to stop. It *was* a conspiracy—both the assassination and the cover-up. Hundreds of thousands of entries on a gazillion websites, and the only people who knew the entire truth were those who'd committed these crimes—and me. And someone knew it.

With everything saved on flash drives, I erased the files from my computer and shut down. I picked up my neglected glass of a gentle, but flavorful, Anderson Conn Valley Pinot Noir that had been breathing so long, it was tired. So was I. I moved my head in circles trying to loosen the kinks in my neck. Pulling myself from the comfort of the recliner, I dumped the stale wine down the sink and decided to make another visit to Greg tomorrow. He had mentioned scramblers and different types of recording devices. I needed them. It was time to become a real spy.

But then I realized that tomorrow was Thanksgiving. There was no way I could face my father, not now. It was enough that he'd impeded my career and sabotaged my love. Now, he had stolen my innocence. He was no longer my father. He was a monster.

CHAPTER EIGHT

"**H**i Berta. It's Kat." I faked a throatiness and coughed a couple of times for added effect. "I'm not feeling well, so I won't be able to make it for Thanksgiving dinner."

Berta, my father's housekeeper, cook and, although he would never admit it, companion of a sort, moaned.

"Please tell everyone I'm sorry. I know how much trouble you go to for these dinners, but I'd be miserable company."

"Your father will be disappointed."

"Yeah, well he'll get over it." His disappointment couldn't approach my disgust.

"I don't know. Your father's been acting funny lately, like something's on his mind. You know how he gets that look, like he's always in control and nothing bothers him. That's when it's the worst. Well, he's been walking around with that funny look all the time these past couple of weeks, and I don't mind saying that he's been a pain in my butt. Get the drinks. Set the table. Cook the dinner—like I don't have a family of my own to feed."

"Sounds like his normal self," I responded bitterly.

"He may not always show it, but he loves you. Your problem is that you take him too seriously. When he gets in one of his snits, just ignore him. I do." She exploded in a guffaw that practically pushed the phone away from my ear. I could see Berta throwing her head back in laughter. I would miss seeing her most of all.

Once she recovered, she said, "I'll tell him you're not coming. He won't be happy. Neither am I."

"I'll stop by when I feel better. Happy Thanksgiving."

Berta merely grunted.

I spent the morning and early afternoon reading, but like the sirens of old who lured sailors to their doom, the vault summoned me. I debated the pros and cons of succumbing to its call. I'd be violating Ben's schedule, and my presence could be detected, but based on the rose I'd received and the men who followed me out of Langley, someone already knew about my activities, so what difference would it make? Also, it was a holiday. Only a skeleton crew would be at work, making it less likely that anyone would monitor my entry via the scanner.

Besides, time was running out. Rehab of the entire area would begin soon, and everything might be lost. Ben would be back on Monday, expecting my preliminary report, and I had a lot of pictures to take. There was so much inside. If I didn't go, I'd never see it. Someone had to—at least, someone who valued the truth. I pulled on some clothes, took care of Scout, and was out the door an hour later.

The convoluted corridors seemed even darker and longer than usual—especially with Jermaine nowhere to be seen. If I did encounter trouble, I was on my own. The thought heightened all of my senses, to the point where I imagined specters lurking in the shadows. The occasional sound had to be the footsteps of a foe. By the time I reached the vault, I was paranoia personified. I took out a wedge I'd brought from home and jammed it under the door.

I pulled on Greg's gloves and removed one box after another, sounding like a cicada as I clicked photos and entered each item by voice onto the spreadsheet. I would read the documents at home. Still, I couldn't help but notice that evidence from the assassinations of Robert Kennedy and Martin Luther King was also in the vault. Pieces of kitchen walls, door frames, and ceiling tiles from the Ambassador Hotel were stored, each with a number of bullet holes—representing far more ammunition than Sirhan Sirhan's gun could have held. I kept snapping away.

I came across audio tapes and the original testimonies of Sandy Serrano, LAPD officer Paul Sharaga, Dr. Marcus McBoom, and photographer Evan Freed, making me wonder if their testimonies were omitted from the criminal investigation of RFK's assassination like those of his brother's. Photos of the crowd were also included, with the faces of two men circled. I instantly recognized the CIA's David Morales, and according to a handwritten note on the back of one, the other man was chief of psychological warfare operations, George Joannides. It was discomforting that they attended RFK's celebration for winning the California primary. Even the Secret Service didn't provide protection for candidates back then. Given my newfound distrust, I assumed that they were there to witness RFK's death.

It was getting late. I logged off, pocketed the scanner, and placed my camera and computer in the case. Taking one last look to ensure that I had all my belongings, I was still amazed that my gloves left no mark in the dust frosting each box. I left the vault and pressed the button inside the podium to close the door, confident that no one could detect my presence there. As I walked down the empty hallways, it was becoming increasingly clear why the vault might make others nervous. It held evidence from not just one assassination, but three, and who knew what else? I wasn't even halfway through. The silence and isolation of the corridors held me captive. At last I reached the elevator, my escape from Langley's hell. I punched the button harder than normal and didn't exhale until I reached the ground floor.

Instead of returning to my office, I detoured to Greg's, hoping that my expanded security clearance would allow me entry into his lab. An old friend like him wouldn't mind if I picked up some of the scramblers he'd shown me. When I arrived, I saw that the lights were on and heard Springsteen playing inside. I knocked on the door and opened it before he could answer. "What are you doing here on a holiday?" I asked.

"Hey there." He swiveled around quickly on his stool. "You're not the only one with a top-secret project. I thought I was the only idiot working on Thanksgiving. What are *you* doing here?"

"It's that project I'm working on. Tight deadline, I'm afraid. By the way, thanks for the scanner and software. I can't imagine how long it would take without them."

"No problem." He stood and walked toward me as though he wanted to keep me away from whatever it was he was working on. "Whatever I can do to help."

"Well, there is something." I began, trying not to look over his shoulder. "You said you had scramblers?"

He beamed with pride and began lifting various objects from shelves. "Well, sure I do. What do you need? I got 'em for computers, cell phones, GPS devices—you name it."

"I could use them all, that is, if you don't mind."

He stuffed his hands in his pockets, but I see his fingers were wiggling inside. "Must be some project," he said, sounding hopeful that I might elaborate.

"It is. I'd love to tell you about it, but just like whatever it is you're working on over there, it's RYBAT. You know I'd tell you if I could."

"Got it." He turned back to the equipment and picked up the first item. "This one here plugs into your computer port. No one can tell what messages you're sending or what websites you've searched." He handed it to me. "This one plugs into your phone, where the headset goes. No one can intercept your calls—incoming or outgoing." He gave me that one as well.

I picked up the devices and looked them over. "You mean, if someone took my computer, they could figure out what websites I visited? What else could they find out?" Panic enveloped me as I thought of how much I had researched using my computer.

"On most computers, we can identify every keystroke that someone has made, never mind what websites they've been to." He said it proudly, but when he saw a glimpse of horror on my face, he thought for a bit and then his eyes lit up. "But not if you use one of these babies." He pulled out a laptop from a drawer and turned it on. "A block is programmed into it. No one can learn anything from it as long as they don't know your password and security code." The screen lit up and various icons appeared. "And, if someone tries to mess around with it, you know, enters the wrong password and fails several times, or enters the wrong security code, the RAM will automatically self-destruct."

"Really? How does someone get one of these?" I took a closer look. Given the amount I had researched lately, this could be a godsend.

"For you, it's free. Just don't tell anyone where you got it. They'd have my head." His smile was as wide as the Potomac.

I hugged him. He blushed. "Take it, it's yours, but really, you can't tell anyone, okay?"

"Promise." I squeezed his arm and turned to leave.

"Wait a second. Look at this." He sprang to the counter and pulled out a pair of glasses that looked like something out of Star Trek and handed them to me. "Made these before plans for Google Glass were sketched out on someone's cocktail napkin."

"They look a little dorky. What do they do?" I asked, while examining the glasses.

"They're a voice-activated, hands-free computer with GPS capabilities among other things. They use CIA satellites for positioning, which makes them faster too. Try them on." I did and looked back at him. "Okay, name a destination," he said.

"Crystal City Mall." A map appeared in my visual field, with printed directions at the top. "Wow. Would these tell me what restaurants have an opening if I needed to make a last-minute reservation?" I chuckled, as I handed them back.

"And more. Say you're in Afghanistan and have told the GPS where you want to go. Not only will it give you the route, but it will also tell you if there are any bad guys along the way—built-in heat sensors. I'm working on a detection device for IEDs as well. State of the art, if I do say so myself."

"They could come in handy. You could make a fortune."

"Take them. They're yours. I'm working on a newer model with more bells and whistles."

"Thanks. I mean it." I stuffed the glasses in my bag. "I've got to get some work done before it gets too late. Maybe we can catch up next week."

"That would be great. I can't wait to hear about your project. If you need stuff like this, it must be pretty interesting. Just like your old operative days, huh?" he asked.

"Hardly," I said, smiling. As I walked toward my office, I could hear him humming along with "Thunder Road." I stopped briefly by my desk to check on things and then left for the night, praying that the only being waiting for me was Scout.

A generous glass of a 2006 Caymus was calling my name, and I hoped that its robust flavor would do its magic. Once home, I pulled on my old sweats, poured myself some wine, placed some cheese and crackers on a plate, and settled into my recliner. I listened to several voice mails before my father's paralyzed me.

In a voice saturated with sarcasm, he said, "You must have made a miraculous recovery if you're not home to answer the phone. Or perhaps for some reason..." he paused poignantly, "...you are avoiding me. We need to talk."

I blew out the air I had sucked in upon hearing his voice. My father never called. The last thing I wanted to do was talk to him. I had more pressing concerns.

Removing Greg's computer from its case, I logged on and began downloading all of the pictures I had taken earlier in the day, swirling the wine in my glass while I copied the perilous information onto flash drives. I erased all incriminating files from my old computer—web searches, pictures, scanned documents—everything except for Ben's inventory, which was a legitimate assignment. As long as I could keep Greg's computer safe, I would be safe. At least that's how I consoled myself.

My apartment was too quiet, and I was keenly aware of every creak in the floor, the banging of the heating system, and sounds from the street, so I rose and inserted a Beach Boys CD into my stereo. I had created the ultimate non sequitur of an evening; sipping fine wine, downloading evidence from the crime of the century, and humming along to "Don't Worry Baby." Right, I thought to myself, as I returned to the comfort of my recliner and sipped some more wine.

Knowing that Langley would be sparsely occupied on Friday, I decided to work from home. There was so much reading to do, and I needed to work on my report. Sometime in the afternoon, the phone rang. Checking the caller ID, I was relieved to see Pam's name.

"Hey, girl, how was Thanksgiving with the two-headed monster?" Her voice was cheery and provided necessary relief from the task at hand.

"I didn't go. The last thing I needed was another one of his lectures or commentary on my personal life." It was so good to have someone I could vent to.

"Don't blame you. Any news on the Rob front?"

"He's coming for dinner tomorrow night, but I'm not too optimistic. I think he just wants someone to hang out with."

"Don't give up. Give it time. He and Trevor were talking about something in the study, and I couldn't help but overhear him mention your name."

"Really?" I perked up. "What did he say?" This was the best news I had heard all day.

"Something about how good you still look, not much else. You know Trevor. He likes to do the talking." She giggled.

"Speaking of Trevor, how is he?"

"I've hardly seen him. He's out. If I didn't know better, I'd swear he had another woman on the side."

"Oh, Pam. He wouldn't, would he?" All I could think of was that Trevor might be attractive to impressionable co-eds.

"Just kidding. Probably just end-of-year school stuff—you know, midterm exams, grades, students panicking. Must be getting to him though. He went out after Thanksgiving dinner and when he came home, he went straight to his study and lit up his pipe. He knows I detest that thing."

"That doesn't sound like him. Are you sure everything's okay?" My gut was in overdrive.

"I asked him the same question. He swore that it was, but then he said something odd." She paused, as though selecting her words. "He said that maybe I shouldn't be trying to play matchmaker with you and Rob."

"What? That's crazy. That's what girlfriends do for each other." I faked a laugh to cover for my growing unease. It sounded more like a twitter.

"Must be a guy thing. Don't sweat it. I think Rob's interested. Let me know how the date goes and hang in there, kiddo. Have you heard from Beau?"

"He called, but asked me out for the same night as Robbie, so I couldn't go. I think he was miffed. Maybe he's not all that interested."

"Or maybe he's playing it cool."

We hung up with me promising to tell her how things went with Robbie. Still, Trevor's behavior was lodged in my head. Despite my efforts to put it aside, it preoccupied my thoughts as I returned to my reading, mostly about the CIA's role in overthrowing the governments of Guatemala, Iran, Vietnam, and others. I finally had to put it down when I read that Diem was assassinated three weeks before JFK. That couldn't be a coincidence.

I thought back to college. My protest of the war had been so naïve—based on the number of Americans dying in a foreign place that no one had ever heard of. Linking arms with Robbie as we marched down the street was an added benefit. Had I known then what I knew now, had we all known, could we have made more of a difference, or was this beyond anyone's capability to stop? Kennedy had tried, and look what happened to him.

But it wasn't just about Kennedy now; it was about King and Bobby and who knew what else? Maybe the vault hid many more skeletons of the military-industrial complex, and I was rattling the bones.

CHAPTER NINE

I had an entire day to prepare for Robbie's visit and take my mind off what I had read the previous night. After a quick run with Scout, I headed toward the store a few blocks away. Robbie used to like chips and salsa—did he still? Maybe some crudités or stuffed olives? Hmm, drinks. He liked beer, but he drank wine at Pam and Trevor's. I bought two magnificent steaks, a couple of potatoes, and some fresh, delicate asparagus. I was acting like a schoolgirl, and it felt fine.

Once back at my apartment, I checked the time—only one o'clock. How would I fill the next six hours? Resisting the urge to go back to my computer, I vacuumed, wiped counters, cleaned the bathrooms, ironed, and did my nails. As if stuck in beltway traffic, the hands of the clock had only crept to four p.m. Like an addict, I needed another fix. I pulled out Greg's computer, logged on, and opened my spreadsheet. I would never know why, but when I came across the name Marita Lorenz, something inside made me check her out on the CIA's database.

Many links emerged so I began clicking, reading, and then thinking. I visualized a sunny Florida day in November.

> *"Come on, Marita. We don't have all day."*
> *"I'm coming Frank. Who's in the other car?"*
> *"Oswald and the Cubans. Bosch and Diaz will ride with us."* He opened the door and climbed in.
> *"Can you open the trunk?"* she asked. *"I want to put my suitcase inside."*

"No room." He stepped out of the car and popped the trunk. Marita saw pistols, rifles, and ammo. "See? What did I tell you?"

Frank Sturgis had lured her away from Castro and recruited her to work undercover—both as an operative and as his mistress. Seeing the guns was something she was accustomed to.

The convoy drove all the way in the rain. When they reached Dallas, they pulled in to a tawdry hotel that charged by the hour, not the day.

"I'm going to freshen up," she said as she left the main room. The Op-40 men spread a Dallas street map on the table and studied it. By the time she returned, Hunt and Ruby had arrived.

"The hit is on," Ruby said. "They changed the route, just like we wanted." The men smiled and lit cigars.

The next day, Marita sat in the hotel while the men left for their mission. She jumped when the phone rang.

"Hey babe. It's me, Frank."

"I saw the news..."

"We got the bastard. Everything was covered in advance. No arrests, no real newspaper investigation—very professional."

She replaced the receiver just as she heard him say, "I'll see you when things die down."

I sat bolt upright in my chair. Oswald couldn't have been with them, I thought. He was working at the book depository. Suddenly feeling chilled, I rubbed my arms. This was probably one of the fake Oswalds that my father created.

I checked my watch—6:30. Damn! I leaped from the sofa and rushed into the bedroom, flinging open the closet doors. With all the time I had today, I'd never bothered to think about what I would wear. I climbed into black skinny jeans created by some sadistic designer, pulled on a burgundy, cashmere V-neck sweater, and stepped into some low heels.

I stuck in some hoop earrings and fastened a matching necklace—favorites that always reminded me of a former hippie in Sausalito who'd made me feel young again for a night. I took two swipes with a brush through my hair. It would have to do.

Dashing to the kitchen, I retrieved the appetizers from the refrigerator and started slicing vegetables for the crudités. I ripped open the dip container and crammed it on the plate between them. I dumped some tortilla chips into a bowl and splashed the salsa into a smaller side dish. The beer was cold. The wine was cool if he drank white and room temperature if he wanted red. I shoved some James Taylor CDs into the player. The buzzer startled me as I placed the spread on the coffee table and exhaled.

"Wow—you're prompt!" I said, yanking open the door while my heart jack-hammered in my chest.

His hands were jammed in his pockets as he shuffled inside. "I've been driving around your neighborhood for the last half hour. Parking around here is impossible." He chuckled as he walked toward the living room. "Nice digs."

"Thanks. Can I get you something to drink?" It was so good to see him. I wanted to give him a hug, but decided to follow his more subdued lead.

"A beer would be great." He smiled upon seeing the munchies and chomped on a chip as he surveyed the room. "How did you find this place?"

I answered as I went to the fridge to grab his beer. "It's convenient to nearly everything, and I love Shirlington Village. It's like a small town nestled in the big city."

He took in the pictures on the wall, the wine rack, and the furnishings. "I see you still like Sierra Club photos."

"Yeah, but these are actual photos, not like the posters we taped to our dorm walls in college." I handed him the beer and sat down on the sofa, hoping that he would join me. He munched on another chip, still viewing my décor. "Do you still hike?"

"Not as much as we used to," I said, trying to bring our past back to life, "but I'd like to."

"We should go sometime."

That sounded promising. I jumped on it. "Just say when."

"It's too late to go this year, maybe next spring."

Finally he sat down on the sofa, a little farther away than I had hoped, but the evening was young. I didn't want to wait until next spring. I had to come up with a winter activity. "Do you cross-country ski? I've heard there are some nice places in the mountains."

"Uh, sure. Maybe after the holidays." He took a swig of beer and chewed on a carrot. "What's for dinner? I'm famished. Haven't eaten all day."

"Your favorite—at least it used to be. I'll get it started. Can't have you fainting from hunger on our first—I mean the first time you come for dinner." Stupid. I think he knew I was going to say first date, but he let it go—still a gentleman. I rose to start the meal.

"Hey, it can wait a bit," he said, pulling me back to the sofa. "You've got enough chips and dip here to feed the city." There was that endearing crooked smile again. I couldn't help but comply. "Tell me more about what you do. We never got to that at Pam and Trevor's."

"Not much to tell you, really. Like I said, it's a boring desk job at State." I tried to return his smile, but could only manage a defective replica. "I sit at a computer all day."

"I'm disappointed. I thought you'd be tilting at windmills like in the old days." His eyes twinkled, but I could sense his disappointment. Oh, how I wanted to tell him everything.

"Me too, but sometimes things don't always work out the way you planned. Before you know it, days have turned into years and years have turned into careers. I don't know where the time has gone."

"Did your dad get you your job?" His tone was innocent, but the question still prickled like a burr.

"No, I think he wanted me to marry and have his grandchildren." What another stupid thing to say to a man who had proposed to me, a man I'd foolishly rejected. He looked away, so I changed the subject. "Doesn't really matter now. I'm so close to retirement." I rose to start dinner, hoping to break this line of questions. "Do you still like your steak medium rare?"

"How is your dad?" He followed me into the kitchen.

I clanged the pots a bit too loud as I pulled them from the shelf and then yanked the steaks from the refrigerator.

"I hit a nerve, didn't I? Sorry," he said, as he placed the steaks on the broiling pan, piercing them with a fork and lightly applying some Montreal rub that I had placed on the counter.

"Forget it. We have a mutual avoidance pact. I live my own life and make my own choices." I slid the steaks into the oven, desperate to change the subject. "And now, I'm choosing a robust Sonoma Cab with an exquisite finish that will perfectly complement these steaks. You do like Cabernet, don't you? If not, I could get you something else. I have white wine, more beer, scotch...whatever you want." Calm down, calm down, I admonished myself.

He pulled the potatoes from the oven. "You worshiped him."

"I did once, but not now. Yes, I love him. After all, he is my father, but...," I sprinkled some olive oil and basil into the pan and turned to face him. "I resent the control he had over me. My life could have been so much different." Fearing I'd said too much too soon, I turned to the potatoes, smashing them with unusual vigor.

"How?" Robbie snapped the ends off the asparagus and began to sauté it in a pan, stirring it with a wooden spoon. It amazed me how naturally we fell into our old ways.

"Oh, I don't know," I answered, but was thinking that Robbie and I might have shared a life together. "Maybe I would have had a more exciting career, or maybe I wouldn't be alone." As soon as I said it, I regretted it. I moved toward the wine rack so he wouldn't notice the crimson tide that washed across my face.

"You could have had both." His voice was low, but he instantly compensated with a forced laugh. "It's not too late. You're bright, energetic, and you certainly don't look your age."

I smiled gratefully, but said nothing. Instead I handed him the bottle to open while I returned to the stove and stirred the asparagus hissing in the oil. "You've aged pretty well yourself, Robbie."

"You're the only one who still calls me Robbie." A warmth permeated his voice, and I could feel tension leave my shoulders and spine.

"Everyone else calls me Rob." He turned the corkscrew and removed the cork, rubbing the wet end in his fingers and smelling it. "You still know how to treat a bottle of wine."

"Would you rather I call you Rob? It sounds like a thief." I pulled a couple of glasses from the shelf and poured the wine, allowing it a few minutes to breathe.

"Not in a million years." He smiled again, but as soon as I allowed that to calm me, he stunned me with his next question. "Your dad, he was CIA, wasn't he?" He said it so lightly, as though it was nothing. He brought the glasses to the small dining table that was squeezed between the cramped kitchenette and the living room.

"How did you know?" The tension flowed back, bringing a tide of angst with it. I couldn't let my father, or even the mere mention of his name, ruin things again. I gored the steaks with a fork and dropped them onto a small platter.

"Just a hunch. He always struck me as a cold warrior—serious, distant, always guarded with his words, but still managing to get his way."

We filled our plates and carried them to the table. I lit the candles while Robbie swirled his glass and enjoyed the wine's bouquet. He toasted, "To reunions!" We tapped glasses. I took a sip, this time only lightly swishing it around my tongue. "Perfect."

"Let's not talk about my father anymore, okay? I want this to be a pleasant evening." I tried to say it as a joke, but was completely serious.

"Fair enough, but he really wasn't all that different from the rest of his generation. Don't take it personally; I don't."

"What do you mean?" I managed to ask just before shoving a piece of meat in my mouth.

"At the risk of making a gross generalization, I think that our parents taught us how to love our country—blindly, willing to sacrifice anything and everything for it. We 'boomers' tried to keep the country honest." He took a sip of wine and paused. "You know, both are important."

"Hmm, I guess so. They got us through the Depression, World War II—we wouldn't be here if it weren't for them, but it seems like the ends always justified the means in their world. As long as you were white, male, straight, held a job, and went to church, you were okay."

"Then we came along, protesting flawed wars, unseating unscrupulous presidents, and generally being pains in the ass," he snickered. "Ah, those were the days—flower power meets the silent majority; not trusting anyone over thirty, the generation gap, and the best music in the world. Now here we are, way over thirty and hearing our music in elevators."

His tongue was plastered in his cheek, and his winsome smile made me want to reach out and pull him close to me. "Speaking of music, we need some more." I rose to insert another CD.

"Allow me." Robbie stood and walked to the entertainment center near my desk. "You can learn a lot about people by their CDs."

I sat back down and grinned as I thought about my recent attraction to country music. "Is Josh Turner a deal breaker?" I looked back down at my plate, scooped up some veggies, and took another sip of wine, thinking that, for the most part, the evening was going well. I looked at Robbie hunched over the CD rack, turning his head sideways to read the titles. But then he rose, and horror descended on me as I realized that he was no longer looking at CDs, but at my computer. There was Marita Lorenz, with her dark eyes, brown Patty-Duke-styled hair, and a smile that made Mona Lisa look gregarious. I could see him stiffen as he read about her on the CIA's database. I placed my fork on the table and instantly was at his side, trying to distract him.

"Why are you reading about Marita Lorenz?" he asked.

A strange tingling rendered my body taut and inert. "It's nothing. Just something I came across on the History Channel." It didn't work with Trevor; why was I trying the same lame excuse now? Robbie's skepticism was obvious.

"No one looks up Marita Lorenz unless they're into the Kennedy assassination—are you?" He turned toward me and studied my face. I wasn't sure what he was seeking.

I answered with a question of my own. "Why? Are you interested in the Kennedy assassination?" This could open up a whole new line of conversation, one that might provide an interesting twist on things and maybe some context for what I discovered in the vault.

"I guess you could say I'm a bit of a conspiracy buff." He smirked, as though bracing for my response.

"Really? I mean, you seem so grounded. I thought conspiracy nu... buffs, were kind of eccentric." Damn. I was stepping on one verbal IED after another.

"You were going to say 'nuts,' right?" He seemed simultaneously amused and annoyed.

"Sorry, my boss's words. When he talks, the two words seem inseparable." I rubbed my hands and looked down.

"Why is your boss discussing Kennedy?" He walked back to the CD rack and renewed his search for some music. He pulled out several CDs; it looked as though he was going to stay a while.

"What about the singers you wanted to hear at the bar?"

"They play every Saturday. We can go another time. So, about your boss?"

"Um, it just came up. Besides, it's not important. It was over fifty years ago—water under the dam or over the bridge or whatever the saying is," I said, trying to keep my voice light.

After inserting the CDs, he rose and turned abruptly to face me. "Kat, it *is* important. At least we 'conspiracy nuts' think so." Then, in a more strident voice, he continued, "Aren't you tired of the lies, the deceit? Don't you want to know the truth before we die?"

"Would it change anything?" Sensing his dismay at my response, I asked earnestly, "Let me rephrase that. How would it change things?"

"Maybe if people knew what the government was capable of, they'd take their votes more seriously and hold elected officials more accountable."

"You give people too much credit. I'm not sure anyone really cares about the Kennedys anymore."

"That's the problem. They should. Government shenanigans are alive and well, thanks to everything they've gotten away with. All you have to do is read the paper—IRS, electronic eavesdropping, Benghazi, government shutdowns..."

My skepticism must have been obvious because he added, "I'll admit, they've done a good job of marginalizing us; I can elicit rolled eyes and stifled yawns with the best of them." He attempted a smile, but it was short-lived. "Do *you* think JFK's assassination was a conspiracy?"

His eyes glowed like intense blue flames that could burn me if I wasn't careful.

I took a second to select my words. "I think it was a conspiracy and the government covered it up." I looked up briefly to gauge his reaction. He wanted to hear more. "What I don't understand is why they continue to do so after so many years." He smiled—for real this time. I was relieved. "When did you get interested in the assassination?" I asked, trying to remediate my chances with him. "I don't remember you mentioning it when we were in college."

"It would be easier to answer when I wasn't interested." He chuckled. "I've been into it for as long as I can remember."

"Tell me about it." I brought our glasses and the wine bottle to the sofa, where he joined me, swallowed a few sips, and after a few prods, began relating his personal journey, beginning with that day in 1963.

"I was only eleven and was home sick from school. My best friend came running over to our house to tell me about the assassination. I spent the rest of that weekend glued to the TV, watching everything I could—maybe because Kennedy campaigned in our town and I got to see him in person. When I saw Ruby, who looked like every gangster I'd ever seen, shoot Oswald that Sunday morning—right on national TV—I knew something wasn't right, even though I was just a kid." He finished the last of his wine. "Turns out, it wasn't."

"Ruby said he shot Oswald because he felt bad for Jackie. I take it that you didn't believe him," I poured some more wine into his glass, hoping he'd continue.

"Gangsters wouldn't care about Jackie Kennedy, but there was something else." Robbie leaned forward, obviously into the story. "My dad was reading the newspaper the day after, and he threw it down on the table with an audible snort. He said something like, 'First, they report that there may have been multiple gunmen and that maybe that it was an international plot. Then, poof! It's just a lone assassin, Oswald. Within hours, they've got his whole life history in the newspaper—before he'd even been charged with Kennedy's murder!' I can still hear him ranting, 'How could they have produced that so fast if he was just some anonymous nut case?'"

"So, you've been at this a long time," I said, while my thoughts drifted to the vault. "Who do you think did it?"

"I'll tell you if you tell me why Marita Lorenz is on your computer. I mean, the real reason."

I stiffened once more, knowing that he would see through any attempt I made to throw him off. "I'll make you a deal," I began hopefully. "I'm going to retire soon, within a year. After that, I'll tell you whatever you want to know."

"So this has something to do with your job? Are you CIA, like your dad?" His voice was casual, nonchalant—in complete contrast to the steel rod that was now my spine.

It was my turn to go on the offensive. "I'm curious, why would a conspiracy theorist know about my dad?"

"I'll tell you if you tell me the real reason you were reading about Marita Lorenz." Though somewhat misshapen, his smile disarmed me once more—especially as it was now accompanied by a gentle touch of his hand as he brushed some errant strands of hair from my face.

"Robbie. Can we change the subject?" I took his hand and held it. "It's been over thirty-five years since we've seen each other. Surely we can find other things to talk about."

He thought for a bit and, with a gentle chuckle, said, "Remember your junior year, when we went camping and that bear appeared?" I smiled at the memory. "You seemed so calm, like you wanted to pet it. I half thought you might."

"I remember when the provost called you a meddlesome muck-raker," I laughed. "Me, of all people, dating a rebel."

"You had a little rebellious streak, as I recall."

"I learned from the master," I said, unable to keep the smile off my face, which now mirrored his.

"At the risk of becoming a pest, do you have plans for tomorrow?"

"What did you have in mind?" I asked, taking hold of his hand as the wine took an even stronger hold of me.

"How about coming to my place? There are some great jogging trails. We could run together, like we used to. You do still run, don't you?"

"Not as fast as I used to, but if you're willing to slow down for an old lady, I'd love to. May I bring Scout?" The dog raised its ears at the mention of its name and turned to look soulfully at Robbie.

"How can I refuse a face like that?" He cupped Scout's snout in his hand. "Of course, the more the merrier." He checked his watch and gasped. "I'd better go before I wear out my welcome. It's two a.m.!"

This was the Robbie who'd won my heart so many years ago and was coasting to another victory now.

That night I lay in bed, thinking about our evening and his response to seeing Marita Lorenz on my computer. Thankfully, there was no indication that it was a CIA database, just the picture and accompanying text. Robbie seemed so much more engaged once he saw her photo—even canceling our date at the bar. I wondered whether he'd invited me over the next day so he could probe more. Maybe he felt I was a kindred spirit. Or maybe he sensed that my job made me privy to information he craved.

I'd once harbored such great hopes of a life of excitement, a life of intrigue, a life of passion—the Holy Grail so many had sought, but few had found; some because they didn't recognize it, some because they gave up too soon. But that ship had sailed long ago. Had I given up, or had I been too weak to pursue it? Why had I let my father deny me my passions? What was it Robbie said: that we were at the point in our lives when, if we were going to make a difference, it was now or never. With sixty staring me in the face, it was time to chart a new course. I had a second chance at passion, both at work and, God willing, with Robbie. Two dreams were dawning, and yet I was wide awake. What were his last words? Something like, "Just don't go petting any bears, okay?"

CHAPTER TEN

When the alarm hollered at eight a.m., I threw on some running clothes and packed a bag with clothes for afterward. At least, I hoped there'd be an afterward. Robbie hadn't said anything about that. As I drove through the national park to the peninsula, serene views of the Potomac River met me at every bend. I saw the sign for Mason's Neck and soon after, entered the drive of a massive spread that fronted a stately brick mansion. A small, stone carriage house sat just inside the open wrought-iron gates. I parked at the end of a curved bluestone pathway that led to its green front door, which matched the working shutters on each window. I knocked a couple of times, using the brass anchor affixed to the door, and then tugged on my running jacket and pulled at my tights.

Robbie appeared, wearing a sweat suit and a broad smile. "How do you like my little slice of heaven?" he said, as he waved his arms across the panorama around us.

"It's beautiful! Is that really Beau's house up there? It's huge."

"He only lives there half the year. He usually goes down south in November, and I watch his house while he's gone." He surveyed the big house. "I'm amazed that he hasn't left yet."

"Must be nice," I said. Robbie welcomed me in, and I took another quick peek at Beau's house. It would be awkward running into him here. "Have you stayed in touch with Beau since college?"

"No. When I came east for the job, I attended a lecture at Georgetown. It was called something like 'The Legacy of the Cold War' and was given by none other than Pam's husband. She was in the audience and we recognized each other. We got together a few times, and she mentioned that Beau had a place for rent. It just sort of fell together." He pulled on his sneakers and as he was lacing them said, "There's a great five-mile trail that goes around the peninsula. Are you up for it?"

Shortly, we were on the move with Scout, true to his name, trotting just ahead of us. Except for the evergreens, the trees were bare, their fallen leaves now crunching like cereal with each of our footfalls. Small bushes with prickly stems ushered us to a path along the bay where, despite the nip in the air, fishermen and kayakers floated upon the water. I inhaled the crisp air deeply, as if it were a decongestant that cleared my head of the city's chaos. Robbie set a relaxed pace, for which I was grateful.

"So Beau must have a great job," I said, hoping to hear more about him from Robbie.

"Hmm, sort of. I guess you could say it was a family arrangement."

"What kind of family arrangement?" I asked innocently, not wanting to betray Pam's confidence.

"It's not really my place..."

"Oh come on. You can tell me."

"He got a job with an oil company when he graduated. His father was some sort of bigwig, but he's not..." I could see Robbie search for words, "... really one of them. He's more like a high-powered lackey for the CEO. He's kind of vague about it, but I don't think he likes it."

"Why not? He's seems to be doing well."

"I think he resents being bossed around. They tell him to jump and he's leaping through dozens of hoops. Here today and then, boom. He's gone on another trip."

"That must be tough. No wonder he has no family." I said, still fishing.

Robbie didn't even nibble. Instead he said, "We get together for drinks occasionally. He lets me live here for next to nothing. He's a good guy."

For the remainder of the run, Robbie pointed out various sites and some of the unique features of the area. I was grateful that he was doing all the talking as I needed every breath to keep up with him. Eventually, we rounded the turn and began running back to the house, our faces pink from exertion and glowing with perspiration.

"Race you back!" he said. With that he took off; Scout followed close behind. I arrived several minutes after them, totally winded. He came out of the house with two glasses of water. "Here's to..."

"...two aging baby boomers who can still manage a five-mile run." I finished, clinking his glass.

He showed me to the guest-bathroom shower and gave me a towel, adding, "Don't be long. I'll be waiting."

I took the quickest shower in history, at least my history, and pulled on a pair of jeans and a green sweater accessorized with a silk scarf. The aroma of eggs and bacon drew me to the kitchen where Robbie's feast waited. "So much for running," I said.

He smiled affectionately. "You have nothing to worry about."

"I could say the same about you. I guess being a freelance reporter has its perks. You can set your own hours and get regular runs in." I mused upon how nice that sounded. "I'm jealous."

"You said you're going to retire soon. You'll be able to call your own shots then. Any idea when?"

"I have one last assignment, and then I'm gone."

"Must be a big one to keep you working." He took a sip of coffee, but his eyes never left mine as he gauged my response.

I thought it odd that he would say that. What would make him think it was a big assignment? And why was he watching me so closely? Was he interested in Marita Lorenz or me? In an effort to steer the conversation away from work, I answered, "I'm thinking more about what I'd do afterward. Any ideas?" He sipped some orange juice, but his eyes remained on me.

"You don't need my help." He took my hand.

A smile crept across my face. "But I'd welcome it." He didn't bite, so I tried again. "The other night you said you'd changed. How?" I took his hand and studied his scar.

"Hmm, emotionally I'm not the person you knew. Professionally, I've done okay. Unfortunately, there will always be corruption to investigate, criminals to expose."

"What was your biggest story?" I asked.

"It had to be the one that earned me this." He pointed to his scar. "I wrote about the illegal importation of immigrants, slave trading really. Using young girls as prostitutes. Torturing them if they didn't cooperate. Drugging them to make them docile. Tying them up in semis for long trips in the hot sun. Some of them died from the heat, literally baking to death. My story resulted in immigration reform, but at great cost." His eyes glistened momentarily. I knew he was thinking about his wife. "It's hard to talk about, but you need to know."

"I'm glad you told me, but is it really worth it? I mean, why do you do it?"

"This is going to sound trite, but I'd rather die pursuing the truth than live ignoring a lie. It doesn't matter if it's those poor girls from Mexico or Kennedy's assassination. It's what makes me tick, Kat." His eyes begged me to understand.

"Just like Superman. A reporter by day who flies all over the place to right wrongs. I admire you, I really do. But how do you deal with the danger? Aren't you scared all the time?" The mere thought prompted me to lean closer and rest my hand on his.

"Well, yeah, but someone has to make these people pay." He looked at me like the young boy who'd confronted "Shoeless" Joe Jackson with "Say it ain't so." And found out it was. "I guess my kryptonite is that others get hurt, people I care about." Unconsciously, he touched his scar once more as though this act might somehow dull his pain.

In that small cottage, with the aroma of eggs and bacon still scenting the air, Jackson Browne asking us to rock him on the water, and Robbie's scar flashing *warning, warning* like a neon sign, I knew I could never tell him about the vault and its contents. He'd already lost too much and had been in harm's way too often. It was time for someone else to step up; like me. The vault was my issue and the threats I received were mine, not Robbie's. He didn't need any more sorrow in his life. This was even more important than the oath I took when I joined the CIA or my promise to Ben. No, there were too many reasons to keep what I knew to myself. No matter how many times Robbie asked about Marita Lorenz, I would not yield. I would protect him from himself, honor my promise to Ben, and not dishonor the Agency.

I collected our dishes and brought them to the kitchen. Robbie washed and I dried. In an effort to lighten my obviously somber mood, he splashed me with a few drops of water. I snapped my towel at him lightly. He wiped off my nose with his finger. I closed my eyes and smiled. He had disarmed the bomb ticking inside me.

"Come on, let's try out that hot car of yours," he said playfully.

"You're on."

Even though it was November, we put the top down, like two crazy teenagers; that's how we felt—especially with The Who singing "My Generation" on the car stereo. I pulled my hair back into a ponytail, while his curls blew freely.

Within two hours we had found our way to Charlottesville, where it all began. Strolling down the UVA quad, we reminisced about the freshman-year keg party where we first met. Not used to the freedom of college, I drank too much. Giggling, slurring my speech, and weaving like a child's top, I bumped into him and said something like, "You're cute." He took me outside for some fresh air and held on tightly enough to prevent me from careening headfirst into the pavilion gardens or the security guard who watched us with more than casual interest. We walked and walked and walked until I could see straight and form an entire sentence.

"You stopped by the next day to see how I was doing," I remembered fondly.

"You were one hurting pup. I felt bad for you."

"A lot of guys would have taken advantage of the situation." I pulled him close and buried my head in his shoulder.

"I'm not like a lot of guys."

I nodded. He wasn't.

"Do you remember how we'd sneak out at night and dress Thomas Jefferson up as Santa Claus for Christmas and like a leprechaun for Saint Patty's Day?" I asked, as we walked by the rotunda.

"Oh yeah, I remember all right. We'd be nice and warm in your room, and you'd make me go outside in the middle of the night and climb that silly bronze statue. Ole Tom was one cool dude in the winter, and I mean that literally."

"I made sure you got plenty warm when we returned to the dorm." Robbie wrapped his arm around me. I felt so secure, so wanted, so happy.

"In some ways it feels like yesterday," he sighed. "So what are you doing tomorrow?"

"It depends. What are you doing?" His eyes glowed like lanterns, providing light and warmth for whoever was lucky enough to be with him. And then he flashed that smile again, making me tingle from my toes to my neck. It was a half smile, really. Only one side of his mouth rose, exposing one tiny corner tooth that turned slightly inward, as if God had decided no one could be that perfect. But it was also a smile that radiated appreciation, joy, and a belief in life's possibilities. It began slowly and grew, carving a deep dimple in his right cheek. The best part was, I saw it often that day, and each time I felt lucky.

We walked down Rugby Street, then by the Corner, over to the Chapel, and found ourselves outside Alderman Library. By the statue of Icarus, we stopped. "Do you remember what happened here?" Robbie asked.

"Our first kiss," I replied.

"The first of many." Oblivious to the few students who had returned early from Thanksgiving break, he kissed me intently. "Couldn't help myself."

"I'm glad," I said as I held onto his arm like a comforter. "This has been so nice, like traveling back in time and rewriting our history."

"I wish it was that easy," he said as the sun escaped from the sky. "But we *can* determine our future."

The wind began to kick up. I zippered my jacket and wrapped my arms around my chest as though wearing a straitjacket.

"You look just like a co-ed. Want to go on a date with me?"

"Sure, where?" I said, enjoying the banter.

"I know a place with some fantastic hot chocolate." We walked briskly to the car, taking one last look at the campus: the thick white columns, the stately rotundas, the curving brick walkways, and hibernating gardens—the place where we first began. Robbie pressed the remote ignition, raised the convertible top, and we headed back toward Mason's Neck. Once again, the soundtrack of our lives accompanied us on the ride. Robbie tapped the steering wheel to the beat of each tune and sang along in his lilting baritone, joining Alvin Lee. "I'd love to change the world, but I don't know what to do."

Then looking at him I chirped, "So I'll leave it up to you."

He smiled. "You can change it too, Kat."

I sat quietly until the next song, when we both accompanied Neil Young. "Tin soldiers and Nixon's coming. We're finally on our own." Mostly, I watched Robbie being himself—a sight even more beautiful than the hills that rolled by.

"Those were strange times, weren't they? I guess what I miss the most is that at least we cared enough to want to change things." I said wistfully.

"Some of us still do. I guess that's how I became your garden-variety conspiracy nut. We deserve—no, we *need* the truth."

"If we did learn the truth about JFK's death, what would people do with it?"

He didn't respond, just kept staring ahead, with an occasional glance in the rearview mirror. At first I thought he was contemplating his answer, so I contented myself by listening to the oldies and thinking about the memories each one inspired. It was dark outside now, and the road was just a black ribbon, with only our headlights illuminating the dashed lines that split it in two. A hangnail moon ducked behind wispy clouds. Robbie must have been enjoying driving the car. He would speed up and then, when he sensed me getting nervous, slow down. But inexplicably, he did this several times. Each time, he watched the rearview mirror. I thought he was checking for cops, who might not take too kindly to such speed on these back roads.

"You never answered my question," I commented, mostly to interrupt his Mario Andretti imitation. I sighed with relief as we turned onto the highway, but then the car lurched forward. He shifted into overdrive—eighty, ninety, and then a hundred miles per hour.

"I'm glad you like the car, but could you slow down just a bit? Please?" I clutched his leg.

He gave me a sidelong glance and in a steely voice, so unlike anything I'd ever heard from him, said, "Hang on, we have company."

The car swerved abruptly into the adjacent lane. Before I could assess the situation, he swerved back. I stared at him and saw intensity contort his face as he tightened his grip on the steering wheel. I held onto the dashboard and turned to see what had caused his response. A dark sedan matched our every move, and it was gaining.

In and out of traffic, we veered back and forth. I was thrown into the door and then back into Robbie. We sped up to avoid some cars and then braked violently to avoid others, our disorientation heightened by the darkness and speed. At one point, Robbie slid onto the shoulder to avoid a slower car, causing the rumble strips to growl. My car screeched as if in pain as we grazed the guard rail. We swung back onto the highway as though we were playing some horrific video game. But it wasn't a game. We could get killed. We could kill.

That's when I heard the shots—rat-a-tat-tat—an automatic. I yanked Greg's GPS glasses from my purse, shoved them onto my face, and screamed, "Find the nearest police station!" A bullet shattered the back window, sending glass everywhere. A map appeared across my eyes. I yelled, "There's a police station off the next exit. They won't follow us there."

Robbie nodded and at the last second jerked the steering wheel to the right, sending us flying down the exit ramp at more than seventy. His eyes darted back and forth from the road to the rearview mirror. The other car also squealed onto the ramp, but roared off as we swerved into the parking lot cluttered with police cars. We sat hyperventilating to expel the tension. I was shaking. I think Robbie was too.

"Are you okay?" He leaned over and grasped my hand. I wasn't, but said yes anyway. "We should report this," he stated quietly.

Far too quickly I responded, "Can we just go back?" Seeing his quizzical expression, I added, "What can the police do? We have no information—no license number, and there are a million sedans. They'll just ask a lot of questions that we can't answer." I tried to subdue the pounding in my chest. "Please, let's go back."

He pressed, but relented when I said, "Trust me, the police can't do anything."

He said nothing, but seemed perplexed as we drove back to the road, proceeding much more deliberately. I assumed that my assignment was responsible for the chase and was dumbfounded by Robbie's next words.

"I'm sorry I put you through this. They've found me. You're not safe. I was nuts to think that we could have a life together. Maybe it would be better if..."

"Don't, Robbie. Please." I pulled off the glasses and said, "I'm not going anywhere..." I kissed him gently on the lips and caressed him, "... except home with you."

CHAPTER ELEVEN

Scout's wagging tail and blissfully ignorant eyes greeted us when we reached Mason's Neck. We took him out for a quick stroll into the cold, starless night. I could feel the presence of an omnipotent force that made me shrink with wonder and, tonight, fear. Each rustle of the bushes gave us a start. We scoured our surroundings for skulking figures lurking behind the massive pines or in the shadows created by the bright lights of Beau's estate. We hurried back to the carriage house, both of us opting for a glass of scotch instead of the promised hot chocolate. Its warmth mended my frayed nerves, but I couldn't stop thinking about the car chase and how much worse it could have been.

"You sure know how to show a girl a good time," I teased, trying to neutralize the charged atmosphere.

"If anything had happened to you..." he began, unable to finish.

"It didn't. Let's forget about it," I said, knowing full well that it would be impossible. I would have to call Ben and tell him about the incident, but I couldn't now, not with Robbie so distraught and not if I were to keep confidentiality. Robbie would wonder who I was talking to. The call would have to wait until tomorrow. I knew that Ben would not be pleased.

"I didn't think they'd follow me here. I thought I could start over, pursue other things." Robbie was talking to the floor, not me.

"Like what?" I asked, trying to calm him with a gentle caress.

He pulled away; we locked eyes. "I want to show you something that I've never shown anyone before." He led me down the hallway to his study. I followed willingly, curious but also gratified that he was sharing something important with me. He flipped the switch and illuminated a small room, whose walls were covered by a forest's worth of books. The desk was cluttered with notes, a computer, and an open bag of chips. "Look at this section here."

I scanned the titles: *Rush to Judgment, The Killing of a President, JFK and the Unspeakable,* and hundreds more. "My god, Robbie, have you read all of these?"

"And then some. See this stack of papers?" He pointed to a pile several feet high. "I got these through the Freedom of Information Act. You see, my interest in the assassination is not a hobby; it's more like an obsession."

"And no one else has seen this? Not even Beau?" He shook his head. Gazing at the numerous volumes, I made a feeble attempt to lighten the mood. "Well, you've raised being a conspiracy nut to an art form."

"Don't, please. It's been over fifty years, and we still don't know what really happened because our own government won't tell us. Even history textbooks state as fact that Oswald was the assassin, perpetuating the lie from one generation to the next."

"Robbie, you're a journalist. Don't you think the media would have exposed the truth?" I was fishing to see what he knew.

"The media was silenced. William Pawley of *Life* magazine sat on the Zapruder film for twelve years. James Angleton, the CIA's head of counterintelligence operations, ran a completely independent group of journalist operatives. The CIA owned or subsidized more than fifty newspapers, news services, radio stations, and periodicals. Even the president of CBS News, Richard Salant, told *Variety* magazine that he had no intention of airing the network's seventy-plus hours of assassination outtakes because they did not support the notion that Oswald acted alone."

"But there must have been other independent news outlets," I responded as I continued to read titles.

"There were, but those who did speak out were discredited—or worse."

"What do you mean, 'or worse'?" I recalled the list of people on the death list. Several were reporters.

"Have you ever heard of Dorothy Kilgallen?" He didn't give me a chance to respond. "She interviewed Jack Ruby, said she was going to break the Kennedy case wide open, and boom—she dies. Drug overdose. Before she could publish a single word."

"I find it hard to believe that a free press could be suppressed so effectively." But even as I said it, I remembered her name, also on the death list.

"Because you find it implausible, or because you don't want to believe it?"

"Both, I guess." My spirits plummeted—especially when I remembered the file in the vault entitled "Media Campaign." "What about Watergate? The *Washington Post* let Woodward and Bernstein write about that."

"Sure, but only when Nixon decided to end the Vietnam War. Nixon threatened Hunt that if he ratted about Watergate, he'd tell everyone about what really happened with the Bay of Pigs which, according to H. R. Haldeman, Nixon equated with the assassination."

"Robbie, I want to believe you, really I do, but it's too..."

"Convoluted?" he asked and then continued. "You don't know the half of it. Did you know that in 1947, when Nixon was a congressman in California, he arranged things so Jack Rubenstein would not have to testify in front of Congress?"

"Jack Rubenstein? You mean Jack Ruby." Robbie was on a roll. I enjoyed that he was opening up to me.

"Bingo." He shuffled through a few more papers. "Here it is." He put on his glasses and read, "It is my sworn testimony that one Jack Rubenstein of Chicago...is performing information functions for the staff of Congressman Richard Nixon, Republican of California. It is requested Rubenstein not be called for open testimony in the afore-mentioned hearings."

My jaw dropped as I absorbed this last piece of news. "So Nixon had links with organized crime, including Ruby, and was using his office to protect them?"

"And probably himself." Robbie read further, "Committee staffer Luis Kutner later described Ruby as 'a syndicate lieutenant who had been sent to Dallas to serve as a liaison for Chicago mobsters.' You see, in exchange for Ruby's testimony, the FBI eased up on its probe of organized crime in Dallas. In 1959, Ruby became an informant for the FBI." He looked up and must have seen the look of disbelief on my face, for then he added, "Does that really surprise you?"

"I'm rapidly approaching the point where nothing surprises me," I said, still scouring the titles, astonished by how much of his life Robbie had dedicated to finding the truth.

"Now, let's see, despite everything Nixon did, he gets pardoned and by who? Ford—the man Nixon *appointed* to fill in after Agnew was dropped as vice-president for taking kickbacks while governor of Maryland. Ford, who was on the Warren Commission, said he pardoned Nixon so the country could heal. Bullshit. Nixon knew what went down in Dallas. He was there. Ford had to pardon him; Nixon could have exposed Ford's role in the cover-up.

The phone rang and Robbie picked up. "Yeah, sure. I see." He held up his hand, indicating that he needed a few minutes of privacy. I walked back to the living room and sat. While I did, my mind wandered as I recalled Robbie's words.

> Two men sat in an office, housed in the congressional chambers. Their jackets hung on the back of their chairs; their ties were loosened. "Gerry, we've got a problem. Remember how we thought we had three shots to explain all the wounds? Turns out that one hit a guy named Teague. Bounced off the curb, and a piece of cement hit him in the face. You know what that means?"
>
> "Damn. Now we have to explain everything with two shots. There's no way." His tone was solemn as the dire consequences of this new development sank in.
>
> "And one of those was the head shot. That means we have to explain Kennedy's throat and shoulder wounds, plus all of Connelly's wounds, with one shot," Specter added.
>
> "Do Johnson and Hoover know?"
>
> "You're Hoover's mole, you tell me."

Ford shot Specter a look of disdain, but could not refute the charge. He didn't like Hoover preempting the commission's mandate any more than others on the panel did. But even a rubber stamp has to have some credibility or the whole thing would blow up in their faces. He couldn't afford that. He had ambitions of his own.

"Look Arlen, I don't give a rat's ass about Johnson. All I care about is keeping a lid on this. If it gets out that Oswald had company, maybe the Cubans, we're all going to hell. It's bad enough that Ruby keeps nagging me to bring him here to DC so he can spill the beans."

"That's all we need. If the world finds out that Kennedy was killed by a conspiracy, maybe even a coup, and Johnson goes to jail for all his shenanigans, we'll look just like a banana republic. McCormack's next in line. He'll be so busy trying to please everyone, nothing will get done. The Reds will have a field day."

The two men sat in silence, poring over the autopsy sketches, straining to find something—anything—they could use to make the story stick. It was getting late. Maybe it was the hour. Maybe it was the sense of impending disaster. Maybe some sort of survival instinct kicked in.

"Hey, how about this?" Ford asked. "Kennedy's arm was leaning over the limo like this, right? "He bent his arm and held it level with his shoulder. "That would pull his jacket up. So, even though from the looks of the jacket, it appears that a bullet entered over his shoulder blade, it could have entered here, below his neck."

"The docs say that the neck shot came from the front," Specter countered.

"Nothing can come from the front. Everything has to come from the book depository. Did you see the wound? It's huge. It had to come from the back."

"They did a tracheotomy through the wound. That's why the wound was so big. Not because it came from the back"

"You want World War III? Work with me here. The jacket's hiked up, so the bullet really entered here." Ford pointed to a spot four inches below the neck. *"It comes out the front and goes into Connelly's shoulder."*

"What about Connelly's wrist and leg wounds?"

"I don't know. The bullet exits Connelly's shoulder and caroms off his wrist and then enters his leg."

"No one will believe it. The docs at Parkland will go nuts."

"We'll sit on them. It has to work. I don't speak Russian and I don't want to learn now. Edgar will make it work, you'll see."

"We're honorable men, Gerry. Why are we doing this?"

"Because if we don't, the country is screwed. Unfortunately, as counsel for the commission, you'll have to present this."

Specter groaned. He hadn't wanted to be on the commission. No one did, except maybe Dulles who couldn't wait to bury Kennedy. But Ford was right. It had to be done.

"There you are," Robbie said as he entered the living room.

"Who was that?" I asked, startled by his sudden appearance.

"Just some guy I'm hoping to interview. Where were we?"

"You were talking about Ruby, Nixon, and Ford..."

"Did I mention Hoffa?"

"No, but let's take a break." I stroked his arm. I didn't want conspiracy talk. I wanted him. It was not meant to be.

He cupped my face in his hands and said, "Sure, but this is important to me. You need to know that, if you and I have any hope."

"If it's important to you, it's important to me," I said with total sincerity. "What are you going to do with all of the information you've gathered?"

"I'll tell you, but don't laugh." He paused, and I returned his look with an equally earnest one. "I'm writing a book of my own, one that connects all the dots, from JFK to weapons of mass destruction to the NSA's eavesdropping—with facts, not speculation."

"Don't take this the wrong way, but don't you think that's a bit of a stretch? Besides, didn't you say that too much has been suppressed or destroyed?" I felt so hypocritical asking the question knowing what I did, but I wanted to get inside his head a little further. It might help me understand what I saw in the vault and maybe Robbie as well.

"That's part of the problem. Even with the Freedom of Information Act which, by the way, resulted from Watergate, there's still so much that's missing, and most of the players are already dead." His fist landed hard on the stack of papers. "Those bastards will never have to answer for what they did and keep doing."

Being chased and shot at strengthened my resolve. Telling Robbie what I knew would place him in greater danger. As much as I wanted to give him the information he needed, I couldn't.

But then another thought emerged. After thirty-five years apart, Robbie and I just happened to run into each other, right after I was given my assignment. It seemed too coincidental. Had someone arranged for that and, if so, who? Ben obviously knew what I was doing. Jermaine probably had a pretty good idea. Whoever threatened me must know. But none of them knew Pam and Trevor. How could they arrange for me to meet Robbie at Pam and Trevor's party? And why would they want me to run into Robbie?

It occurred to me that I hadn't responded to Robbie as the wheels turned inside my head, so I quickly added, "Does anyone else know about this book?"

"Doubt it. You're the first person I've told, although a lot of people know about my interest in the assassination. Requesting all of this information has probably put me on somebody's list somewhere. Is that a deal breaker?"

"No, I admire you for it. You are not like anyone I know." I held my forehead to his chest as we stood surrounded by silent tomes with so much to tell. "I feel so much closer, knowing what's important to you."

I wanted to drown in the blue pools of his eyes. The passion that made me love him so many years before was now completely revived. "I have a lot to learn and hope you'll be patient with me."

He must have sensed my desire, because after several serene moments, he said, "It's getting late. We're kind of new at this, and I want to do it right this time—you know, take it slowly, but after what's happened, I don't want you driving alone tonight. Please stay. I can sleep on the couch."

I protested but, in truth, part of me was relieved and part disappointed. He was right. We had time. I didn't relish the idea of venturing into the frigid night with only my fear to keep me warm. Robbie dug out an old UVA T-shirt which I donned while cleaning up in the bathroom. He fluffed pillows and spread blankets in preparation for his night on the couch. When I came to say good-night he stood up, turned off the lights, and embraced me tenderly. I melted into his arms, unaware of the ticking clock or the wind blowing outside. Eventually we drew apart from each other, but as we did, I looked over Robbie's shoulder to the lights of the big house. That was when I saw Beau watching from his window.

CHAPTER TWELVE

I left Robbie's early, thinking about the work I needed to do. As much as I wanted to stay, I couldn't. Someone wanted me dead, and I needed to find out who.

The phone was ringing when I entered my apartment. Hoping it was Ben, I lunged toward the receiver. It was Pam. I removed my sneakers and tossed them across the room in frustration.

"How did dinner go?" she asked, with way too much energy for a Monday morning.

"You won't believe the weekend I had."

"Good or bad?"

"Uh, good, really good." I said, hoping she wouldn't detect my anxiety. "And we're getting together again tonight. I can't talk. I've got to get ready for work."

"Don't over plan. Be yourself. I'm sure that the two of you have changed over the years. Take some time to get to know each other again."

Then I had a thought. Maybe Pam could shed some light on things. "I did learn one thing about Robbie. Did you know he's into the Kennedy assassination?"

She laughed. "That's the understatement of the year. You should hear him and Trevor go at it. I swear they'd go on all night if it weren't for me." I said nothing. Sensing the delay in my response, Pam added, "Is it a problem?"

"No, not at all. I just found it, uh, unique." I had to stop myself from chewing a fingernail.

"Well, if you could endure an evening of JFK redux, how about the four of us going to dinner some night this week?"

"Sounds like fun. I'll mention it to Robbie when I see him later." We hung up, with me promising to let her know what night worked best. I undressed and jumped in the shower, enjoying the hot water ironing out the knots in my neck and back. Reluctantly, I left its warmth and wrapped myself in a robe. On my way to the kitchen, I noticed the message light blinking on my phone—maybe Ben had called. I punched the buttons, only to hear Robbie's gentle baritone tell me that something had come up and he needed to talk to me. My tension returned and I called him immediately.

"Hey there—got your message. What's up?" I asked, twirling my hair in tight rings around my fingers.

"There's this guy I've been hoping to talk to. He finally agreed to an interview this afternoon. It's important. I'm not sure how long it will go, so would you mind...?"

"Of course not," I jumped in. "Do you want me to bring dinner? It'd be one less thing to think about." Perhaps he wanted me to cancel, but I hoped that my preemptive offer would be an acceptable compromise.

"Um, okay. I guess that would work. Thanks." He definitely sounded tentative, but that was better than not seeing him at all. We agreed to a seven o'clock rendezvous. He said I could get Beau to open the door if I arrived before him. That would be awkward.

When I finally got to work, I called Ben. His phone rang incessantly, but he didn't answer. He'd promised that I could reach him 24/7. Damn. Where was he? I left a message for him to call me ASAP. What I had to say couldn't be left in a voice-mail message. I'd try again later. I needed to tell him about the car chase. It worried me that he didn't answer and made me wonder if he might be in danger as well.

I spent the day on the computer, trying to learn more about various conspiracy theories and the players featured in each, while waiting for Ben to return my call. No wonder conspiracy buffs had become marginalized: their list of suspects was endless and strained credibility—the Cubans, the Russians, holdover Nazis, the mob, Johnson, Nixon, the CIA, Hoover, the Secret Service, right-wing segregationists, Big Oil,

Mossad, Jackie, and even space aliens. The bottom line, I realized, was that whoever was responsible not only had to arrange the shooting, but had to cover it up as well. Few had the power to do that.

When my eyes started to blur, I left work and ran to the store to pick up some food for dinner, something we could cook together. Sharing the meal's preparation made us seem even closer, like the old days. I got to Robbie's promptly at seven and was relieved to see his Prius in the driveway. No waiting. No chance of seeing Beau, only Robbie—or so I thought. I knocked on the door. Beau answered. I managed a self-conscious smile.

"Ah, Kat. Rob said you might be stopping by. He's in the shower."

Beau didn't seem to be miffed about my overnight visit to Robbie's. What a relief. "Sorry, I didn't know you'd be here. I only brought enough dinner for two," I responded, "but we might be able to stretch it a bit."

"Far be it from me to horn in on your evening." The mismatch between his eyes and his smile was disturbing. I thought I detected anger behind his gaze, but maybe I was overreacting. He ushered me into the living room. "May I fix you a drink?" he asked.

"Thanks, but I'll wait." He turned his back as he poured an overly generous portion of bourbon into a tumbler of ice. I deposited the groceries on the kitchen counter and reluctantly returned to the living room, opting for a chair instead of the sofa.

"So, it looks like I'm losing out to O'Toole again." He said it lightly, even chuckled, but his laughter did not ring true. How long could a shower take?

"So tell me, what have you done with yourself since UVA?" I asked.

He shared a superficial account of how he had stayed with the family business—oil—but then moved to the policy side of things and that's why he lived in the DC area. He and his wife had three children, but divorced several years back. She got the children. Though dating, he was not seriously involved with anyone. Work-related travel made it difficult to develop relationships, he said.

I studied him carefully. He was gorgeous, charming, and wealthy. What was wrong with me? Why was I more attracted to Robbie? At last, Robbie walked in, dressed in a robe, his wet curls plastered against his head. "Sorry, running a bit behind. Beau offered to keep you entertained, so I took a quick shower."

"Kat's brought dinner for two, so I guess I'll be running along," Beau said. Turning to me, he said, "Nice to see you again. Maybe next time, the three of us can get together." He gulped the remainder of his drink and gave me his mock salute. I watched him leave and then rose to give Robbie a peck on the cheek, which grew into a legitimate kiss.

"Sorry about that. Beau popped in just as I pulled into the driveway," Robbie said, as he began to towel dry his hair.

"No problem. It was a little awkward, that's all."

"Why?"

"Beau asked me out after the party, but you beat him to it. Just like college all over again."

Robbie laughed. "Don't sweat it. He's fine."

I rolled my eyes. Men could be so dense when it came to dating.

"He even asked how your job is going. I think he really cares about you as a person," Robbie said.

"My job? Why would he ask about my job?"

Robbie shrugged his shoulders.

Not wanting to discuss Beau further, I asked, "How did your interview go?"

"It didn't. The guy blew me off again." He snorted in frustration. "Happens all the time. Make yourself at home, and I'll get dressed."

I returned to the sofa and scanned the magazines on the coffee table—*Runner's World, National Geographic, The Economist*—and then noticed a book sitting on the corner, *Plausible Denial: Was the CIA Involved in the Assassination of JFK?* I read the back cover, which described the book as an account of Mark Lane's successful defense of the *Spotlight* after it published an article claiming that Hunt was involved with the assassination. Hunt sued, won the first time, but then lost on appeal. I thumbed through the pages, fearing what I might find. Lane deposed CIA stars: Richard Helms, Stansfield Turner, David Atlee Phillips—my father's boss, G. Gordon Liddy...and there she was, Marita Lorenz. Thankfully, my father's name was not listed.

I was enjoying a brief moment of relief when Robbie entered the room, looking fresh and irresistible. I threw the book down and rose to hug him again, but not before he noticed. "Some light reading, eh?"

"Just killing time," I answered, as I wrapped my arms around him.

"Why didn't you kill time with *Runner's World*?" He gently pushed me away and searched my eyes.

Disregarding his question, I asked, "I'm curious, does Beau know you're interested in this stuff?"

"He pretends to be interested. Sometimes he asks me if I've discovered anything new, but I think he's only trying to make conversation. Mostly, he's dismissive. Says it's in the past, and why bother?"

"Of course he would. He works for the oil companies. Does Mark Lane mention others in his book, like Johnson or Big Oil?" Robbie's expression was devoid of any romantic nuance.

He picked up the book and said, "Lane was focused on the CIA because of the Hunt case, but others have mentioned the great white fathers of Texas. According to LBJ's mistress, Madeleine Duncan Brown, there was a party at the Murchison house the night before the assassination. She said that Nixon was there; so were Hoover, other oil barons, bankers, the Mafia, the mayor and sheriff of Dallas, media moguls—even Jack Ruby.

"So you're saying that Johnson knew about it before it happened?" Although I feigned disbelief, it fit with my own thoughts that were beginning to take shape. "You're kidding, right?"

"I wish I was. Come on, let's take Scout out."

We walked hand in hand along the road in silence as the moon rose in the sky. Scout disappeared into the woods. The longer we walked, the more the cold around us dissipated. Even in the waning light, I could see Robbie's eyes sparkle and dent at the corners. We got back to his house around eight and spontaneously began preparing dinner together, steaming the rice and vegetables and broiling the fish.

Carrying our plates to the sofa, we sat close, clinked glasses, and took first bites. As romantic as the evening had become, the book stared up at me, daring me to ignore it. I asked, "If Johnson knew about the assassination plot beforehand, why didn't he stop it?"

"Knew about it? He probably was in on the planning." Robbie chomped on some green beans.

"Come on, Robbie. How gullible do you think I am?" I punched him playfully, jaded by the plethora of conspiracy theories I'd read about earlier in the day.

"Think about it. Kennedy made a lot of enemies in three short years. If LBJ's mistress was telling the truth, they all were at the Murchison party—well, except for the Cubans. Who had the most to gain?"

"It sounds like they all had a stake in it, like in *Murder on the Orient Express*." I was thinking out loud, momentarily forgetting his passion.

"Please don't trivialize it." Disappointment darkened his face.

"I'm not, honest. But in that book, everyone on the train helped kill the victim. It sounds like the same thing, like they all played a part." I brushed a crumb from his shirt. "I'm still not convinced that figuring it out will change anything."

"Maybe I watched too many Superman shows as a kid. I actually believed in truth, justice, and the American Way. Back then, I thought the American Way was a good thing. Maybe if we can find the truth, we can find our way back."

"Do you really believe that, Robbie? There are still a lot of good things about our country."

"I love my country, with all my heart, Kat, but I want it to be the best it can be. What was it Bobby Kennedy said?" He looked up at the ceiling while searching his memory bank for the words. "'There is always a tendency in government to confuse secrecy with security. Disclosure may be uncomfortable, but it is not the purpose of democracy to ensure the comfort of its leaders.'" Then turning to me, he added, "Somehow the assassination lifted the veil and all the warts became visible. The problem is, more and more warts appeared. If it had all stopped with JFK's death, maybe it would have been different."

"You're saying it didn't?" I asked. He was letting me in again. I held on tightly to his every word.

"They got away with it once, so why not try it again? I'm afraid that it still goes on."

"Let me get this straight. You're saying that Kennedy's assassination was a prelude to everything that followed. How could that be? Different administrations, different political parties." He couldn't stop now. I was hooked.

"Let me ask you a question. While Democrats and Republicans have been in and out of office, what has remained constant?" Before I could answer, he jumped in. "The military, the intelligence community, and the power brokers who pull their strings."

"You said that rogue CIA agents were involved with the assassination. Now you're saying the whole intelligence community is committing illicit acts? Do you know how many men and women risk their lives daily to protect us? Bin Laden would still be out there if it weren't for, uh, them." I wiped my mouth with my napkin and added, "I think that your obsession has made you paranoid."

"And I think that you're unusually defensive."

His scrutiny was unsettling. I looked down at my plate, but could feel his eyes on me. "I am not being defensive, just ..."

"...being your father's daughter. Is that it? Or maybe you followed in his footsteps. You seem to care more about this than most people. First, Marita Lorenz, and now you're defending the CIA. Why them and not the other members of the intelligence community?"

I said nothing while he calmly took another bite and washed it down with some wine. "You work for them, don't you? You're CIA."

It was as if he'd stabbed me with a dagger. "What? I...I...What makes you say that? I told you. I work for the State Department; I never said anything about the CIA."

"You don't have to. I can see it in your face." He slammed his fork down. We sat in a silence so uncomfortable that it caused a physical ache in my chest.

I couldn't take it any longer. "For the sake of argument, let's say I do. It doesn't change the fact that there are good people who work hard to protect the country from those who would do us harm." He didn't respond, so I took a breath and continued, "Okay, fine. Do you know how I spend most of my days? I read manifests, thousands of them, looking for people of interest so they don't hijack planes and fly them into buildings, or blow up trains, or..."

The phone rang and Robbie sprang to answer it. After a few uh-huhs, whats, wheres, and whens, Robbie slowly placed the phone in his pocket and turned to me. "I gotta go. That was my contact. He can meet me now."

"Now? Are you kidding? We just sat down to eat."

He shrugged and pulled on a coat. I called Scout. Despite the distance between us, I asked, "Is it safe? Will you be okay? Can I go with you?"

He shook his head. "I need to go alone. Will you be okay driving home? You can stay here if you want, but I don't know how late I'll be."

"I'll be fine," I answered.

"Text me when you get there?"

We walked to our respective cars in tortured silence. I pressed the remote ignition, opened the door for Scout, and then climbed in. I slammed the door shut. Maybe it was time to give Beau a call. He wouldn't abandon me for an interview or care that I worked for the CIA.

CHAPTER THIRTEEN

During the drive home, I recalled what Robbie had said about the Murchison party, and my thoughts began to wander about LBJ and his cronies.

It was late and Clint's party would be breaking up. That was good. His actions from here on out would be watched closely, and the fewer people who saw him here the better. He needed to be careful. Tonight's gathering would seal the deal, but first he had some cat herding to do. As the car traversed the rolling hills and passed a regiment of stately oaks, he knew he had no choice now, not with that prick, Bobby Kennedy, riding his ass. It was this or jail, and he knew it.

At last, they pulled into the drive of the Murchison estate. The ladies, if you could call them that, would be socializing in the library. Once he arrived, the men would convene in the conference room. How many times had he and Clint hoisted a few in that room? How many deals had they brokered there? Clint wasn't the same since his stroke, but he could still pull the right strings, and he ruled with an iron, albeit withered, fist.

As he strode into the foyer, he could feel the eyes of Texas upon him. As soon as Murchison saw Johnson arrive, he said, "Come on, boys."

The men entered the conference room; some shuffled, others couldn't wait to get the meeting underway. "Let's get started. We don't have much time," Johnson said, gazing around the room. He saw his oil buddies, H.L. Hunt and Sid Richardson, as well as his attack dog, Mac Wallace. The rest were allies at best or potential liabilities, like Nixon who sat brooding in the corner.

A lone black man slouched against the wall. That would be Hoffa's eyes and ears, Larry Campbell. Hoffa wormed his way into everything like a chigger under your skin, but with Bobby Kennedy's "Get Hoffa" squad in high gear, Hoffa had more pressing concerns, like going to jail for one. Johnson didn't miss the pain in the ass. Hoover and his partner, Clyde Tolson, were whispering to each other up front. The mobsters, Marcello, Civello, and Campesi, clustered to one side. Everyone seemed to be there.

True to form, Hoover jumped in first. "We got the fall guy. It's all set up, Lyndon. Byrd arranged for him to get a job at his book depository three weeks ago. I've got his biography all set for the press."

"Who is he?" Johnson asked.

"Name's Oswald. He's been working in my organization, but he's a snitch," Marcello answered in his heavy accent. "Bertrand and Banister served him up. Oswald thinks he's infiltrated the plot and is keeping Phillips informed. Little does he know that Phillips is with us." Marcello's bitter laugh sounded like paper shredding.

"What about the shooters?" Johnson asked, all business.

"Six men." Wallace answered. "All aces. I'll be on the sixth floor with a couple of others. A couple of Marcello's boys will be at the Dal-Tex building, and Phillips has a couple behind the fence if needed."

"You should let us handle it. We don't need the others." Marcello jumped in.

Johnson stabbed the air between himself and the mobster with a rigid finger and glared at him, eyes ablaze.

"Dammit, Carlos. Your boys will be there. You'll get your fucking revenge. I'll be damned if I'm going to owe the mob." Then more calmly, he continued. "What about the police?"

Bill Decker, the sheriff of Dallas County answered. "Obviously not all the boys are in the know, but the ones we need are. Don't you worry, LBJ."

"We even changed the route so it will go right through Dealey Plaza," said Earl Cabel, the mayor of Dallas. "They'll have to drive real slow around those turns on Elm and Houston." A man Johnson knew all too well stepped forward and thrust a piece of paper at him. "Here ya go. It's right here."

"Thanks Jack. You be sure to keep those Secret Service men out late partying tonight." Ruby was key to the whole plan. Johnson had to play him just right. "That reminds me, where will I be sitting in the motorcade?"

"Way back, away from the shots," the sheriff responded.

"Who's the lucky guy who gets to ride with Kennedy?" Johnson asked.

"Connelly."

A fellow Texan, thought Johnson, but his remorse was fleeting as he promptly asked, "Now about the press..." He knew his TV station wasn't a problem, and the Feds controlled numerous other outlets, but he had to be sure.

"We've got men on the ground to grab film and strong-arm witnesses. We'll feed the press our information." This was from Hoover, not exactly a local. But then the oilmen chimed in. They all felt that the press wouldn't be a problem. They owned most of the local news outlets. Still, Johnson couldn't be sure. There would be too many people. They couldn't stop them all.

"Some schmuck doesn't cooperate, they're gonna take a little trip," Civello replied, his acid tone searing all *humanity from his voice, leaving Johnson, no stranger to extreme measures, unnerved.*

Johnson stared around the room. He didn't trust half of these people, and the other half could screw up. The hit wasn't the problem. The aftermath was. "You all know what's at stake here. We're in this together. If we fuck this up, we're all going down, got it? Any questions?"

The room buzzed as the reality of what was to happen set in. "What about Bobby?" one of the mobsters asked. "He's killing us."

"If this works and I'm president, I can assure you that he won't be my attorney general." Johnson answered irritably. "Besides, do you really think he's stupid enough to continue his crusade once his brother's taken out?" Johnson removed his glasses and looked at the man with obvious impatience.

"What about Cuba?" another asked.

"God dammit. We're talking about killing a sitting president. We can deal with Cuba later." He took a deep breath. He couldn't lose it. Not now. He lowered his voice. "Each of us has our reasons, but we're all agreed that the SOB has to go, right?"

This time the response was laced with greater enthusiasm, making him feel a bit better, but not much. So much could go wrong, and if it did, not only would he go to jail for his ties to Sol Estes and Baker, but he'd be hung for treason. But if they succeeded, he'd be president and would have the power he craved. "All right gentlemen, let's do it."

They all stood as Johnson headed for the exit. Once he entered the main room, his mistress, Madeline Duncan Brown, caught his eye and ran over to meet him. "Shit, not now," he thought.

"Hi Lyndon. I didn't think you were going to make it with all that's going on. Do you have time...?"

He stared at her. She was the last thing on his mind right now. "Not now, sweetie." He forced the endearment. "Maybe after tomorrow."

"Tomorrow?" she asked.

"After tomorrow, those SOBs will never embarrass me again. That's not a threat. That's a promise."

She watched his back, stymied by his words and the tone in which he delivered them. She would forget neither.

Before I knew it, I was back in Shirlington. My reverie had distracted me from my irritation with Robbie, but now it returned. So what if I worked for the CIA? I was proud of what I did, and he wasn't going to guilt trip me into thinking otherwise. Still, I texted him and was glad that, despite everything, my safety was important to him. At least he cared, even if I was "one of them."

With an unanticipated free evening, I hauled out my computer and pondered my preliminary report. Should I include everything? Or should I hold some items back until I learned more about their significance? If I reported on all of it, Ben might shut the project down, and I wasn't ready for that. Scanning the list was daunting; there was so much. I decided to exclude the brain for now, since I didn't know what else, if anything, was in the alcove. The brain sent me running away before I found out. It was getting late, so I wrote an introduction that described the room's location, access, and dimensions and printed the report.

Around midnight I went to bed, but sleep was fitful at best. Robbie called sometime after one a.m. "Hey Kat. Just wanted you to know that I'm home."

"I'm glad you're safe. How did it go?"

"Okay. I'll tell you about it tomorrow. I'd like to make amends. I overreacted, I'm sorry. Could I come by tomorrow night?"

"Sure. I'd like that." I was relieved but in truth, I felt he had overreacted as well.

We hung up and I sank back into bed. The issue with Robbie seemed to be resolved for now, but there was another one lurking—Ben. He had never called back. He was supposed to return tomorrow. It was time for a frank discussion. I could only hope that he would be there for it. I had to know why he requested this information and what he was going to do with it. He owed me that, especially if strange men were leaving roses on my pillow and nearly killing us on the highway.

But then I thought about the threats. Ben said that someone was just trying to scare me, that if he'd wanted to kill me, he would. The men on the highway were definitely trying to kill us. Had the efforts of my adversaries intensified, or were there two different parties at work? Or was one group after Robbie and the other one after me? Should I call Ben now? What could he do at this hour? No, it could wait until tomorrow. I would confront him with everything that happened, demand an explanation and more security than his *Sports-Illustrated*-reading bodyguard provided. Ben had to know more than he was letting on.

Then I began to think about the vault. Why hadn't the evidence been destroyed if it was so threatening? Was it actually Kennedy's brain in the canister I had held? Was the organization that I had devoted my life to really involved somehow? If not, why was the evidence at Langley? Why did Ben want it inventoried? And how could my father justify helping with the cover-up?

My thoughts returned to Robbie. He knows how the CIA operates. He couldn't expect me to betray confidences, could he? It wasn't as if I was part of the cover-up. I pulled the comforter close to my chin and shivered at my next thought. By keeping what I knew secret, I *was* part of the cover-up. What a choice: either keep what I knew in confidence so we could both be safe, or expose what really happened that day in Dallas, inviting harm into our lives.

Once at work, I stomped straight to Ben's office. His light was on. I pounded on his door.

"Ah, Hastings. I've been expecting you." Ben sat sipping coffee and shuffling through some papers. "What have you got for me?"

"Where have you been? I've been calling you and left you messages to call me back. You never did. You said you'd be available 24/7. You weren't." I made no attempt at a calm demeanor.

"I never got your messages. Are you sure you called the right number?"

"I entered it in my phone like you said. I've reached you using that contact number before."

"Then they've compromised my phone," he muttered, more to himself than to me.

"Who's 'they'?" I looked at him, waiting for an answer, but none came. When I could stand his silence no longer, I said, "You told me to call if anything happened. Well, it has." He sat forward in his chair. His eyes looked like small onyx stones. "You said no one knew about what I was doing," I continued, "but I've been chased by men in a car who shot at me, and I've been threatened. What's going on?"

He disregarded my question and sat back in his chair with a distant look on his face. After a weighty silence, he asked, "How much more is there to do?"

"There's still a lot in the vault that I haven't even touched, but I'm not scheduled to go back until Thursday." I could feel my pulse pounding away and tried desperately to erase any emotion from my voice. "You haven't answered my question."

He contemplated this information for a few more maddening moments, the tips of his index fingers touching under his chin and repeatedly gliding up to his lips and back. Just when I thought I would explode, he muttered, "I don't know."

"What do you mean, you don't know?" Any remaining restraint disappeared. I jumped up from my chair. "Who are these people? How do they know what I'm doing? Are they going to kill me? What aren't you telling me?"

Ben remained placid and thoughtful. I wanted to throttle him.

"I warned you that there might be people who didn't want this information revealed. I don't know how they found out. Have a seat and stop ranting." He stuck a pen between his teeth like a cigarette. "If they renovate that part of Langley, everything in that room will be destroyed.

You're touching history, and if it's destroyed, any chance of knowing what really happened will be destroyed with it."

"With all due respect, history is the last thing on my mind right now. Survival is."

"Understood. Show me what you've got, and we'll figure out where to go from there."

"I've prepared your preliminary report as promised," I began, waving the bound copy in front of him, "but you need to answer my questions."

Despite my best efforts, I could not match his tranquility. He reached for the document, but I snatched it back. He stood and planted both hands on his desk, leaning across and surveying me sternly. I waited for some admonition about just doing the job and following orders, but none came.

I was still standing and asked, "Why stop at a list? If the truth is to be known someday, why not put it all in the National Archives?"

"There are those in the Agency that think it'd be best if the truth never came out, that we should just let the conspiracy nuts speculate all they want and discredit anyone who may be getting close to the truth. If this got out, the Agency would have a lot to answer for, and now, with the terrorists looming, North Korea and Iran having the bomb, and Syria about to explode, we can't afford to have our wings clipped. There's too much at stake."

Now I was confused. Ben had said that I was touching history and that if the evidence was destroyed, the truth would never be known. Now, he wanted to protect the Agency. He was driving me nuts.

"Why does anyone care? The people who did these things are mostly dead," I retorted, trying more to reassure myself than to argue the point.

"Your father isn't. Neither are a few of his old cronies."

"What's my father have to do with it?" I snapped back.

His eyebrows arched, wrenching his eyes wide open. "So you really didn't read anything?"

"You told me not to," I said, looking away, unable to meet his gaze.

"Give it to me. Now." Anger marred his calm façade, and his outstretched arm felt threatening. Grudgingly, I handed him the report, hoping my trump card wasn't wasted. Ben took a few minutes to read it and as he did, his face grew ashen and drawn. He chewed on the pen. At last he spoke. "This is worse than I thought."

"There's more. This is just a few days' worth." I leaned forward and put my hands on his desk. "Now about the threats..."

He took a deep breath. "They could be coming from inside the Agency or out. I honestly don't know." He stood and walked to the front of his desk, sitting directly in front of me and motioning me to sit.

"Kennedy was seen as soft on communism and that ticked off people in the Company, the military, and on the right."

"So they killed him? The election was the next year. People could have voted someone else in. I thought we were a democracy." I finally sat down, but just on the edge of my seat.

"Kennedy was too popular. He and Jackie were the American equivalent of royalty." Ben paused and then turned to me. In a much more intense tone, he continued, "Besides, who do you think 'they' were? Sturgis, Morales, Phillips, and your father were all in Dallas that day. I don't think they were there to wish Kennedy well."

"Maybe they were there to investigate the threats that had been made," I responded out of desperation.

Ben didn't comment, but walked over to the window and gazed out at the gray sky as he began, "When I was in Nam, about a hundred years ago, I had a desk job and saw many of the memos meant for the generals' eyes only. There were two in particular—NSAM 263 and NSAM 273. The first was signed by Kennedy mere days before the assassination and called for the withdrawal of a thousand military personnel stationed there, with a promise of complete withdrawal within the coming year. The second was signed by LBJ just days after Kennedy was killed and called for a major escalation of force. Such an about-face in four days." Ben hesitated, as though he was deciding whether to continue. "I was told to keep my mouth shut if I wanted an honorable discharge at the end of my hitch."

"Did you ever tell anyone?" I asked.

He turned toward me and sat back in his chair, clasping his hands behind his head. "You're the first. And there's more. Too many people with too much power didn't want the war to end; it was a cash cow."

"But it *did* end," I said, still teetering on the edge of my seat.

"But not before Johnson's oil buddies had made their money."

"So, it could have been the oil guys *and* the CIA?"

Ben grunted. "Don't forget the right-wing racists like Milteer who told an FBI informant, Willie Somersett, that they were going to kill Kennedy with a high-powered rifle shot from an office building. Hoover never told the Secret Service, nor did he tell them about Marcello's planned hit. The Secret Service was operating with a quarter of the normal coverage. They partied until the early hours of the morning. They allowed Kennedy to ride without the bubble top. They pulled agents off the back of Kennedy's car and left him exposed. They changed the motorcade route so Kennedy's car would have to slow as it passed by tall buildings. They moved the autopsy to Bethesda. Some have claimed that a Secret Service agent who was in the back-up car, Hickey, I think it was, shot Kennedy by mistake. I guess an accident is more palatable than a coup."

"Okay, Ben, I give up. Who *didn't* kill him?" I'm sure that what my father had called my "pouty look" was all over my face. "Besides, if it was all so complicated, and there were so many different parties involved, how could they possibly keep it so secret?"

"Any network of conspirators that is capable of murder, each with some hold over the other, would have little difficulty in maintaining secrecy." He stroked his jaw hard enough to make it glow red. "Anyone of them might want to threaten you."

I jumped from my seat. "You knew all this, and yet you put me on this assignment?"

"You're the one who's constantly complaining about how boring your job is," he fired back. Then, in a lower tone, he said, "I guess I overestimated you."

That hurt, and he knew it. I sat back, collected myself, and more calmly asked, "So what do I do?"

"I want you to finish this assignment and then go away for a while. Once they're convinced that you'll keep quiet, maybe they'll leave you alone."

"They're trying to kill me." I said, through gritted teeth.

"You might as well finish because you already know too much."

"You know it now, too," I responded, hoping for some empathy.

He stood once more, shoved his hands into his pockets, and turned his back to me. "You're not the only one getting threats, Hastings." I inhaled deeply and could feel goose bumps burst from my skin. "You said Thursday is your next scheduled day?" he asked.

"Yeah. I could go tomorrow, but Jermaine wouldn't be there since it's not on the schedule."

"Who the hell is Jermaine?" He wheeled around, looking both baffled and enraged.

"The guard you sent." Ben's glare deepened. More nervously, I continued, "He said that you assigned him to be there while I was working in the vault." Ben's stare made it obvious that he didn't know anything about Jermaine. I had been in Jermaine's Hummer, and he knew where I lived. The thought made me weak.

"I didn't assign anyone to be there." Ben turned abruptly, scattering papers and sending pens flying. "Finish and get out of town—fast. I'll find out who this Jermaine is."

I knew I couldn't wait until Thursday.

CHAPTER FOURTEEN

I spent the rest of the day consoling myself with the fact that I would see Robbie that night. I raced home to prepare dinner for his arrival around seven, but seven came and went—and then so did eight, nine, and ten. I repeatedly tried his cell phone, but could only leave messages, hoping that he would call me back. I knew what he was working on, that he met with questionable people, and that if I was in danger, he probably was as well. Worried did not begin to describe what I felt.

Sleep was useless, so I stayed up reading scanned documents from the vault. Though the import of many escaped me, there were enough to make me quake with disbelief. Sometime around two or three a.m., I made my decision. Schedule or no schedule, I was going to the vault. I changed into jeans, a sweater, and sneakers. I pulled my hair back and applied no make-up. It was time to finish what I could, to dig in deep. Somehow, I knew that this was my last visit, and it was time to get dirty.

I packed differently for the day. Maybe it was the growing fear spawned by Robbie's absence, the disturbing conversation with Ben, the discovery that Jermaine was a fraud, and the knowledge that my life was in danger. Whatever the case, I removed the pepper spray from my purse and inserted it into my computer bag. I packed two sandwiches instead of one and some fruit, candy bars, and a couple bottles of water. It would be a long day. At least, I hoped it would. I wanted to document as much as possible before bidding the vault good-bye.

The early hour and the anticipation of a late night ahead made public transportation impractical, so I drove to work. Besides, I might just need a car at the end of the day—to see Robbie, to get home quickly, or to escape. Its back window was still shattered from the bullet, but

Robbie had covered it with a plastic sheet affixed with duct tape. A vicious scrape on the passenger side looked like an evil grin, taunting me. I winced upon seeing the battered vehicle and realizing how close we came to injury or even death.

With little traffic on the roads, I was at Langley in minutes. I didn't stop by my desk, but walked purposefully to the ancient elevator. Each creak and groan heightened my already tense state. The door opened with a screeching sound that shattered the silent, dark corridors. I practically leaped out to distance myself from its unnerving cacophony. Without trying, my footfalls were noiseless. I knew the way now and reached the room quickly, but before entering, I looked down the hallway in both directions; I detected no sound and saw no movement.

Somewhat reassured, I ducked in and pulled the door shut behind me. At this early hour, I didn't think to wedge it shut. At the control panel, I pressed the button to open the vault door and shut off the lights to the exterior room, my flashlight illuminating the way. Once inside, I closed the vault and activated the door to the small panel inside. With limited time, I decided to go for those things that were most hidden. I pressed the remaining button and once again heard only soft, white noise which was somehow comforting. I left it on.

I shoved aside the canister containing the brain and reached deep into the back of the small chamber. I felt something long and hard and pulled it out. A rifle. It had a smooth wood stock surrounding a dark metal cylinder, with a small tag looped around the trigger guard that read "7.65 German Mauser bolt-action rifle." It was signed by H2. I groaned. I remembered reading that Roger Craig, a Dallas policeman, said that the gun that was found on the sixth floor was a Mauser, not a Mannlicher-Carcano. My god, I was holding one of the guns that might have killed Kennedy. I began snapping pictures in a frenzy, until I was startled by the sound of a door closing. I heard voices, muffled at first, then clearer as they approached. I froze. The button I hit must have been some sort of intercom. Whoever was talking didn't sound happy, and all that separated me from them was the door to the vault.

"Who the hell put Kat on the job?" My father's voice; I'd know it anywhere.

"Douglas. I had nothing to do with it," the other voice responded.

"How much does she know?"

"I checked the list she gave him. There's some bad stuff, but everything in the vault is bad."

"Is the stuff from the back chamber on it?"

Every muscle in my body constricted as I thought of what I had seen. Beads of sweat formed on my brow, and though the door to the vault was shut, I crouched down behind the rear shelf.

"No, not yet. She's due to go back in tomorrow, but maybe she hasn't found the panel. She may never find it." Thank God I left the brain off Ben's report.

"See that she doesn't," my father snapped.

"What are you saying? You don't want me to..."

"No, of course not. Just rattle her. Make it bad enough to make her want off the case."

"We've tried. She's as stubborn as you are." After a brief silence, the voice asked, "Do you think she'll blab to the press?"

"I'm not sure, but if she tells O'Toole, he'll spill everything." My father uttered Robbie's name like a curse. He knew about us.

"O'Toole?" the voice asked and then laughed bitterly. "The California mob is already onto him. They're just waiting for the right moment to burn him." I thought about his no-show last night and prayed that it hadn't already happened.

"And just what makes you so sure of that?" my father asked. I had heard that tone so many times, and it never boded well.

"We've had a tail on him since he's been east. He ordered a shitload of info using that damned FOI."

"If they kill him, Kat will jump off the deep end and tell all." I heard my father swear several times before adding, "Douglas did this on purpose. He put her on the case knowing I'd have to protect her."

"You can't protect her from the others."

"I still have some contacts. If I can convince them that she'll keep quiet..."

"What if she knew that squealing would get you indicted? There's no statute of limitations on murder—especially the murder of a president. We're screwed."

"I'll make sure she doesn't talk. Give me a few days."

"How are you going to do that?"

"Remember Atsugi and those mind-control experiments? I learned a few things from Stanley Gottlieb."

I heard a sharp intake of breath. "Geez, H2. You are one tough bastard." I heard steps as one of them walked around the room.

"If we can get rid of the stuff in the vault, no one will be able to prove anything. When are the renovations scheduled to start?" I could imagine my father cracking his knuckles. He always did that when he was agitated.

"Next week. Benning's men are supposed to box the stuff and destroy it. He doesn't want the Company compromised in any way."

"A vanishing breed. It's not like the old days is it, Carson? Phillips would be turning over in his grave."

"Yeah, we watched each other's backs, no matter how bad it got," Carson added. "Shit, Liddy was willing to get killed to keep Nixon in power."

"Nixon..." my father spat. "I don't know who was the bigger jackass, him or Johnson."

"Yeah, these presidents actually think they run the country." Carson cackled bitterly.

"Well, now we've got another mess to clean up, but this one's personal. I'll get Douglas for this." My father's voice dripped with venom. I prayed that they would leave soon. It was getting hard to breathe. The dust, the claustrophobic space, the diminishing oxygen—I was feeling light-headed, but willed myself to remain alert so I could hear the rest of the conversation. Survival depended on it.

"You want me to get rid of the stuff now? I could get some boys..." My spine stiffened. Carson was standing right outside the vault. I could hear him tapping on the wall.

"Tonight. When no one's around," my father interrupted. "But let's take one more look. I want to get an idea of what Kat's found."

As he walked to the podium, I whisked my computer to the back, closed its lid, and covered its blinking lights with my coat. I pulled the pepper spray from my computer bag and held it with rigid fingers. I plastered myself against the back wall and prayed—hard. The chill of the vault disappeared. Sweat dripped from my brow. Terror peeled the lids from my eyes. I clenched my teeth. Every nerve was on red alert. I strained to remember any trace of my presence that they might see.

The door slid open. The silhouettes of the two men appeared, visible between the boxes of papers and various canisters. They stepped inside. Carson was several inches shorter than my father and definitely heavier. I held my breath as they each scanned the shelves on either side, occasionally picking up a small box and looking inside.

"It doesn't look like anyone's been here. She couldn't have gotten too far."

"That's my Kat." It almost sounded as though he said it with pride. "Meticulous to a fault. She'd leave no trace which, unfortunately, made her perfect for this job. If Ben hadn't been so clumsy, we'd never have known about this until it was too late."

"You think she'll cooperate?"

"Don't know. We haven't had what you'd call a close relationship." He paused, then in a more reflective tone, added, "I never wanted her to join the Company. I didn't want her to find out about me. If she's read anything in here, she probably hates my guts more than she already did, if that's possible."

"This isn't good, H2. Let's get out of here."

My father turned to leave and then took a final look back, seemingly right at me. Had some sixth sense kicked in? Just when I thought he would walk straight to me, he shook his head and left. I exhaled.

I didn't dare move for several minutes. When I heard the outer door shut and was convinced that they were really gone, I opened the vault door and sucked in fresh air as though I'd been drowning. Maybe I was. They needn't do anything else to terrorize me. The greater horror was what they'd said about Robbie. He was in danger and I had to let him know, but by doing so, I would have to reveal what I'd been doing. If I talked, my father would most likely go to jail—not that he didn't deserve it. I rubbed my neck and moved my head in circular motions, trying to unwind the accumulated tension. I needed to finish the job today, before the vault was cleared of its contents and any hope of the truth coming to light disappeared.

But first, I had to call Robbie and prayed that it wasn't too late.

I closed the vault, and after checking the hallways to make sure no one was around, I ran toward the elevator. Once I could see bars on Greg's cellphone, I entered Robbie's number, and waited. After what seemed like an eternity, the phone switched over to voice mail. "Robbie, it's Kat. I can't tell you how I know, but they're going to kill you." These last words cut like shards of glass, making my voice hoarse and unrecognizable. "Please call me. Let me know you're safe." He hadn't returned any of my calls from last night, and now I'd missed him again. Maybe they had already found him.

With newfound energy, I sprinted back to the vault and pulled the trunk labeled "Nagell" under the small chamber. I stepped on top of it and reached further inside. I felt several manila envelopes and pulled them out. "Original Autopsy Photographs," they read. Then I found more envelopes labeled "Original Autopsy X rays." Even in my ignorance, the fact that these items were here could only mean one thing. The Warren Commission never saw this evidence. If these differed from the official photos, as I suspected, it meant that the military personnel who conducted the autopsy at Bethesda were complicit in covering up any frontal shots. I tore open the envelope with the X rays and snapped away like a paparazzi.

There was one last task I knew must be done. I took a deep breath and reached into the small chamber, slowly pulling the canister from its perch. Bracing myself for the stench I knew would come, I unscrewed the lid and turned my nose away from its formalin-laden fumes. I carefully lifted the mangled brain with gloved hands and placed it on the overturned lid.

While photographing it from every angle I could imagine, I noticed the glint of metal. Placing my camera on a nearby shelf, I probed the tissue with my gloved finger until I felt something hard. I extracted the tiny tail end of a bullet lodged within. I took a picture of it and jammed the fragment into my pocket. After placing the brain back in its container and returning it to its hiding place, I found the envelope containing other bullet fragments. Then I pilfered film reels and pictures. I stashed everything I could fit into my satchel. If they were going to destroy it anyway, why not?

It was getting late. I had to leave before my father's buddy, Carson, returned with "his boys." Taking one last look at the vault to ensure that everything looked undisturbed, that I had collected all of my possessions, and that the small chamber was shut, I left. Still, I felt no relief, nor would I until I was home behind a locked door, cuddling Scout and answering a phone call from Robbie saying that he was safe. I hurried down the corridors and outside to the parking lot, feeling the weight of the stolen evidence. I climbed into my car and roared off.

Scout greeted me with the enthusiasm I craved. He was the closest thing to security I had. I hugged him and held him close for several minutes before feeding him and then taking him to the dog park. While he rolled in the mud on the riverbank, my mind rewound to the conversation I heard from the vault. I had always thought my dad was a hero. Sure, he was brusque and said "move on" when we skinned our knees, but ultimately I thought he was good and strong. Despite his stern attitude, I knew that he cared. But now, there was no denying it. He was every bit as guilty as those who had pulled the trigger, because he covered their tracks.

And now he was going to keep me quiet. But how? Would he really use some method from Atsugi on me? And how else was Carson going to scare me away from the job? My thoughts returned to Robbie. I pulled out my cell phone and called him again. I left another message—this one even more urgent. Saying the words into the receiver rekindled my fears. I quickly called Scout and returned to my apartment.

Scout stood in silent resignation as I bathed him—all that work in the river for nothing. Before I could make any headway, the phone rang. I lunged for it, leaving a soaking-wet dog the run of my apartment.

"Hi," said Robbie. I exhaled with relief. "I would have called sooner, but someone stole my cell phone. I didn't mean to worry you."

"It's so good to hear your voice. I've been worried sick." I could feel my chest loosen and my breathing return to normal. "Who stole your phone? Where are you? Why didn't you come over last night? I was a wreck."

"Whoa, one question at a time!" His laughter was maddening. "I was at this roadside diner in the middle of nowhere, meeting with my contact. Anyway, I put my phone down, and some guy grabbed it and ran off."

"But that doesn't explain why you didn't show up." I made every effort not to sound irritated, now that I knew he was safe.

"I'm getting to that." He didn't sound at all defensive, just frazzled. "We decided to go somewhere more secluded to finish our conversation. When we were done, my contact left, and by the time I got to my car, the tires had been slashed. No one was around. Someone must have tailed me there. I was worried that it was a trap, so I hightailed it through the woods." I thought back to the conversation I had heard outside the vault. Carson said they had a tail on Robbie. "No phone, no car. I was stuck and had to hitch a ride home. It took most of the night."

"But you're all right?" I asked.

"Fine, a little beat, but fine."

"Robbie, we have to talk. Can you come over tonight?"

"Sure. What's going on?"

"They know about us. They're tracking you down." There was silence on the other end of the line. "Are you still there?" I asked.

"Yeah, I'm here. I guess we do need to talk. How did you find all this out?"

"I'll tell you in person tonight. It's complicated." I walked like a sentry patrolling my living room, trying to think on my feet. I bit my lip before adding, "Be careful, they might follow you here."

"To quote the Stones, 'Wild horses couldn't drag me away.'"

I made a mental leap to the last line of the song, "Let's do some living after we die."

CHAPTER FIFTEEN

Robbie arrived at eight. I threw myself into his arms and kissed him hard on the mouth. I hugged him and didn't want to let go. He was alive. He was here. I could feel the strength both in his arms and in his spirit.

"What a welcome! I should stand you up more often." I couldn't speak. I could only bury my head in the opening of his shirt and feel his skin upon mine. He placed his index finger under my chin and gently lifted my head. "It's gonna be okay." I wanted to believe him.

After a few moments locked in his embrace, I drew back. "You must be famished. How did you get here? Did anyone follow you?" Sentences and questions erupted like shots from a semiautomatic.

He hung his jacket on the coat rack as he laughed and said, "You know, you really need to let people answer one question before you ask another. Yes, I'm hungry. I rented a Zipcar, and I'm pretty sure no one followed me. Now, what's for supper?" He rubbed his hands together to warm them as we entered the living room.

"I'm afraid it's what we were going to have last night. I'll reheat it, if that's okay. I got home late. There was no time to get something fresh. I would have, but you see ..."

"Kat, relax. I've never seen you like this." He hugged me once more. "Tell me where everything is and I'll fix it. Have a seat and I'll bring you some wine." He deposited me on the sofa and uncorked the bottle of wine standing on the counter. He made two plates of leftovers, popped one in the microwave, and brought me a glass of wine. We clinked glasses and sipped while he nuked the food.

"Such service," I said, trying my best to smile. He put two placemats on the coffee table and brought the heated dinners over.

After a couple of bites, he said, "Talk to me."

I took a large sip of wine and then began. "That car that chased us, well it's not the only thing that has happened. I told you that I have a big assignment at work. Since I've been on it, strange things have been happening." I told him about the rose, being followed out of Langley, that he was being tailed and that some people from California were going to kill him. "And when you didn't show up last night, I thought the worst."

"Does this have anything to do with Marita Lorenz?" he asked. I said nothing, so after a brief "humph" he continued. "So whoever is doing these things knows where you live, has been in your apartment, and knows your routine. Are you sure this is because of your assignment?"

"What else could it be? It all began when my assignment did."

"Why didn't you tell me this sooner?" he asked.

"I thought that someone was just trying to scare me. Now that we've been chased and shot at, I think they're serious and..." I paused, dropping my fork on my plate and turning to him added, "I think my father's involved."

He turned abruptly, his eyes incandescent with rage. "Your father?"

"I overheard him talking to this other man. I can't tell you how. You're in danger, Robbie. They're going to tell the people who are after you where you are so they will kill you." He pulled me close, resting his chin on the top of my head, and linking my arms in his as we tried to gain strength through the comfort of each other. "Would you stay tonight?" I asked.

He took my hand and led me to the bedroom, lowered me onto the bed, and embraced me gently. Making love with him was even better than I remembered. He still knew how to please; his generosity was boundless, his fingers slow and soothing. This was not a conquest, but a healing balm, a celebration of the good things in life hidden in the cracks between the surrounding lies and danger. Afterward, we spoke of the tragedy of our past and the triumph of finding each other again.

While I basked in the afterglow, he fell asleep. I envied him. He seemed so calm—almost too calm. Why wasn't he more distressed by what I'd told him? I envied him, but also felt an increasingly familiar churning in my gut. I tiptoed from the room, logged onto my computer, and downloaded the last set of photos from the vault onto a flash drive. While I was at it, I made a copy of the report I would give to Ben. The sooner I could erase the files from my computer, the better. By five a.m., I could not keep my eyes open any longer and returned to bed.

"Where have you been?" asked Robbie groggily.

"I couldn't sleep, so I did some reading. Sorry if I woke you."

"What kind of reading?" he asked, propping himself up on one elbow.

"If I am going to sleep with a conspiracy buff, I thought it best to know what he was talking about," I replied, hoping that would suffice.

"I'm not a conspiracy buff in bed, but I do enjoy investigations." He smiled with eyes not yet fully ready for the coming day. "Come on, let me at least hold you in the couple of hours we have left." We snuggled, the heat of his body soothing mine.

I woke to the sounds and smells of bacon sizzling in the pan and coffee dripping into the pot. Utensils clanged and dishes clattered. I enjoyed the momentary luxury of lying in bed and gazing out the window. It looked bleak outside, a stark contrast to the warmth and comfort of my apartment and the company of the man I loved.

"Good morning, sleepyhead." Robbie appeared at the bedroom door, shirtless but wearing jeans and a broad grin. "Breakfast is served." He held a tray with a steaming cup of coffee, a glass of orange juice, and a plate piled with bacon, eggs, and toast, with a single red rose standing in a small vase.

"It looks amazing! How long have you been up?"

"Hmm, I guess since 6:30. I walked Scout, and by the way, it's nasty out. Then I made breakfast."

"Have you eaten?" I asked between bites.

"About two hours ago."

"Two hours ago? What time is it?" I looked at the alarm clock—8:30. "I have to get to work." Grabbing my robe, I rose from bed.

"Whoa, Nellie. You slept two hours at most. Call in sick. Even the CIA can spare you for one day." He removed the tray, eased me back onto the bed, and climbed in next to me, wrapping me in his arms and nuzzling my neck. I convinced myself that I could work from home after Robbie left. There were still files to download and a final report to write. I rolled over, picked up the phone, and dialed Ben's administrative assistant, telling her I'd be working from home today. She took the message and said that Ben had called in sick and wouldn't be at work either.

I stared at the phone in silence as I contemplated her words. Ben never missed work. Something was up.

"I've got a proposition for you," Robbie said, with a mischievous twinkle in his eye. "How about you stay at home today and get some rest. I'll take Scout and do some reading. When you're ready, you can come over, leave your car, and we'll drive together to meet Pam and Trevor for dinner. Then we can go back to my place tonight and, if you're willing," he smiled roguishly, "we can pick up where we left off."

"I completely forgot about them." I thought for a moment, wondering if it made sense to keep our dinner date with all that was happening. But maybe a night out would provide a much-needed distraction, so I added, "It sounds like a great plan." I pulled him close to me. "Thank you, Robbie—not just for breakfast, but for being here. Waking up with you beside me or hearing you in the kitchen or the shower...just knowing that you're near makes all the difference in the world."

"Do you mean it?" He stroked my face with the back of his hand. His eyes seemed even bluer in the morning, like the sky on a summer day. His freshly shaven face was soft, inviting my lips to visit. His hair was tousled, curling elfishly around his ears and across his forehead like so many commas and question marks.

"I've never been more serious." I inhaled his scent. I couldn't get enough.

"I could stay in bed with you all day, but..."

"I know. You have work to do. What's on tap for today?" Our tryst was over, at least for now. I propped myself on one arm and leaned over him.

"You sure know how to get a man out of bed," he rolled over and pulled away. "J. Edgar Hoover." I looked at him skeptically, so he continued. "Hoover purportedly received a memo from the Miami office indicating that Marcello was putting a hit on Kennedy. Hoover should have alerted the Secret Service, but he didn't. He hated both Kennedys—especially Bobby."

I sat up, pulling the blanket over my bare chest. "You're accusing the highest ranking law-enforcement officer in the country of abetting the assassination? Come on."

"Like the CIA, the FBI and the Mafia overlapped a bit. Hoover thought Kennedy was immoral and kept a file on his dalliances. He also thought Kennedy was an arrogant, elitist prick who was soft on communism. More importantly, Hoover thought that JFK, if reelected, would force him to retire on January 1st of 1965."

"Do you think he would have?" The analyst in me returned. I honed in on every word, especially as I thought about the files I had seen that were labeled "FBI."

"Definitely. The Kennedys hated Hoover too. As attorney general, Bobby was Hoover's boss. When Bobby began prosecuting members of the mob, Hoover would not cooperate, so Bobby conducted his own investigation without the FBI. Hoover was livid. Bobby undermined his power. Hoover couldn't protect his mob buddies."

"What about Johnson? Did Hoover have anything on him?" It felt so strange being stark naked and having this conversation.

"Of course. He knew about Johnson's mistresses and his sordid history in Texas. But Johnson played Hoover's game; they understood each other. In Hoover's eyes, Johnson was far preferable to Kennedy."

"I'm sorry I asked," I muttered. "Was there any part of government that was clean?"

Robbie snickered. "Sure doesn't seem like it, does it? Well, enough about Hoover. I'm sure you have better things to do than listen to me drone on about him." He cuddled me briefly. "Just one more kiss."

"I could get used to this."

"What? Talking about Hoover?" he teased. I tossed a pillow at him, sending him scampering from the room. Within minutes, he was back, completely dressed, hair combed, and ready for the day.

"Now you get some rest, okay? I'll see you around six."

I wrapped myself in a robe and saw Robbie to the door. After a long sensual good-bye, he was gone. I secured both locks on the door, wedged a chair under the knob, and returned to my bedroom, indulging in reflections of the night and morning. Somehow, being with Robbie made the horrible events of the past couple of weeks disappear. I was falling in love all over again, but as soon as I admitted it to myself, Marita Lorenz reared her head. I couldn't deny that Robbie's interest in me had seemed to escalate after he saw her on my computer. And why was he friends with Beau, an oilman? Robbie was unnerved by the car chase, to be sure, but what about everything else? Shouldn't he be frightened as well?

I couldn't think about that now. I had work to do. I logged on and set to it. By four, I finished downloading what was left of the photos and put the finishing touches on my report. Seeing the entire list was overwhelming—especially now that certain items had become more significant after listening to Robbie. Originally, I had entered each item in the order I had found it, but for the report, everything was organized by type and topic. When I got to the items in the alcove—the brain, the rifle, and the autopsy reports—I realized that, by themselves, these items could prove a conspiracy at the highest levels of government *and* could get me killed. Carson and my father seemed relieved to think that I hadn't found the alcove and its contents. If I omitted them from the report, maybe I'd be safe. Ben wasn't showing his hand, and I wasn't sure that Robbie was either. Why should I?

Confident that the photos, the scanned items, and the inventory were successfully captured on the flash drives, I reviewed my report one last time. If Ben was shocked by the preliminary report, this one would finish him off. I hid the flash drives in the pockets of my parka, which hung in the back of my closet, and buried the satchel underneath my dirty laundry. I didn't want any rose-bearing intruders to find them. I'd have to find a better hiding place, *and soon.*

I showered, dressed, and was on the road by five. I tried calling Ben several times, intending to tell him about the conversation between my father and Carson outside the vault—even if it meant acknowledging that I hadn't stuck to his schedule. Once again, there was no answer. I didn't know whether to be worried or relieved.

I made it to Robbie's, expecting him to be ready for dinner, but only Scout greeted me at the door. I scratched his head and looked around the living room. There was no sign of Robbie. A band of tension tightened around my chest as I crossed the room, peeking around corners and calling his name. I crept down the hall. Still no response. Expecting the worst, I walked into his sanctuary only to find him still scanning papers and jotting notes. He looked so studious with his reading glasses, concentrating to the point where he didn't react as I entered. Relieved, I gently touched him on the shoulder. "At least Scout is happy to see me."

Robbie remained seated and chuckled. "He just beat me to it. He's been sleeping all day and hasn't been reading Hosty's notes to Hoover."

"You could at least say 'Hi.'" I crossed my arms and flashed a mock scowl.

He grinned sheepishly. "Sorry, I didn't hear you."

"So what's got you so preoccupied?"

"Oswald. Did you know he was a contract agent for *both* the FBI and the CIA? His FBI informant number was T-179 and he was paid $200 a month. He had a CIA number too. I guess that makes him a colleague of yours." He smirked. "His trip to Russia, his involvement in Fair Play for Cuba...I think they were intelligence-sponsored activities that enabled Oswald to infiltrate and inform. Take Oswald's ordering the Mannlicher-Carcano through the mail. It was 1963. Why would anyone living in Texas buy a gun through the mail when he could go to a local gun shop and pick it up without leaving a paper trail?"

"I see what you mean. If he used the gun, he'd be signing his own death warrant."

"I don't think he did. No one would buy that kind of rifle to kill someone. It was inaccurate, dangerous, and difficult to get off rounds quickly. Even the Italians called it the humanitarian rifle because it was so bad at killing people."

I glanced at my watch, but my anxiety had less to do with making Pam and Trevor wait than thinking about the Mauser with my father's initials attached. If Robbie and the policeman, Roger Craig, were right, the Mannlicher-Carcano must have been planted. Did my father do that, too? "So why did Oswald buy it, if it was such a bad gun?'

Robbie saw me glance at my watch and took it as a hint. He rose from his chair and headed toward the bedroom to get dressed. I followed to enjoy the show. "Maybe it was another one of his jobs. Maybe the FBI wanted him to investigate the use of the mail to make illegal-arms purchases, I don't know," he said, as he changed his shirt and stepped into another pair of pants. I snatched a tie from the rack and tossed it to him.

"Do I really have to wear this thing?" he asked.

I nodded and said, "Maybe Oswald intentionally bought and planted a bad gun so that the shooter would miss," I said.

"Never thought about that. It's a possibility." Robbie wrapped the tie around his neck and fumbled with the knot. "Imagine how he must have felt when he realized that he'd been set up to take the fall."

"Can you prove it?" I asked. I was conscious of the time but interested in his answer.

Robbie put on his jacket, looking fantastic, and answered with a simple "No."

"You ready?" I asked.

"As I'll ever be." We left the house and, once in the car, switched topics and talked about Pam and Trevor and the urbane, peaceful life they led: he as an academic and she as an antique dealer. Would we ever enjoy a similar peacefulness? Between Robbie's quest for truth and my own current project, peace was beyond our reach—maybe because we were grasping for something else.

CHAPTER SIXTEEN

B y the time we arrived, Pam and Trevor were already seated, holding hands like newlyweds and talking quietly. They definitely didn't look as if they were having any problems, as Pam had joked; quite the contrary. The restaurant they selected was a cozy bistro with small tables, a casual atmosphere, and a cuisine that featured seafood with an Asian flavor—light, but tasty. We enjoyed a window seat that overlooked the street filled with Christmas shoppers, bundled in heavy clothes and moving quickly to flee the frostiness of winter. No sooner had we exchanged greetings when a waiter stopped by to take our drink orders. Robbie ordered a beer while the rest of us opted for wine.

Conversation began with our various plans for the holidays. I admitted that mine were still up in the air, which drew questioning looks from everyone at the table. Pam asked, "Don't want to deal with Dad?"

"Something like that," I replied. Robbie jumped in to say that I could spend Christmas with him, a response that seemed to amuse Pam and Trevor.

"Seems like the two of you are hitting it off," Trevor chimed in. "It figures—you both have something in common." Seeing Robbie's questioning look, he added, "Kat grilled me on Op-40 after you left our little soiree. I figured that she'd do the same to you of all people, Rob." I shrank into my seat, feeling totally exposed. "Speaking of which, how *is* your work going?"

Robbie glanced at me before answering. "Good, but now that Kat is on the scene, I'm going to have to find more hours in the day to get anything done." He winked in my direction, igniting a pleasant series of sparks inside.

"What are you working on now, Rob?" Pam asked. I gave her a discrete elbow.

"Well, I haven't told anyone but Kat. I trust you two will keep it confidential. In fact, Trevor, I'd welcome your input both from a publishing and historical perspective."

"Happy to help in any way that I can," Trevor offered. Robbie explained the basis for the book he had in mind. Trevor thought for a moment, sipping his wine slowly. The rest of us sat in silence, waiting for his response. "Interesting concept, Rob, but you know that subject still rattles people in this town. Besides, how will you be able to link all those events together, with so many missing pieces?"

"I know, but what I've collected so far is incredible. Maybe if I could get it published, there would be enough of an uproar that the rest of the information would be released."

"I know a publisher or two that might take the chance. Although, of course, now you can self-publish. You know, most mainstream publishers won't touch it," Trevor replied.

"I'm prepared for that, but I have to try. It's way past time that the truth came out, don't you think?" Robbie asked.

"Hmm, not sure it ever will." Trevor puffed his lips and then added, "I can help with the historical context, but as a silent partner. I want to keep my job."

Trevor was about to launch into what must have been a familiar spiel about the Cold War, because Pam's eyes rolled and she took my hand, saying, "Now I know why you elbowed me. I thought we'd make it to the entree before he started."

"It's okay, Pam. I'm interested to hear what Trevor has to say," I said.

Robbie studied me, his eyebrow arched in curiosity, but then he turned his attention back to Trevor saying, "That's the thing. The stuff that happened in the fifties and sixties is still going on. The Kennedy assassination gave them the hubris to continue."

Trevor gulped down his wine and asked for another glass. "So you think that the actions like those of the Mexico City office continue today?"

I thought about my father's associates—David Phillips, David Morales, and the others. "What about the Mexico City office?" I jumped in, ignoring Pam's betrayed "not you, too" look.

Trevor paused before responding, eyeing me closely, but Pam came to my rescue. "Answer Kat's question, dear. Then maybe we can get back to enjoying our dinner."

He sighed and began. "Where to start?" He took a swig of wine as soon as the waiter placed his glass on the table. "Well, in the fifties, the Mexico office of the CIA, along with the banana companies and Somoza, staged a coup in Guatemala, where Marcello was thought to have major influence. Right there, you have the seeds for the CIA, the mob, and business conspiring to overthrow a government," Trevor began.

"Was Hunt there?" I asked. Robbie turned abruptly to face me, impressed.

"He was there, all right. In fact, in 1958 he organized an anti-communist confederation, headed by the guy who was also Marcello's lawyer. Incidentally, one of Banister's men was also part of it." Trevor was on a roll. The professor couldn't help himself.

"Was Hunt involved in the coup?" I asked.

"The people you really should be asking about are John Roselli and John Martino."

"I've read about them. They helped with the Guatemalan coup too, right?" I said, eliciting another quizzical look from Robbie that made me draw back a bit.

"One and the same," Trevor replied. "Martino began with the Atlantic City mob, installing security systems in Havana casinos for Trafficante. He was also involved with the Nixon-authorized CIA-Mafia plots at the time of Bay of Pigs. Importantly, he ran much of his activity from the Mexico office. Martino told people that he worked with Ruby in Havana; Ruby met with Roselli in Miami in early October, 1963."

Robbie jumped in to help clarify things "You see, Martino and Roselli were the interface between the CIA and the mob."

"Yeah, certain parts of the CIA and the mob were like this," Trevor crossed his index and middle fingers. "But there's a very interesting story," Trevor looked briefly at Pam, "and then I'd better stop before Pam makes me sleep on the couch tonight."

I was insatiable. "Please, I'd like to hear it."

He gave Pam a sheepish look. "If my better half will indulge me." Pam nodded, but her eyes indicated it would be the last time. "After the Bay of Pigs and Martino's release from Havana jail, Roselli and Martino established themselves in Key Biscayne. Does that ring a bell?"

"Wasn't Key Biscayne where Nixon had a place?" I answered. Trevor nodded, displaying an uneasy expression. I couldn't figure out why he had such a problem with my interest and not Robbie's.

"Uh, yeah," Trevor said. "Anyway, encouraged by Nixon's folks, they mobilized a new Cuban resistance to Castro, working with the old CIA-mob alliance, including Carlos Prío Soccarrás, Tony Varona, Gerry Patrick Hemming, David Phillips, and Frank Sturgis. All of these guys had been at the Lake Pontchartrain training camp."

"That's the one where anti-Castro Cubans were trained by the CIA," Robbie explained for my benefit.

I was already thinking back to the vault and the trunk labeled "Nagell," which held films and pictures of these people and Oswald at the training camps with the Cubans.

"Yep. Martino formed a hit team that went to Cuba in 1963. It was backed by the CIA, organized crime, William Pawley of *Life* magazine, and a New York financier who was close to the JFK White House. The hit team even used William Pawley's boat to go to Cuba. Its crew was a bunch of covert-operations Hall of Famers, plus Richard Billings who would write the exclusive story for *Life*. Even though the raid was organized by Trafficante and Giancana, who wanted to overthrow Castro to get their casinos back, it was sanctioned by Kennedy."

"There were plenty of raids on Cuba and attempts to hit Castro, Trevor. Why is this one so important?" I asked. A shadow of concern darkened Robbie's face. My zeal was too transparent; I was revealing too much.

Trevor, in his best professorial tone, continued, "First, it further demonstrates the precedent for cooperation among the mob, members of the CIA, the anti-Castro Cubans, and the media. Second, some people think this mission was used to blackmail the more mainstream parts of the CIA and *Life* magazine into covering up the assassination later on."

"Is that why *Life* magazine sat on the Zapruder film so long?" I asked, leaning in even further. Pam was looking around the room at the other diners, almost as though she wanted to join them rather than stay with us.

"Probably," Trevor answered, "and there's one last tidbit. When the Church Committee investigated CIA-Mafia activities, they subpoenaed Giancana and Roselli, but both were murdered before they could testify." Trevor sat back, finished with his account.

"Ironic, isn't it?" mused Robbie, "JFK sanctioned the very activities that ultimately led to his death." He took a sip of beer and gave me a sidelong look.

"But you said that JFK's assassination was just the beginning," I began. "What do you mean?"

Trevor realized that I was not satisfied and grimaced; I couldn't tell if I had irritated him or if he was wrestling with some inner misgivings. "Why don't you take it from here, Rob? This is more in your area of expertise." Trevor wanted out.

"The power elite knew that another nuclear war would result in a global holocaust. They wouldn't be able to make money from wars anymore. Kennedy's actions were viewed as appeasement. He wanted to deal with the Russians and end the Cold War. The best way to do that was to dismantle the CIA, including its clandestine subunit, the office of policy coordination."

"Wait a second. Kennedy wanted to dismantle the CIA?"

"Yep," Robbie answered. "If Kennedy succeeded, the OPC would not be able to initiate lesser skirmishes around the world—Korea, Vietnam, Afghanistan, Iraq, and so on. These skirmishes still enabled global businessmen—the ones with the real power—to keep their coffers full without precipitating Armageddon."

"How can you call these skirmishes?" I banged my glass a little too hard on the table as heat rose inside me, causing my face to flush and my hands to form knots.

"I think what Robbie is trying to say is that a real war requires a mission—like preventing Hitler from taking over the world," Trevor interjected.

"This is what I hope my book will address." Robbie's voice was full of energy, and his eyes burned brightly. I encouraged him to continue. "Think about it. Who created the insurgency in South Vietnam? The CIA. Who had the greatest amount to lose when Iraq invaded Kuwait? Big Oil. Who trained Osama bin Laden? The CIA. Who provided information on weapons of mass destruction? The CIA. Who benefitted from all these conflicts? Big business: oil, defense contractors, bankers." Robbie kept his voice low so diners at adjacent tables wouldn't hear, but the stridency was still there.

Seeing Pam look down at the floor, out of either boredom or irritation, I yielded. "Okay, I get it." But something inside wouldn't allow me to completely let it go without one last rebuttal. "But I still don't get how Kennedy's death had anything to do with Iraq or Osama bin Laden."

In a condescending tone, Trevor responded, "Fletcher Prouty wrote a book, *JFK: The CIA, Vietnam, and the Plot to Assassinate John F. Kennedy*. You should read it. Maybe you will see your organization in a new light."

"You're a spy?" Pam gawked at me as though she was seeing me for the first time. I shot her a look, and she immediately sat back in her seat.

"No, I'm not a spy. I do desk work, nothing exciting." I stared down at my glass of wine, trying to regain composure, but my nerves were in overdrive. I couldn't return her gaze. How did Trevor know I was CIA? I'd never told him. Did Robbie? I looked over at him, but his face revealed nothing. Realizing that I had pushed too hard, I took a long sip of wine. "I'll check it out," was all I could say.

The table was quiet until Pam jumped in, sounding a little skittish. "Okay, enough shop talk. Our poor waiter has been by three times to take our order and couldn't get a word in edgewise. I'm famished!"

"Good idea, dear," Trevor responded, after checking my face one last time. He had blundered by revealing that he knew I was CIA and was eager to change the subject. "Rob, stop by sometime and we can discuss your book then."

"Great. I can share some of the new stuff I've found, as well." Robbie sipped his beer and assessed me. He registered my disappointment at being excluded from the invitation.

I could have grilled the two of them all night, but Pam was right. This was a social occasion, and it was difficult to be social when everything that was said had me straining to remember items I had seen in the vault. When the waiter returned yet again, we ordered. I selected a pan-seared halibut, opting for a crisp Chardonnay in lieu of my usual Cabernet. We spent the remainder of the evening discussing holiday plans, Pam's antique business, and college memories. Pam invited me to join her at an upcoming auction, which sounded like fun. There was no further mention of anything to do with Kennedy.

In fact, the evening became quite jovial until Pam said, "Maybe next time we should invite Beau. He'd love to join us, I'm sure."

"That might be a little awkward," I said. "My seeing Robbie might bring back old college memories."

Pam laughed. "He wouldn't care about that. Since his divorce, he's had a different woman on his arm every time we've seen him."

"What happened? I mean with his divorce." I asked.

"The usual—irreconcilable differences. She left him, but not his money. He had to pay a bundle. More than anyone I know." Then in hushed tones, Pam added, "She must have had something on him—either that or she had a very good lawyer."

"That's enough, Pam," said Trevor. "We shouldn't be airing Beau's dirty laundry."

By the time Robbie and I dragged ourselves home, it was almost eleven p.m. Scout was his usual bounding bundle of energy, greeting us at the door, leash in mouth. Once he was harnessed, we made a U-turn out the door. Robbie held Scout's leash in one hand and mine in the other as we walked down the path near his house. Beau's Christmas decorations were already up. It would have been a perfect evening except for the question that had gnawed at me since dinner.

"Did you tell Trevor that I work for the CIA?"

"I was wondering if you'd ask me that. No. I didn't. I don't know how he knew."

"It's strange. Trevor and Pam are friends with Beau. Beau works for Big Oil. You and Trevor believe that the CIA is in lockstep with big business, including the oil companies. Am I being paranoid, or is there a connection here?" It was almost as if I was thinking out loud more than conversing. I couldn't deny the obvious; Robbie was friends with all of them, too.

We walked a bit further in silence, hand in hand. "It does seem a little weird. But if Beau and Trevor had some sinister agenda, why would they be so supportive of my work? I'm trying to expose the covert actions of the vaunted military-industrial complex. If they're part of it, I don't think they'd encourage me the way they do."

"Maybe they want to keep tabs on your progress." I squeezed Robbie's hand. "Do you trust them?"

"It's hard to know who to trust anymore." He stopped and turned to face me. "Do you trust me?"

I jerked my head and stared at him in surprise. "Of course," I responded too quickly.

"But you won't tell me about your assignment," he countered.

"I can't, but I will—when it's safe. For both of us."

"It may never be safe." He took my hand and resumed walking. "Until I know what you're up to, I can't keep you safe."

"Is that the real reason you want to know what I'm working on?"

"That's the most important reason."

I wanted to be satisfied with his answer. But I knew that he did have other reasons, and I was betting that Marita Lorenz was one of them. "Once I'm done with this assignment, I'm leaving the Agency. When I leave, I'll tell you everything."

Robbie nodded silently. He wasn't satisfied with my answer either, I could tell. We returned to his cottage and readied ourselves for bed. There would be no lovemaking tonight. My questions and doubts made romance impossible. Robbie rolled over and slept the sleep of the innocent while I lay awake, thinking about work tomorrow and whether Carson and his boys had cleaned out the vault.

Then I pondered the wisdom of telling Ben what I had heard, which meant admitting that I had violated his schedule. Then I began thinking about the flash drives. If someone was desperate enough, they'd search my apartment, looking for anything that would implicate me. I needed to stash them somewhere, possibly a safety-deposit box, but it couldn't be in my name. That would be too easy to locate, but it wouldn't be right to place anyone else in jeopardy. And what about Trevor? He knew a lot of the same things that Robbie did, *and* he knew I was CIA. How?

So many thoughts; so little sleep. Maybe that was why I heard footsteps on the gravel driveway. I crept to the window and peeked through the curtain. Beau was walking outside, his head down and shoulders hunched, as though bearing the weight of the world. Maybe the approaching holidays made him miss his children. Maybe the job demands that prevented him from traveling south for the winter were taking their toll. That mock salute of his was just a prop to convey the air of a carefree bachelor, but now, stripped of his façade, he seemed so alone, so vulnerable. He glanced briefly at my car and then to Robbie's cottage. Maybe I also contributed to his melancholy. I felt so badly. Pam was right. We should all go out some night and have some fun. Beau looked as if he could use it.

CHAPTER SEVENTEEN

Sometime during the small hours of the morning, I decided to play dumb about all I had seen or heard. That meant visiting the vault as scheduled, knowing that it was probably empty. I stopped by my office and found nothing amiss except that a burgeoning stack of reports and manifests now perched precariously on my desk. I'd get to those later. I chatted with a few co-workers who had arrived early, helped myself to a cup of coffee, and checked my e-mail.

By eight, I was on my way down to the dimly lit corridors I now knew so well. Jermaine was at his station, reading a weight-lifting magazine. He looked up, flashed his neon-bright smile and greeted me like a long-lost friend. I debated the wisdom of confronting him, with just the two of us alone in the remote maze of corridors. There was no telling how he would respond. As long as I was continuing the ruse with the vault, I might as well continue the ruse of believing that he was my "protective guard."

"Good morning. Nice to see you again. Back at it, huh?" Jermaine said.

"Hi, it's been a while," I responded, looking at him intently, searching for any sign of awareness of changes in the vault. Perhaps he thought that our ride together sealed my acceptance of his presence. "When did you arrive?"

"I've been here since six a.m. You usually come down a little earlier, don't you?"

"Yes, but I had to take care of some things at my desk. Quiet, as usual?"

"Like a tomb." He smiled once more and picked up his magazine. "Well, don't let me hold you up. You have a nice day."

Upon reaching the meeting room, I scanned my badge. It still worked. I sucked in a deep breath before opening the door and surveying the room. Nothing seemed out of place. So far, so good. I pressed the buttons on the control panel and watched the door of the vault slide open. I flipped on the lights. Even from the podium I could tell they had come. The shelves were empty; the floors bare. I walked tentatively toward the vault, as though half expecting someone to jump out.

Once inside, I realized that whoever was here had done a thorough job, and even though I had expected as much, it threw me. All the evidence was gone. I pressed the buttons on the panel inside toward the rear. The small chamber opened. It, too, was empty. History would be denied, except for what was listed on the inventory or was in my possession. Even though I knew it was going to happen, I felt violated, betrayed, and very angry.

I could tell Ben that I'd come down here as scheduled and found the empty vault. It would leave him with an unfinished report and ignorant of what I had heard yesterday. If the thieves assumed they'd removed everything before major damage was done, maybe they'd leave Ben and me alone.

But it didn't feel right. I'd always been honest with Ben. I could tell him that I was here on an unscheduled day, hand over the remainder of the list, and tell him what I overheard. Ben was in danger, too. I owed him as much. I should have called him last night. I was knee-deep in quicksand and sinking fast. I would not mention the flash drives and the items I'd taken. They were my insurance. With slow, deliberate steps I left the room.

"What are you doing back here so soon?" Jermaine asked.

"Someone has cleaned everything out. I need to tell Ben."

The gregarious banter disappeared; gone was the canyon-like smile. He stood and asked me to show him the vault. I debated the wisdom of doing so; he was an imposter. But maybe if I took him there, he would reveal something about himself. Besides, the evidence was gone. Once in the room, he said, "This is a crime scene now, Agent Hastings. Did you touch anything? Move anything?"

"Of course I did. It was part of my assignment," I responded. "Maybe they moved up the renovation schedule and relocated the items."

"I would have known." He was all business now; I hardly recognized him. "I don't know what you were doing in this room, but the fact that someone's been here and cleaned it out indicates that the items you saw were highly sensitive. That explains why those guys in the car followed you out of Langley. You may be in danger. Has anything else happened?"

"I have to talk to Ben," I responded. "There are several things I need to discuss with him."

"Like what?" He glared at me as he moved closer and reached for something in his pocket.

As he did, I jabbed my hand into my own pocket, reaching for the pepper spray and holding it tightly inside. He pulled out a card and handed it to me. I released the pepper spray and took the card from him, but remained silent.

"Okay, fine, have it your way, but if anything else happens, call me at this number immediately. Memorize it, and let me know when you leave for the day."

I agreed, and examined the card briefly. There was no name, no title, no organization—only a hand-written phone number. I shoved it in my pocket and left, feeling his gaze upon me and praying that he didn't suspect that I knew he was a fraud. I ran to Ben's office, dreading the conversation we needed to have. His light was off and his door was locked. I took a moment to assess the situation, long enough to realize that my pulse had quickened and neurons were firing. After checking several offices, I found his administrative assistant in the copy room and asked her where Ben was.

"It's the strangest thing. He didn't come in again today. He didn't call or let me know he'd be out."

That wasn't like Ben. I asked her for a phone that I could use in private. She unlocked Ben's office, and I called his emergency number.

"Douglas," he answered.

My relief was great, but transient. "Ben, it's Kat. I need to talk to you. It's urgent."

"Where the hell have you been? I've been trying to reach you," he shot back. Oddly, it was good to hear it.

"I went to the vault. My cell phone doesn't work there." I was chewing my nails.

"So you're at Langley?" he asked.

"Yes, in your office," I answered, as I scanned the room, looking for anything that might shed some light on events. "Where are you?"

"Go somewhere safe, and use your cell phone to call me back at this number." He recited a new phone number that I hurriedly jotted down.

I ran outside and called him again on Greg's phone, with the scrambler activated. He told me to meet him at the Watergate in an hour and to bring my computer. I was supposed to ask for a Tom Peyton when I arrived. I was to tell no one where I was going. Ben's precautions heightened my anxiety, as though that was possible.

I asked the guard at the front desk to get me a cab and walked to the stand. Traffic was light as we crossed the Key Bridge, and we reached Foggy Bottom in about twenty minutes. I looked up at the high-rise building and thought it was odd that, of all the places we could have met, Ben chose this one. I crossed the checkerboard floor of the massive lobby, brightened by sunlight streaming in through floor-to-ceiling windows, to the dark-wood reception desk that was bookended by alabaster pillars. I asked the desk clerk to contact Tom Peyton and waited by a colossal vase of fresh-cut flowers placed upon a polished, round table in the lounge. I was too hyper to sit, so I strolled around, trying to admire the artwork and flowers.

Ben rushed into the lobby and led me to the elevator. "There are too many people here. Let's go to my suite. There's a sitting area where we can talk."

We rode the elevator to the top floor, neither of us saying a word until he opened the door to a spacious room, classically appointed and offering a magnificent view of the Kennedy Center and the Potomac. "What have you got for me?" Ben asked, not wasting any time on small talk.

"I went to the vault today; it was empty." I saw his face blanch momentarily, but he quickly salvaged his businesslike demeanor.

"So, what you've given me is all we have?" He sounded resigned, as if somehow he had expected this news.

"Ah, no. That's what I need to tell you about. I'm not sure where to begin."

"Spit it out. I don't have time for this."

"I went Wednesday. I wanted to get as much of the evidence catalogued as possible. You mentioned renovations, and then there were the threats. I..."

"You disobeyed my orders," he stated flatly.

"Yes, and I'm sorry, but I did get more information. And there's something else you need to know." I hesitated, trying to regroup and select my words.

"I'm listening." His impatience was evident by his fingers, now drumming rapidly on the end table at his side.

I told him what I had heard when I was in the vault: the muffled voices, the threats, and insinuations. I told him that one of the men was my father.

"And you're just telling me this now?" he boomed. His crimson face looked as though it would explode.

"I tried calling you several times, but you didn't answer."

"Shit." He hit the wall. "Do you have any idea what's happened in the last forty-eight hours? A little warning would have been nice." He knocked his coffee cup to the floor. It shattered. He stood and kicked a few of the pieces aside. "Do you have my report?"

I pulled out my computer and opened the report. He took it from me and read while I shifted in my seat. "When you said to finish up and get out of town, well, it made me nervous," I said as he scanned the document.

"You should be nervous. I had some interesting visitors stop by the house last night. My wife and I were unharmed, but it could have been much worse. I've sent her out of town to stay with some relatives while I stay here. Don't tell anyone that you saw me."

I stared at him, not knowing what to say. I could feel the blood drain from my face. All I could manage was, "I'm sorry."

"Forget it. It's done. If they were going to kill me, they would have last night. Even if you had told me, I probably wouldn't have assumed they'd act so soon. At least you were able to finish the job. You did finish the job, didn't you?"

"There were a few boxes left, but I got most of it." I thought about the alcove within the vault and the particularly incriminating items it held, but after hearing the conversation between Carson and my father, the fewer people who knew about this, the better.

"Have you heard from your father?" I told him I hadn't and he followed with, "It's time for you to go away."

"Ben, I think it's time for me to leave the Company." It just popped out of my mouth, as though the idea had been percolating inside and bubbled over

"If you do, I can't protect you. Just take a little trip for a week or so. The job is done. Let the dust settle. I can do damage control while you're away."

"If I can figure out who's on a plane or train, so can someone else. Carson said that Jennings is an ally. You work for him, don't you?"

"Jennings? Well, isn't that interesting?" He said it more like a statement than a question, pausing while he absorbed the information. "That explains a few things. Jennings has a lot of power in the Company." He drew his hand across his chin, as though checking for the closeness of his shave. "I'll make a couple of calls while you're driving back. You'll be a new woman." For the first time that afternoon, Ben Douglas cracked what would almost pass for a smile. I was going undercover.

"What about this Jermaine guy?" I asked. "He was down there again today. He gave me a number and told me to call him if I ran into any trouble." I showed Ben the card. He crumpled it up and threw it in the trash can.

"Why'd you do that?" I went to the can and pulled out the card and returned it to my pocket.

"I checked him out. He's JSOC, Joint Operations Special Command; you know, Delta Force, the Seals, the air force's special tactics squadron.

He's legit. I just don't know whose side he's on. If you call him, you'll be tipping your hand to whoever sent him to watch you. We can't have that, not now."

I nodded in understanding. Everything was happening so quickly, and there was so much to do: open a safety-deposit box, hide the evidence, and arrange for Scout's care, not to mention, pack. "When should I leave?"

"As soon as you can get your ass out of here. If not tomorrow, then definitely the next day. Don't see your father before you go. If he calls, don't answer. He can't know you're leaving until you're already gone. I don't want him on to you anymore than he already is."

"Got it," I replied quietly. My father was now a full-fledged adversary.

As I gathered up my things, Ben said, "Leave your computer with me. I'll get you a new one. Any idea where you'll go?"

"Not a clue." As I pulled the door to his suite closed, I could hear Ben already on the phone, making arrangements for my new identity. At least my computer was clean. I had erased everything except Ben's report. Greg's computer was another story all together. That one would not leave my sight.

The blinking light on my desk phone nagged at me. Forcing back my mounting anxiety, I punched the keypad and listened. Four messages later, there it was. "This is your father. Meet me for dinner. I'm thinking steak and some nice wine. Call me."

Yeah, I thought, when the Orioles win the pennant. There was no way—not after what Ben had said. I desperately needed to talk to Robbie, but he'd told me he wouldn't be home tonight. With no legitimate computer, I dove into the paper monolith and didn't come up for air until it was time to leave. I packed my things and walked out the door to the bus stop. But as soon as I left the campus, Jermaine's familiar brown Hummer pulled up beside me.

"Get in," he ordered.

I quickened to a trot, grateful that I hadn't worn heels that day. Once again the Hummer was at my side. Jermaine snapped, "I said, get in."

I ran. The Hummer pulled over ahead of me and Jermaine jumped out. I veered into a wooded area between the road and a housing development. He caught up to me, grabbed me around the waist, and pushed me back toward his Hummer. I reached for the pepper spray and as I did so, he twisted my arm behind me, sending the pepper spray flying from my hand. He laughed. "You thought you'd stop me with pepper spray? Come on, get in the car. We need to get out of here. You're not safe."

"Where are you taking me? And don't tell me Ben authorized this. You've been lying to me the entire time."

He nodded, but said nothing until we hit the main road. "Some men were seen entering your apartment building. I'm thinking that they went to your apartment. Does your building have a concierge or any type of security? Is the parking garage well lit? How many times do you use your car in a normal week? Do you leave your apartment at night?"

I sat quietly, not answering a single question, consoling myself that if he wanted to kidnap me, he wouldn't be taking me to my apartment.

"I'm trying to help you," he insisted. Jermaine pulled into the circular drive and parked the car there, with its flashers on. He was instantly at my side door before I had a chance to collect my purse and button my jacket. After opening the front door, he covered the distance to the front desk in just three strides and asked the concierge if he'd seen two strange men enter the building. The concierge shook his head, no. We proceeded to the elevator, which carried us to my floor.

I unlocked the door to my apartment and knew immediately that something wasn't right. Scout was not there to greet me. I called his name and ran into the room but was passed instantly by Jermaine. I screamed "Scout!" but to no avail. Jermaine ran into my bedroom as I ran to the guest bedroom. I found Scout in the guest bathroom, behind its closed door.

Jermaine ran to the bathroom. "He's been in there all day?"

"I guess so. I never use this room." I scratched Scout's head. He looked fine, but uncomfortable. "I've got to take him out."

"I'm going with you."

Scout dragged me faster than I could walk. The cold of the night felt like a bucket of water thrown in my face and left me shaking. "For the sake of argument, let's assume you didn't shut Scout in by mistake, that someone was in your apartment and put him in the bathroom to get him out of the way. Why? They didn't toss the place. Tell me the procedure for guests when they arrive. Do they have to register with the guard?"

I shook my head, no.

"Are there security cameras? Would you recognize anyone that didn't belong in this building? Do you have anything that someone else might want?"

I thought of the evidence hidden in the closet and tensed, but did not respond. That was one secret I wouldn't share—especially with Jermaine.

"Since they didn't toss the place, we should check for bugs," Jermaine said. When we got back from the walk, he examined the phone receivers, unscrewed the light bulbs, and looked behind pictures, inside cabinets, and under furniture. He scoured the place relentlessly until he reached behind the flat-screen TV. Working his long fingers into the small space between the TV and the wall, he reached in, felt around, and pulled out a minuscule microphone, holding it up between his thumb and index finger.

I started to speak, but he held his finger to his lips and motioned me to follow him to the hallway. Once the door was shut, he said, "There may be more, I don't know, but someone wants to know what you have to say and who you're saying it to. Just to be safe, don't use your land line. Don't have any confidential conversations in your apartment. And for goodness' sake, don't go out by yourself tonight. Keep your door locked."

"Why should I listen to you? You abducted me. You've lied to me." Harsh whispers conveyed my anger.

"I was trying to keep you from getting killed. If I was working against you, why would I be searching for bugs?"

"How do I know you didn't plant them yourself?"

"You don't," he sighed. "Yes, I lied to you. I had to."

"Tell me about JSOC," I said smugly, folding my arms across my chest and eliciting a transient rise of his eyebrow.

"You've been checking up on me, I see. I don't blame you." He thought for a moment and then answered, "A buddy of mine says we're the dark matter, the force that orders the universe, but can't be seen." A deep laugh escaped his throat. "At first, we went after Al-Qaeda, Hamas, and the other terrorists. Now we're watching bad guys here at home, too."

"Who assigned you to me? And don't say Ben. He was livid when he found out about you."

His face was pinched; his words, clipped. "The people you're tangling with play for keeps. They have harsh ways of getting information from people, and believe me, they will. You will suffer. The more you know, the more they can find out. It's enough that you know that I'm JSOC. Any more than that can endanger others. I can't allow that."

His words stabbed me like a hidden shiv, but I couldn't let on. "Right." I placed my hand on the door and waved him off. "I think you should leave."

Ignoring me, he reentered my apartment and gave the room one last scan. "Somehow you have to find a way to trust me," he said, turning to me. "I'm the only one you can." Then he smiled. "Besides, I'm one of the good guys."

Although not convinced, somehow I felt ever so slightly better.

He left, after giving me numerous additional instructions. I closed the door and propped myself against it, feeling drained of all emotion and energy.

The evidence.

With a burst of adrenaline, I ran to the bedroom and plunged my hand into the pocket of my parka and then the laundry basket. Everything was still there. A tsunami of relief crashed over me. I sat on my bed and held the bullet fragment in my hand, staring at it in disbelief. This had killed Kennedy. It changed history, and now I could set things straight. It was time for some wine—lots of it. I craved the oblivion where I wouldn't have to feel, think, or fear. But I did have to find a place to go where no one would think to look for me—not Jermaine, not Ben, and definitely not my father.

CHAPTER EIGHTEEN

The cell phone rang, shattering the tranquility of my apartment. I was well into my second glass of wine.

"Hey, Kat, it's me." Robbie's voice was a balm for my ragged nerves.

"Where are you?" I clutched the receiver so tightly that my hands were shaking.

"On my way to your place. My interview bailed again." I could hear the traffic in the background and the frustration in his voice.

"I'll meet you at the entrance, and then maybe we can drive for a while. I need to talk to you in private." Just knowing Robbie was so close comforted me more than the wine ever could.

"Your apartment's not private?" His voice rose an octave.

"Not anymore. I'll explain when I see you." I gnawed a knuckle as I tried to decide just how much I could say when I saw him.

"I'll be there in ten minutes."

I didn't even bother to turn Joni Mitchell off as she was singing "Free Man in Paris," an old favorite, now so incongruous considering my current state. I was alive, at least for now, but not unfettered like Joni. I brushed my hair, pulled on my parka, grabbed my purse, and pounded the elevator button, shifted from one foot to the other, and pounded again. After what seemed like an eternity, the door slid open and I joined three or four people inside. When we reached the lobby, I jogged to the entrance of the building and scrutinized every car that entered the driveway. A blue Ford Fusion with the Zipcar logo pulled in and flashed its lights. I saw Robbie's welcome face inside.

"Where to, Nanook?" he laughed. I wrapped my arms around him and kissed him hard, with an urgency that erased his smile. "Hey, it's okay. We'll just tour the city."

"Robbie, there's so much to tell you. I don't know where to begin." I felt safe for the first time that day and relaxed in my seat.

"We have all night." He stroked my face and patted my hand. "Take a few minutes. When you're ready, let it fly." He shifted into drive and we were off.

I placed my purse on the mat by my feet, unzipped my parka, and pulled it off, hearing its precious cargo clank inside the pocket. I looked behind and beside the car, not knowing for what exactly, maybe to see if someone was following us. While horns honked and motors revved outside the car, Robbie turned off the NPR station and took my hand. "What is it, Kat?" he asked.

"My boss, Ben Douglas..."

Robbie stomped on the breaks, causing me to lunge forward as he shot me a look of alarm.

"What's wrong?" I tried to read his face in the shadows of the car. "Why did you stop?"

"It's, uh, nothing. I just remembered something that I was supposed to do. Uh, sorry, you were saying?"

"I don't believe you."

"It's nothing. Really. Let it go." He stared straight ahead, seemingly unable to look me in the eye.

"You're sure?" I asked, still studying his face.

"Yes, now tell me what's happened." He took my hand as if gentleness could persuade me to believe him. I'd deal with that later.

"Anyway, Ben is the one who gave me the assignment I keep mentioning. He wants me to go away until everything dies down. He's creating a new identity for me." Then I paused. He must have sensed that I was contemplating my next words, because he remained silent for a full cycle of the stoplight. "Robbie, there's more, and I swear I'll tell you everything after I leave the Agency. But for now, you and I are in trouble. My place has been bugged."

"It seems as though we both have a number of things that we've been keeping from each other, and because of that, neither of us is safe," he said.

"What have you been keeping from me?" I could hear the edge in my voice. I thought he'd been completely open about all he knew and his speculations. He said nothing, so I continued. "I admit it. I've kept many things from you, and I'm sorry, but it's my job. What's your excuse?"

"Let's talk about that later. We have more important things to think about."

My frustration grew. "If I get burned…"

"It sounds like you may already be burned." His voice was somber and low. "We need to focus on how to stay alive."

"Ben told me to go away until things blow over. I'd like you to go with me, but I haven't figured out where." I could almost see his thoughts popping like firecrackers. "Would you?"

He tapped out a rhythm that sounded like "Tusk" on the steering wheel. I remembered him doing that in college when he considered his options. Then his eyes brightened. "I've got an idea. You keep asking me about the assassination. Let's go to where it all began—New Orleans. There's a guy there who is willing to talk to me. I was going to see him next week, but maybe he'll meet me sooner. He used to run with Roselli. He calls himself Joey. He claims that he was a member of Hoover's hit squad."

"Hit squad?" I shuddered at the thought. "Never mind. You can tell me about that when I'm a little more sane. Is it safe to talk to him?"

"He says he's clean now. Gave up the life years ago. He's become a recluse and hasn't talked to anyone yet, as far as I can gather. Says he wants to set the record straight before he dies."

"It sounds risky; are you sure?" One more thing to fuel the fires of my anxiety. Great.

He stroked my arm and said, "You'll have a new identity tomorrow, and after tonight, I will too. How would you feel about dating a man with short, blond hair who goes by the name of Tom?"

Trying to match his tranquility, I answered, "Okay, but don't tell my boyfriend."

We drove around until we ended up in Adams Morgan, known for its wide array of ethnic restaurants. Robbie announced that he was starved and at that moment, a Cajun restaurant appeared before us. "Kismet," he exclaimed. "If we are going to New Orleans, what better way to prepare? But first, let's ditch the Zipcar."

"Yeah, I was meaning to ask. What's wrong with your Prius?"

"Long story. Let's just say that my car has become a little too recognizable." Fortunately, the nearest Zipcar location was just a couple of blocks from Eighteenth Street and a short walk to the restaurant. We entered the cozy bistro and were greeted by Dixieland jazz and the smell of jambalaya. Though a mere hole-in-the wall on a street full of other small restaurants, it was packed with raucous patrons—a perfect place to blend in. The host led us to a table for two crammed against the back wall, below Mardi Gras posters, dangling beads, and a variety of masks. Robbie ordered an Abita beer while I, still trying to calm down, asked for a Cajun martini. Our drinks arrived promptly, and we raised our glasses. "To truth, justice, and the American Way," I toasted.

"To my partner in crime," Robbie said, as he clinked my glass.

"To New Orleans, the city that care forgot," I followed, almost beginning to giggle. I could feel the tension abate for the first time that evening.

He took my hand and added, "To us." I drew back involuntarily. Perhaps I didn't trust him as much as I thought.

The waiter returned for our orders. Robbie chose the jerk chicken while I went with the crawfish étouffée, hoping for prompt service as the martini had taken a detour, bypassing my stomach and going straight to my head.

"Do you ever think how our lives would have been different if we had we stayed together?" I mused.

"Only every day," he smiled gently, "but maybe it was meant to be this way. Maybe this time, we'll appreciate it more."

"I was so stupid. I let my father bully me into marrying Nate. I didn't think I had a choice. He had a way of..."

"Getting his way?" Robbie's smile morphed into one more rueful.

"How did you learn about my father?" I asked, swallowing another gulp of fire.

"Thanks to FOI, I've learned a lot about him. You're welcome to read what I have, although you may not want to. "

"Try me." I was hanging on his every word.

"He was part of the Mexico City office under Scott and Phillips, which means he probably helped create the Oswald persona and then helped Phillips frame him." Robbie's words, combined with my memories of the files I had seen, painted my soul gray.

"No wonder you can't stand my father," I said, more to myself than to Robbie.

Robbie's smile disappeared. "He's not my favorite." He took a sip of beer. "So tell me about your new identity."

"I don't know who I'll be yet, but as soon as I do, I'll fill you in." I started to say more, but stopped when the waiter arrived with our orders. We dove into our meals, savoring bites and moaning with delight.

I was still nursing the embers of my martini when Robbie asked, "Do you trust your boss?"

"Ben? Of course," I answered reflexively, but then began to ponder his question further.

"But he did put you on a dangerous assignment."

"I work for the CIA, remember? There are lots of dangerous assignments. Besides, he was threatened as well." Why was I defending Ben?

"Did he tell you that, or do you know that for sure?" he asked. I sat quietly; I didn't know for sure. "And what about this Jermaine fellow? Do you trust him?"

"He's been friendly, very professional, and he alerted me to the men following me out of Langley. He found the bugs in my apartment, but he lied to me. He told me that Ben put him on the assignment, but Ben had never heard of him." I mentioned nothing about JSOC.

"Let me play devil's advocate for a second. Maybe he knew those guys were following you and was trying to gain your confidence. It could have been staged. What if he pretended to look for bugs and faked pulling one out from behind your TV?"

"I don't know," I answered feebly. My assumptions were crumbling beneath the weight of Robbie's questions.

"What about your father? What lengths would he go to in order to prevent you from talking to anyone? Would he harm you?"

"He's my father." I glared at Robbie, but then sat back, asking myself—just how far would he go?

"I'm just saying that you don't really know who you can trust. Take me, for example. How do you know I'm not just playing along, hoping to get information from you?"

"I can't believe you said that. You don't know what I'm working on. Besides, how did you know we'd meet at Pam's? You haven't hounded me for any information. And you've been threatened as much as me." Other diners were looking up; I continued in a more hushed tone. "You're the only person I do trust." As soon as I said it, I knew it wasn't true. I was trying hard to convince myself that I could trust him, and that could be a big mistake.

"I was hoping to hear that, Kat. You can trust me, honest." He crossed his heart and raised his hand. "Forever." He took my hands in his and added, "I just want you to be careful. We both have to be." He pulled away and took another swig of beer. In a lighter voice he added, "When we get to New Orleans, we can *laissez les bon temps rouler*. I'll even treat you to a private tour from a conspiracy buff's perspective."

"What about your work?" I asked.

"I'm an investigative reporter, remember? My time is flexible. Besides, since my hit man is in New Orleans, I can combine business with pleasure." He smiled over the rim of his glass.

"But how can you travel incognito? You can change your appearance, but you still have the same identification."

"Got it covered, thanks to a pal of mine who just happens to have short, blond hair and doesn't need his license anymore."

"Okay, professor. I'm your willing student." I took a final swig of my martini—still potent after more than an hour.

"One more thing. If they do have your apartment bugged, let's use it to our advantage. When we're back, follow my lead, okay?" His voice was hushed and a little conspiratorial.

"I will follow you anywhere." My eyes beamed, and my heart meant it; my brain was not as sure.

"Even to the grassy knoll?" he asked

"Even to the grassy knoll," I laughed. Once again, we'd hit the reset button and could move forward.

All the way back to Shirlington, the cabbie was playing rap music and talking on his cell phone, oblivious to our conversation. Nonetheless, we stuck to benign topics like the economy, sports, and the approaching Christmas holiday. We arrived and both checked out our surroundings. Catching each other in the act, we chuckled as we climbed the stairs. Robbie held the door as we entered the lobby and hurried toward the elevator.

"Wait a second. I might as well check the mail while I'm here." I unlocked the box and flipped through the usual bills and catalogues. A plain white envelope caught my attention. It had no address or stamp. I opened it immediately and became a stone, staring at the words with horrified eyes until Robbie ripped the paper from my hand and read...

You've ignored our warnings and now you will pay. If you open your mouth about anything you've seen, you are a dead woman. The same goes for your nosey boyfriend. We enjoyed meeting your dog. It'd be too bad if something happened to him. You can run, but we will find you. By the way, we watch you run every day.

I seized the paper, but it was too late. "Kat, about your assignment. I know you can't tell me anything, but..."

I pulled Robbie's arm urgently. "You don't think they'd hurt Scout, do you? We've got to get upstairs right away!"

He ran behind me as I raced toward the elevator. Someone had been to my home again and found a way to get the note into my box. Suddenly I was assessing everyone I saw. Was the man by the newspaper rack looking at me strangely? Was the woman sitting in the lobby watching my movements? Was the desk clerk a real desk clerk or a plant?

"Scout is going to need to go out. Would you like me to walk him?" Robbie asked.

"I just hope he's still there!" Taking a deep breath, I unlocked the door. Scout's happy face and bouncy demeanor flooded me with relief. I squeezed Scout's neck and released a sigh from my innermost depths. Robbie removed the leash from its hook and took my hand as we retraced our steps to the elevator and went outside. Poor Scout was denied a long walk once again; neither of us wanted to tarry too long.

The stores and restaurants were winding down for the night, as customers left for home. My suspicions continued unchecked. I looked at each person who passed and avoided shadows, alleys, and trees. The wind gusted down the main street, funneled by the buildings on either side. I was glad to be wearing my parka, not only so I could hold on to its invaluable contents, but for its warmth and comfort. "Robbie, I need to get out of here. It's getting to me."

"We will, I promise. What will you do with Scout?"

"I guess I'll have to put him in a kennel. We've never been apart." The thought broke my heart. "When can you leave?"

"Late Monday, early Tuesday. The guy who's been blowing me off promised to meet. Do you want to stay at my place over the weekend?"

"Yes, please," I said. "I don't need any more visitors. My home isn't safe."

We returned to my apartment, ready for the ruse in case anyone was electronically eavesdropping. We quickly peeked in all of the rooms to verify that everything was in order and hung our coats in the closet. Robbie poured us each a nightcap from the bottle of Caymus I had opened the previous night. With each sip, the tension ebbed until I was merely neurotic. We engaged in small talk, but then I gave Robbie a signal, indicating that I was ready.

"So your boss told you to take a vacation, huh?" he began.

"Yeah, I guess I should. I've never really taken more than a few days off. It's time. Do you want to come?" I had to remind myself to speak in a normal voice.

"I wish I could, but I've got a lot of catching up to do at work." He winked. "Where are you going?"

"I don't know, maybe New York. MOMA has a couple of new exhibits I'd like to see, and I've never been to Radio City for the Christmas show. That might be fun. Maybe I'll go to a Broadway play. I have a few friends who live there. I'll probably look them up as well."

"How long will you be gone?" he asked.

"I don't know. A week, maybe? I'll drive up so I can be flexible." Even though we'd practiced in the car, it seemed so awkward—especially since we didn't even know if anyone was really listening.

"I'll miss you." He held my hands, willing me to press on with the charade.

"Come up for the weekend." I shuffled a few papers for sound effects. "Here's the hotel where I'll probably stay."

"I might just do that. Save the Broadway play for then, okay? We'll have a nice dinner first. I know this great Italian restaurant in the theater district."

"That would be wonderful. Are you sure you don't mind taking care of Scout until then?"

"Of course not. We're buddies, aren't we, boy?" Robbie scratched the dog's head, sending his tail into hyper-wag. "I'm beat. How about you?"

"Exhausted. Let me check my voice mail and I'll be right in."

Robbie lunged at the phone before I could retrieve my messages. "It's late. Why don't you check them tomorrow?" He pointed to the ceiling. If someone was listening, they would hear the messages as well and know that I had heard them. Instead, I reviewed the callers' names only. The first message was from my sister. The second was from Pam. The third one made me tremble—my father. I looked at Robbie. He held a finger to his lips. We readied ourselves for bed and turned in. Once silenced by the cocoon of the comforter and wrapped like vines around each other, he whispered, "Don't tell anyone where you're going—not

Ben, not Jermaine, not Pam, not your sisters, and most of all, not your father, okay?"

I whispered, "My lips are sealed."

"I'm sorry to hear that." I could almost see his grin.

"I so want to be out of here." I curled up in his embrace, thankful for his resilience, his calm, but at this moment, mostly his body.

He took my face in his large hands and kissed me with a firmness that was pleasing, but also terrifying because it made me realize that he, too, was frightened but was trying to be strong enough for both of us. I clutched him, and at that moment knew that despite any doubts I had, I loved him as much as any woman can love a man and that if we somehow survived this, I would be his for the rest of my life—however long that might be.

CHAPTER NINETEEN

We spent a blissful, but all too fleeting weekend at Robbie's, enjoying long runs delectable meals and easy conversation. Sometimes we acknowledged our plight; most times, we tried not to. With so many details to address, we seldom succeeded.

I called the kennel and fortunately, they had an opening for Scout. No, I didn't know how long I'd be away, maybe two weeks. Yes, I had a record of his shots. No, he'd never been in a kennel before. Yes, he gets along well with other dogs. Yes, I would bring his food and, yes, he should be exercised every day. One item checked off the list. I would miss him terribly.

Next, I called Pam to explain that I couldn't go to the auction with her as we had planned. "That's too bad," she said. "We were hoping that you, Rob, and Beau would join us for dinner afterward. Beau will be disappointed. He was looking forward to seeing you." She asked what had come up. I explained that I'd told Robbie I needed a break and he asked me to accompanying him on an interview. True, but vague enough.

The last item, the plane, required some thought. It might be better to make flight arrangements at the last minute. If we didn't know what we were doing, no one else could either. The ten a.m. flight to New Orleans still had open seats. That might work.

When Monday arrived, we woke to a gray morning, not yet illumined by the sun or announced by the alarm. Robbie, Scout, and I set out for a quick three-mile loop. The peace of our surroundings did nothing to assuage the tension that cramped each muscle and rendered my feet like cinder blocks. What had once been an enjoyable routine now seemed fraught with apprehension. Robbie did his best to keep things light by teasing me about my hapless Orioles or discussing the latest affair that had sent a congressman packing. Nothing worked. I could only manage monosyllabic responses and a quickened tempo.

Once back and showered, we promised to stay in touch and hugged each other a little harder and longer than usual. Robbie dropped me off at Langley and left to tie up his loose ends. I checked my e-mail and voicemail. There was a message to call a Hans Schmidt. I did so immediately. It was Ben. He told me to meet him at the Hyatt within the hour.

Another message was from my father. All attempts at civility were gone. He demanded to speak with me immediately. That wouldn't happen. After talking with a few co-workers for the sake of appearances, I called a cab and was off. Traffic was heavy on the Georgetown Parkway and by the time we crossed the Key Bridge, it was gridlocked. Nothing was moving except my digestive tract, which seemed to be in overdrive, either from last evening's dinner or my now chronically hyperactive nerves.

The trip to New Orleans would be a blessing as long as we could flee DC unnoticed. While staring out at various monuments, cars, pedestrians, and a few tardy birds that had yet to fly to warmer climes, I was mentally packing my suitcase and reviewing a checklist of what needed to be accomplished before leaving. The flash drives and evidence were a problem. I didn't want to bring them to New Orleans with me, but where could I stash them before we left?

What would have been a fifteen-minute trip without traffic took forty-five. Ben would not be happy. I quickly exited the cab and stepped into the ultramodern lobby of polished wood floors, marble display counters, and mirrored glass which reflected the naked trees shivering outside. Ben did not seem to be on a strict budget. Using a lobby phone, I asked the operator for Hans Schmidt. A second later, Ben was firing questions at me like a verbal Uzi. Where had I been? What was going on? Had I spoken with my father? When was I leaving? Had there been any more threats? There was hardly enough time in between to answer any of them. Clearly, his anxiety level equaled mine. I rode the elevator to his floor, anticipating another barrage.

He pulled open the door and immediately said, "We don't have a lot of time." He walked back to the table and picked up a folder. This is for you. It contains a passport, a driver's license, and a profile of a woman named Carla Banks. She is an IT specialist for Microsoft and lives in Seattle. Study it, and be ready for any questions that might be asked of you. If you fly, don't check your bags. They could be searched while out of your possession. Do not carry your normal identification on you while you are using these."

I took the envelope from him and began paging through the documents inside. "Who knows about this besides you?"

"Someone I trust implicitly." He was all business, but I could tell he had more to say.

"So why a different hotel and name?" I asked,

"The measures I'm taking are not your concern," he said, waving his hand dismissively. "But there is something I want to discuss with you." He placed his coffee cup on a black lacquered end table and said, "You've been seeing a guy named O'Toole. Dump him."

I sprang from my chair. "What? Why?" I couldn't figure out how he knew.

"He's trouble. They're onto him, and the target on his back gets bigger every day. If you hang around with him, you're as good as dead. Worse, they might use you to get to him."

"You don't understand. I ..."

"No, you don't understand. This isn't a game. It's time you smartened up. O'Toole has been sticking his nose where it doesn't belong, and he's gotten the wrong people angry."

"Ben, everything he's done is legal. He's an investigative reporter."

"And using you in the process?" Ben's eyes were inches from mine. "Doesn't it strike you as odd that he shows up out of nowhere right after you were put on this assignment?"

"A college friend invited us to a dinner party. It was a coincidence. He doesn't know what I'm working on."

"So you say. If he cares for you, why would he put you in danger?" His voice could cut wire.

"I refuse to believe that he's using me. He hasn't asked me for anything."

"Yet," Ben said. His face was red, and for the first time in thirty years, he tugged at his tie and unfastened the top button of his shirt. This one act frightened me more than anything up to this point. I had never seen his perfect Windsor knot loosened—not even during the heat of a Virginia summer. "You've got to trust me on this. If you keep seeing this guy, you are in danger. They *will* kill you. I can't make it any plainer than that."

My defenses sprang to DEFCON5. Even though Ben was trying to protect me, his accusations were too personal, his orders too intrusive. In a voice so stiff that even I failed to recognize it, I said, "I'll think about it. Is there anything else?"

"When are you leaving?" I told him I wasn't sure. "Make it fast." He paused and touched my arm. "And for God's sake, be careful."

It was only when I was sitting in the cab that my pulse slackened. I had never told Ben about Robbie, but he knew. The man I'd trusted for my entire career was telling me to stop seeing the man I loved. And based on the conversation I had overheard outside the vault, my father knew as well and wanted the same man dead. The men in my life were driving me insane.

I didn't return to work. Instead I went home to pick up the evidence and then drove to a bank in Alexandria. As Carla Banks, I obtained a safety-deposit box and placed the evidence inside, wondering if it would ever be seen by anyone again.

I returned home and dug out warm-weather clothes for the trip south. My carry-on suitcase was jammed with clothes, but even so, there were nowhere near enough outfits to last one week, let alone two. After my bag was packed, I pulled Scout's vaccination record from a file and did a quick scan of my apartment, realizing that I would have to move when I returned. The worst part was that I had no idea who was robbing me of my privacy and my way of life. My enemy could be a stranger, a friend, or...my father.

I leashed Scout and we descended to the parking garage. With both suitcase and dog in tow, I unlocked the car with the key fob and then pressed the automatic ignition, though the car was an aisle away. A thundering roar reverberated throughout the garage—so loud that I didn't hear my own scream as I recoiled back toward the door. Glass rained down upon the asphalt of the garage floor, and acrid smoke billowed around me. An orange hydra of fire devoured the cloth of the convertible roof and sprang from spaces that used to be windows.

Scout barked. I heard footsteps running toward me. My hands shook involuntarily, and my legs threatened to give way. Events slowed and strange voices spoke. "Is that your car?" "Are you all right?" "I'll call the police." "Is there someone we can call for you?" I didn't move—even as coughs racked my body. My already injured BMW was now gone, destroyed, assassinated.

Someone took me by the arm, yanked me inside, and called the police on his cell phone. Someone else brought me water and ushered me to the bottom step of a stairwell. My legs were suddenly boneless. Scout looked at me, confused and concerned, licking my hand and rubbing his head against my leg.

Shock is an odd thing. It splits you into several minds. The first one is numb, unable to feel or think or function. The second becomes a spectator, watching what is happening but somehow remaining separate from it all, floating above and looking down on events. The third becomes empathetic, hoping that others weren't hurt. But these minds don't coalesce, and the result is a zombie-like inertia where the face stares blankly while the mind reels in disparate orbits.

The sirens of the fire trucks and police cars pierced the air. Several maintenance workers covered their faces and opened the door to meet the emergency vehicles, shouting directions to one other. High-pressure fire hoses, like a thousand car washes, vied with the sirens for decibels. More trucks, more police cars entered the garage. The chaos was disorienting. I wanted to run away, but knew I couldn't. There would be countless questions that I couldn't answer, the most important being my own.

I don't know how long I sat there before a policeman said, "You are one lucky lady. Evidently not a popular one, though. Are you okay?" I nodded robotically. "Any idea who might have done this?" I shook my head. "How long has it been since you last drove your car?" asked another policeman.

"I'm not sure, a week, maybe?" I gratefully took a glass of water offered by a stranger.

"Where were you planning to go?" he asked.

"On vacation."

"Who knew you were going?"

"Uh, no one."

I stood abruptly and said, "Officer, I need to make a phone call. It's important. Can we continue after?" At first, he pressed me to continue to answer his questions, but as I became more insistent, he finally relented. I took Scout to the lobby and found a secluded spot behind some fake, potted Ficus trees in a wood-paneled alcove. My eyes focused on the number of people flooding the lobby. My ears sensed the murmur of their conversations as they learned of the explosion.

I called Robbie, and hearing him was a tonic. My head cleared. The vibrato of fear left my voice as I told Robbie everything. He said he'd come right away. He said everything would be fine. He said he loved me.

I hung up and held onto Scout. It was as though he could somehow feel the turmoil I was experiencing. I don't know how long we sat, with my arm draped around his neck and my head on his shoulder, or would have if it weren't for the large man now towering above me. "Jermaine. What are you doing here?"

"I was listening to the police scanner and recognized your address. What's happened?" His face was impassive, but he could not conceal the concern in his voice.

"My car exploded when I hit the remote ignition. The police are down there now. I need to go back."

"I'll go with you." We returned to the garage where many people had gathered—police, firemen, maintenance workers, hotel management, other residents. There must have been a hundred people or more. "Wait here," Jermaine said, as he left to speak with the officer in charge. Jermaine flashed his ID. They spoke for several minutes, away from the chaos of the scene, and then Jermaine returned. "I'll take you up to your apartment. They'll call if they need you."

"Thanks. You've rescued me again." My feeble attempt at humor was wasted on him.

"You don't make it easy," he said, as we rode to the sixth floor. "I may not make it next time." His voice was kind and gentle, but still laden with tension.

"Excuse me. You lied to me. You won't tell me who sent you. What do you expect?" By the time we reached my apartment, I had calmed down a bit and asked, "What did you say to the police?"

"Forget about that." Jermaine took Scout's leash and helped me to my feet. "The cop said something about you taking a trip?"

"Ben wants me to get away for a while."

"And when were you going to tell me about that?"

"I wasn't."

"You need to tell me your plans. How can I protect you, otherwise?" he said, as he scanned the room and poked his head in a few doors.

"We've been through this."

"Your car's been blown up. Strange men are following you and bugging your apartment. Who found the bug? Me. Who told you about those two men who followed you out of Langley? Me. You may not trust me, but I'm all you've got."

He asked about the explosion, when I'd last driven the car, who knew it had a remote ignition, and a dozen other questions, until the buzzer sounded. I pressed the intercom button, heard Robbie's voice on the other end, and let him into the building.

While waiting for Robbie to arrive, I picked up the phone and dialed Ben's number. It went straight to voice mail. "Damn. His phone's off again," I said, more to myself than Jermaine.

"Not good. Maybe you *should* leave."

There was a knock on the door. Jermaine beat me to it and opened the door. "I'm Jermaine Biggs, and you are...?"

"Rob O'Toole. What are you doing here?" Robbie's face was marbled with curiosity and consternation.

I rushed to him. "Robbie, it's so good to see you!" Ignoring Jermaine, I wrapped my arms around Robbie and held him firmly. Scout bounded to Robbie and licked at his hands.

Robbie dropped his bags and scratched Scout on the head. "Hey, fella." Turning to Jermaine, he said, "So, what's going on?"

"Someone has it in for your girlfriend," Jermaine answered. "You've been spending plenty of time with her. Why don't you tell *me* what's going on?"

"Who the hell do you think you are?"

"I suggest you stand down, Mr. O'Toole," Jermaine replied in a steady, but stern tone. "I'm here to protect her. I'm just stating the facts."

"Facts? Let me give *you* some facts, buddy. Her apartment's been bugged for I don't know how long. She's been followed, chased, threatened, and shot at. We both have. I'm trying to get her away from whoever is after her." I'd never seen Robbie so furious. "Those are the facts."

Jermaine glared.

"You haven't leveled with her from the start. Why should we trust *you*?" Robbie's rage was growing by the minute.

Turning his back on Robbie, Jermaine looked at me and said, "I know you have no reason to trust me with all that's happened and the little I've told you," Jermaine began, "but you must. I can't make you tell me where you and tough guy here are going, but it sure would make life easier—for both of us." I remained silent. "I see. Well, in that case, I suggest you give me a number where I can reach you. You still have mine, right?"

I nodded and asked, "What about the mess downstairs? The police won't let me leave without questioning me."

"I'll handle them." Jermaine looked at Scout and then asked, "What are you going to do with your dog?"

"He's going to a kennel," I answered sadly.

Jermaine shook his head. "Let me take him. Once whoever bombed your car realizes that you've left, they may kill him in retaliation." I looked at Robbie; he shook his head. Jermaine continued, "At some point, you have to trust me."

"Why?" I asked.

Jermaine smiled ruefully. "What choice do you have? Who are you going to call? The Agency? The police?" He kneeled down next to Scout and petted him gently. "I had a dog once. Named him Shaft. After the detective. My father loved that movie, so we watched it a million times. Mama hated it. Shaft was a mix, too. They make the best dogs." Scout wagged his tail; Jermaine had won him over. "Big dog with a heart to match. He watched out for me when I was a kid. Scout reminds me of him." Jermaine stood and faced me. "Now, what kennel is he supposed to go to?" Scout was now rubbing his head against Jermaine's leg.

"We'll take him." Robbie said.

"Have it your way." His eyes bore into Robbie's. "I just hope he's still there when you get back. You better get out of here. The press is probably already downstairs."

CHAPTER TWENTY

After Jermaine's admonition, it was difficult to leave Scout at the kennel. What if someone killed him while we were gone? His gentle face haunted me long after we hailed a cab and asked the driver to take us to the Crowne Plaza at Crystal City. We rode in silence. Once we arrived, Robbie pulled a wad of bills from his pocket and thrust them into the cabbie's hands. "You didn't see us, right?"

The cabbie looked at us, confused, but then caught on. "Right, never saw a thing."

We lifted our bags from the trunk and strode directly to the recessed bank of reception desks. Robbie asked for a room, using his alternate identification. Though I knew Robbie was traveling incognito, I was taken aback when the receptionist asked, "And what credit card will you be using, Mr. MacGregor?"

"Cash," Robbie answered. The receptionist seemed surprised, but handed him the printout and asked if we needed help with our bags. We declined and made our way to the elevators, double time. "Glad she didn't check my license too closely." He smiled, but when he saw the fear still present on my face, he added, "We'll get through this Kat, or should I say, Carla? By the way, how much cash do you have on you?"

"Ten thousand dollars." Astonishment erased Robbie's smile, so I quickly explained, "Robbie, I'm an analyst. I've spent too many hours of too many days finding persons of interest by monitoring their use of credit cards."

"Okay, Miss Secret Agent, but it's not Robbie. It's Tom now, Tom MacGregor," he said, kissing my lips.

"But Tom is blond." I mumbled, nuzzling his neck.

"In an hour or so, I will be, too." Robbie smiled. "That is, with a little help from Coiffures by Carla." Somehow, I managed a small grin.

Once in the room, Robbie turned on the flat screen TV, rapidly flipping channels. "Just want to see if your explosion made the news yet."

"I've been thinking," I began tentatively. "Do you think we should travel separately?" He recoiled as though I had slapped him in the face. "I mean, maybe we would be less conspicuous."

"What are you saying?"

I brushed back my hair and flung my arms out in exasperation. "I don't know. Everything is happening so quickly."

"We're stronger together than apart. Has someone said something to you?" He stared at me, and the longer I took to respond, the surer he was. "Who was it? Don't hold out on me now. Please."

Finally, I couldn't take it any longer. "The last time I saw Ben, he said to dump you."

"Ben Douglas said that?" Robbie asked and then moved next to me, crouching a bit so he could look me in the eye.

"Yes, and that they're onto you, and that if I stay with you I'm in danger. They might use me to get to you. After tonight ..."

"Is that what you want?" His azure eyes glistened. "Because if it is, I need to know now. There's too much at stake. Are we in this together or not?"

"Of course I want to be with you." I caressed his face and held it close. "Robbie, I'm not leaving this time. I'm just trying to figure out the best thing to do. They are looking for a couple, not two individuals."

"But if you and I fly separately, they could bring one of us down and the other wouldn't know it, and worse, would be alone. I don't want to be without you."

"Really?" I rubbed his scar tenderly. This time he didn't push my hand away.

We stood as one, each gaining strength from the other, until that wonderful smile crept across his face. "Now I think it's time for my extreme makeover. I've never been a blond before. I've heard they have more fun. What does Carla look like?" I pulled the papers from my bag and showed them to Robbie. "Hmm, not bad looking. Hair's a little shorter, face a little rounder, but she does resemble you. You're not going to cut your hair, are you?" he asked with dismay.

"No, I was going to pull it back under my cap."

"Not that Orioles cap, I hope. Besides, they've seen you jogging in that. Here's a Red Sox hat, use this." He handed it to me.

"No way, I groaned," I pulled out a blue cap with no logo and stuffed it into my jacket pocket. "Let's get started."

"Where did you get that hat? Government issue from the looks of it." He removed some dye and scissors from his bag.

"Another gift from Greg. Who knows? It might come in handy," was all I said.

We converted the bathroom into a salon. It broke my heart to snip away Robbie's beautiful curls, but I drew the line at a buzz cut. Tom MacGregor's license picture would be a challenge. He was older. His hair was sandy colored, not blond. He was stockier, more resembling a football player than a runner like Robbie, but it was all we had. Two hours later, my handsome Irishman had converted to a rugged Scotsman.

"Not bad," Robbie remarked as he viewed himself in the mirror. "If you ever leave the CIA, you could open a barbershop."

"What do you mean, 'if'? As soon as this mess is all over, I'm gone."

"This mess is just beginning, I'm afraid." Robbie rubbed his head vigorously to shake out the loose hairs. "We can leave for a little while, but it will still be here when we get back. It would be nice to know who's after us."

I picked up the empty dye box and scissors. "I'm not sure that knowing will help or provide much consolation."

"But what about you? Who's after you?" he asked, as he returned the scissors and dye to his bag.

"Maybe your friends from California are trying to get me, too. Why don't you let me toss those things?" I asked.

"No, I'll get rid of them somewhere else. No need to advertise our new look."

I realized that he was adept at this type of thing. It was both reassuring and disconcerting.

He thought for a moment and said, "I doubt it's them. It's got to be your project. Maybe your esteemed colleagues at the Company are after you. Maybe if you would tell me what you're working on..."

"Robbie, I've told you. I can't. Please don't." My eyes begged him, but my heart wanted to tell him everything.

"Even if it means getting killed because of it? Thank God you had a remote ignition. What if you had been in the car?"

"Want to hear something ironic? It was my father who insisted on the remote ignition. His paranoia saved me."

Robbie scowled. "You say you trust me, but how can I believe you? How can I help you if you won't tell me what you're doing? Maybe we could figure out who's behind this. Maybe we could..." Robbie paused, in deep thought. His forehead creased and his eyes looked beyond me, toward the window. "Does it strike you as coincidental that Jermaine just happened to show up right after it happened?"

I thought for a moment. "He always seems to be there, doesn't he? He walked me out of the building when the guys in the car followed me after work. He forced me into his Hummer and found bugs in my apartment, and then he shows up after the explosion. I can't figure out how he knows when these things are going to happen."

"I'm not saying it's him, but there's something odd about his timing. I wish we knew who he worked for."

"You said something else," I began. "Something about Beau..."

"We've known Beau since college. Now who's paranoid?"

"There's something I haven't told you. The last time I was at your place, I couldn't sleep and I heard someone walking around outside. It was Beau, and he was staring at your house."

"Oh, come on. First of all, Beau is nocturnal. Second, he's under a lot of stress at work. He told me so the last time we had a drink together."

"It was two in the morning."

His brow wrinkled, and he began working his jaw as though he was chewing a phantom piece of gum. "Okay, I admit that's a little strange, but I can't believe that Beau has anything to do with this."

"Well, we can't dwell on that now," I said. "We have to figure out how to get out of here." I massaged my temples while I spoke, as though trying to prod myself into coherent thought. "Let's get the tickets now. The airport will be empty. Fewer people to see us. Tomorrow will be busy. If we have the tickets and take carry-ons, we can go at the last minute."

We took the shuttle to Reagan airport. It was late. A few lonely stragglers plodded down the concourse. The man behind the desk glanced at our respective IDs and issued the tickets without comment, although seeing over a thousand dollars in cash woke him up a bit. Robbie mumbled something about paying down our credit cards, and the agent smiled. It must have been a long day, or he had seen enough oddities in his time that our story was just heaped upon his pile of jaded experience.

We rode back to the hotel, took a couple of scotch nips from the mini-bar and turned on the news. There was nothing about the car bombing. We looked at each other in disbelief. Jermaine had certainly taken care of things.

The next morning, we saw the *Washington Post* lying outside the hotel-room door and skimmed through it. We gave each other wary looks as, once again, there was no mention of the car bomb. Did Jermaine really have that much clout, or were other parties squashing the story? At eight, we took the hotel shuttle to the airport, each riding alone, checking in individually, going through different security lines, and sitting in opposite ends of the gate area. We boarded separately and sat in aisle seats, four rows apart. I so wanted to hold Robbie's hand and feel him next to me on the plane. Instead, I scoured the faces of the people around us in the hallways, the gate, and on the plane. If someone was watching, I couldn't tell.

CHAPTER TWENTY-ONE

The rain spat on us as we landed at Louis Armstrong Airport, toting our carry-on luggage and hastily making our way to the exit. I waited on the sidewalk outside while Robbie retrieved the car. People met friends and family, policemen shooed cars away from the pick-up area, and taxis waited for their next fare. No one seemed to be lurking or taking any notice of us. Still, it was a relief when Robbie pulled up in a gray Chevy Malibu. I had brought Greg's glasses and stated our destination, which instantly registered on the lenses. Those CIA satellites were doing their job. Soon we were motoring down I-10, passing Lake Pontchartrain en route to the Big Easy. In Metairie, Robbie exited the highway onto Route 90.

"I thought we were going to the French Quarter," I said.

"I want to show you something first. Think of it as your first class in JFK 101." Daylight waned and an eerie feeling descended as we dissected the strip of scattered gas stations, bars, and adult book stores, surrounded by acres of swampland. With no family or friends within a thousand miles, I was at Robbie's mercy.

In a clearing, Robbie pulled into a gravel driveway, pockmarked with puddles from the recent rain. Upon a failed attempt at a lawn sat a white, one-story, wood-frame building hooded by a tile roof. A couple of air conditioners hung out of the windows. In front, a sign read "Mosca's, established 1946." An occasional car passed, but otherwise no one was around.

"Why are you stopping here?" I asked, scanning the area furtively.

"It's suppertime." He unbuckled his seat belt and hopped out of the car.

With some hesitation, I unstrapped myself and joined him in the parking lot. "Here? With all of the great restaurants in New Orleans, you want to eat here?" We walked inside and were greeted by the smiling portraits of an elderly Italian couple peering down at us. The smell of garlic was overwhelming.

"Provino Mosca." Robbie pointed. "He was rumored to be Al Capone's driver in Chicago."

"And what does he have to do with Kennedy?" I asked in hushed tones.

"Before Mosca's, this place was called the Willswood Tavern. There was a lot of gambling in this area during the forties. After a day spent losing, winning, or fixing races, gamblers came here for huge portions of Italian food. It was Carlos Marcello's unofficial headquarters, where he administered his own brand of justice."

A dark-haired, mustached man appeared and guided us past the plain, dark-wood bar, which seemed small by today's standards. There were no flavored vodkas or rums, no blue or green liqueurs, just the basics; that is, except for the dozens of bottles of Italian wine standing like soldiers on the shelf to the right of the bar.

We sat at a table bedecked with a plain white cloth, a small lamp, salt and pepper, and a jar of grated parmesan. The waiter handed us a couple of menus and quickly walked away. I looked around, thinking that the Olive Garden suddenly seemed like fine dining.

"Couldn't we just have a drink here? I'm feeling like the mob could bust in at any second." I meant it.

"I want you to get the full flavor, if you'll pardon the pun." He took my hand. I still couldn't get used to the sandy-blond hair that framed his beautiful face.

"When Mayor LaGuardia closed down his operation in New York, Frank Costello brought five thousand slot machines to New Orleans for Marcello to run. That's how Marcello got started and then his empire mushroomed. Speaking of mushrooms, I'm starved. What looks good to you? "

"Didn't you say that Hoover was friends with Costello?" I scanned the room and the few people inside. A man, probably in his fifties, sat at a table in the corner, occasionally looking up at us. Waiters glanced our way as they passed by. My paranoia was rampant.

"You're a quick study." Robbie smiled and stroked my hair from across the table.

Even his affection could not calm me down. "You said Marcello wanted JFK killed. Why not other members of the mob?" I asked.

"Oh, they wanted JFK too, but Bobby Kennedy had made Marcello's life miserable—multiple indictments of his buddies and him, deportation, IRS inquiries, getting Marcello's colleagues to rat on him. Maybe Marcello hated the Kennedys a little more than the rest, but not by much."

I nodded in understanding, letting his words sink in.

"I'm going with the Oysters Mosca, you?"

I hadn't even looked at the menu and picked the first thing that jumped out at me. "I guess the Shrimp Mosca." Reflexively, I scanned the room again. The walls were covered in bead board, punctuated by charts of Mosca family history and pictures of Mosca family members. Frank Sinatra was crooning from a jukebox. The waiter returned, and Robbie ordered a Greco di Tufo, *prego*. I smiled at his attempt at Italian, but the waiter did not. "This doesn't seem a fancy enough place for a Mafia chief," I observed.

"The 'Little Man'? The 'Mafia midget'?" Robbie laughed. "By the end of his career, he was the richest of the Mafia dons, also one of the most ruthless. He built a mansion in Marrero, about ten miles southwest of New Orleans—red-tiled roofs, Corinthian arches, eight bedrooms— one of the most ostentatious homes on the west bank of the Mississippi. It was his way of letting everyone know how important he was. In New Orleans, he was more untouchable than Elliott Ness."

"So, is this where he plotted the assassination?" I practically whispered, hoping Robbie would quiet down as well.

"No, probably not here. Marcello had another place in the swamplands, called Churchill Farms. He claimed it was used for duck shooting, but everyone knew the bayous were good for hiding bodies."

Robbie proceeded to tell me a story about a meeting with Marcello and three men, one of whom was Edward Becker. At one point, Becker commented on the way Bobby Kennedy was treating Marcello. Marcello started stomping around the room, ranting and screaming, "Don't worry about that sonofabitch Bobby, he's gonna be taken care of!" When Becker cautioned Marcello about the trouble that would cause, Marcello said, "In Sicily they say if you want to kill a dog, you don't cut off the tail. You go for the head. That meant the president."

"I thought you said that Johnson or the CIA was behind it." This was maddening. Every day it seemed as if Robbie contradicted himself.

"I know it gets confusing. A couple of weeks later, Santo Trafficante, Marcello's friend and Tampa mob boss, was discussing business with a Cuban named José Alemán. Trafficante berated Robert Kennedy and said that he and his brother were in for some serious trouble. Alemán said that he thought Kennedy would be reelected, and Trafficante replied, 'You don't understand me, José. Kennedy's not going to make it to the election. He is going to be hit.'"

I remembered the transcripts in the vault. I was sure one was from a conversation between Alemán and two FBI agents from the Florida office. That must have been the one Robbie told me about, the one that Hoover did nothing to prevent.

"Even if Hoover really didn't know about the hit, which I doubt," Robbie continued, "I'll bet Costello told him about it. Costello and Marcello were tight. Hoover and Costello were racetrack buddies." Robbie looked around. "It gets worse, but I'll tell you about that later. It's getting a little crowded in here." Others started filing into the restaurant and were greeted warmly by the man at the door, who had barely spoken a word to the two of us. "Regulars," Robbie muttered. "I heard that frequent customers are treated like family. In this place, that could have a double meaning." He winked.

Our meals arrived. We should have split one of them; the portions were huge. The small room was now swollen with diners, and the noise level rose several notches with laughter, crying children, and shouts from the restaurant staff as they called in orders to the kitchen. "This is fantastic," I said. "And I'm glad you're having garlic, too."

"They say garlic is an aphrodisiac." Robbie flashed his mischievous smile.

"Like we need that." I shoveled in one forkful after another, not sure if it was from hunger or just that the food tasted that good. A while later, I took one last swallow of Shrimp Mosca and laid my fork down. The meal won. I was stuffed; I'd had too much wine and too much Mafia ambience. It was time to go. Robbie signaled the waiter for the check. We paid in cash.

We hopped back onto the highway, crossed the Huey Long Bridge and entered the Crescent City, New Orleans. Turning down Poydras Street, we found the Hilton Riverside and entered its spacious lobby, crossing the gray-and-white windowpane-tiled floor to the massive, light-colored, wood reception desk. The receptionist handed us the key to a huge room with windows overlooking the steamboats, shops, and bridges that lined the mighty Mississippi. The view would be better enjoyed tomorrow when we took a jog around the city. The bed was too inviting, and the garlic too effective.

While Robbie was in the bathroom, preparing for bed, a tone sounded on his cell phone. I picked it up and read, "It's on—day after tomorrow at ten. You know where to go."

"You got a message," I shouted through the door. Opening it a crack, I handed the phone inside. When he came out, I asked him who it was.

"My contact. The meeting's on—Thursday," he answered tentatively.

"Great," I responded with enthusiasm. "That gives us an entire day to explore the city."

"Let's hope he doesn't change his mind."

CHAPTER TWENTY-TWO

The next morning, we pulled on our running shorts and T-shirts, eager to begin the day with a jog along the river. I gathered my hair into a ponytail and pulled it through the hole of Greg's anonymous baseball cap, activating the camera and recorder.

Unlike the intensity of our nocturnal activities, which fed a carnal hunger, the casual intimacy of our run reassured my soul. We marveled at the Mississippi, apparently oblivious to its reputation as the bully that swamped the city during Hurricane Katrina. Today, it was the idyllic waterway of Huck Finn and Jim, on which riverboats, tankers, and shrimp boats paused before beginning their day's work. We loped along the pavestones of the Moon Walk that would soon feel the weight of thousands of tourists. Diehard gamblers were checking their pockets for loose change, wondering how they could have lost so much at Harrah's the night before.

Passing the aquarium, we jogged by Woldenberg Park and turned onto Decatur Street. We gazed at the majestic Saint Louis Cathedral and its cone-shaped towers, guarded by Andrew Jackson on his rearing horse. His namesake square had not yet woken for the day. A few street vendors and artists were unfolding their stands and displaying their wares in hopes that the right person would walk by. If not, *"C'est la vie,"* as they say in *le Vieux Carré*. Across the square, the Jax Brewery peeped above the trees. With no musicians, no tourists, and little conversation between the artisans, it was quiet and peaceful—unlike the French Market across the street, which teemed with people sipping their chicory-laced coffee to jump start the day.

We took a left on Barracks Street and another left onto Bourbon Street, which was still recovering from last night's revelries. Street cleaners swept away the French Quarter's hangover, and a few looked up, wondering how tourists like us could function this early in the morning. We trotted by oyster bars, jazz bars, and open-walled bars where men cruised other men. In the light of day, Rue Bourbon seemed like an aging actress in desperate need of makeup.

Outside Chris Owens Club, Robbie paused. "This was once the site of the 500 Club," he said. "It's much nicer looking now. In 1963, it was a strip club." I looked at the edifice with its slick "500 Bourbon" address over the door and gave Robbie a questioning look. "Another one of Marcello's joints," he explained.

At the end of Bourbon Street, we turned left onto Canal and after a battered dark-green street car passed, we cut across the double-lane thoroughfare and took a right onto Camp Street toward Lafayette Park. Robbie stopped short and only after a few steps did I turn back to join him, asking him why he'd stopped outside the federal courthouse.

"This used to be the site of the Newman Building, known locally as the Banister Building." Robbie trotted around the corner to Lafayette Street. "Oswald used the 544 Camp Street address on his Fair Play for Cuba pamphlets. Guy Banister's office was on the other side. Out of all the office space in New Orleans, Oswald and Banister just happened to be in the same building. Some coincidence, huh?"

I had read about Guy Banister and wondered how a guy could go from being the former head of the FBI office in Chicago to working for Marcello. While Robbie scoped out the grounds, I let my mind wander.

Banister sat behind a rustic desk in the old brick building. The heat and humidity were stifling. Even the Cubans who came and went complained. While proofing the galleys of his racist magazine, the Louisiana Intelligence Digest, *Banister pulled a bottle of whiskey from a drawer in his desk and took a slug, wiping* his mouth on his sleeve afterward. He sat back smugly, thinking about the saying that no man could serve two masters, but he wasn't just any man. Besides, serving the mob and the FBI didn't present that much of a problem— especially in New Orleans.

After finishing his edits, he put the galleys in a pile for his secretary to correct and began flipping through his files: American Central Intelligence Agency, Ammunition and Arms, Anti-Soviet Underground, B-70 Bomber Force, and Civil Rights Program of JFK, until he got to Operation Northwoods and Operation Zapata. Opening the folders, he inserted some papers that included a list of new recruits in the fight against Castro. They'd need more guns. He'd have to call Ruby to get 'em and Ferrie to fly 'em in.

It had been much harder to attract volunteers after the Bay of Pigs—a wholesale slaughter in which he'd lost some close friends, thanks to Kennedy. He'd get his. Banister snickered at the thought.

He checked his watch, returned the files to the cabinet, and locked it. He stood and wiped his brow with a handkerchief before walking to Oswald's office. "Damn, it's hot," he thought as he knocked on the door.

"Time to go?" Oswald asked, looking up from his desk.

"Yeah, we got an hour's ride ahead of us."

They rode to LSU to debate the school's new policy on desegregation. Part of him hated setting Oswald up like this. They'd worked together for a while now, but it needed to be done. Oswald had to look the part of the pro-Castro communist for the plan to work. And let's face it, he thought. Anyone who supported desegregation had to be a communist.

After the debate, Banister slapped Oswald on the back. He had held his own. "Good job, Ozzie. Your Uncle Dutch knew what he was doing when he sent you to me. Let's go to Mancuso's and get something to eat."

"Hello," Robbie called, snapping me back to the present.

"Wasn't Banister the one who pistol-whipped some guy into the hospital?" I asked. "Something about the guy saying that he remembered seeing Oswald, Ferrie, and 'all those Cubans' hanging around Banister's office?"

"One and the same. Ten days after the Warren Commission hearings concluded, Banister died and his files went missing. What I wouldn't give to know what was inside." His subtle nudge made me uncomfortable. I knew what he was driving at. "Let's go. There's more to show you."

I was already a couple of steps ahead before Robbie started. Between breaths, I asked, "So, if Banister engineered this whole thing, why did Jim Garrison prosecute Clay Bertrand?"

"Bertrand was a bigger fish. He owned the Trade Center in New Orleans, which probably explains his involvement with Permindex. Maybe Permindex enabled everyone to coordinate their roles in the plot."

We ran back to the corner of Camp and Canal, where Robbie pointed out the spot where Oswald passed out the pro-Castro leaflets. "This is where Bertrand's International Trade Mart stood. Interesting that Oswald passed out leaflets here, huh?" I cocked an eyebrow in agreement. From there, we sprinted back to the hotel and showered. We could now justify some beignets at Café Du Monde.

Robbie waited in line for coffee and beignets while I found a table near one of the thick, beige pillars and sat in a Naugahyde-cushioned chair. The cold, hard vinyl permeated my jeans, making me crave the warmth of the coffee more than its chicory flavor. Even though it was a weekday, Café Du Monde was buzzing with tourists scanning maps and planning their day's activities. It seemed strange to be so anonymous in such a crowd.

That's when I noticed a gray-haired man wearing a tattered baseball cap, faded jeans, and a Saints T-shirt. He sat back in his chair, five tables away, with one leg crossed over the other, and was speaking on a cell phone. He was staring directly at me, but looked away as soon as our eyes met.

When Robbie arrived, bearing the morning's repast, I said, "I think we're being followed. Don't look now, but there's a guy over there," I discretely pointed, "who's been watching me the whole time I've been sitting here."

"Do you want to leave?" Robbie asked.

"Not just yet. I want to see what he does."

"Are you sure you're not being paranoid again? How could anyone know we're here? The only person who knew we were leaving town was Jermaine, and we didn't tell him where we were going." Robbie took a sip of coffee and then added, "That guy really bugs me."

"Jermaine's not the only one who knew we left town. Ben knows, and so does Pam."

"You didn't tell them where we were going, did you?" I shook my head. He added, "Besides, we trust them. Can't say the same about Jermaine."

I looked over to the table where the man remained, despite having finished his coffee and beignet. Robbie caught my eye and said, "I think we could lose him in the French Market if you're game."

I nodded. We jumped up quickly and dashed out of Café Du Monde toward The French Market. I glanced back and saw that the man had left his table. We entered the market and dodged tourists and vendors as we weaved our way through the crowd. Exiting through the rear, we circled back and saw the Moon Walk streetcar. We sprinted toward it and hopped on. After finding seats in the rear, we hunched over and hoped that if the man was really following us, we could lose him.

Once back at the hotel, I asked Robbie if it might be best to leave New Orleans.

"Not yet," he answered while looking out the window, presumably to see if anyone was lurking below.

"Then we should get another car and change hotels." If someone knows we're here, they must know where we're staying and what we're driving."

Robbie agreed, so after packing our belongings and checking out, we drove to a rental agency and exchanged cars. While Robbie drove, I called another hotel and made a reservation for the night.

As we passed 640 Magazine Street, Robbie pointed and said, "This was the site of O'Reilly's Coffee. Oswald worked there and met a brilliant cancer researcher, named Judyth Baker, who worked for a woman named Mary Sherman at the Ochsner Clinic in New Orleans. O'Reilly's was probably just a front. Oswald and Baker were hired on the same day, and both left their jobs on the same day. Another coincidence, right? Rumor has it that Oswald and Baker were having an affair."

"Why would a brilliant scientist bother with a loser like Oswald?" I asked.

"I'll bet the FBI or CIA crafted Oswald's loser image, who knows?"

"I assume this has something to do with Kennedy, right?" Between taking in everything Robbie was telling me and straining to remember what was in the vault, my mind was racing. Still, I didn't recall anything about Judyth Baker. I was snapping pictures so fast, I couldn't read everything. Maybe there was something about her on the flash drives. I'd have to take a look.

"Dr. Alton Ochsner was a famous surgeon who had links to the intelligence community. He hired Mary Sherman to develop a bioweapon in order to kill Castro with a cancer-causing monkey virus. Right-wing politicians and the Texas oil barons sponsored the project. Not only were Oswald and Judyth Baker involved, but Oswald introduced Baker to Ferrie, Clay Shaw—aka Clay Bertrand—and Guy Banister."

"Baker said that?" I asked, as we drove on and I surveyed the passing houses and their unique architecture.

"Yep, it took her thirty-eight years to summon the courage." That explained why I'd seen nothing about her in the vault. Her testimony was too recent. Robbie pulled in front of a gray stucco house on Louisiana Parkway. It had two porches, one on each story, beside a tall and narrow, arched window. The house number, 3330, was posted outside. "This was Ferrie's house. His secret lab was down the street, at 3225. He may have been observing the virus-injected mice to see if they developed cancer. Remember how Ruby claimed that he had been injected with cancer cells and he had to tell people what he knew before he died? Guess what he died from—cancer, just four years after he was imprisoned. Another coincidence?"

"So what's Oswald have to do with the cancer project?"

"According to Baker, Oswald had learned how to handle the materials and volunteered to take them to Mexico City where the CIA was supposed to arrange their transport to Cuba. His contacts never appeared, so he tried to go to Cuba himself, hence the request for a visa. Hurricane Flora hit Cuba hard so the project was called off, but the paper trail was established and was later exploited to paint Oswald as a communist."

My father's smear campaign must have been a breeze with all this background. "Do you think they knew that Oswald was an informant? Maybe that's why he was picked as the patsy. You know, as retaliation," I said.

"Possibly, but I think it was Oswald's activities that made him the perfect choice. Anyway, Baker said that she and Oswald were both going to get divorces and marry in Mexico. She said he knew about an assassination ring and volunteered to investigate it. He thought the CIA would help him escape to Mexico after he provided them information. What he knew probably got him killed."

"What about this Mary Sherman? Didn't you say that she led the project?" Robbie drove a bit further and pulled in front of a large apartment building at 3101 Saint Charles Avenue.

"Mary Sherman lived and died here," he said, motioning toward the complex. "She was found stabbed in the heart, arm, leg, and stomach and suffered massive burns, probably to cover up the stab wounds. The crime was never solved. But, hey, this was New Orleans in the sixties." Robbie laughed sarcastically.

"Did she have a chance to testify first?" I asked, anticipating his answer.

"She died right before the Warren Commission began its hearings in New Orleans. Another coincidence, right?"

"Okay, but everyone involved with this project died except Baker. How did she manage that?" I asked.

"She said David Ferrie warned her to be quiet or she'd be killed. She's been in exile outside the States since then." Robbie noticed my skepticism and added, "Okay, some people don't believe her. That's the problem with this murder. Not only is there missing information, there is misinformation muddying the waters. When a witness does come forward, he or she is often discredited."

"Why haven't I heard about Judyth Baker?"

"The History Channel developed a series, one segment of which was called 'The Love Affair,' about Baker and Oswald. Another one, called 'The Guilty Men' described the alleged involvement of LBJ. Lady Bird and Johnson's aides filed complaints, along with Carter and Ford. A private party bought the rights to the series, and they never aired again in the United States. Who has that kind of power?" Robbie shook his head in disgust, but then grinned. "But you can find the videos on YouTube." I loved it when he enjoyed small triumphs.

We finished our tour with a drive by Oswald's house at 4905 Magazine Street. A sad, ramshackle building stared back at us, crying out for paint. It seemed like too pathetic a structure to have housed such an infamous tenant. What secrets haunted his dreams? Who may have met him there? Was he the predator or the prey? Did he even feel safe in his own home?

I slumped in my seat and exhaled deeply. Robbie asked me what was wrong, to which I could only reply, "I'm tired, hungry, and my brain is saturated. Can we go back and get something to eat?"

"You haven't lost your appetite after hearing all of this?" Robbie brushed my cheek. His hand was warm, and he instantly changed from instructor to lover.

"Not for food, but with everything I've learned, I have lost some faith in the good ole US of A."

"I think that's why some good people played along. They couldn't let the American people lose faith during the Cold War. Believing the lie was preferable to fearing the truth." Robbie gazed at the road ahead, and even though he seemed lost in thought, he was able to maneuver through traffic and find our new hotel, where we parked the car and checked in.

Once settled, Robbie said, "I'm thinking Cajun, how about you?"

"Sure, anything as long as I can get a decent glass of wine."

"Great. You see, I, ah, took the liberty of making a reservation at K-Paul's before we arrived. Otherwise, we'd never get in. It's my favorite."

"It's a good thing I'm hungry. Otherwise, I'd accuse you of plotting a conspiracy."

He groaned.

CHAPTER TWENTY-THREE

We walked to Chartres Street and saw a line of ravenous patrons waiting outside the restaurant; I was glad that Robbie had planned ahead. Walking under yet another lacy, wrought-iron balcony and past the sign that read "K-Paul's Louisiana Kitchen," we entered a plain dining room with red-checkered tablecloths, broad-plank wood floors, and zydeco music playing in the background. When told that we had a reservation, the maître d' looked relieved and led us to a table for two under a huge ceiling fan that hung idle, unnecessary on the cool, dismal day.

I pulled off the cap and loosened my hair, shaking my head so my hair fell loosely. Robbie smiled appreciatively. But when I splurged and ordered a bottle of Cakebread, his eyes took on a look of mild concern.

"You may wish you had ordered a beer. The food here is plenty hot," he said.

"There's always water."

"That won't work, trust me," he smiled knowingly.

"I do. Trust you, that is." I think I meant it. I wanted to mean it.

"I'm glad, because if you keep what you know a secret, you'll be just like them." His tone was serious as he pulled my menu down so he could look me in the eye.

That stung. "You have to trust me, too," I responded. We sat in silence, separated by a transient emotional rift, until I asked, "What are you going to have?"

"Probably the gumbo and then the étouffée. How about you?"

"I was thinking the pear salad and the blackened redfish, although I'm not sure how red wine will go with it. My father would be appalled."

"Not to worry. I don't think that your father and I will be having any conversations any time soon."

"I wonder if I will be. My cell phone has been shut off since we left. I'm sure he's tried to reach me. He's been calling like crazy lately. It's a special phone invented by a friend of mine at the Company. Supposedly, no one can track me while I'm using it, but why take the chance?"

His forehead wrinkled, and his mouth opened slightly. "What are you saying?"

"Are you kidding? I've spent the better part of the last ten years using cell phones to track people of interest. Anyone who uses their cell phone can be located through triangulation of cell towers." I looked at Robbie with growing concern. "Yours isn't on, is it?"

"Of course it is. I have to keep my phone on in case my contact tries to reach me. Besides, I have a new cell phone, remember?"

"A new phone doesn't matter if it's in your name. That may explain how someone knows we're here."

"Damn." He cringed. "But I've got to see this guy. He knows stuff."

I took a gulp of wine, not even tasting it, wishing it was stronger. "They'll be on us in no time."

"Then we'll leave New Orleans right after I meet with him, but there's one more problem."

"Only one?" I asked wryly.

"If he calls, and that's not a given, it could be anytime. He holds all the cards, I'm afraid. That's how it usually works."

The food arrived, and once the waiter left I said, "It sounds dangerous. When are we going to see him?" I took a bite and chewed robotically, not even tasting K-Paul's renowned dressing.

A fault line fractured the landscape of Robbie's face. "Well, that's the thing. I was thinking I should go alone. I don't know if it would be safe for you. He's not the most..."

"No way. If something happened to you, I'd never forgive myself."

Robbie sipped his beer, swallowed slowly, and clasped my hand across the table. "Kat, he's killed people. I can't put you at further risk."

"I'm going," I declared. "If this guy doesn't want to tell you his story with me around, I'll wait outside, but I'm going with you. Besides, we need to leave right after. You won't have time to pick me up after your meeting." Robbie sighed and relented. We finished our appetizers just in time for the arrival of the main courses. We could smell the hot pepper well before the waiter arrived with the blackened redfish. I regretted not ordering a beer to cool its heat. One bite and I lunged for the glass of water.

Robbie shoveled some étoufée onto his fork and held it motionless for a moment. "Let me do the talking. I'll figure out some way to explain you. He may take precautions, like making sure we aren't packing a gun. Put your purse in the trunk, or else he'll probably look through it. He's older than dirt, so he may have others around to protect him." He saw my eyes harden with impatience at his orders. He must have assumed it was due to fear because he asked, "You sure you want to come?"

"For the last time, I'm coming with you." We were in this together, for better or for worse, whether we trusted each other or not. There was no going back; not now, not ever.

By the time we finished our meals, my tongue was numb, but my brain was worse. Maybe it was because we'd finished the bottle of wine. Maybe my apprehension had spread inside me like Judyth Baker's monkey virus. Maybe it was because I was seeing a side of Robbie I hadn't seen before—fearless, but concerned; determined to find the truth and share it with me. Ben Douglas might say that Robbie didn't want me to accompany him because I might blow his chance to get the story. Ben Douglas had suggested that Robbie was stringing me along to get information from me. But where was Ben Douglas? Why hadn't I been able to reach him?

As we strolled through the French Quarter, drunks were already leaning against buildings and making catcalls to passing women. The lanterns now were bright, casting odd shadows under the porticos. Music blared from the doors of the jazz clubs. The aging actress, Rue Bourbon, was now adorned with the makeup of the night, making her seem younger and livelier. Her littered streets and tawdry shops were camouflaged by bright neon signs, music, and laughter that flowed from the many establishments that she wore like a shawl. Revelers ruled as they spilled into the streets, sipping hurricanes and allowing us to pass unnoticed to the banks of the Mississippi to watch the boats, the moon, and other couples holding hands.

Robbie hugged me tightly and kissed the top of my head. We stood locked together for several moments. People walked by. Ship horns sounded in the distance. The din of crowds from the casino was constant. The stale, salty smell of dead fish rose from the river. The night darkened, and the moon hung higher in the sky.

"Let's go back. I'm ready for bed, and for you," I said. This time, it was I who took his hand and led him back to our room. At that instant, I knew I had the strength to get us through this somehow.

It was four a.m. Thursday morning when Robbie's cell phone rang. The meeting was on. If we were late, "Joey" would be gone. We packed immediately and woke a sleeping receptionist so we could check out.

Robbie had used his phone. They could find us now.

CHAPTER TWENTY-FOUR

We embarked upon a long, wordless drive across Lake Pontchartrain to Mandeville. Traffic was light as I gazed out on the murky, brackish water. Robbie broke the silence by noting that Lake Pontchartrain was the site of many voodoo rituals. Hearing this amplified my now-chronic anxiety as I realized that this was also the site of the training camps for anti-Castro Cubans. Ferrie, Oswald, and David Atlee Phillips had all been here and were captured on the film and pictures that I found in Nagell's trunk.

"I wonder if my father was ever here," I said, more as a thought than an intended question.

Robbie shot me a look of astonishment and then stared ahead, not certain how to proceed. "So you know about the training camps." I nodded. "This must be hard for you. I've never been a fan of your father's, for obvious reasons, but I can't imagine what it's like to learn the truth about him."

"It is hard. I always thought that he was a patriot; you know, risking his life for the country. I just assumed that his demeanor was a by-product of the pressure he was under. I was always afraid that, one day, we'd get a message that he'd been killed. I'm sure that's what my mother thought."

"Did you know what he did for a living when you were young?" Robbie's tone was devoid of any judgment or negativity.

"Not when I was really young, but occasionally we'd overhear my mother talking to her sister and telling her how she feared what might happen to him. The day of the assassination, when I came home and found her crying in the den, she said something that always stuck with me. 'He might not make it back this time.' I'll never forget it."

"You think he told her what he was doing?" he asked, glancing in the rearview mirror.

"No, but she knew. It seemed like every time something big happened—you know, coups or assassinations—he was on a business trip." It rolled off my lips so easily, but hearing myself say it was staggering. I gazed out at the road, the massive bridge that spanned the lake, and the airplanes that soared across the leaden sky. "What I don't understand is who paid for all of the covert things the CIA did. Surely, some desk jockey like me would have found out about these illicit activities."

"Drugs. The CIA managed one of the biggest drug-running operations in the world. They brought the drugs in from Southeast Asia, using their own airline, Air America, or their shipping company, Sea Supply, and the mob distributed them. Marcello's organization controlled the docks down here." He said it as though it was the most natural thing in the world.

"Wouldn't somebody somewhere have leaked that?" I asked.

"Some have."

"So it wasn't just Big Oil and defense contractors who wanted to perpetuate the war," I said, thinking out loud.

"Bingo. Vietnam made the CIA all sorts of money."

I stared out the window, unable to talk. Robbie looked at me, his blue eyes now dulled by sadness for eliciting such a response. "I'm sorry. I guess I've become so jaded by all of this, it no longer has the effect it once did. I should be more sensitive."

"The more I learn, the more my soul shatters. In less than one month, everything I've done, everything I believed in—it's all been tainted."

Robbie asked, "What was it like with your dad? I mean, was he a normal father? Did he play with you guys, take you to movies, go to church, mow the lawn? Did you go on family trips?"

"It's hard to describe, really," I answered as I watched the scenery go by. "When he was around, which wasn't very often, my two sisters and I vied for his approval. He could be attentive, but I wouldn't say that he was affectionate. Sometimes, it seemed like we were the most important thing in the world to him. Other times, it seemed like we were a nuisance."

"What about his relationship with your mother?" The Beatles were playing on the radio; I think it was "A Day in the Life." Robbie turned it off, indicating that he was genuinely interested, not just making conversation.

"I never saw them hold hands, and I never heard him say endearing things to her. I asked her about it once, when I was older. She was a very religious person and told me that when she said 'I do,' it wasn't just a promise to my father, but also to God. I asked her if she ever regretted making that promise."

"What did she say?"

"That my father wasn't the only one who made sacrifices for his country." I shook my head at the memory. "I miss her, Robbie."

He rested his hand on my thigh. "Do you think your father loved your mother?"

"In his own way, yes, but I think he loved his job more. I remember one time, though. It was in the early seventies, I think. He missed my prom night, and I was devastated. All of my friends' fathers were around, snapping pictures and telling all the girls how beautiful they were. My mother apologized repeatedly for him, and I knew she ached for me. He returned a couple of days later. I was angry. Like a typical teenager, I stomped my feet. I cried. I stormed into my room and slammed the door. He came upstairs, knocked softly, and asked if he could come in. I yelled no, but he entered anyway, picked up a stuffed animal, and sat on the bed next to me. I turned away and he placed one hand on my shoulder, and with the other, he nuzzled my teddy bear against my cheek. Like a ventriloquist, he spoke through the bear, saying, 'Your daddy is so sorry he wasn't here for your prom. He wanted to be. He brought you something.'"

"What was it?" Robbie's voice was low and gentle.

"A locket with a picture of him and me from when I was about five years old. I was on a swing and he was standing beside me, smiling. He said it was his favorite picture. He pulled out his wallet and showed me a larger version of the same picture. He told me he carried it with him everywhere."

"You're kidding. Do you still have the locket?" Robbie looked at me compassionately.

I reached down my blouse and pulled the chain out, opening the locket and gazing at the picture. "I wear it every day," and as I inserted it back in my blouse, added, "It reminds me of that moment when my father was human. Anyway, that night I hugged him and asked why he had to be away so much. He said that only his country could keep him away from me."

"He really believed that what he did was for the good of the country?"

"He loves our country, more than anything or anyone." We watched as the trappings of civilization yielded to the back country of Louisiana. "He loved me until I pursued my career. Then he changed. He never understood my divorce; women were supposed to forgive the weaknesses of men. He still thinks that Nate is a good man. By divorcing Nate, I bucked the natural order. I didn't accept his world, and he didn't understand mine."

Robbie took a moment to absorb what I had said and then asked, "Was he always that way?"

"No, but by the sixties, he was a stranger. I didn't help matters. All these new ideas, the music, the wild clothes—they fascinated me. You remember how even the newscasters wore wide ties and thick sideburns? My father thought the country was in ruins."

"He must have loved it when Nixon appeared on Rowan & Martin's Laugh-In." Robbie scoffed at the thought.

"I don't think he really liked any president, to tell you the truth, but he'd also tell you that it was his job to serve. As time went on, I think he began to feel that, in some ways, they were all the same. Sure, their policies might differ on the surface, but in the end they're all figureheads, controlled by the power elite."

"Hmm, I'd hate to think that your father and I agree on anything."

"That *would* be amazing." I took a deep breath and exhaled. "I wish I could remember more of what he was like in the beginning, that man in my locket, the man my mother loved. She must have seen something in him."

CHAPTER TWENTY-FIVE

W e rode in silence until we came upon a rutted, unpaved road. We might have missed it except for the hand-written "Keep Out" sign attached to a rough-hewn pole stabbing a mound of dirt, leaning precariously, as though it could topple at any moment. The road split a marshland from which sprouted wild grasses, vine-covered trees, and God only knows what kinds of snakes, alligators, and other animals too sinister to imagine. We rode deeper and deeper into the swamp. The road narrowed and we bumped over potholes the size of cauldrons, testing the shock absorbers as well as our nerves. Every twist and turn made us more wary of what might be around the bend. If we had to leave in a hurry, we couldn't. Neither of us said a word. If someone killed us here, no one would ever know.

No sooner had that thought crossed my mind when we heard an engine hacking. I turned in my seat and saw a black pickup truck following us. I shivered when I saw the driver. He was the man who had been watching us at Café Du Monde, and now he was smiling like a gator that had cornered its prey. A rifle sat in the gun rack behind his head. A Confederate flag waved from his antenna. Country music blared from his radio. Robbie checked his rearview mirror and gave me a sidelong glance.

"The guy that's following us—he's the one from Café Du Monde I told you about. Do you think he's Joey?" I asked. Though my voice was steady, a cold sweat covered my skin.

Robbie took another look in the rearview mirror. "Can't be. Joey's got to be over eighty." Robbie slowly reached inside his jacket, pulled out a small revolver, and placed it on the seat. "Here, take this." He pushed the gun toward me and asked, "Have you ever shot a gun?"

"Where did you get that? You didn't bring it on the plane, did you?"

"We're in New Orleans, remember? I made some calls. They don't call it 'the Big Easy' for nothing."

I slowly picked up the gun and opened the chamber. It was loaded.

"I see they trained you well," he smirked. "I want you to stay in the car. If something happens to me, protect yourself."

We drove with our escort close at hand, until the road abruptly ended in grass and gravel, behind which sat a seedy cabin covered by a battered tin roof. Wisps of smoke escaped from a rusty pipe of a chimney. A tan-and-white pit bull stalked in front of the cabin, eyeing our car with suspicion, ready to attack. His teeth gleamed ivory white, and his lips curled into a sneer.

Robbie pulled the car to a stop and shut off the engine. "Let's wait until that dog is leashed. They'll come to us."

Sure enough, the door opened and a stooped, bald-headed man, who I assumed to be Joey Cravanno, limped his way down the cinderblock stairs. Simultaneously, the driver of the pickup climbed out of the cab and ambled toward us. "Here are the keys," Robbie said. I began to protest, but he continued, "If they come out and I'm not with them, you need to leave right away." I carefully shoved the gun into the waistband of my jeans and pulled my jacket over it.

"You're early. What's the broad doing here?" the old man rasped, in a voice that sounded as though he gargled with shrapnel.

"She's my assistant. She won't be a problem. She can wait in the car."

"That wasn't the deal," he replied, looking me over like a prize heifer. "Get out of the car." Robbie did; I didn't. "Search him, Frank."

The man from the pickup moved toward Robbie. I could feel the cold, hard barrel of the gun digging into the small of my back and prayed he wouldn't frisk me as well. The thought of his hands on my body was not only disgusting; it petrified me. Robbie held his hands above his head as the man named Frank patted him down.

"What's this?" Frank asked as he reached Robbie's pocket. My heart leaped into my throat.

"It's my tape recorder. Joey said no notes. This is the only way I'll get everything just as he says it."

"It's okay, Frank. Anything else?" the old man snapped.

"He's clean, Pop." Frank hooked the dog to a fraying rope that lay like a copperhead on the ground. It didn't look strong enough to hold him. Frank pulled out a gun and pushed Robbie ahead of him.

They were about ten feet away when the old man grunted, "I want that broad where I can see her. Bring her in, too."

Frank leered and waved his gun at me, motioning for me to join them. I slowly exited the car, being careful to keep the gun hidden. "We don't have all day," he snarled.

I walked toward them with hesitant footsteps. Frank and Robbie kept walking and when they reached the door, Frank pushed Robbie inside and held the door for me. He grabbed my arm and yanked me inside.

"Come on, come on," yelled Joey. "Get your asses in here—quick." Fortunately the old man's impatience distracted Frank; he didn't frisk me.

Robbie looked at me sorrowfully. I could tell that this was just the scenario he'd feared. Somehow I wanted to reassure him, but reassurance was in short supply.

The old man pointed to a sagging couch, its threadbare material stained and tattered. We crossed the bare, scuffed floor, passing a couple of ratty old chairs. An odor of mold mixed with woodsmoke fouled the air. The only sounds were the static from a police scanner and the crackling wood fire burning in the stove. The windows were coated and only where someone had rubbed, could anything be seen through them. There were no curtains. The walls were naked. No one could live here, only exist. The old man lowered himself into one of the chairs, evoking a groan from its wooden supports and propelling motes of dust into the dank air. Frank remained standing.

"Sit down. It's not the Hilton, but make yourselves at home. We'll be here a while. We've got lots to talk about," the old man smiled wickedly, revealing crooked or missing teeth.

"You said we'd be alone," Robbie stated.

"Well, I guess that makes us even. You brought your so-called assistant, and I've got my son. Let's just say he's my insurance." I swallowed hard, unable to take my eyes off Frank and his gun. "What's your name, missy?"

Before I could speak, Robbie jumped in. "She's Carla Banks, and leave her out of this."

"Yeah, and I'm Barack Obama." The old man's laugh sounded like a rusty door hinge. He saw my face go white and added, "Don't worry, sweetie. None of us use our real names in this business."

"Just one question before we begin; why are you willing to speak with us? You've kept quiet for so long. Why now?" asked Robbie.

"Well, sonny, it's like this. I don't expect to draw too many more breaths in this life, and there's a truth that needs to be told. Shitheads like you need to learn from the people who were saving the country and making history in the process."

"With all due respect, Mr. Cravanno..."

"Respect my ass," he boomed. His eyes caught fire, and he glared at Robbie with a look of evil and death. "Now you listen, and listen well. You turn on that recorder and shut the fuck up before I get Frank here to keep you quiet."

Robbie hit the "record" button and placed the tape recorder in front of Cravanno. I folded into a cocoon, trying my best to disappear into the cushions of the musty couch. "Whenever you're ready," Robbie said quietly.

"You'd better print this just like I tell it, or you won't be printing anything anymore, got it?" Joey said. Robbie nodded. Cravanno cleared his throat, eliciting another wheeze. He spat on the floor near my feet and began. "I grew up in Brooklyn and joined the army—fought in France mostly, a little bit in Sicily. I came home a hero and was honored by our ward chief. You don't need to know his name, only that he was tight with Mr. Costello. Back then, the best future for a punk like me was to join the mob, become a made man. You see, Mr. Costello was tight with Mr. Hoover, but you probably know that."

"Just to be clear, you mean Frank Costello and J. Edgar Hoover?" Robbie asked.

The man snapped, "You show some respect, boy. It's Mr. Hoover and Mr. Costello to you." He settled back into his seat. "I don't care what any of you bleeding hearts say. They were loyal Americans."

Robbie apologized. The old man ignored him and continued. "Well, Mr. Hoover arranges a meeting with me one day. I didn't know it was going to be with him, but here I am sitting in the back room of some New York bar and he walks in—just him, no one else. He sits across from me and says, 'I need your help. Frank Costello says you're a good man, that I can trust you.' Well, me, I get all puffed up like a rooster in a hen house. The head of the Feds wants me to help him and has the blessing of Mr. Costello. He passes me a gold coin and says, 'Whenever someone gives you one of these, it means I need you. You in?' he asks. Well, of course I'm in." The old man motioned to Frank, who came to his side. He whispered something in his ear, and Frank left the room.

"Let's see, my first job was a hit in Hawaii. The Jap asshole who killed our boys in the Bataan Death March was feeding the CIA dirt on China. Mr. Hoover knew this guy was scum and didn't deserve his cushy life, but he also knew he'd never get this guy in court, not when he had the CIA in his pocket. I went to this dick's fancy resort, lured him into a secluded spot, offed him, and dumped him into the water where he became chum for the sharks. That felt good."

Frank returned with a black-velvet bag and handed it to his father, who opened it and dumped its contents onto an overturned crate that served as a table. More than twenty gold coins spilled out, as if he had just won at slots. "There's one here for each job I did for Mr. Hoover." I gasped and he glanced over. "Seems your girlfriend is a little skittish." He looked at me with eyes narrowed by the rutted brow that squeezed them.

"I'm fine," I lied. I shot Robbie a look of apology and discretely wiped the sweat greasing my hands on my slacks.

"Well, you're not here to listen to all of my jobs, just one—Dallas, right?" He didn't wait for an answer. "I didn't know they were going to bump Kennedy off, but I'm not sorry they did. He was trashing everything we accomplished in the war. He fucked up Cuba, was playing nicey nice with the Ruskies, bringing them damn niggers into schools with our kids, and squeezing my friends in the mob. Meanwhile, he's screwing every woman he can find and pretending that he's some sort of prince. Worse, he was going to fire Mr. Hoover, a man who had dedicated his life to keeping the Reds out. So what if Mr. Hoover was tight with the mob? Back then, our interests were the same, just for different reasons."

He removed a pack of cigarettes from his shirt pocket and lit up. After a couple of puffs, he began again. "Makes me pissed just thinking about it. Where were we? Oh yeah, Dallas. That Friday night, after Kennedy got whacked, I got a call to meet a guy at this restaurant in Brooklyn. I heard the news. I knew what was going down before I got the coin. The guy gave me a key to a locker at LaGuardia and told me to get there early the next morning. I go home, pack my things, and am at the terminal by five a.m. In the locker was a round-trip plane ticket for Dallas and the names of two people I'm supposed to hit. One's a cabbie and the other is a show girl at Ruby's club. Both of them were talking too much about Ruby, saying he knew Oswald or that Oswald showed up at the club. They had to be shut down or the story wouldn't work."

"Excuse me," Robbie asked. "What do you mean about the story?"

"Don't bait me, sonny," Joey snapped. "You know as well as I as do, that Oswald was the fall guy he claimed to be. If Oswald lives, he talks. Couldn't let that happen." He took another drag from his unfiltered cigarette, sending an inch-long ash to the floor. He ground it in with his foot. "I wasn't the only one down there, either. Between the mob, the CIA, and Mr. Hoover's squad, we bumped off a lot of people who couldn't keep their mouths shut. That guy at the overpass, the one who said he saw a puff of smoke from behind the fence—fucking idiot. He was asking for it. Then there was the guy who saw a man running out the back of the book depository. There were lots of car *accidents*, if you know what I mean. The guy who said that Tippit's shooter didn't look anything like Oswald—that one got screwed up. His brother was shot by mistake, but at least it was enough to get the guy to change his story. I don't know how many we got, but Mr. Hoover's story stuck—at least until worms like you started crawling out from under rocks."

"So, why are you telling a worm like me all about this?" asked Robbie calmly.

"Because it's time Mr. Hoover got credit for cleaning up the mess these damn politicians get us into. He kept us all safe. Killing the Kennedys was no different than killing the Krauts."

"Did you say Kennedys? You mean both of them?" asked Robbie, trying to keep his voice steady.

"And King, don't forget King. We got 'em all. Oswald took one for the team, whether he wanted to or not. He was one of us."

"Oswald worked for the Feds?" Robbie asked. I was squirming. I knew he wanted explicit statements, but he was getting Joey angry.

"Get your head out of your ass, boy. Oswald, Ruby, others too. The reason Ruby got away with so much was because he was feeding the Feds information. Who do you think bailed him out of his money problems? Fucking asshole goes walking around Dallas like a pimp with pretty girls to sell, flashing thousands of dollars in his pocket. I heard that the night he whacked Oswald, he was a nervous wreck until the guard told him Oswald croaked. If he had screwed up the hit, he would have been sorry. He had a sister, you know."

"So the Feds paid Ruby off?" Robbie asked.

"The Feds, the mob; what difference does it make? He got paid for the hit on Oswald. They tried to get Roselli and Trafficante to rat on us, but we took care of them too. Bullets around the mouth for breaking the code of silence, omerta. You see, the mob had rules; it had honor. We took care of our own, and if someone broke the rules or brought dishonor to the family, we took care of that, too."

The tape recorder clicked, and Robbie began to replace the tape with a second one. Cravanno grabbed Robbie's hand. "You've got your story. Now get out before I change my mind and feed you and your girl-friend to the swamp." He laughed bitterly. "Just tell it like I told it, you hear me?"

"Yes sir. Word for word," Robbie answered, pulling the recorder off the table and rising to leave. I jumped up behind him.

"One more thing. Whoever is after you knows you're in New Orleans. If I were you, I'd get the hell out of here. I want my story told, and you lying in a ditch somewhere won't make it happen. The sooner you leave, the sooner I can get out of this rat hole."

"You don't live here?" Robbie asked.

"Like I said, Mr. Hoover took good care of me." The old man's leer made me feel even dirtier, if that were possible.

The interview was over. Robbie put the cassette into his pocket and picked up the recorder before taking my hand and following me outside. Frank fell in behind.

We were about twenty feet from the house and another thirty from the truck when Frank growled, "Hold it right there. You two aren't going anywhere. Now give me that tape." Frank leveled a gun at Robbie, who slowly reached in his pocket, pulled out the tape, and handed it over. Frank threw it on the ground and stomped on it, shattering the plastic cassette with zeal. I discretely reached behind my back and felt for the gun.

"Pop may want his story told, but the people paying me don't. In fact, this is the end of your little game." He cocked his gun. "I'm going to get a bundle for this. Now, who wants to be first?" The devil himself could not have laughed more wickedly. Frank was going to kill us; I was sure of it.

Without a second to form a conscious thought, I whipped the gun from my back and fired. Frank fell backward and hit the ground with a thud. The gun fell from his hand. An expanding red circle appeared on his chest, and his face was fixed in disbelief. Robbie kicked Frank's gun into the swamp and looked up at the house. Cravanno had seen the whole thing, and he had a shotgun pointing right at us.

"Don't worry. I'm not going to shoot you. I want my story told, like I said. If you hadn't killed that worthless sonofabitch, I would've. Now, get out."

His rheumy eyes never left us as we sprinted to the car. We sped out the driveway onto I-190, hitting bumps hard enough to bang our heads on the ceiling of the car.

I was trembling, and Robbie placed one hand on my thigh while keeping the other on the wheel. "You had to do it, Kat. He would have killed us on the spot. He had no intention of letting us go." He waited for my response. Getting none, he continued, "You saved our lives."

I still couldn't respond. My heart was racing. My hands were shaking. I placed them flat on the seat and willed myself to composure, staring straight ahead as trees lashed the windshield and pebbles sprang from the tires. When we reached the main road, I finally exhaled as if I'd been holding my breath the entire time. I handed the gun to Robbie, as though getting rid of it could purge my shock. Cravanno said he would kill his son without a moment's hesitation. How could a father do that? Then I thought about my father. Suddenly I was cold and shivering. Would he do the same?

Once on the highway, I finally spoke. "Could we pull over? I need to get my phone. It's in my purse."

Robbie veered onto the shoulder, sending gravel flying. He pressed the trunk release. I hopped out to retrieve my purse and ran back to the car, not wanting to delay our escape. We sped onto the road while I rummaged through the junk inside. I had to call Ben. I had killed a man. That was when I felt an object the size of a matchbox and pulled it out.

"Oh my god." I shouted. Robbie abruptly turned to me, causing the car to swerve.

"What is it?" he asked. His blue eyes darkened; his voice was strained and sharp.

"Someone planted a tracking device in my purse. It's been here since we left Washington. They've been able to track us the whole time. We have to get out of here—*fast*."

"Give it to me," he ordered. "After a brief inspection, he threw it in a drainage ditch next to the road. "This should throw them off. It might buy us some time."

My head was spinning as I contemplated our options. "Do you think Joey was telling the truth?" I asked.

"I've heard about Hoover's hit squad but, until now, I never knew whether it really existed. I'm convinced—this guy is for real."

"Do you think he'll have second thoughts and send someone after us?"

"Don't know, but while we're jettisoning things...," Robbie pulled over, got out of the car and heaved his phone into the water—just another secret kept by Lake Pontchartrain. Climbing back in, he said, "We'll use your spy phone. It will be safer. Three cellphones in three weeks—that's got to be a record."

I dialed Ben's number. Once again there was no answer. I banged my phone on my thigh." Dammit, where is he?"

"What's wrong?" Robbie asked.

"Ben's still not answering his phone." I could swear that Robbie seemed to shift in his seat, sitting up a little straighter and clenching his jaw. "I'm worried, Robbie. Ben's been hiding out in different hotels. He sent his wife back to the Midwest. I heard my father say that he would get Ben for putting me on my assignment."

"The assignment that you won't tell me about." He stared at the road, his face unreadable: I couldn't tell if he was angry or teasing me.

"Yeah, that one." I nudged him playfully, trying to eliminate some tension, but it didn't work. We were on our own. I'd killed the son of a hit man. They knew where we were. We had to get away, but we also had to restore good feelings between us, so I added, "But I will tell you everything as soon as I can."

He was quiet for several moments, until the frostiness thawed a bit, when he said, "What really ticks me off is that, after all of that, I've got nothing to show for it. The tape is gone. Shit."

I removed my hat and pointed at it. "Don't worry. I got it all, with video." His look of admiration almost made the entire experience bearable.

"You're amazing." He reached out and pulled me close. "My own secret agent. Who would have thought? By the way, where'd you learn to shoot like that?"

"Survival can be a great motivator." I nestled my head against his shoulder. "I can't wait to get out of here."

"Yeah, but where should we go?"

I answered with a single word. "Dallas."

CHAPTER TWENTY-SIX

We ditched our Chevy Malibu at Avis and picked up a Nissan Sentra at Hertz to throw whoever was after us off our trail, opting to drive the eight hours to Dallas so it wouldn't be as easy to track our movements. Merging onto I-10, we headed west through the bayous into the heart of Cajun country, passing oil and sugarcane refineries. A few plantations fronted by archways of massive oaks could be seen in the distance, a reminder of a different time and way of life. Swans preened on the edges of lakes. Puffy, white thunderclouds floated overhead in the distance.

But then the scenery changed. Spindly trees dripping in Spanish moss looked like skeletons wearing tattered shawls, tiptoeing into the swamp. Thorns the size of penny nails strangled honey locusts. Abandoned geriatric barns tried valiantly to stand erect, like World War II veterans at a parade, while makeshift houseboats lay marooned on the shore of the great Atchafalaya Swamp. Rusty railroad bridges supported tracks that led nowhere. It was majestically ominous. Few trucks and fewer cars passed. Already unnerved by the words of Joey Cravanno, our surroundings further heightened our apprehension.

Lynyrd Skynyrd was on the radio, singing "Sweet Home Alabama," and Robbie hummed along. Neither of us had spoken for about half an hour. In any other place, we would have been comfortable with the silence. But in this foreign world of swamps, bayous, training camps, and killers, I felt a change inside, the emergence of an alter ego. We were hiding. We were running. We were seeking a truth and risking our lives to do it. I'd killed a man, yet I'd never felt more alive in my life.

After lunch in Lafayette, Louisiana, we merged onto I-49. I slept until we hit Opelousas and then took over the wheel so Robbie could nap. With Greg's glasses handy and Charlie Daniels singing about the devil and Georgia, I thought about everything that had happened since that fateful day in Ben's office.

My mind drifted back to the conversation between my father and Carson outside the vault. Why did he really enter the vault? Did he know I was there? Was his conversation with Carson for my benefit? Is that why he mentioned the alcove? The most important evidence was there—the brain, the Mauser rifle, and the autopsy photos. Was he trying to tip me off? He also mentioned the mind-control experiments at Atsugi. Why? Slowly, the jigsaw pieces of the mystery were falling into place, and I hoped that Robbie would complete the picture when we got to Dallas. Where we went from there was another mystery.

Robbie woke when I exited I-20 to merge onto US-80. The city burst from the plains surrounding it. I took the Elm Street exit and followed it to Main.

"Thanks for driving." He gave me a peck on the cheek. "I really crashed."

"My pleasure. You didn't miss much in the way of scenery—flat plains as far as I could see and then, boom—we're in the city."

He rubbed his eyes and stretched, looking at his watch as he lowered his arm. "Guess we should find a room, huh?"

"Robbie, I want to stay somewhere really special tonight. My nerves are shot, and I could use a little pampering. What do you think?"

"I'd be happy to pamper you." I knew he was grinning. Suddenly, he lurched forward and pointed. "Turn here!"

I veered into the driveway of the Adolphus Hotel on Commerce Street. As we got out, a gentleman was at the car, ready to assist us with our luggage. "Robbie, it's beautiful, but so old. Can't we stay in a place that's a little more modern?'"

"If we're going to do Dallas properly, we've got to stay here."

"Why?" I asked.

"Ruby's Carousel Club was right across the street. Beverly Oliver saw Ruby and Oswald together there on several occasions. Madeleine Brown met Lyndon Johnson at the Adolphus during a post-election party. She's the one I told you about; you know, his mistress? One of Ruby's girls, Shari Angel, claimed she saw Johnson and Ruby together at the Adolphus several months before the election. This is also where Nixon stayed before the assassination."

We handed the keys to the valet, removed our bags from the trunk, and walked under ornate arches through large glass doors into the dark, wood-paneled lobby. It felt as if we had entered the living room of a Rockefeller or a Vanderbilt with its massive wood columns, potted palms, flowered-print carpeting, and paneled ceiling. An elaborately carved Steinway sat idle, waiting to be played. I half expected to see some old Texas oil barons smoking cigars while sitting in leather chairs positioned under crystal chandeliers and in front of massive paintings.

The Adolphus had a room available, and after checking in, we took the elevator to the twentieth floor. We gazed through floor-to-ceiling windows down at the city where JFK spent his last day. Robbie stood behind me, his arms wrapped around me like a stole. He whispered in my ear, "Who gets to take the first shower?" I turned and suggested that we both could.

I gulped down breakfast at the Bistro. I couldn't wait to begin the day. I was ready for more. The zeal I felt yesterday was just as robust today and was growing; my need to learn more was insatiable. With Robbie's understanding and the information I had, we really might be able to solve the crime of the century, as a team, but only when it was safe to tell him everything. The prospect was intoxicating. We could rectify all those years that history was cheated and finally satisfy a generation scarred by the lies of its fathers.

As soon as Robbie finished his coffee, I jumped up and pulled on my running jacket. "It's a beautiful day. Let's go."

"Just like the day of the motorcade, sunny and bright," he said.

We jogged west on Commerce Street. The morning's rush-hour traffic had diminished, but many cars still streamed down the road with horns honking, engines racing, and radios blaring. Six or seven blocks later, we cut through the John F. Kennedy Memorial Plaza, zigzagging our way to Elm Street. At the corner of Houston and Elm, I stopped short. There it was, the Texas School Book Depository, rising like a sphinx with an unsolved riddle. Seeing the building in person was startling. Robbie pointed up. "The infamous sixth floor."

He ushered me to the seven-story, austere brick building that now housed the Dallas county administrative offices. "Okay, stand right here and look up at the sixth-floor window. Amos Euins, standing right where we're standing now, claimed that he saw a man who looked like Oswald, holding a gun with the barrel sticking out of the window. Do you really think anyone could make an identification from this distance?"

"I read that there was a sniper's nest created by piles of boxes in front of the window. Wouldn't a gunman be hiding behind those?" I asked.

"You'd think so. Let's go up." We entered the building, paid the entrance fee, and rode the elevator to the sixth floor.

The first thing we saw was an exhibit covering the early sixties, then we passed the *Trip to Texas* exhibit, before reaching the sniper's nest which overlooked Elm Street. "Look here." Robbie pointed. "Imagine that Kennedy's car is coming from Houston Street. If I want to kill him, I have a great shot as he's coming toward me, not after he's turned onto Elm. I'd have to shoot through that tree as he's going farther and farther away. That doesn't make sense."

"But if the assassin shot when the car was coming toward him, wouldn't he have attracted attention to himself?" My voice was low and barely audible. "I think he had to wait for some signal so all the shots were fired at once, making it difficult for people to count them or identify where they were coming from."

Robbie looked at me and smiled, like a teacher whose student had aced the exam. "Good point. Especially these guys; they were professionals. Maybe the guys up here wanted to be seen so the shooting could be blamed on Oswald."

"Any idea who they were?" I asked, surveying the room and the other visitors within.

"Maybe three guys—one at each of the windows. A man named Loy Factor claims that Malcolm Wallace, LBJ's hitman, recruited him for the job. The night before, a woman named Anne picks him up. Ruby's in the car with a guy that they called Oswald."

I thought back to the vault and couldn't remember seeing anything about a Loy Factor, but I *had* seen Malcolm Wallace's fingerprint. "Are you kidding? How come no one's ever heard of Loy Factor?"

"There's a lot that people don't know about." Robbie walked from window to window. I followed as he continued, "But this wasn't the only building shooters fired from." I followed his finger to a building adjacent to the book depository. "Supposedly, Nicoletti and Roselli were on the second floor of the Dal-Tex building, over there."

"If what you say is true, why didn't anyone see the real shooters leaving the book depository or running from the Dal-Tex building?"

"People *did* report seeing men running from the back of the book depository and getting into a car. Remember what Joey said? One of the witnesses was killed after the event. Then there were the three 'tramps' who weren't dressed like tramps at all. In fact, all three were known killers—Chauncey Holt, Charles Harrelson, and Charles Rogers. When they were discovered in a boxcar, about an hour and a half after the assassination, they told the police that they were working undercover to catch smugglers. The fake IDs were made by Chauncey himself. Holt was part of a documentation mill for the CIA, forging documents and spreading disinformation. He confessed to the whole thing."

"Why didn't the police arrest the tramps?" I asked as I stared out the window, trying to imagine the motorcade passing and checking out the angles from the sixth floor, the grassy knoll, and the Dal-Tex building. It all looked so easy in hindsight.

"To the cops, if they were real cops, the tramps were 'colleagues.' Their pictures were taken, but they were let go without any statements or fingerprints recorded."

"What makes you think they weren't real cops?" I didn't doubt him. I just needed to know what was real and what was supposition.

"There's a picture of two cops walking with the three tramps. Their uniforms differed from those of the Dallas city police, and each wore a different hat." Robbie walked to the other window; I followed. "When Harrelson was arrested for the murder of a cop later on, he said that he could clarify 11/22/63 as he called it and that he had been involved in it himself. He retracted his statement later, saying he'd been high on cocaine." Robbie looked around the room and ushered me ahead. "This place has gotten too crowded."

"Okay, but one more thing. Where was the real Oswald during all of this?"

"Carol Arnold said she saw Oswald sitting alone in the lunchroom at 12:15 p.m. JFK's motorcade was running late and passed the book depository at 12:30 p.m. If he was a shooter, expecting Kennedy to pass by at 12:20 p.m., why would he be sitting in the lunchroom? Less than two minutes after the assassination, a policeman charged into the book depository with the building manager and saw Oswald on the second floor, calmly sipping a Coke."

"I see what you're saying," I said. "Oswald couldn't have done everything they said and make it to the second floor, but even if he could, wouldn't someone have seen him running down the stairs?"

"Victoria Adams watched the motorcade from a window on the fourth floor. As soon as the shots rang out, she left the window and ran down the stairs. Oswald would have had to pass her. She testified that she neither heard nor saw anyone on the stairs."

"Why didn't the Warren Commission believe her?" I asked.

"I doubt they ever heard her testimony. Federal agents constantly tried to make her change her story. There's one more thing. A law clerk, Lillian Mooneyham, who worked over there," he pointed, "said she saw a man in the window moving boxes three to five minutes *after* the assassination. If Oswald was in the lunchroom by then, someone else must have been up here."

"Let me guess. Her testimony was never heard, either." Robbie nodded. "Why didn't these people come forward when the Warren Commission report came out? They had to know it was a sham."

"They were scared."

We left the window, passing by the model of Dealey Plaza and then by an exhibit called *The Investigations*. I thought I heard something like a "tsk" coming from Robbie. "Over here," he said, pointing to a spot near the back stairs. "That's where they found the gun. When the police first saw it, they called it a Mauser, not a Mannlicher-Carcano."

I grimaced as I remembered the rifle in the vault, labeled with my father's initials. "Do you think anyone *did* use the Mannlicher-Carcano?" I asked, whispering.

"Not to kill JFK, but maybe to help frame Oswald. Some think Oswald placed it here on the orders of his handler, David Atlee Phillips." Robbie saw the horror in my face. "Sorry, I know this is hard."

"It's okay, go on." Inside I was thinking something altogether different; that my father might have planted the Mannlicher-Carcano to frame Oswald and then removed the Mauser to cover for someone else.

"And get this...the three shots heard on the police radio were not evenly spaced. According to at least forty-eight witnesses it was more like bang......bang, bang. In other words, the last two were shot almost simultaneously."

"So one person couldn't have fired them, not with a bolt-action rifle."

"You got it."

"Okay, but if the real Oswald wasn't a shooter but knew about the plot, why was he hanging out in a lunchroom?"

"He was near a phone. Maybe he was waiting for instructions. When the call didn't come, he bolted. Judyth Baker said Oswald had infiltrated the plot and wanted to thwart it, but was double-crossed." Robbie guided me toward the elevator. As we descended to the first floor, he looked at me with disappointment and said, "You know, I've told you a lot of things that would blow most people away. You haven't even reacted. I don't get it."

"It's a lot to take in. I'm, uh, just trying to keep it all straight." My head hummed like a computer, processing Robbie's data, noting what fit and what didn't.

He closed his eyes and slumped against the elevator wall. "You know what I think? I think you're trying to convince me that you're being supportive of my work when, in reality, you're preoccupied with your project and are using me help you." He left the elevator first and walked ahead of me, not waiting for me to catch up.

I'd been busted. Still, I protested, "I didn't even know that you were into conspiracy theories when I ran into you at Pam and Trevor's," as I trotted to catch up.

Robbie wheeled around and took me by both arms. "You ran into Beau, too. He's got a lot more to offer than me, and he's interested in you. He told me so. So why me and not him?"

"Because I love *you*." It was true. I had hoped that would placate him, but was wrong.

"And the context that I can provide. Is that it?" He released my arms as several tourists approached. We walked out of the book depository and into Dealey Plaza.

"Please, be patient with me. It will be worth it, I promise," I said, as we moved toward the grassy knoll. It all seemed so much smaller than I thought it would be. I sat on the cement block where Zapruder shot his famous film and let my mind drift back fifty years.

People line Elm Street, buzzing with excitement. For the first time ever, a sitting president was visiting their city. Roars from the crowd crescendo as the motorcade approaches. The charismatic man and his elegant wife smile and wave as they ride by, basking in the atmosphere and the enthusiasm of the crowd—so unexpected on Johnson's turf.

But others in the crowd—rogue CIA operatives, the mob, the FBI, right-wing fanatics, Cubans—look around surreptitiously. They came to witness, firsthand, the "big event," and gloat in its aftermath. Their nemesis, the president of the United States, would die, and if things worked out as planned, a patsy would take the fall for it. They look up at the buildings, searching for the shooters and hoping they hit their mark. They catch one other's eye and wink. Any second now.

The umbrella man stands to the right, by the curb—in perfect position to signal the shooters positioned at various points in the plaza. The limo slows almost to a stop and is now mere feet away. The umbrella goes up and then bang, bang, bang, bang, bang, bang. *Kennedy's head explodes. The umbrella man's companion pumps his fist and speaks into a walkie-talkie.*

Shock and disbelief stun the crowd. Euphoria morphs into screaming, crying, and running. Bedlam descends as bystanders charge the grassy knoll or stare up at the book depository. Cops question witnesses. Newsmen vie for scoops.

And all the while, several men are breaking down their weapons, stuffing them in their coats and casually walking toward a car or the street, behind the depository, or in the rail yard. Men with fake ID's accost people with cameras and seize their film.

The limo speeds away, taking the fallen president to Parkland and leaving behind a void, first in Dealey Plaza and then the entire nation.

"Hey, come here. I want to show you something," Robbie yelled. I shook off the image and joined Robbie behind the stockade fence. Some of Robbie's kindred spirits had left graffiti, such as "America lost its innocence here," "This is where the real killer stood," "Why are we still lied to?" and "Oswald was framed."

"James Files claimed that he fired the head shot from here," Robbie said in a subdued voice, still smarting from my reticence to share more. "He also said that he and Nicoletti hit Kennedy at the same time. That's consistent with the police radio recording. It would also obscure the entry and exit wounds in the head." Robbie further related how Files claimed that he'd used a Remington XP-100 Fireball—a powerful, deadly accurate pistol that was given to him by David Atlee Phillips.

"Phillips was my father's boss," I said quietly. This was hitting me hard. "Do you believe Files?"

"Yeah, he knows too many details that were verified much later."

"Such as...?"

"Files said that he bit the casing of a .222 caliber shell and left it behind, like a macabre trademark. In 1987, two Dallas residents found the casing when they went digging around the fence. A UCLA anthropologist dated the casing to 1963. An orthodontist confirmed that there were teeth marks on the shell.

I thought about the fragment I had removed from the brain. If it was the same caliber, it might confirm Robbie's contention. I scrambled for words. "Is that a common type of bullet?"

"I'm no expert, but I do know that Files said that the gun he used was a prototype with limited availability. Supposedly, the CIA had access to it. The next year's version of the gun, the one that was available to the public, used a .221 caliber bullet to reduce the fireball upon shooting."

"So what's missing is the actual bullet," I said, treading cautiously.

"Yeah, if we had that, we'd know for sure that the CIA or some such agency was involved. That would clinch it."

I could clinch it. I had to find a way to determine the fragment's caliber and give Robbie his truth. I watched him intently. He honed in on the big X painted on the street to identify the site of the head shot. I could read his imaginings, his pain, and anger. I walked silently behind him and put my arms around his waist.

"You okay, Robbie?"

"So many years have passed. I can't let them get away with it, Kat. So many wrongs." Robbie lowered his head and slowly shook it back and forth. "Sorry, it always gets to me when I come here." He looked back at the book depository, the Dal-Tex building, up at the stockade fence, and across the street to the south knoll. "You want to hear something weird? They never found out what happened to Kennedy's brain. It went missing after the autopsy. It could tell us everything."

I stiffened. A lump formed in my throat, making it hard to swallow. I looked away to hide my discomfort. This was torture.

"What's wrong?" he asked.

I scrambled for an answer, one that rang true. "I'm sure that my dad was here that day. I'm wondering where he stood. What was his role?

Did he know who the shooters were, where they stood, how they got away?" I looked around and could feel tears welling up in my eyes. The scene blurred. I sucked my lip and stopped the tears before they fell.

"For you it's a bunch of names—Johnson, Hoover, Phillips, Marcello, Hunt. For me, it's my father. Do you have any idea what it's like to realize that the same person who read me bedtime stories and held me during thunderstorms might have helped kill a president, let an innocent man take the blame, and then lie to our country?" I searched Robbie's eyes for comfort and compassion, but they were strangely absent. His grief, or maybe anger, was too strong. "I need to confront him. I need to tell him what I know. He may not have to answer to anyone else, but he needs to answer to me."

"I don't believe that your father answers to anyone." Robbie's voice was cold and stiff.

I blanched. How could I expect Robbie to cut my father any slack? After a moment or two, he trotted off, calling over his shoulder, "There's more to show you."

CHAPTER TWENTY-SEVEN

We traversed Dealey Plaza, with Robbie pointing out where Lee Bowers stood when he saw the men behind the fence. He showed me where James Teague was hit in the face by concrete that splintered after the first bullet missed. He pointed out several spots where additional shooters may have stood.

"Are you sure?" I asked.

"I don't have proof, if that's what you mean." I detected an accusatory tone in his voice.

The rising deceit burned like acid in my stomach. To help neutralize it, I muttered softly, "You will."

He shot me a strange look as we ran onto Commerce Street, to Houston, across the viaduct, through Lake Cliff Park to North Zang Boulevard, and then turned left onto North Beckley Avenue, stopping in front of house number 1026. Robbie stopped and turned to me. "Guess who lived here."

"Oswald?" I answered, while catching my breath.

"Bingo." Robbie walked toward the house for a closer look. "A policeman, Roger Craig, testified that he saw Oswald run from the depository and enter a Rambler station wagon. Oswald purportedly said that the car belonged to Ruth Paine and to leave her out of it. He also said something like, 'Now everyone will know who I am,' like his cover had been blown or something. By the way, Craig's death was a little odd to say the least—just one of many."

Thoughts of the death list resurfaced. I remembered Craig's name and didn't even bother to ask Robbie why his death was odd. With confusion distorting his face, Robbie continued, "What I still don't get is how could Oswald be seen running from the book depository and get in a car, but also be on a bus and in a cab."

"You said that there may have been more than one Oswald." Robbie seemed puzzled by my recollection. He'd told me that, hadn't he? Or did I recall that from the vault? I quickly recovered by asking, "But what I don't understand is, why would Oswald return to his house after the assassination and go to the movie theater? If I'd shot a president, I would have bolted from Dallas."

"But what if he didn't shoot the president? He'd have no reason to run." Pointing to a window, Robbie said, "That's where Oswald's landlady was standing when she heard him come home, around one o'clock. She saw a police car outside. It honked and then drove away. Oswald left the house about five minutes later." Robbie took my hand. "Now, you and I are going for a little walk."

Robbie checked his watch and began walking briskly to East Fifth Street and then turned left on East Canty. When we hit North Patton, we turned right and then turned again onto Tenth Street. Halfway down the block, we stopped. He checked his watch—twelve minutes. "Eyewitnesses said that Tippit was killed here between 1:11 and 1:15. We were walking pretty fast. No way could Oswald walk this distance in seven minutes."

"Maybe the eyewitnesses were off by a couple of minutes. It happens. Besides, Oswald *was* carrying a gun."

"That's the thing. Oswald's gun was fully loaded when he was captured, and he didn't have any extra ammo. But there's something else. One of the policemen at the Tippit murder scene testified that he had marked the shells with his initials, but no initials were found on the shells later produced by the police. The really screwy thing is, Oswald carried a revolver. Revolvers don't eject shells, yet four were found at the scene, *and* they differed from the type of bullets found in Tippit's body."

I thought of the shell casings from the Tippit murder in the vault and wondered whose gun they came from. A chill crawled down my back, but I had to press on. "So if Oswald didn't kill Tippit, who did?"

"Files, the shooter I told you about, claimed that a guy came to his hotel room the afternoon after the assassination. He asked Files to get rid of his gun for him because he had to 'burn a cop.' Tippit was the only policeman killed in Dallas that day. And get this; the guy Files' buddy was supposed to shoot was Oswald, not Tippit. When he didn't, Ruby had to."

"So the real Oswald is at the theater. What about the other one?" I asked.

"That may have been the guy who ran into Files's apartment. Some say he was also in the movie theater, as was Ruby. Evidently, Oswald kept changing seats, maybe to locate his contact. His contact snuck out of the theater when the police stormed in. There's a witness who swears he saw Oswald in a red car in a nearby parking lot. How could he, if the real Oswald had been taken into custody?"

"Now I know why it's so easy for the general public to dismiss a conspiracy—it's too much to believe. This one lives with that one who knows this one who works for this agency who associates with these people. Robbie, how do you expect the average person to believe all of this?"

"I know. I've been dealing with it for most of my life, but think about it. Forget what you've been fed by the government, the press, and history books. It comes down to this. If Oswald was a lone assassin and everything was as the Warren Commission claimed, why wouldn't the government just release all of its files? What would there be to hide?"

"So, if the lie, no matter how big it is, is repeated over and over, you wear people down and finally, no one bothers to question it anymore," I said in a subdued voice, barely discernible even to myself. He nodded. "Is there anything else you want to show me, Robbie?"

"You look pretty beat. Maybe you've dealt with enough for the day." He brushed some hair from my eyes.

I shook my head. "There's something else, isn't there?"

"Yeah. You sure you want to hear it?"

What I really wanted was to be back at the hotel, where I could wash the slime off my brain and sit comfortably with a drink; I craved the numbness. But our work wasn't done. "Go on," I answered.

"It's about what happened at Parkland Hospital. And then, I promise, that's it for the day." He jogged slower than usual which, at this point,

I didn't mind. "Every doctor in the ER described both an occipital and a parietal head wound to the president—both front and back, meaning the shooters had to be in front and in back as well. The official autopsy photos only show the frontal wound; the back of Kennedy's head seems uninjured. Somebody altered them."

I tried to look amazed, but inwardly I cringed. I had seen the originals.

"There's more. One of the doctors probed a bullet wound with his finger. The wound did not go through all the way."

I stopped jogging and stared at Robbie incredulously. "But that would mean four definite shots, not three."

"You got it." He beamed. "Supposedly, the location of the wound was moved to fit the Warren Report's explanation of how it all went down."

I felt like Atlas, my shoulders bent from the weight of all I had learned, both from Robbie and the vault. I was just about to cry uncle when Robbie added, "At the hospital, they wrapped Kennedy in sheets so the satin lining of his expensive bronze coffin would not get stained with blood. When the coffin was unloaded at Bethesda, Kennedy was in a plastic body bag and was removed from a standard-issue military coffin."

"Wait a second. Are you saying that JFK's body made a detour somewhere between Parkland and Bethesda?" He nodded. "Why? Did they alter his injuries before performing the official autopsy at Bethesda?"

Robbie searched my eyes; I could read his mind. He wanted confirmation, not questions, from me. I returned his gaze evenly, silently prompting him to finish. The tension between us grew. "You know what's odd?" he asked.

"It might be easier to ask what *isn't* odd in this whole mess."

Robbie smirked and continued, "Lyndon Johnson called Parkland Hospital himself and asked Dr. Charles Crenshaw, who was busy trying to save Oswald's life, to get a confession out of him before he died."

"But if he did get the confession, it would have solved the whole mess. Why not try?"

"Doesn't it strike you as odd that Johnson is being so hands-on at this point? He's just stepped into the presidency and Oswald's confession is his top priority? It's also interesting that Johnson sold his Halliburton stock the day before the assassination. Johnson called Hoover and said that he wanted something issued so the public was convinced that Oswald was the real assassin. Oswald hadn't even been killed yet, let alone tried in a court of law." Robbie raked his hair with his fingers and released a huge sigh. "So the American people are left with the pack of lies known as the Warren Commission report while others know the truth." He looked at me askance. He now lumped me with them. We ran back to the Adolphus in a silence, his trust in me shattered.

Robbie had shared everything he knew with me, willingly. I gave nothing in return. I felt like a cheat—worse, a murdering cheat.

CHAPTER TWENTY-EIGHT

By the time we returned to the hotel, showered, and dressed it was midafternoon. My brain was saturated with everything I'd seen and heard, and I was pensive about our next steps. With his phone drowned in Lake Pontchartrain, Robbie went to the business center to check his e-mail, but perhaps also to get away from me.

I turned on my cell phone and was stunned by the thirty-two messages that maxed out my voice mail. Ten were from my father. The first few conveyed his irritation at my lack of response, but in subsequent calls, his voice was louder, more strident. He asked where I was. Was I safe? He wanted me to get off the project and quit the Agency. I needed to call him, but didn't dare do so until we were en route back to Washington. Another call was from Pam. Then I listened to the message from Jermaine.

"Agent Hastings, I'm afraid that I have some very bad news," he said. "Ben Douglas died in a car accident last night at nine p.m. He was alone and driving southbound on Leesburg Pike. The official word is that he had been drinking and lost control of his car. He crashed into an embankment and was dead by the time the police arrived. I'm very sorry. I took Scout from the kennel. He'll be safer with me. I've also been monitoring activity at your apartment complex. I'll tell you about that later. Call me as soon as you can. We need to talk."

I didn't listen to any other messages. I went numb. My legs felt like lead weights as I repeatedly crisscrossed the room, trying to keep my head from spinning out of orbit. Ben was dead. Or was he? I had only Jermaine's word and he had lied to me before. Maybe this was a ruse to bring me back. I called Ben's assistant, and the second I heard her voice, I knew it was true.

"It's just awful. He'd been acting so unusual. It must have finally gotten to him. Oh, Kat, I can't believe it." Then all I heard was sobbing and finally, she said she had to go. The line went dead.

I ran down to the business center and found Robbie at a computer, typing away.

"I've got to tell you something, but not here. It's important."

He must have seen the panic in my eyes because he immediately logged off, stuffed a paper in his pocket, and followed me back to the room. His restrained manner indicated that my reluctance to fill in his missing pieces still stung.

"There's something I want you to hear," I said, as we entered our room. I played Jermaine's message for him and could see his face go blank while his chest heaved with deep breaths. His fist rose to his lips and then he began to pace, as I had only moments ago.

"Ben didn't drink," I said quietly. "Either he went off the wagon, or someone is trying to make it look that way."

Robbie sank into a chair and looked off in the distance. When he finally spoke, I hardly recognized his voice. It was so strained and thin, devoid of its normal lilt. "Let's take a walk." It sounded more like a command than a suggestion. We descended to the lobby in silence. Robbie took my hand and pulled me outside. Day had yielded to dusk. Halos framed the streetlights. Cars honked in traffic like geese desperate for home. Signs flashed. Commuters walked with post-work deliberation.

Taking my hand, Robbie walked north, maneuvering us between pedestrians, across streets, and finally yanking me into a small Irish pub, where several men in suits clustered at the bar, watching ESPN. We found a table on the far side of the room. The first words I heard from Robbie were "Redbreast, neat, water on the side." I stuck with scotch. Robbie's eyes darted around the room several times, and only when the waiter returned with our drinks and left did he speak. "We need to get back."

"I know." The thought scared me to death, but there were issues and people to deal with.

"Take a look at this." He withdrew the paper I had seen him stuff into his pocket and handed it to me. It was an article from the *Washington Post*.

Car Explodes in Shirlington Garage

Late Monday afternoon, the owner of a green BMW 325 convertible triggered an explosion upon pressing its remote-access ignition. The car was parked in the garage of a large apartment complex in the Shirlington section of Arlington, VA. Several additional cars adjacent to the BMW sustained significant damage. Police and fire departments were summoned to the scene by hotel employees. The garage is still being cleared of debris by police, who are searching for additional clues. Other than the owner, there was no one in the vicinity when the car exploded. There were no injuries. Police briefly interviewed the owner of the vehicle at the scene, but the owner has disappeared and remains unavailable for further interrogation. The owner's identity is being withheld until further information is available. Anyone with information concerning this incident is asked to contact the Arlington, VA police immediately.

I looked up at Robbie with perplexed eyes. "This makes it sound like engine trouble. There's no mention of a bomb or foul play, and it makes it sound like I ran away and wasn't cooperating."

"Someone is squashing the story. It's been delayed and details are missing. No reporter would accept this."

"Jermaine took care of things after I left. Maybe JSOC has the power to suppress the story." I dropped the paper on the table and stared mindlessly at the TV, where a basketball player thumped his chest after making a slam dunk. My gaze returned to Robbie. "The kennel wouldn't release Scout to a stranger, but Jermaine said he has him. If he's telling the truth, he must have taken Scout without their permission. Why would he do that? And how?"

"Like I said, we need to get back." Robbie downed his whiskey and threw some money on the table.

The city air was a welcome alternative to the stale beer fumes of the bar. All I could think of was that if they killed Ben, I could be next. We would be walking right back into it. But I had to find out more about Ben's death. I needed to talk to Jermaine and hoped that I could get Scout back. I also had to figure out what to do with all the evidence.

And as much as I hated the thought, I needed to confront my father and maybe try to understand his participation in the conspiracy, although it was hard to imagine how anything he might say could diminish the overwhelming sense of shame and betrayal I now felt.

But then another thought emerged. It was quite possible that the only one who could help me might be my father. The prospect sickened me. It would mean swallowing my pride and revulsion. I wasn't sure that I could do it. Besides, given our chilly relationship and all that had happened in the last few weeks, I wasn't sure that he would or could help me.

Somehow, one foot followed the other, and we found ourselves at the bustling hotel entrance, pretending that nothing was wrong and we didn't have a care in the world. Oscars had been won for lesser performances.

Once back in the room, Robbie began to think out loud. We'd leave tomorrow, not tonight. We'd go straight to his place. I'd make my phone calls from there. We needed to discuss what to say to my father, when to meet him, and where. Same with Jermaine. I'd go to work on Monday, as usual, and find out what I could about Ben. Robbie would go to the paper and see what he could dig up about the car bomb and Ben. We'd meet after work at my apartment to see if everything was in order.

His stream of consciousness was incessant, so finally I just burst out, "Wait a second, do I get a say in this?"

Robbie stopped and looked up, startled by my interruption. I continued, "Think about it. Ben was driving on Leesburg Pike. That's between where I live and his house. Why would he be driving there at night? I think he was trying to find me." I also began to walk around the room, as though the two of us were engaged is some desperate tango. "But until we have more information," I continued, "we can't really know what happened. We don't even know if the report is legit. If he was murdered, who knows what lies have been used to cover it up?"

Robbie rubbed his forehead as though spurring his mind to think. "When you checked your calls, were there any messages from Ben?"

"No, and it worried me. I tried to call him several times before we left and couldn't get through. I was afraid that something had already happened to him."

"If he was trying to find you, wouldn't he have called first?"

He had me there, but where would he be going if not to my place?

"Do you have access to his office? Was he working on something that may have put him in danger? What was his reputation at the Agency? Did he have any enemies?" Robbie asked.

"Now who's not waiting for an answer," I replied, the weight of the day unleashing rare sarcasm. "Ben was tough, but fair, and brutally honest. Do the right thing, but don't make waves. A Company man all the way. Ben wouldn't betray his oath to the Agency. It was his life."

"But you said he was close to retirement. Maybe he was going to blow the whistle about something after he left the CIA."

"I never said Ben was going to retire," I shot back. Then I stared at Robbie, as a new realization dawned. "You seem especially concerned about Ben's death. Why?"

He looked away. Once again, he was a stranger, with his sandy-colored hair and somber demeanor. I walked over to him and looked him in the eye. "What is it? What aren't you telling me?"

His voice was quiet and, at first, hard to hear. "Ben wasn't looking for you that night. He had some information that he was supposed to hide in the wheel well of my car."

I wanted to scream, but was speechless. Ben was going to Robbie's house? How could that be? How did they even know each other?

Robbie saw my face blanch but continued, "Since he was traveling south, my guess is that he never made it."

I remembered the conversation I overheard the day I got the assignment. Ben was telling someone that he might have something for him. Could that have been Robbie? Regaining my composure, I asked, "What kind of information?" although I knew the answer.

"He said he had information that's never been released. He wanted the truth to come out after he retired. I agreed to not use anything until he left and was safe." He watched me closely, looking for a glimmer of understanding. "You wouldn't happen to know anything about that, would you?"

"You've known all along." Now, rage replaced shock. My hands knotted into balls of flesh and bone, my knuckles threatening to burst from my skin. I was shaking. In a voice even I didn't recognize, I shouted, "I was just Plan B in case things didn't work out with Ben, is that it? Is that all I mean to you?"

"No, of course not. I love you, and the last thing I want is for you to meet the same fate as Ben. He was the contact that blew me off the night you came to my place. Now I know why. He told me he had someone taking inventory of an old Op-40 room that might contain missing evidence. Between what I saw on your computer, your grilling Trevor, and then finding out that Ben was your boss, I realized it was you. That's when I knew I needed to take you away. You are more important to me than whatever he was going to give me."

"Especially if, by winning me over, you might still get your information, is that it?" I wanted to pound him.

He pulled me to him and forced me to meet his eyes; his anger now alloyed with disappointment. "Dammit, Kat, you said you trust me. Was that a lie?"

"Trust? How can you possibly ask me that now? You played me. You're worried that I may have an accident, like Ben, and you'll never get your precious information." I turned my back to him, not wanting him to see my vulnerability.

He moved close behind me, gently resting his hands on my shoulders. "I am worried about you—the chase, the car bomb, the threats. It all scares me to death. I can't let anything happen to you."

"Or your information."

"Stop it!" he yelled. "It's not about that. I didn't tell you because this was the very thing I was afraid of. I was sure that if you knew about my arrangement with Ben you'd think I was seeing you for the same reason." He stomped toward the window.

"So, now, who's not trusting who?" I asked.

"Okay, okay, maybe I should have told you. I'm sorry. But we've only been seeing each other a few weeks. It was too soon to know how you'd react. How did I know that you wouldn't rat Ben out to the CIA? What if you decided it was best not to see me? I was hoping that by sharing everything I knew, you'd trust me. If your oath prevented you from telling me what you knew, you could put the pieces together. It's not about who reveals the truth, only that the truth gets out." Then, in a sorrowful, softer voice he delivered the kill shot. "The Kat I knew once upon a time, the one who wanted to pet bears and take on the world, would have fought for the truth."

"I'm not sure that she still exists," I said, barely aloud.

CHAPTER TWENTY-NINE

Once we turned in, neither of us could sleep. The distance between us had widened to a chasm. As we lay on our respective sides of the bed, the events of the day, everything Robbie had shared about the assassination, his relationship with Ben, and the breach of trust between us ricocheted in my brain.

The enormity of our predicament was crushing. As much as Robbie knew, he still was speculating extensively. He had expected that Ben's information would fill in the blanks. Now, unless Ben had somehow preserved the information and figured out an alternate way of getting it to Robbie before he died, I was Robbie's only hope. But all Ben had was a list. The contents of the room had most likely been destroyed.

That meant that I was the only living person who knew and could prove exactly what was in that room, and whoever killed Ben knew it too. Although I fully intended to give Robbie the information after I retired, I had to somehow create the impression within the Company that I was as trustworthy as those CIA agents who carried these secrets for years without reprisal—like my father. Otherwise, Ben's fate would be my own. But I had no idea how to do that.

And what about Robbie? He seemed trustworthy, but once upon a time so had Nate; so had my father. Was it worth getting killed so Robbie could have his Pulitzer, his truth? Didn't he understand the position he placed me in when we began to date? He had to know that I'd be suspect, given his reputation, yet he pursued our relationship anyway. If he really loved me, would he have done that? The only way I'd ever know would be to give him what I had and see if our relationship continued. That way the world would know the truth about the "big event" and I would find out my own personal truth about Robbie. Both were important to me.

Was there a way to do both? Could I somehow gain the trust of those who'd killed Ben and reveal what I knew to Robbie without getting killed? I didn't see how, certainly not at two a.m. and certainly not by myself. I had to span the gulf that now divided us. "Are you still awake?" I asked. Robbie grunted. I sat up and pulled the sheet around my chin. "I can't stand this."

"I'm listening."

"I killed a man. My boss is dead. People are trying to kill us."

"And after all that we've been through, you still don't trust me."

"What about my oath?" It was a question to myself, but Robbie pounced on it.

He jumped upright. "Are you kidding me? You and I are on the verge of destroying our relationship again, and you want to honor the oath of an agency that threatened you, that may have killed Ben, and probably helped kill Kennedy and others?" He released a disgusted moan. "Unbelievable."

"It may be the only way I'll survive. I'm expendable. I could go to jail for violating the CIA oath of secrecy, or worse. I'm as good as burned."

"May I remind you that they're trying to kill you even though you haven't said anything?"

His point found its mark. I rocked back and forth while I searched for words. "Well, you know what I've been working on. What is it you want to know?"

"What did you find?" He propped himself on an elbow. I could feel his eyes searing me.

I began to tremble and could feel my skin prickle as my face grew warm. I couldn't deny him, not now. "I don't know where to begin. There were films, photos, bullets, transcripts, autopsy reports..."

"What do you mean, 'were'?" He jostled the mattress as he sat up and moved closer to me, hanging on my every word.

"They cleared out the room. It's gone—everything."

I could hear him gasp at this last bit of news. Then he became silent as the consequences of what I said sank in. I paused, reluctant to continue. "There's something else." He took my arm gently, urging me to continue. Even so, I had to force the words from my throat. "I found his brain."

"What?" he shot back. "I mean, I believe you but...what did it look like?"

"Half of it was gone, maybe more. The front and back were both blown out. It was a mess."

He exhaled deeply. "Front and back?"

"Yeah," I answered quietly.

With resignation he asked, "So what Ben had was it?" I didn't answer right away, so he added, "Then it's over. We can't prove anything now. Dammit." He was now mere centimeters from my face. "But you know what you saw."

"And what I scanned, photographed, and kept."

His face brightened by a thousand watts. He hugged me—hard. "You have it? Where? Is it safe?"

"It's in a safety-deposit box under Carla Banks's name. I've wanted to tell you, but between my oath, my promise to Ben, and my fear for our safety, I didn't think I could. Now that Ben is gone, none of that matters."

"I could kiss you."

"I could use a kiss right now." He gently pressed his lips on mine. We didn't pull apart. All the while I was thinking that now we really were in this together, with no clue how we could extricate ourselves, let alone survive. His embrace was comforting but could not dispel my fears about our impending doom. After several moments I said, "Could I ask you one big favor?"

"Sure, what is it?"

"Put it all together for me. Tell me how you think it happened—start to finish."

He sighed with exasperation, but several moments later he began. "Everyone says it's too complicated, but it's really not if you think of it at a high level."

"Then it shouldn't take long for you to explain it."

He took a deep breath. "First, there's the 'big event' itself. It probably began with a few people griping about the Kennedys—maybe the mob bosses, Hoffa, or some of the rogue CIA agents. Once the seed was planted, it grew. Somebody like Roselli, who was an interface between the mob and the CIA, spreads the word and the underpinnings of the plot are in place. Hoover gets wind of it through his wiretaps and tells his buddy, LBJ. Johnson realizes that with Kennedy out of the way, he can avoid jail and get the power he's always craved. The thing is, he doesn't want to owe the mob, so he tells his hatchet man, Ed Clark as well as his Big Oil cronies to take care of things. Some umbrella organization like Permindex or 8F, the power mongers in Texas, enables them to coordinate roles."

"But they didn't pull the trigger," I said.

"That's the next tier. Clark gets Mac Wallace involved. The mob and the CIA recruit the other hit men."

"So where does Ruby fit in?" I asked.

"Ruby acts as a go-between. He was seen all over the place that day."

"But Ruby didn't have the kind of power to control events after Kennedy was killed."

"You're right. Big Oil ensured that certain members of the Dallas police cooperated. The government, probably the CIA, infiltrated the Secret Service. Phillips and your father, with the help of Banister and Ferrie, set up Oswald as the fall guy. That's the third tier."

I sat up and pulled my knees to my chin, still perplexed. "But what about the cover-up? With so many people involved, I don't see how they could keep it all quiet."

"Using info dug up by Hoover, LBJ blackmails Earl Warren to lead a commission comprised of people Johnson can control—none of whom are fans of Kennedy. Hoover determines what the Warren Commission sees and doesn't see. He also publishes a report citing Oswald as the lone assassin which preempts any in-depth investigation by the commission."

"But what about all those witnesses you mentioned? Why didn't they talk?"

"The mob, the CIA, and Hoover probably killed over one hundred people whose testimony contradicted the lone-assassin explanation, like our friend Joey said. They harassed peripheral witnesses until they changed their testimony. Finally, they spread disinformation to throw people like me off, sending us fishing in a pond of red herrings. It's all there, nicely compartmentalized. It's so big that it facilitates plausible denial. No one person can blow the entire operation."

"I don't know," I said, skeptically. "The press would have exposed it."

"The CIA, Big Oil, and Hoover used their influence to muzzle the press, either by ownership or by appeals based on national security."

I wrapped my arms around my chest, trying to simultaneously shield myself from an unseen horror and yet absorb it all. He had made it sound simple. Suddenly I was cold, lonely, and scared; even though the man I loved was within reach, he was a million miles away. Robbie must have sensed my vulnerability.

"Am I close?" he asked.

"I really don't know, Robbie."

"Come on, Kat. I've told you everything." His frustration returned.

"I knew they were going to clear the room, so I took as many pictures and scanned as much as I could. I didn't know what was important, so I wasn't sure what to take. I was afraid it would all be lost." I gulped reflexively. "I haven't read much of it."

He flopped on his back and groaned. I could almost hear him thinking. "Does anyone else know this?"

"No, just you." I hesitated an instant before adding, "I wanted to be sure you wanted me more than the information." He groaned again, so I continued. "That night when you came to dinner, it was all small talk until you saw Marita Lorenz on my computer. Then you became Cary Grant—smooth, funny, and attentive, inviting me to your place the very next day. What was I supposed to think?"

"I was interested from the start. I didn't know what you were working on until that night in the car when I found out Ben was your boss and nearly drove off the road. That's when it all came together."

"You had no idea before then?" I was stunned.

"When I found out you were CIA, that, coupled with seeing Marita Lorenz, made me wonder. Then, when all the crazy stuff began to happen, I grew suspicious and I began to worry about you. If you were the one doing the work for Ben, I knew you'd be in trouble."

"Why didn't you say something?"

"I could ask you the same question. If I had said something, would you have denied it?"

"Probably," I answered. "I don't know. I don't know anything right now."

He held me close and spoke softly in my ear. "Then know this. I love you." He touched my cheek and rested his hand on my chest. "The thought of anyone harming you terrifies me. You have to trust me, Kat. We have to trust each other."

We lay there, each taking comfort from the touch of the other. The only sounds were the cars in the street and the hum of the heating system. But I couldn't fall asleep, and neither could Robbie. Finally, I asked, "You still awake?" I asked.

"Yeah."

"There's something about my father's involvement that doesn't ring true."

"What do you mean?" Even in the dark, I knew his reporter's instincts were on alert, creasing his brow and crinkling his eyes.

"His initials were on the forms citing the multiple Oswalds. There were so many mistakes. My father doesn't make those kinds of mistakes."

"They had to scramble. Make things happen quickly. Oswald got his job in the book depository just three weeks before the assassination. They only had hours to incriminate him afterward."

"It doesn't jibe." I began working my hands. "I need to know more about my father. I need to know what his motivation was. I can't believe that I have spent my entire life trying to gain his respect. Can you imagine what that feels like?"

"No, but I do know one thing," he said as he held my face. "Be very careful when you do meet with him. There's no telling what he will do to find out what you know."

I pondered that as several minutes flashed, one by one, on the clock. "He may be the only one who can help us. I'm not sure, but I think he made those mistakes on purpose. Maybe Ben knew about them and thought my father would be supportive. Maybe that's why he put me on this assignment."

"You don't think it was just because Ben thought you were trustworthy and proficient?"

"There are many people he could have chosen who meet those criteria," I said dismissively and my mind kept swirling. "There's something else. I heard my father mention Atsugi. I think he was trying to tip me off."

"How so?"

"Don't know, but I'm going to check into it," I said, drained by what I had revealed and how it would change things between us. "Do you ever think there will come a day when you and I can lead a normal life? I mean, will we always be plagued by Dallas?"

"If it was just Dallas, I'd say yes, but it's not. After everything you've seen, I bet you know it too. Fifty years later, what would be the harm in acknowledging a conspiracy? The government could claim that we no longer do business that way, but as you know, I'm not convinced. The military-industrial complex is alive and well, and there's plenty of money to be made and power to be had. Dallas is just another bump on the highway to hell."

"So you're saying that we may never have a normal life together." Robbie fell onto his back. I could almost feel him searching for the right words.

"You know me well enough to know that I can't let this stuff go. If I let them silence me, what good am I to anyone? I will have betrayed myself. I can't live with that."

"I've waited a long time for you, Robbie O'Toole. I've put myself at risk for you. I've violated my oath of secrecy for you. And now, you're telling me that this is the way it will always be?"

"I hope not, but maybe. We are the last generation who was alive when JFK was killed. We have to make it right."

"So you're saying that history is more important than us."

"I'm saying that unless your desire for the truth is as strong as mine, then there is no 'us.'"

"I was such a fool to believe that this could work."

"Kat, don't." He tried to stroke my face, but I turned away. "It's just that I've spent most of my life pursuing this, and now, it's all so close. You hold the answers that I and many others have been seeking for years." We sat motionless as the clock continued its march toward morning.

"Robbie, I'm so confused. Though terrifying, it was also exciting when it was just you and me, on our own, sharing the intrigue, but now, with Ben gone..." I threw up my hands and let them fall like dirt on a grave. "I know it wasn't an accident. Who else will die? You? Me? We can't run forever."

"I agree, but if we don't stay with this, he will have died for nothing. *We* may die for nothing. We have a responsibility."

He was right. We could be killed. After a moment or two, I spoke. "They'll be looking for the two of us, travelling together. Maybe we should return separately. I'll go to my apartment, call Jermaine, get Scout, and go to work—like nothing's amiss. You do what you have to do."

"Will you give me the information when we get back?"

My gut churned. "I will give it to you. I'm just not sure how and when. I need some time to figure it all out."

He replied sharply, "We don't have time."

CHAPTER THIRTY

It was a lonely flight. Our respective trips included layovers in different cities; mine connected in Cincinnati, his in Chicago. Neither of us wanted to be coming from Dallas. I landed at BWI; he landed at Reagan. I took a Blue Van; he took a cab. It felt as if I'd been away for eons. I paused before unlocking the door of my apartment and steadied myself for what I might find inside.

I tossed my keys on the table in the foyer and looked around. Nothing seemed out of place. I walked into the living room, unable to quell the uneasy feeling inside, but found nothing unusual; papers were where I left them, books were shelved neatly, and the remote control sat on the pile of magazines as I remembered. In the bedroom, I opened drawers; my clothes were folded neatly within. I opened the closet where garments hung in the same order as always. The bed was made and the throw pillows arranged as I'd left them. Entering the bathroom, I found the towel neatly hanging; the bathmat was draped across the rim of the tub as before. I checked the second bedroom and bent down to examine the storage bins under the bed. Their contents appeared to be undisturbed. Still, something didn't seem right, but I couldn't identify what it was. Perhaps my paranoia was playing tricks on me.

As I was drinking a glass of water, I noticed that the light on my answering machine was not blinking. I had numerous messages on my cell phone. Why were there none here? I hit the message button, and there were no calls waiting. Very few people knew I was out of town. Had someone listened to them and erased them, or had none arrived? If the police were investigating the car bomb, wouldn't they get a warrant and search my place? If so, it should be obvious that they were here. Instead the place was almost too neat, even for me.

My worries flew to Scout. I went to the lobby and called Jermaine to grill him about why he'd removed my dog from the kennel. He answered promptly.

"It's about time you called," he answered. I could sense that he was trying to remain composed. "We have a lot to talk about. Will you be going back to work?"

"What about Scout? Why did you take him out of the kennel? You had no right."

"I know how much that dog means to you, and there's no way I was going to leave him in a place where others could find him. They wouldn't think twice about using him to get to you. He's fine. I'll bring him by now, if you'd like."

"Yes, please." I couldn't argue with his logic, but still felt he had overstepped his bounds. I didn't even know if he had any boundaries, and now he was coming to my home.

"I'll be there in twenty minutes."

I dialed my father's number. A sense of foreboding reduced my fingers to stubs that could only poke at the keypad.

"Where the hell have you been?" he snapped upon answering. "I've been worried sick about you." He sounded sincere.

"Father, I had to leave in a hurry. There was an incident... "

"Are you in Washington now? We need to talk."

"Yes, we do," I agreed. "Would you still like to meet for dinner?"

"Come to the house tomorrow evening. I'll have Berta fix us something."

I told him I'd be there at seven and dialed Pam's number. "Hi Pam. It's Kat. Sorry I haven't been in touch. I just got back."

"Hey there. How was the vacay with Robbie?" She proceeded to fill me in on Trevor's activities and what their children were doing. Then she asked, "Are you and Robbie free the Saturday before Christmas? Trev and I were thinking of a pre-Christmas dinner before chaos ensues."

"Hmm...that's a week from this Saturday, right? I can't believe how fast time is going by. I'll have to get back to you. Things have been... hectic." It was difficult to match her light-hearted banter, so I kept it short. She filled in the details. After we ended the call, I went back to my apartment.

Minutes later, there was a knock on the door. I dashed to answer it. When I saw Scout, I smothered him with hugs and kisses, realizing just how much I'd missed him.

"I don't mean to interrupt your reunion, but we need to talk," Jermaine whispered. "I don't trust your place. Let's go for a walk."

A public place sounded good to me, better than being alone with him in my apartment. I pulled on a jacket and locked the door. Once outside, we wended our way to the park. The sun sagged in the sky, providing light but little warmth. Brown leaves rustled beneath our feet, and the trees looked as if they could snap in two with the slightest gust. We walked briskly; it was the only way Jermaine knew, and every dozen steps, I had to trot a bit to catch up. Deep in the park, the part I seldom traveled, Jermaine broke the silence.

"I guess you're wondering about your car."

"Not just the car. I want to know about Ben. Do you know anything about that?"

"First things first. We took over the investigation. The police weren't happy about it, but they've been cooperative."

"Someone was in my apartment. Was it you?"

"What makes you say that?" he asked. I told him about my voice-mail messages.

"I checked to make sure that nothing was sabotaged," he said. "And yes, I did try to listen to your messages in case there were any more threats, but someone else beat me to it. I guess they were trying to figure out where you went."

"First you took Scout from the kennel without my permission and now this? Who the hell do you think you are?"

He turned sharply, towering over me and reinforcing my vulnerability. "Excuse me, Agent Hastings, but I'm trying to help you." He started walking again, constantly looking around and intensifying my misgivings as he did so. "I've been watching your place. I've seen a couple of men come and go. I wanted to make sure they didn't leave anything behind. By the way, whoever planted that bomb was a professional. You're lucky you had a remote ignition and used it."

"Maybe whoever did it knew I had remote ignition and was trying to scare me."

"Doubt it. Even if they knew, they couldn't be sure you'd use it. There are a lot of folks who get in their car before turning it on—whether they have remote ignition or not. No, I think the same folks who killed Mr. Douglas were trying to kill you."

"Do you have proof that Ben's death was no accident?"

"His steering mechanism was compromised—made it look like he was drunk, but here's the kicker. We think he was dead before he crashed. There would have been more blood otherwise. The tox report showed no alcohol, but did show high levels of Xyrem in his hair—a good thing they checked, because it disappears from the blood and urine within eight hours."

"Ben wouldn't have let someone drug him. He's smarter than that. What's Xyrem?"

"Xyrem is better known as the date-rape drug because it's colorless, odorless, and can be easily slipped into drinks, even water."

"But wouldn't it be obvious he was drugged? How could they claim it was alcohol related if this showed up?"

"Xyrem is a form of gamma-Hydroxybutyric acid, a substance found in the central nervous system. It's used to treat alcoholism. This made it easy to claim that Mr. Douglas was an alcoholic who went off his treatment."

I continued walking in silence as I processed this information. Eventually, I said, "He never had a chance, did he?"

"Nope, and if you don't listen to me, you won't either." He said it so matter-of-factly, but his point hit home.

"I need to get another car and find a new place to live."

"Don't get a car. They'll just try it again. Keep your current place, but rent another. Use your new identity." I stared at him. How did he know about my new identity? Noticing my incredulity, he added, "I know you better than you may know yourself, but that doesn't matter now."

His statement was unsettling, but he was right. There were more important things to consider now.

"I'll keep an eye on your place, but you'll have to go in and out occasionally to keep up appearances," he said.

"But won't it be easy for someone to follow me home from work? They can figure out where my new place is."

"Not if you follow my instructions, but that hasn't been a high priority for you." This time, his smile was forced.

"Things have a way of changing, Jermaine."

"For your sake, I hope so. How's your tough-guy boyfriend? Is he still in the picture?"

"I hope so, why?" Now he really was overstepping his bounds.

"Tell him he doesn't look so good in blond hair." I stopped short. How did he know? "Come on, I'm a professional. I wouldn't be much of a bodyguard if I couldn't figure out where you went and how you got there." He paused while I scooped up nature's call. "I think I have a pretty good idea what you've been up to, and if you don't mind me saying, the folks you're up against will do anything to keep you from blowing the whistle."

"I took an oath when I joined the CIA." I looked him squarely in the eye, trying to convince him I was telling the truth.

"So why are you seeing someone who's been investigating the assassination for so long?"

"We dated in college and I ran into him at a friend's party. He tells me a lot about his work, but that doesn't mean I've told him anything."

"Uh huh." His eyes repeatedly shifted to the right, the left, behind, and back to me.

In too strident a voice, I stated, "You don't believe me." Lying seemed an all too common response now, and I wasn't very good at it.

He turned and met my eyes. "What I believe isn't important. How are you going to convince the people who are after you?"

"I don't even know who they are. So much has happened."

"Like what?"

"I'll level with you if you do the same with me."

"I can't, and I've told you why."

"Until I know more about you, I'm not saying anything. I've got to go. By the way, I'm supposed to have dinner with my father tomorrow night."

"You better be careful, ma'am."

"It's my father, for God's sake."

Jermaine left around four, but not before he confirmed that I would be at work on Monday. Ben's death and the various incidents I'd experienced had taken their toll, and despite Jermaine's unwillingness to come clean, I was beginning to feel strangely safe around him.

I walked down to a private spot in the lobby, punched Robbie's number into my cell phone, and was relieved when he answered on the third ring. I told him about Pam's invitation. He said that Beau had already told him. I filled him in on Jermaine's advice to rent a second place, and he tersely concurred. I told him about dinner with my father, and he grudgingly agreed that I needed to confront him. "So, how were things at your place?" I asked.

He answered in a clipped voice. "Fine, nothing unusual, except Beau is still around and is planning to stay north until after the holidays. We're going out for a drink tonight."

I hated the notion of them comparing notes about me. There was too much tension between Robbie and me already; we didn't need any more. When we hung up, an ache descended upon my soul, erasing the intimacy of the past few days. Although I'd shared the secrets of the vault with him, he was angry that I wouldn't give him the evidence as soon as we returned. As wrenching as it was, however, I had a more immediate concern—dinner with my father.

I opened Greg's computer and accessed the CIA database, looking for anything that might shed some light on the methods used at Atsugi. There wasn't much; many files had been purged by Dulles years ago. But I did find a few things that might help. They had to.

CHAPTER THIRTY-ONE

The cab turned into the snaking driveway, and passed through the wrought-iron gate, anchored on either side by brick pillars. The lawns, demarcated by a repetitive refrain of white wood fencing, were free of leaves; their once-green grass now faded to the color of straw. Under other circumstances, this vista might seem downright idyllic.

I stood in front of the imposing federalist brick house, replete with floor-to-ceiling windows, three chimneys, and an oak front door, now adorned with a wreath illuminated by a floodlight. Candles poked through additional wreaths hanging in every window except for the one in the living room which displayed a brightly lit, eight-foot-tall Christmas tree, loaded with ornaments. This was obviously Berta's doing, as my father had never hung an ornament in his life. I pressed the doorbell and Berta appeared, with her arms open wide and her smile broad and welcoming.

"It's good to see you." She gave me one of her famous bear hugs, and the warmth of her embrace melted the icicles inside me. Berta took my coat and pulled me inside. "Kat's here," she bellowed. Turning to me, she said, "Your father told me to get the nicest steak I could find for your dinner tonight. He wants it to be special. I know he's a crusty old goat, but inside, I think he's missed you."

I smiled, mostly to placate Berta, and entered the kitchen. Some carrots sat on the counter. I took one and was munching when my father appeared, dressed in tan corduroy slacks, a green-and-tan tattersall shirt, and a green pullover sweater with leather patches on the sleeves, looking every bit the country squire. "Well, if it isn't the ghost of Christmas past," he said, pleased with his stab at humor. "Can I get you a drink?"

"What are you having?" I asked in a monotone.

"Talisker, but I also have some Dahlwinnie. That's a nice lady's scotch," he said. I followed him into the den while gritting my teeth.

"I'll have what you're having, with some ice on the side." I watched his every move.

"If you must. Never understand why you want to dilute a good single malt." He pulled a small snifter from the bar and poured a healthy dose. "To your health."

"Interesting you should say that, Father." I said, after sipping the strong, peaty liquid.

"And why is that? Are you ill?" His eyebrows formed little mounds above the rim of his glass.

"No, but my car suffered a mortal blow." I gazed at him, looking for any glimpse of understanding.

As usual, his face was a mask of feigned indifference. "How so?" he asked.

"It was bombed. Fortunately, I started it with the remote ignition. Otherwise, I would have been killed. That's why I left town."

This time he couldn't hide the shock on his face. "Kat! Why didn't you tell me sooner?" His reaction seemed genuine. He rose and paced back and forth, sipping scotch but not speaking until he stopped in front of me and said, "This is very serious." He pulled me close to him in a way he hadn't held me for many, many years. "I was worried that something like this would happen. It's that stupid assignment Douglas gave you. He had no business getting you involved in that mess."

"Father, Ben is dead." He pulled back, not seeming to know how to respond. It was apparent that he either knew or expected it. "So you knew about my assignment," I said in a detached voice, swirling the scotch in my glass.

"Yes, but I won't say how. I suppose you've learned some things about me along the way." He took a long sip of his drink. "Let's save this discussion until after Berta leaves, if you don't mind." He stood and walked to the tree, adjusting an ornament here and there. "So what are your plans for Christmas? Your sisters have asked if you will be joining us."

"I'm not sure yet. I guess it depends on what happens at work and if there are any more incidents. It may not be safe for me to stick around."

"I see. Have you spoken to anyone about Ben?" He gauged my eyes, my movements, looking for some hint of deceit.

"No," I lied. "Tomorrow I hope to see Ben's boss and discuss recent events with him." I said it plainly, knowing that any emotion would trigger an outburst I'd regret.

"That would be Jennings?" he stated more than asked. It amazed me how much he still knew about the Company. I nodded. "I don't know him well, but have heard he's a good man," he said.

"Your buddy Carson seemed to think so."

His eyes blazed. "So you *were* in the vault. I thought so." He poured another scotch. "We have many things to discuss. Can I give you a refill?"

I shook my head. The Talisker tasted like a bog, and no amount of ice would render it palatable. "Perhaps some wine with dinner." I saw my father's expression change just enough to indicate a fleeting thought, but once again, his impassive façade reappeared.

We exchanged small talk about the family, RG3 and the Redskins, and the continuing NSA scandals, until Berta announced that dinner was served in the dining room where two places were set—one at the end of the table and one to the side. A perfectly grilled porterhouse steak lounged on a china platter surrounded by beans, mashed potatoes and gravy, corn, and biscuits. As usual, Berta had prepared enough food to feed a platoon.

"In honor of the occasion, I brought a bottle of Opus 1 cabernet from the cellar," my father proudly proclaimed. "I think you'll like it." He poured the wine, and we were ready to dive in when Berta asked if there was anything else. My father told her that everything was fine and dismissed her for the night.

She gave me a big kiss on the cheek and whispered, "It'll go fine. His bark is worse than his bite. He loves you, even if it doesn't always feel that way." I smiled and squeezed her hand.

Mere seconds after the door shut, my father jumped in. "Tell me what you know." He speared a piece of meat and chewed it vigorously.

"You already know about my assignment. Ben asked me to find a room that had been mentioned in a document he came across. If I found the room, I was supposed to tell him what it contained. I had strict orders to confine my efforts to inventory, not analysis. I found the room, took inventory, and gave the list to Ben."

"That's it?" His skepticism was obvious.

"What are you suggesting, Father?" I took a sip of wine and swirled it around my tongue. It was smooth but bold and complemented the steak perfectly—a great choice, I had to admit.

"I know what was in that room. I put some of it there. I can't imagine anyone disciplined enough to not investigate its contents."

"Then perhaps you underestimate me. I follow orders." I took a bite of the tender filet and returned his piercing gaze. "But even in making a list, the significance of what was in there was clear. It doesn't mean I'd betray my oath of secrecy."

"Then why are you seeing O'Toole? You know he's been digging for dirt about Kennedy for years." He forcefully placed his fork on the table and tilted closer.

"We ran into each other at a friend's party. I didn't even know he was investigating the assassination until we had several dates. Just because he's interested in it doesn't mean I've told him anything. He knows I monitor the movements of suspected terrorists, but not much else. "

"Uh huh. And does he know about your car?"

"Yes. We were also chased home by some men who shot at us. Robbie thinks these incidents are because of his work, not mine."

"And he is willing to put you in harm's way? Not much of a boyfriend, if you ask me."

"I didn't." I took another sip of wine. "He's seeking the truth, Father, as are many people who've been lied to for many years. It's because of people like you that people like Robbie exist. You created them."

"I don't disagree, Kat," he said solemnly.

Involuntarily, my forkful of steak halted in midair. I had expected a defensive reaction, anger, or denial—not this.

"But please don't lump me in with the others."

"Why shouldn't I, Father? At this point, I would love to hear anything that might separate you from the ones that killed Kennedy."

"You don't know what it was like to work for Phillips, Hunt, and the others. They were zealots and got in with some thugs—people who killed government leaders all over the world. To them, Kennedy was just another bad egg. Then Johnson got involved, and the whole thing exploded." I noticed that he was clenching his knife tightly, holding it more as if he was ready to attack than eat a steak. "They left it to people like me to whitewash the whole operation, and if you judge me for anything, judge me because I was happy to do it." He threw his napkin on the table, pushed his plate away, and clasped his hands in a tight knot.

"The country couldn't have handled the knowledge that its government had killed one of its own—not with Castro and Russian missiles ninety miles away, and Khrushchev's threats driving people under their desks or into bomb shelters. If it had gotten out that the Cubans had been involved, it would have started World War III. Hundreds of millions would have died. The Russians had us by the balls and wouldn't let go."

"And that justifies a coup d'état?" I fired back.

He drained his glass. "Kennedy wanted to put the Company out of business. Phillips, Hunt, Dulles, Cabell, McCord—they all hated him. When they found kindred spirits in the mob, Johnson, the oilmen, the Cubans—well, it just all came together. Phillips delivered Oswald on a silver platter, and I helped him do it. I had to. I had a family." He stood to pour himself some more wine and spilled some on the server. "Damn. Get me a towel."

How typical, I thought. Why didn't he just wipe it up with his napkin? He was always treating me like a maid. I went to the kitchen and returned with a towel. "Here you go, Father. Tell me more about Mr. Phillips."

He snorted. "Phillips was a piece of work. Demanded total allegiance. Any dissent and you were toast. I heard him boast that he could kill more people with his typewriter than others did with their shotguns. Problem is, shotguns are for keeps; typewriters aren't, as evidenced by O'Toole's foolishness." He took a sip of his wine and assessed me. "Drink up. We have to finish this bottle. It's too good to waste. You can stay the night."

The second I took a sip, I knew something was different; slightly sweet and chemical. The time had come. All those years spent savoring wine had paid off in this one moment. His conversation with Carson outside of the vault replayed in my head. He had warned me about mind control, and I was prepared. But why had he warned me if he was trying to get information from me?

He watched me closely as I pretended to swallow. I scooped up some mashed potatoes and meat and faked a choking fit, discretely spitting the wine into my napkin and taking another sip as though I was washing the offending food down. I motioned that I was going to get some water. I ran to the kitchen and spat the wine into the sink as I filled a glass with water from the tap.

"I hate to waste good wine, washing down my food like that," I said upon my return. A moment later, I took another sip of wine, discretely wiped my mouth, and spat the wine into the napkin.

"There's plenty more. Are you all right?" His gentle bearing belied the situation.

"Just swallowed wrong." I repeated the wine-and-napkin maneuver a few more times during the subsequent conversation. When we finished our meal, I cleared the table and stuffed my napkin, now red with wine stains, into my purse. I removed a clean one from the drawer, crinkled it a bit, and placed it alongside my father's on the kitchen counter.

When I returned to the dining room, I asked, "Where were we? Oh yes, you were telling me about Mr. Phillips." The drug was supposed to take effect in a few minutes, so I spoke more slowly. "Tell me something, Father. What difference would it make now, after all these years, if the truth did come out?"

I could see he was appraising me, looking for a sign of diminished capacity. "It's a Pandora's box. One discovery would lead to another, then to another." He continued to drone on; I decided it best not to speak.

By now, the drug would be in full effect. I let my eyelids flutter, then close. I could hear the grandfather clock ticking in the hallway. I could feel his breath against my cheek. "Can you hear me, Kat?" I nodded, but said nothing. Inside I was quaking from the fear of blowing my ruse and nervous about what was to come. He left the room and several minutes later, returned with someone else.

I could hear the new person settle into the chair opposite me. He had a strong but pleasant scent. I didn't dare open my eyes. The stranger flicked my cheek and seemed satisfied with my lack of response. So that's why my father tipped me off—to fool this other man.

"She's out. Let's start," said my father. The stranger adjusted his chair as my father began asking benign questions about my age, where I lived, who I was dating, and how I liked my job. But then he asked a more personal question. "Have you slept with O'Toole?"

Instantly, I could hear the voice of The Who's, Roger Daltrey, playing in my head. "For I know that the hypnotized never lie." I had to tell the truth and did. There was a short break in the interrogation. I was certain that the two of them exchanged glances.

"Okay, let's start." My father shifted in his seat; the other man seemed to come closer. "Have you spoken to anyone about what you found?"

I nodded. My father paused, and then he rattled off several names, including Robbie, Trevor, Jermaine, and Ben. The only one I acknowledged was Ben. Hearing Trevor's name was a blow. I willed myself not to react.

"Did you find a secret compartment in the vault?" I furrowed my brow a bit, as though I was confused by the question. He repeated it, using slightly different wording. "When you were in the vault, did you find a small compartment in the back wall? I shook my head, no. Another moment passed.

"Has O'Toole figured it out?"

I shrugged.

"Did you tell him anything?"

I shook my head, no.

"Is there any record of the contents you found other than what you gave Ben Douglas?" I shook my head, no. I heard my father sigh with relief.

We sat in silence for several minutes. I didn't move. My father and the other person stood and walked to the far side of the room. "It worked," my father said. "Satisfied?" The other man must have nodded, because my father added, "You won't hurt her, right?" My father's voice sounded uncharacteristically pleading. I didn't hear an answer.

There was some rustling, as if the other man was gathering his things. My father escorted the man to the door and returned, sitting down next to me once again. "Can you hear me?" I nodded. "You will not remember our conversation. You will stay the night. Tomorrow, you will tell your boyfriend that you will not see him anymore. It's over. Do you understand me?" I nodded.

Robbie. How could I pull this one off? Then I thought about poor Scout missing his late-night walk, but there was no way around it. I had to continue the charade. My father knew who was threatening me and who had killed Ben. He had to do this to get them to stop, didn't he? In a twisted sort of way, he was trying to help me, wasn't he?

I thought my father was done, but then he spoke again. "We've had our differences over the years, but I want you to know I'm proud of you. I know you're trying to do what you think is best. That's all any parent can hope for." His voice became softer and filled with emotion. "Let's put our differences aside and start over." I shrugged. Even doped, I wasn't sure I could pull that one off.

He stood and lifted me under my arms. I tried my best to seem like dead weight as he dragged me to the den and onto the sofa. He removed my shoes, lifted my legs, and helped me lie down. He draped an afghan across me and stuffed a pillow under my head. Then he did something he hadn't done in decades. He kissed my forehead softly and turned out the light.

≪≫

"Well, lazybones, it's about time you got up," my father greeted me in a cheery voice.

"I must have had more wine than I thought. I don't even remember going to the den. What time is it?" I stretched and yawned.

"Eight. I thought you were going to work today."

"I've got to get home! Poor Scout will be ready to burst, if he hasn't already." I poured some juice into a glass and gulped it down. "What happened?"

"You consumed quite a bit of wine, dear. I couldn't let you drive. Don't you remember?"

"The last thing I remember is that steak. It was to die for." I gave my father a hug. "Thanks for having me over. We should do this more often."

"You're right. We should." He smiled warmly. "I hope you'll come for Christmas. It wouldn't be the same without you."

"Wouldn't miss it." I took a few bites of some toast. "Sorry to run. Any way I could borrow a car?"

"Oh, right. Why don't you take the Lincoln? Here are the keys and, for God's sake, use the remote ignition."

"Always do. A wise man once told me to." I winked and fled to the door. I couldn't maintain my chipper façade much longer. "Love you!" I exclaimed, as I pulled the door behind me. He seemed pleased. Was it because he thought his post-hypnotic suggestion had worked or because he was honestly happy with our exchange? Less like a truce and more like sincere emotion. Maybe both. Whatever the case, I was off the hook for now. I needed to call Robbie and tell him everything.

A thin layer of ice glazed the country roads in Gaithersburg. It wasn't until I hit the highway that it was safe enough to call Robbie. At first, I couldn't tell whether he was being aloof, was groggy, or both. When I told him about my father trying to drug me, he was angry, but then his genuine concern won out. He acknowledged that the ruse, if truly successful, bought me some time.

Given my father's attempt to dissuade me from seeing Robbie, we agreed that it might be wise to suspend visits with each other until Pam and Trevor's dinner party. Otherwise, my father would know that I had faked the hypnosis. The respite would allow me some time to find another apartment and tend to my affairs at work.

Robbie and I ended our conversation awkwardly, both expressing regret over how we'd left things in Dallas, both disappointed that we couldn't see each other until the party and, though unvoiced, both increasingly fearful of the unfolding events. Who was the mystery man that observed the hypnosis? What if my act hadn't worked? What if my father didn't really buy my act, but let the other man think it had been successful? He was an expert, and I didn't really know how people acted under chemically-induced hypnosis.

By the time I got home, took care of my woefully uncomfortable dog, showered, dressed, and left for work, my head was a morass of unanswered questions, most involving the two most important men in my life—Robbie and my father. I didn't know where I stood with either one.

CHAPTER THIRTY-TWO

A new computer sat on my desk, with a note affixed to it instructing me to call IT support. I did so and was told that someone would be coming within the next hour. Most of my voice-mail messages from the last five days were routine, but one stood out. It was from Ben, using a different alias. Hearing his voice filled me with sadness.

"Hastings, we need to meet again. There's something I haven't been completely truthful about."

Now I would never know what it was. The last message was from George Jennings, Ben's boss, telling me to call him when I returned to work. I dialed reluctantly.

"Good, you're back," he answered. "Come up to my office at once. There are some things we need to discuss." I picked up my purse and left, thinking about how I'd tell him that I was resigning from the Agency.

Jennings's administrative assistant sat outside his office. I gave her my name, and she hit a button on the console at her desk. "Agent Hastings is here to see you." Jennings told her to let me in.

When I entered, Jennings pressed his intercom and said to hold all calls. He stood, offered me a seat, and asked if I wanted some coffee or water. I politely declined and sat in a large wingback chair that faced his desk. He remained standing, placed his hands on his desk, and leaned toward me. I guessed that George Jennings was about five years my senior, like Ben. But unlike Ben, he was balding, with a slight paunch that derailed his suspenders to either side. His paisley tie was loose and fell short of his waist. His desk was awash in papers, and Post-its littered various surfaces—his computer, his phone, and his desk. On the walls were pictures of Jennings with various presidents and industry CEOs, as though one would be impressed with his connections, or perhaps intimidated.

"It's nice to finally meet you, Agent Hastings," he began in a cordial tone, taking a seat. "I know your father, a fine man. He and I go way back. In fact, your father took me under his wing when I was a rookie in the Company. How's he doing?"

That wasn't quite as my father had described it, but I let it go. "Quite well, sir. I had dinner with him last evening. I hope I'm half as spry when I get to be his age."

"Still riding those horses of his?" His pressed the tips of his fingers together and sat back in his chair.

"Every day," I replied with a faux smile on my face.

"Good for him. He deserves a life of leisure after the years he put in. Please give him my best the next time you see him."

"I will, sir." I sat quietly, but was growing impatient, waiting for him to get to the point.

"Yes, H2 is an example for us all. I understand that you are a chip off the old block—dedicated, hardworking. Ben held you in high regard." I said nothing. "It's too bad about Ben. He'll be missed around here."

"Yes, sir," I agreed. Here was my opening. "I was on vacation when I heard the news. What happened?"

"Still under investigation, I'm afraid. I'd hate to think that Ben was DWI. Maybe the job finally got to him."

"Forgive me, Mr. Jennings." He asked me to call him George. "Okay, but Ben didn't drink."

"Is that what he told you?" He fumbled with his suspenders. "You know, sometimes people fall off the wagon—especially if they're under a lot of pressure." He glowered at me. I could feel the next question before I heard it. "Do you know any reason why he might be under more pressure than usual?"

I thought a moment before answering. Might as well face it, since he probably knew anyway. It might help me gain his trust. "Ben had asked me to investigate the existence of a special room. He indicated that it was mentioned in a document under review for release under FOI. If

I found it, I was to take an inventory of its contents. I did as ordered. There was some highly sensitive material pertaining to the Kennedy assassination. I gave him my report. I don't know what he did with the information after that, but there may be a connection."

"Have you mentioned this to anyone else?" His eyes were penetrating despite his best efforts to sound jovial.

"I spoke about it with my father last evening, but no one else." The lies began anew. "Ben was adamant about confidentiality. He even took the computer I used to compile my list." I tried not to squirm.

"Did you have any contact with Ben after you supplied the report?"

"He asked me to meet him outside of work."

"And?"

"He told me to go away for a while. I'd received warnings and my car was bombed, so I left town."

"And you've said nothing about this to anyone else." He was very close now; so close I could smell the coffee on his breath.

"No, sir," I answered firmly.

"I see. Did you travel alone?" By now, the genial manner was gone. All that was missing was the naked light bulb and Gestapo uniform.

"I took a vacation with my boyfriend."

"And you've said nothing to him."

"As I mentioned," I began, trying to soften the steel edge that sharpened my voice. "I've said nothing to anyone but Ben, my father, and now, you." I straightened in my chair and returned his gaze, matching his intensity with my own. "I made a promise to Ben, and I kept it. I took an oath when I joined the Agency, and I've kept it. I do not break promises." My insides twisted as yet another lie left my lips.

"I want to believe you, but don't you agree that it's quite a coincidence that your boyfriend has ordered more than three thousand documents about the Kennedy assassination under FOI? He's provided regular updates on conspiracy websites. He's participated in more than twenty panel discussions condemning both the Warren Commission's and HSCA findings. What you saw in that room would be the mother lode to him."

I stiffened with fear. He knew. Everything. I was being tested, and failing would be disastrous to me and to Robbie. The thought made me choose my words with precision and state them firmly. "I suppose it would if I told him, but I haven't." It was time to take the offensive. "Frankly, I resent that you, or anyone for that matter, would doubt my allegiance to the Company. I've been here for thirty years, I received the Intelligence Commendation, and my loyalty has never been questioned."

He withdrew, studying me as he sat back in his chair and hooked his thumbs on his suspenders. For the moment at least, I'd passed. "There are some things you may not know about Ben Douglas," he began. "Ben was once one of my best men, but he acted irresponsibly and without authorization when he gave you that assignment. He's put you in grave danger, as you've already realized. Did you know that he submitted his resignation right after you gave him your report?" He could tell I was stunned. "We think he was going to leak everything. We're not sure who Ben's contact was, but it may have something to do with where he was going the night he died." Jennings stood and plunged his hands deep into his pockets.

There were so many things I wanted to say, so many questions to ask, but now was not the time. Jennings was on a roll. "He's not like your father, or the other dedicated agents that served their country well. I'm beginning to think that you are one of us, just like H2. You've got his spunk, I'll give you that." He chuckled, as though trying to restore a congenial tone. "These leaks, they compromise our ability to do our job. Your dad and his peers kept us safe when the communists threatened. As you, of all people, are aware, our challenges today are different but no less dangerous." He stopped in front of my chair, compelling me to raise my head and look him straight in the eye. "I want you to find out who Ben's contact was and determine whether Ben gave him your report. Not only is it important to the Agency, it's important to the country."

"I understand." Inside I really didn't. His manner changed so abruptly. Had I really convinced him of my loyalty, or was something else going on? Either way, my desire to quit my job vanished. This assignment would allow me to pursue the very thing I had hoped to do—find out more about the information from the vault and who might be linked to it, and do it all with the blessings of the Agency. "I'm happy to help in any way that I can."

"Keep me apprised of your progress. We can't let this out, not now," he said. I stood, and Jennings placed his hand on my shoulder in a paternal fashion. "Ben was right about one thing. You are a chip off the old block. Your father must be proud."

"I have a few questions," I began. "Do we know where Ben's computer is? Or my old one, for that matter? I need to speak to Ben's wife. She might be able to help. What about phone logs or e-mails? Also, may I be included in any reports that come from the investigation of his death?" I paused, hesitant to ask too much. He seemed pleased with my eagerness. Little did he know that he provided me with the means to achieve my ends.

"Ah, the wheels are already turning. Good. I'll check into it and provide you with all that I can. In the meantime, check with Ben's assistant. She may be able to point you in the right direction."

I summoned a businesslike demeanor and left the room quickly to avoid any potential slipups. At my desk, the techie was waiting. He smiled and went right to work. Once the computer was ready, I logged in and checked my e-mail.

Although many messages awaited my reply, one jumped out. It was from Ben, sent the day he died.

> Greetings, Hastings. I'm sorry that I could not say good-bye in person but by the time you read this, they will have retired me. I remember when we first met like it was only a week or so ago. It's always so good to go back in time. You should try it, and soon. Perhaps you should consider retirement as well. If you do, take up golf. It's a wonderful way to relieve the stressors of work. Go to my favorite club where a pro nicknamed "Spoon" will give you some tips on how and where to play. I'd like to leave you with some brotherly advice. First, respect your elders. I met with your father recently, and we shared a glass of wine.

Although his experiences are many and he may put you to sleep as he recounts them, the time you spend with him will be worthwhile, I'm sure. He's not getting any younger. Take some time to read, preferably something other than those mystery novels you like. My son had the right idea. He was a history major and I learned so much from reading his work. Also, be judicious in romance. The Scots are far more trustworthy than the Irish. Finally, read your Bible—even if it's in the john. There's some good stuff in there, and if you can spend eight hours a day at work, you certainly can spare thirty seconds reading the good book.

Enough preaching. It's been a pleasure working with you. You always went above and beyond the task at hand, which I admired and came to expect.

Best of luck in everything you do, Ben

I stared at the note for several minutes. Ben was trying to tell me something, but there wasn't time to decipher it now. I printed the note and stuffed it in my bag so I could study it later at home, in private. There was too much to do. I practically ran to Ben's office and though I half expected it, I was disappointed to see that it had been completely cleared out. Only his desk, chair, and empty bookshelves remained. I hoped that his personal items had been returned to his wife. While I stood there remembering our many conversations over the years, his assistant appeared by my side. She reminded me of Aunt Bee from the Andy Griffith show.

"Oh, isn't it awful? I can't believe he's gone. He was such a good man—a little demanding at times, but honest and strong." She wiped a small tear from her heavily made-up eye, smearing her cheek that was red from too much blush.

"I didn't get to say good-bye," I stated, voicing my thoughts more than in reply. "Did his wife get his personal belongings? Golf trophies, pictures?"

"I have them packed in boxes, just outside. I haven't had a chance to send them yet."

"I'd be happy to take them to her." I thought that maybe I could also look through them before doing so. "I was going to stop by and express my condolences anyway."

"Why, that's so kind of you." We left the room and I followed her as she shuffled to her desk. "By the way, I found this among his things." She handed me an envelope with my name on it, still sealed. I tore it open, only to find a piece of embossed paper with ornate scrolls and lettering that read, "Army Navy Country Club, Certificate of Appreciation." Maybe this was the favorite course that Ben had mentioned.

"Thanks. I'm not sure why he wanted me to have this, but at least it will be something to remember him by. He always said I should take up the game."

"He did enjoy his golf. I'll call maintenance to help get this stuff to your car."

She was about to leave when I asked, "What happened to his computer and files? Ben took my old computer, too. Do you know where that is?"

She turned back to face me and replied, "Oh, your computer was destroyed last week. Ben said it wasn't working and to get rid of it. I did as I was told. I hope that's okay." Remembering how Greg had said that computer searches could be traced, I could only hope that it wasn't examined first. She continued, "Some fellas from upstairs took the rest of his things. I guess with all the sensitive information he saw, they didn't want to take any chances."

"Sounds like you have everything under control," I said. She beamed through glistening eyes and quivering lips. "I'll check with the director to see if he wants me to go through them."

"Are you going to his funeral?" she asked. "It's at Arlington National Cemetery tomorrow at ten."

"Of course," I answered.

"They told me he retired. I can't believe it. He never said a word to me. I was a little hurt, to be honest, but that's just like him, isn't it? He never went in for any fanfare, and he knew I'd want to throw him a party. Now, he'll never get a party." She dabbed her eyes once more. "You know, it's strange, he's been away so much lately, and he never told me when he'd be out. Guess he started his retirement early, but that wasn't like him. Maybe they were right about him hitting the bottle, but in all my years, I never saw anything to suggest that. Something's not right. It makes me wonder...."

"Please," I cut in abruptly, "it's best if you keep your thoughts to yourself."

"I'm sorry. Don't want you to think I'm into idle gossip."

Gossip was the last thing on my mind. We didn't need another person getting mixed up in Ben's death.

CHAPTER THIRTY-THREE

Greg's glasses guided me to Falls Church and the house that Ben had once called home. The midsized ranch was painted gray; how typical of Ben—unpretentious. It sat upon a tastefully landscaped, immaculate yard, also typical. A long driveway, with a basketball hoop to one side and edged with snow reflectors, led to a three-car garage. I pulled halfway into the drive and parked by a slate walk surrounded on both sides by a perfectly groomed boxwood hedge leading toward three low steps, the porch, and a black front door with a tiny peephole. I rang the bell and was about to ring it once more when a petite, gray-haired, red-eyed woman pulled it open with effort.

"Mrs. Douglas?" I asked. "I'm Kat Hastings. We spoke on the phone."

"Please call me Martha. I've been expecting you." She managed a fractured smile and led me inside to a room whose fine décor contrasted with the well-groomed, but plain, exterior. Beautiful vases and prints abounded. Gracefully sculpted Italian furniture sat upon intricate, hand-woven rugs. We passed by the kitchen, which would have met the standards of any top-rated chef with its Sub-Zero appliances, copper pots and pans hanging from an overhead rack, ceramic tile floor, and granite counters. Like Ben, this house's plain exterior masked a complicated, high-quality interior.

"I'm so sorry for your loss. Ben meant so much to me. Is there anything I can do for you?"

She looked like a porcelain doll that would break at the slightest touch. "You're kind to ask, but we're managing. Ben's death was a shock, but there's something I need to tell you. Recently, Ben told me that he trusted you more than anyone at the Company, so you're the only one I can talk to."

I sat in silent anticipation, trying to be patient as she contemplated her next words. "You see, Ben had already sold this house. The night he died, we were supposed to meet at the airport and fly to Nevis to live. No one knew except our children. He arranged for a car to pick me up. I was to bring our tickets. Ben said that he had one last thing to take care of, but he never made it. I was waiting at the gate when I heard my name paged. My son called me with the news. This past week, Ben revised his will, closed our accounts, and submitted his resignation." Martha pulled a tissue from her sleeve and wiped her eyes. "I know the police said he'd been drinking and that's what caused the accident, but Ben didn't drink—he couldn't. He had an enzyme deficiency and if he drank, he got quite ill."

Her revelation, coupled with Jermaine's information, debunked everything Jennings and others had claimed. I wanted to hold her. She seemed so fragile. But I had to find out what she knew. "Was he in some sort of trouble?"

"I was hoping that you could tell me. He'd been acting strange. I'd never seen him so nervous, so on edge." She had twisted the tissue to shreds and now just rolled the remains repeatedly between her hands. "He said that if anything should happen, I should contact this man who would transfer all of our assets into an account for the children and me."

She stood and walked to a bookshelf and pulled out a copy of Kennedy's *Why England Slept*. "He also told me that I should contact you and give you this." I placed the book on my lap while she continued. "I don't understand what goes on at the Agency; Ben never discussed it. But if he was killed, and you were working with him, you may be in danger as well."

The last thing she needed was to worry about me. "I understand, and I appreciate your concern, but right now I'm more worried about you. Where will you go? What will you do?"

"Once I get over losing Ben," her voice cracked and her whole body shook, "I'll be all right. My boys will take care of me."

I gently took her hand. "I have Ben's personal belongings from his office in my car. Would you like me to bring them in?" I asked earnestly.

"I'll call one of the boys." She rose and tottered to the far end of the house. I could hear one of her sons rumble down the stairs. I did a double take. He looked like a thirty-year-old version of Ben—same square chin, same close-cropped hair, although his was dark brown and not gray like Ben's. He was about the same height, and he obviously kept himself fit. "This is Ben Junior. He can help."

"Thanks so much. I'll see you at the funeral tomorrow," I said as I rose to leave.

"I'm not sure that's a good idea. You need to watch out for yourself. Ben would understand."

Her words preoccupied me on the ride back. Now that I seemed to have passed the hypnosis test to the satisfaction of my father and the mystery man, and Jennings seemed satisfied that I was trustworthy, was I really still in trouble? As long as Robbie and I were discreet and my activities remained consistent with what Jennings outlined, I'd be okay. Maybe. But as soon as the thought formed in my mind, another appeared: that behavior would only placate the CIA. What if other parties were involved? Why would Ben give me this book by Kennedy? What about Ben's cryptic note, and what did it mean? So many thoughts were racing through my head, but I couldn't think about them now; I had to finish at work.

I returned to my office and listened to a message from Jennings saying that he had the police reports from Ben's accident as well as some files from Ben's computer. I was to return to his office to pick them up. Once there, he grilled me about Ben's widow. I reported that she didn't buy the DWI explanation and explained why. I mentioned Ben's preparations and concluded that he was aware of the danger he was in and had settled his affairs for his wife's benefit. I told him of their plans to leave town that night. I could tell that Jennings was pleased with my candor; however, I didn't reveal where Ben had planned to go. What I had shared seemed to be enough to earn his confidence.

"Thanks, Hastings. Keep me posted on anything else you learn. Here are the police reports—strictly RYBAT." I agreed, and then he brought out Ben's computer and explained how to access his files. "One of our

IT boys was able to hack into it. Here's the password." He handed me a slip of paper—T!G3R1; a true golfer, I thought. "I don't have time to go through these, and the fewer people who know about this, the better. Let me know what he was into, I mean, everything. You may find something about his contact there. Once again..."

"I know, RYBAT—you got it." It was going to be a busy twenty-four hours.

Back at my desk, I opened Ben's laptop. It felt strange to punch in his password, as though I was invading his privacy. Hundreds of Word documents and Excel spreadsheets appeared. How would I ever get through them all? Upon closer inspection, I noticed file names like "Color as a Theme in the Great Gatsby" or "Less is More: The Writings of Ernest Hemingway" or "Greek Culture as a Basis for Western Civilization." I clicked on one of these and saw Ben Douglas Jr.'s name on the title page of each. These were term papers written by Ben's son. This wasn't Ben's computer at all. Quickly, I called Jennings and told him. He was livid, calling Ben names that made me bristle.

"I'll double-check these files and speak to his wife at the funeral tomorrow. Maybe it was an honest slipup. He could have brought his son's laptop to work by mistake. It happens. Maybe his computer is at his house."

"It better be, or I'll yank him out of that casket and drop-kick him to hell." I realized someone was putting the screws to Jennings.

I packed Ben's computer along with my belongings, called Jermaine, and headed for home, enjoying the luxury of my father's car even though I knew the pleasure would be short-lived; Jermaine recommended that I use rentals from here on. I knew instinctively that Ben hadn't mistakenly brought the wrong computer to work. He wouldn't do that, but then why? I didn't need Ben's computer to tell me who his contact was. How long could I feign ignorance? Then there were the police reports, Ben's e-mail, and the envelope. It was going to be an interesting evening, but where to begin?

Once home, I opened Kennedy's book and noticed that a key was taped to the inside cover as a typed note fell onto my lap.

Kat - If you're reading this, it means that I am dead. If I am dead, I will no longer need the place where I had hoped that my wife and I could spend our final years in peace. It's yours. I advise you to use it because chances are that if you remain, you are at the same risk. I've placed you in considerable danger, and I am truly sorry. My wife will most likely go to live with her family in the Midwest. I've provided for her needs, so do not feel as though you should turn the property over to her—she never wanted to go to the islands. Your identity is secure. The islands are nice. Enjoy, but remember, they're watching your every move.
Ben

By the time I reached the end of the note, my hands were trembling. Ben knew he could be killed, and yet he believed it was worth the risk to deliver the information to Robbie. He wanted the truth to come out, just as Robbie did. Two men whom I admired greatly wanted the same thing. If I didn't already have enough motivation to share what I knew, this settled it. But all I'd given Ben was a list. Robbie would need more than that to prove his theory. I hoped that the answer was in Ben's e-mail. I pulled the e-mail from my bag and read it several times before dissecting it line by line, the analyst within resurrected.

Greetings, Hastings. I'm sorry that I could not say good-bye in person, but by the time you read this, they will have retired me. *He knew he was going to be killed.*

I remember when we first met like it was only a week or so ago. It's always so good to go back in time— you should try it, and soon. *We met for the first time almost thirty years ago, but he referred to a week ago. What happened a week ago? Of course, we met at the Watergate. Did he want me to go back to the*

Watergate, or was he implying that what I had worked on had something to do with Watergate? I left that one and moved on.

Perhaps you should consider retirement as well. If you do, you should take up golf. It's a wonderful way to relieve the stressors of work. Go to my favorite club where a pro nicknamed "Spoon" will give you some tips on how and where to play. *Ben's assistant gave me a certificate from the Army Navy Country Club. I had to go there and talk to someone named Spoon. Perhaps he would tell me what I needed to know.*

I'd like to leave you with some brotherly advice. First, respect your elders. I met with your father recently, and we shared a glass of wine. Although his experiences are many and he may put you to sleep as he recounts them, the time you spend with him will be worthwhile, I'm sure. He's not getting any younger. *Ben was trying to warn me about being hypnotized, but said it would be worthwhile. Did this mean that Ben thought my father was trustworthy? What about him not getting any younger—was my father at risk? Was I supposed to learn something from him before he died?*

Take some time to read, preferably something other than those mystery novels you like. My son had the right idea—he was a history major, and I learned so much from reading his work. *His son's term papers. Ben wrote this, hoping that somehow I might see the kid's computer. I needed to take another look.*

Also, be judicious in romance. The Scots are far more trustworthy than the Irish. *Ben knew about Robbie O'Toole and me; he'd said so. He must have also known about Robbie O'Toole becoming Tom MacGregor. Did Robbie tell him, or did Ben know by some other means? He said I can trust Scots. Did that mean Robbie should maintain Tom's identity? That they weren't onto Tom MacGregor? But Jermaine knew—how? If he knew, wouldn't others?*

Finally, read your Bible—even if it's in the john. There's some good stuff in there, and if you can spend eight hours a day at work, you certainly can spare thirty seconds reading the good book. *This was easy, I thought, John 8:30. I looked up the verse and read, "As he spoke these words, many believed on him." Who spoke— Johnson? Warren? But what would either have to do with Ben? I stared at the note for a while longer, but could not decipher it, so I skipped to the next section.*

Enough preaching. It's been a pleasure working with you. You always went above and beyond the task at hand, which I admired and came to expect. *He expected me to "go above and beyond." Ben must have assumed that I could not stifle my inner analyst and had gone beyond creating a list. And he put me on the assignment anyway, knowing the trouble I'd be in.*

Best of luck in everything you do, Ben. *Thanks a helluva lot, Ben. You have a lot of nerve. No, he had a lot of nerve.*

If Ben assumed that I did more than create a list, was there something in this note that was telling me what to do with it? I went back to the Bible verse, racking my brain, staring at words that made no sense, as the seconds ticked, ticked, ticked by. Seconds, hmm. Thirty seconds. Idiot. Ben wanted me to look up the thirty-second verse of John 8, not the thirtieth verse. "And ye shall know the truth, and the truth shall set you free." That was the Bible verse that Allen Dulles had inscribed in the main lobby at Langley. I guessed referring to that would be too obvious.

A wave of fear and anger, but mostly dread, crashed upon me. Ben wanted me to blow the whistle, now that he no longer could. With the clarity that comes as one climbs the steps to the gallows, I knew that somehow I would. I just wasn't sure when or how. As much as I respected Ben, I didn't want to join him now.

Next, I scanned the police reports. There wasn't a single mention of alcohol, only the GHB that Jermaine told me about. Ben died from a seizure and then brain death, not from traumatic injury. Who gave the press that message, and how did they override the police reports that indicated foul play? Why didn't the police question the story when it appeared? Maybe Robbie could find out who covered that story and who fed the misleading information. How had Jermaine known? It occurred to me that my close call and Ben's demise both resulted from sabotage to our cars—just like the deaths of many of the Kennedy witnesses. Was that a coincidence? The subterfuge was alive and well, even if Ben was not. Someone still cared tremendously about this information fifty years later, and if Robbie was right, I had a pretty good idea as to why.

I stood and began pacing my apartment. Scout's eyes followed me with each turn, each time I brushed back my hair, each time I pounded one hand into the other. Once I was calm enough, I opened Ben's computer and begin to attack his files, beginning with one labeled "Innovations of the Italian Renaissance." The first fifteen pages discussed the history of the Basilica di Santa Maria del Fiore in Florence, Italy—better known as the Duomo. I flipped through pages of timelines and milestones, a description of the competition between Lorenzo Ghiberti and Filippo Brunelleschi for the honor of completing the dome, and Brunelleschi's ingenious inventions that made the dome's construction possible.

Surely this was not what Ben had in mind. I was about to close the file in despair when the name Giancanna caught my eye, then Trafficante, then Hoffa, then Marcello, and others that followed. Ben had cut and pasted CIA files within his son's term paper. As I read further, I realized that this file summarized all of the dealings between government agencies and organized crime.

I thought to myself, if the Italian Renaissance camouflaged the Mafia, what might the Hemingway paper include? I read page upon page about how Hemingway used dialog to advance plot, with examples from *The Snows of Kilimanjaro, For Whom the Bell Tolls,* and *A Farewell to Arms.* Ben was right. I should read more. Sure enough, many pages later, the name Gerry Patrick Hemming appeared. Hemming— Hemingway. Clever, Ben. I realized that this file included information on the Intercontinental Penetration Force, or Interpen—a group comprised of anti-Castro guerrillas, funded by the CIA, who trained at No Name Key in the early sixties. But it went far beyond that. This file was over one thousand megabytes and included accounts of CIA operations well into the nineties.

There was not enough time to read all of the files, but I knew that whatever they contained was way beyond sensitive; the list I'd generated was nothing compared to this. Ben could provide my list to Jennings without raising an alarm by claiming that if the physical evidence in the vault was to be destroyed, the Company would want an inventory for its records. Was this what Ben was referring to when he said he hadn't been completely truthful about my assignment? Was I just a false flag to divert their attention?

Maybe these files were the real reason why Ben was killed, and if so, I needed to get rid of this computer as soon as possible. I could claim that I opened the documents and stopped reading because each was merely a term paper. I'd rather be accused of shoddy investigation than place myself at even greater risk, but would they believe me? Alternatively, I could tell Jennings what each document contained, further justifying his confidence in me. I got some empty flash drives and went to work.

CHAPTER THIRTY-FOUR

Ben deserved better than the raw, gray Tuesday morning of his burial. Six handsome, fully decorated marines in crisp, bright red-and-blue uniforms bore the plain oak coffin to the gravesite, followed by Ben's family and friends. I saw Jennings and gave him a brief nod. I wondered if the older man standing next to him was Carson. After the casket was lowered into the ground, final prayers were voiced, the bugler played taps, and seven guns fired three times each as a final salute. I expressed my condolences to his wife and two boys. They seemed to want nothing to do with the men from the Company in attendance. I walked from Ben's grave with head down and shoulders bowed, alone with my thoughts of Ben, my assignment, and the danger I was in. I jumped when I felt a hand on my arm. It was my father. I did not pull back, hoping to perpetuate the ruse.

"Had I known you'd be here alone, I would have offered to accompany you. I know this must be difficult," my father said. His manner was warm, his voice gentle.

"Thanks. I didn't realize you'd be here, either. It is difficult, on many levels. Although Ben and I weren't close, he was a good man." We walked several steps in silence before I added, "I'll miss his bark. He always called me Hastings; only once did he call me Kat."

"I would take that as a sign of respect." He looked back at his associates briefly and then added, "But he *did* give you that assignment and for that, I'll never forgive him."

"He did respect me. Maybe that's why he gave me the assignment." I removed a tissue from my purse and blotted my eyes. "Why are you here? I didn't think you were too fond of Ben."

"That's not true, Kat. I thought very highly of him, that is, until recently." My father stopped and watched the people still gathered at the grave. "So O'Toole's not here to support you. Not much of a boy-friend—where is he?"

I tensed at first, but then realized I had an opportunity to reinforce his assumption that the hypnosis had been successful. "I guess he's at work. I don't know." I looked at my father and saw a strange combina-tion of sympathy and inquisitiveness. "Things aren't so good between us, Father. Something inside has changed. I'm not sure why, but I don't seem to feel the way I used to. I can't explain it." I could feel his arm relax a bit.

"It's probably for the best. You'll meet someone, I'm sure." I could swear that I saw him look back to the gravesite, catch the eye of Jennings, and nod. "Do you have to go back to work, or can I take you to lunch?"

"Thanks, but I'm okay. Being away for a week has left me over-whelmed. I'll take a rain check, okay?" I gave him a weak smile and kissed him on the cheek.

"I'd like that. We should get together more often," he said.

I agreed, hugged him, and climbed into the car. He seemed genu-inely pleased. It was becoming increasingly difficult to maintain the ruse, but I had to. My life and maybe Robbie's depended on it. I waved good-bye, and as I pulled away, saw my father walk up to Jennings, ges-ture toward me, and say something. I knew it was about Robbie.

I had no intention of returning to work, at least not directly, and detoured to the Army Navy Country Club. I parked outside the pro shop, where signs indicated sales on last season's shirts, shorts, clubs, and bags. A burly, balding man wearing a blue wind shirt, embossed with the club's logo, watched TV from a chair behind a desk that was cluttered with score cards, tees, course maps, and other golf paraphernalia. I asked if someone named "Spoon" worked there.

"No one here by that name, ma'am. Maybe I can help you." I mentioned Ben's name and told him that I'd worked for him. His face fell. "Ben was a good man. I'll miss him. We golfed together many times. Wouldn't have taken him for a drinker. In all the years I knew him, I never saw him touch a drop, and now this. It's a shame, a real shame."

"I don't understand. Ben recommended that I go to his favorite club and talk to someone named 'Spoon.' I'm sure of it."

He chuckled. "Ben's favorite club was a spoon, better known as a three wood. He never mishit with that thing; his shots always went straight and far. When he hit with a driver, he'd slice. Maybe Ben was pulling your leg a bit." Pete turned off the TV and toddled to the desk. "You know, his clubs are still in back. I was going to arrange for them to be delivered to his house. Maybe one of his boys would want them."

"I'll take them, if you'd like," I replied quickly. "I'm stopping by to see his wife later on. The funeral was today, and I just want to make sure she's all right." He thanked me and left to retrieve the clubs.

I perused the room with its pictures of golfing politicos, cases with names engraved on various gold and silver cups, clothing, and clubs. Out the window, I saw long fairways, bunkers, and greens. Although it must be a beautiful course in the spring, today it seemed barren, with vacant trees sticking out from coarse, brown grass. The Washington Monument punctured the distant sky. A few diehard duffers braved the dreary cold of the day to enjoy the longer rolls on the cement-hard ground, taking occasional nips from their flasks. The pool was covered and the tennis nets removed, making me feel abandoned by the sun and its warmth.

"Here they are—custom fit," Pete said when he returned. "Bet Ben dropped a bundle on these beauties." A black canvas bag with "Ping" emblazoned on its side hung from his shoulder. It looked like a grotesque vase with clubs sprouting from its top. "Let me take these to your car." As I followed him outside, he added, "I'm going to miss the rascal. Never saw him shave strokes, curse after a bad hit, or throw a club. He was a gentleman. Please tell his wife I'm sorry."

I promised that I would and drove off, hoping that whatever Ben had alluded to would become clear, because it certainly wasn't now. Once on Columbia Pike, I pulled into a gas station and filled up. While stopped, I pulled the three wood from the bag and examined it. It felt strange to hold a club that Ben once used and enjoyed. There was so much I didn't know about him and now, never would. I pulled off the Marine-Corps-club sock. There were a few scratches on the club face, but otherwise the head was clean, as one would expect of Ben. I was about to re-cover the club when I noticed something inside the sock: a map of Nevis with an X drawn between the botanical garden and Devil's Cove. An address was scrawled in the corner.

Back at Langley, I marched to Jennings's office on the top floor of the NHB and knocked rapidly upon his door. "Do you have a minute?" I asked. He waved me in and flashed his stale smile.

"They sent Ben off in style, eh? Too bad he turned." He assumed a more serious tone. "You look like you've got something on your mind."

"I've found something you should know about. It's about Ben's computer. Remember I told you that I thought he switched it with his son's by mistake? I was wrong. Ben used his son's term papers to embed some very sensitive files. I didn't read them; there were too many. I made a list that describes the nature of the information each file contained and where it was embedded. Here." I handed him a binder which he scanned briefly and waited for his reaction, wondering if this was just another test.

"Damn. He was going to blow the whole wad." Then, as though he had forgotten I was there, added, "Have you told anyone about this?" I answered with a firm "No" and asked if he wanted me to dig further.

"No, just return Ben's computer, and I'll pass it to the boys in NCS. You're in deep enough as it is." He stabbed the air with his pen and said, "I still need you to find out who Ben's contact was. We need to be sure that Ben didn't get this to him or her." I nodded and left his office hearing a faint, "Good work, Hastings," as I left.

I closed the door and thought that if Jennings was testing me, he would be letting someone know what I'd told him. If so, I needed to know what he said. His assistant was away from her desk. I checked the surrounding area and saw no one. This was my chance. I leaped to her desk and pressed the intercom button for Jennings's office just in time to hear him say, "She's clean. She told me about everything on his computer." Silence. "I think we can trust her." Another pause. "Why not wait until she delivers the contact?" Silence again. "Of course it's O'Toole, but we need to be sure there's no one else." Silence. "You want both of them?" Silence. "Shit, she hasn't done anything wrong. It's O'Toole who's the troublemaker, not her. She's told me everything. Besides, how will you explain this to H2? He has friends, if you know what I mean."

So much for my ruse. I had heard enough. It was time to act.

I drove to the bank, praying that everything in the safety-deposit box was still there. I exhaled when I opened the box and saw every bullet, photo, and transcript. I slipped the bullet fragment from the brain into my pocket and then bagged the other items, handling them as though they would break. From there I went to the post office and picked up shipping supplies. I stopped by a Walmart and bought a tape recorder and cassette, knowing after our adventure in New Orleans that Robbie still preferred his tape recorder to more modern technology. My next and last errand was the most uncertain. Maneuvering through the late afternoon traffic, I reached the Watergate and approached the main desk, where a woman toiled over a fax machine, not noticing my presence. I shifted from one foot to the other as I tried to remember which alias Ben used here.

"Can I help you?" she asked finally.

"I hope so. I'm Carla Banks. Did a man named Tom Peyton leave something for me?"

"Hmm, I'll check." She left the desk and was gone for about five minutes before returning with a large package, wrapped in brown mailing paper, addressed to Carla Banks. "Here you go," she said as she placed the package on the desk. "I'll need you to sign, Ms. Banks."

I scrawled a capital C followed by a wavy line and a B followed by an equally unintelligible script and ran from the lobby to my car. I placed the package in the trunk. It felt like a time bomb ticking away, or maybe that was just my heart. The conversation I overheard between Jennings and some mystery person made the decision to avoid work easy.

Scout, unaccustomed to my early arrival, was euphoric to see me throw on a sweat suit and sneakers. I had a lot to process, and a run provided the perfect opportunity to do so. Besides, I needed an antidote to the fear that now consumed me. The day was bright and the fresh air invigorating. I was sure it was just what I needed. I was wrong.

I rounded the corner and immediately saw two men in suits and sunglasses walking briskly toward me. I wondered if they had followed me from the office or were waiting for me when I got home. If they followed me from the office, they would know about my stops at the bank, the post office, and the Watergate. If they'd been waiting for me to get home, then maybe there was hope. I needed help, but didn't know who I should call. Keeping an eye on the two men, I pulled out my cell phone and punched Robbie's number. No answer. The men were getting closer and I was growing more desperate—enough so that I punched Jermaine's contact number, praying that he really was one of the good guys. He answered on the first ring.

Trying my best to remain calm, I said, "Two men are trailing me. What should I do?"

"Where are you?"

"About a mile from my apartment."

"Leave your cell phone on, and run like hell. I'll find you."

I caught a break. The lights were in my favor. Scout and I sprinted across the street, hoping to get home behind locked doors. The men in black needed to wait for cars to pass before they could follow. All those years I'd spent running might now save me, but could I cover the distance before they caught up? They pushed through people on the sidewalk as if they were scything a field of wheat, precipitating a barrage of curses as people dropped their packages or fell to the ground. I wasn't going to make it; they were gaining.

Just then, Scout did something he'd never done before. He pulled free and charged the two men. My astonishment was tempered by my fear that they'd shoot him. Releasing a flurry of barks and growls, Scout lunged at one of the men and knocked him into a building. The thug's head hit the brick wall with a loud crack, leaving him dazed and immobile. He crumpled to the ground and sat motionless, his sunglasses knocked from his face and dangling from one ear, his legs splayed at an unnatural angle across the sidewalk.

Then, with teeth bared, Scout tackled the other, chomping on his leg and causing him to fall to the ground, where he lay writhing in agony. His lost his grip on the gun, and it went flying into the street. Scout shook the limp appendage back and forth like a toy. His teeth sank deeper and deeper, hitting an artery and creating a mini-geyser that spilled onto the man's slacks. No matter how hard the man pounded on my poor dog's head with his fist, Scout would not let go.

As torturous as it was, I kept running—three, four, five blocks away, stealing looks over my shoulder every few seconds. The two men weren't going anywhere. I screamed Scout's name, and only then did he release the man's leg and barrel toward me. For the first time in my life, I felt unnerved by Scout's capacity for violence. This wasn't the dog I knew.

I entered my apartment long enough to grab keys and my purse. Scout, his muzzle reddened by blood, raced with me to the parking garage and my father's car with its precious cargo. I called Martha Douglas. It was a rotten thing to do right after his funeral, but I could think of nothing else. I flew to her house.

On the way, Jermaine called. "Where the hell are you? Are you all right?"

"I'm fine, thanks to Scout. He saved my life.

I heard a sigh of relief on the other end. "He's a good student."

"What do you mean?"

"I told you I took him from the kennel. While he was with me, I had a chance to teach him a few tricks." I didn't know whether to be irritated or relieved; I was speechless. He added, "Someone's got to take care of you if you won't let me do it."

"I don't know what to say. Thank you." Another vote in his favor. He really *was* on my side.

"Where are you off to now?" he asked.

"There's one last errand I have to do, and even though Scout took care of those guys, there might be others."

"Call me when you're on your way home."

Martha Douglas stood at the door, holding it open as I carried the box up the walk. She led me inside to the study where Ben's personal effects from the office now sat. I placed the box at the bottom of the pile.

"When are you moving?" I asked. She said in about a week. "I hope to be back to pick this up before then. There are several things I must do first. If I don't make it back, please send the box to the address on top." I gave her an extended hug. "Your husband was an honorable man, Martha. I'm sorry to put you in this position, but I had nowhere else to go. Thanks for doing this."

"Please be careful. My husband died doing what he thought was right. I don't want to see you suffer the same fate."

"Me neither." I ran back out to the car, and when I was five miles away from her house, I called Jermaine.

"I need to go back to Langley. I have a friend there who might be able to help me."

"I'll meet you at the gate in half an hour."

There was no room for argument.

I tore into the drive and flashed my ID to the guard. Jermaine's Hummer was parked just inside the gate. He jumped out as soon as he saw me and climbed into my car, turning to see Scout's bloodied muzzle. As I continued up to OHB, Jermaine removed a handkerchief and wiped the dog clean. "Good boy. Let's get this mess off you."

I yanked the wheel and turned into the nearest parking space, eliciting a tiny squeal from the brakes.

"Try to calm down, okay? We don't need to attract any attention," he said.

Easier said than done, I thought. I took a deep breath and stared ahead. He was right. We left the car and walked casually into the building to Greg's workshop. It was after normal work hours, but Greg didn't work normal hours. The lights were on, and I heard the Eagles singing on Greg's iPad, but no one answered my knock. I turned the knob, bewildered to find it unlocked, and stepped inside; Jermaine remained outside, checking the hallway.

I saw Greg right away, slumped over his desk. His head lay in a pool of blood, next to a gun still in his right hand. My hand shot to my mouth to stifle the scream that begged release from my throat. Jermaine came charging in and stopped suddenly when he saw Greg's lifeless body. He gently held my heaving shoulders and pulled me to a chair, helping me down into the seat.

"He was my best friend in the Company. We've known each other since the beginning. Why, Jermaine? Why?" I couldn't staunch the tears which now flowed freely. Snapshots of our years together flashed through my brain—laughing over coffee, the odd phone call out of the blue, his joy and enthusiasm about his work, attending the weddings of his children. This would shatter them. Shock and despair glued me to my seat.

Jermaine handed me a tissue and walked to Greg's desk. He examined Greg's computer—the one that held Greg's confidential project. "There's something you should see," he said.

I rose slowly and walked to the console. There, on the monitor, was a list of all the websites I had visited on my previous computer. While he was still the CIA director, David Petraeus said that one day, the Agency would be able to monitor the actions of any person of interest by accessing his or her computer and computer-operated appliances. This must have been Greg's secret project. He'd made it happen, just like all the other ideas he brought to life.

But Greg wouldn't spy on me, not unless someone forced him to. I was guessing Jennings. Now he knew what I had been up to. I walked away, unable to look at Greg or his computer. Jermaine came to my side. "You okay?"

"I will be. Just give me a minute." I dropped my head into my hands, sure that I was the reason Greg was dead. "He wouldn't kill himself. He was too full of life. He loved his family, his job."

"I don't mean to be insensitive, but it sure looks like a suicide. Could he have found out something about you? Something that might have sent him off the deep end?" He said it gently, but it still stung.

I thought of Ben and now Greg. This assignment was taking too big a toll. Then I thought of all the people involved with the assassination who had died as a result of what they saw and what they were willing to testify to. That's when I thought of Pitzer, the autopsy photographer who was found dead with a gun by his side. I sprang back to the desk. "Greg was left-handed, Jermaine. He wouldn't have shot himself with his right hand."

"Are you sure?"

"I've known him from my first day on the job. I'm positive." I supported myself on a counter and thought about next steps. "We need to get out of here without leaving any trace. But first, do you have gloves?"

He pulled a pair of driving gloves from his pocket and handed them to me. I put them on as I walked to the bench where I had seen the sheet of sarin-coated fingernails. I placed them inside my pocket.

"Let's get out of here. Someone's bound to be by soon."

I took one last look at the room and Greg, my friend. If they were willing to burn a genius like him, I was toast. "Yeah, let's go."

We checked the hallways before exiting, and fortunately, no one was around. We walked quickly through the building. I nodded to the one or two people we passed on our way out, but once in the car, my defenses crumbled. Jermaine allowed me my silence as I drove to the gate to drop him off.

"I can take you home, if you'd like."

"Thanks, but I'll be okay. I think." Right. I was visibly shaking and scared to death.

"They'll look at the surveillance tapes. They'll know we were here," he observed quietly.

"I thought of that. I don't have much time." I stared straight ahead, but added in a robotic monotone, "I've got to get out of town before I end up like Ben and Greg."

"Good idea. Where are you going now?"

"I guess my apartment. There are a few things I need to clear up in case I do leave."

"I'll follow you home."

I didn't protest.

CHAPTER THIRTY-FIVE

I called Robbie and told him what Jennings had said, about the two men who chased me, and how Scout attacked them. When I got to the part about Greg, I broke down. "Robbie, we have to get away. They're going to kill us." There was silence on the other end. "Robbie, are you still there?" I asked, unable to keep the panic from my voice.

"Yeah, I'm here. I'm thinking. You sure you want me to go with you? I mean..."

"I know things didn't end so well in Dallas, but," I bit my lip. "I need you."

"Where are you now?"

I told him that I was in the lobby of my apartment building. He said he needed to make a couple of calls and would contact me as soon as he could. Back in my apartment, I took a mental inventory of what must be done and who might be after us. I packed a bag. Whatever plan Robbie devised, I needed to be ready *and* have a plan of my own.

True to his word, he called back about an hour later. I could tell that he was trying to remain calm for me. "I'll pick you up in an hour. It's time we got back to the garden."

Not having a clue what he meant, I called Jermaine and told him I was leaving. He asked where I was going, but I told him that I didn't know and promised to leave my cell phone on.

When Robbie finally arrived, he embraced me with a combination of urgency and tenderness. Fear carved deep lines in his brow. His eyes were large and dark.

Robbie, Scout, and I were on the road in minutes. I constantly shifted in my seat while looking at our surroundings and people on the street who might be watching our escape. I was sure that a Buick was following us until it turned off. I thought a white truck was following abnormally close until I saw a man texting at the wheel. It wasn't until we hit I-270 that my breathing returned to normal.

"So, where are we going?" I asked.

In answer, Robbie hit the button on the CD player, and the mechanical electric-guitar riff wailed the first notes. "I came upon a child of God. He was walking along the road. And I asked him, where are you going? And this he told me..." At the chorus, Robbie chimed in, "We are stardust, we are golden, and we've got to get ourselves back to the garden."

"Woodstock? Really? In the middle of winter?"

"You got a better idea?" His laugh sounded hollow. "Tom lives in a Hasidic community near Bethel, New York. We can hide out at his place."

"I thought Tom was dead." Robbie shook his head sadly. I continued, "I don't know. It seems so isolated. I was thinking that maybe we should go to New York City. It might be easier to get lost in a crowd, and if we had to leave, there would be more flights out."

"We have no contacts there. Tom has a lot of friends—people who would do anything for him. Besides, don't you think they'd expect us to go to a place like New York? You didn't guess Woodstock; why would they?" He paused a moment before adding, "I think this is best, trust me."

There was that word again—trust. I had no choice but to trust Robbie. Seeking something, anything, to dissipate the tension within, I said, "I remember you telling me about the time you went to Woodstock. I need to calm down. Tell me again."

A serene smile unclamped his jaw. He joked that if you remember Woodstock, you couldn't have been there. "It was amazing, Kat. My parents were at a family funeral, so my older brother and I decided to go. We'd get back before they got home. We brought lots of peanut butter and jelly, bread, a tarp, a couple of blankets, and some cases of beer. Man, we had no idea what we were getting into—the rain, the mud, the drugs, the music. I never saw so many naked people in my life. It was incredible."

He told me how they hunkered beneath the tarp when the skies opened up and how all these people offered to trade a joint for the tarp. He said they could have made a fortune selling PB&J sandwiches when the food ran out, and beer when the water ran out. He woke to Jimi Hendrix playing the Star-Spangled Banner and sang along with Country Joe and the Fish when they crooned the Vietnam Rag. "It was the first time I heard Crosby, Stills, and Nash," he said. "Love at first listen."

I reflected on how different Robbie's description was from that of my father's. "A bunch of dirty hippies wreaking havoc on the poor town, urinating on their property, running naked in their ponds, no regard for others."

We turned onto 15 North and rode through the Maryland night. Robbie continued, "I still can't believe that half a million people, drenched with rain, sleeping out in the open, hungry and exhausted, managed to get along so well—no fights, at least none that I saw, no bitching about the conditions. We went from baby boomers to the Woodstock generation, galvanized and ready to take on *The Man*."

"What about it stays with you the most?" I asked, grateful for a normal conversation.

He thought for a moment. "Meeting Tom MacGregor. He changed my life."

"How?" I asked. Although I had heard many of Robbie's Woodstock stories when we were in college, this was the first time he mentioned that Tom was there.

He described how he and his brother claimed their bit of turf near a stand of trees that provided shelter from the elements and provided some privacy when nature called. Tom and some friends sat next to them. "Tom left the priesthood right after the Catonsville Nine made some homemade napalm and used it to destroy draft records in Catonsville, Maryland."

"So you took to him because he protested the war?" I asked. "Wasn't that the norm in those days? You could have become friends with half a million people at Woodstock based on that."

"No, that wasn't it." Robbie turned down the music. "There was this kid. He had a low draft number, guaranteeing he'd be called up soon. He had already lost a brother and was scared shitless about going to Nam. He was freaking out on drugs. He said he'd rather die on Yasgur's Farm than in some rice paddy. Tom got him to the medical tent and stayed with him all night—missed Janis Joplin, Sly and the Family Stone, and the Who. By the time he got back, Jefferson Airplane was belting out "White Rabbit."

"Sounds like quite a guy."

"Tom lives his beliefs. He cares for others. He fights for what is right, the truth." Robbie placed his hand on mine. "It's why I became a reporter. I want to find that same truth."

We drove further into the night. Robbie hummed a few songs here and there. I fiddled with the zipper on my parka, unable to take my mind off our situation. I needed to think of Plan B if Robbie's return to the garden proved fruitless.

By the time we passed the exit for Newark, I couldn't take the silence anymore and said, "I remember when we were at school and you came running into my dorm room, screaming that you got a high draft number. We went out for a beer to celebrate."

Robbie gripped the steering wheel tightly. I wondered if he was trying to erase his survivor's guilt.

"Would you have gone if you were called?" I asked, trying to keep the dialog going.

"I've asked myself that same question a million times." He sighed. "I guess I would have then, but knowing what I do now, maybe not. I might have gone to Canada, but I had too much to stay for—like you, for example." I took his hand and held it as we crossed into New York at midnight. When signs on the businesses we passed read Goldberg, Steinberg, and Levi, I knew we were close.

"Why did Tom pick a Hasidic community for his home?"

"He didn't. It picked him. He was a hippie who stayed behind, and the Hasidic community grew up around him. No one bothers him or looks for him here."

"Why would someone look for Tom?" I glanced nervously at Robbie and wondered whether we were trading one crisis for another.

"After he escaped the Catonsville incident, he was jailed for protesting at the convention in Chicago. His actions are more low key now, but he's still at it," Robbie said, beaming.

"I can't wait to meet him," I said, thinking that my father would have written Tom off as another wacko.

"He won't be there. It's probably better; I wouldn't want to put anyone else in danger."

"Is it safe?" I asked, feeling the muscles in my back contract.

"Is anywhere?"

We pulled into an easy-to-miss driveway and saw a small house with a large stack of wood outside. The house sat alone, surrounded by woods on three sides. Though the sky was dark, the moon shone brightly, illuminating our path and guiding our steps as we trudged through the foot-deep snow. Robbie dug behind the shutter, pulled out a key, and opened the back door.

We entered a kitchen that looked like something out of Colonial Williamsburg—large cast-iron pans hung from hooks near an open fireplace. A large drain board slanted toward a metal sink with a water pump to one side. The floor was made of wide, pine planks that creaked with each step. Robbie lit a candle.

"Tom's completely self-sufficient. Raises his own vegetables, cans them, and lives all year long off of them. No fossil fuel, just wood, sun, and lots of blankets." Admiration continued to color Robbie's voice.

"You sure know how to impress a lady," I chided, poking around and trying to imagine what the next few days would be like living here. Beautiful photographs of Yosemite, the Tetons, and Big Sur hung on the walls with framed news clippings interspersed. I looked at one about the Chicago convention, accompanied by a picture of a man being shoved into a police car. Based on the license that Robbie was now using, I guessed that it was Tom. Carved wood figurines sat on handmade furniture crafted from tree limbs, some still with bark, all made by Tom. "Not even a phone or a computer?" I asked.

"He's got a laptop and cell phone. Uses a generator to keep them charged." Robbie must have seen some skepticism on my face and quickly added, "It will be fun—just you and me, roughing it out here in the woods." He wrapped his arms around my waist, squeezing the air from my Michelin Man parka.

We explored the tiny confines a bit more, reading some of the clippings, and checking for more candles until we realized that dawn was just a few hours away. Robbie led the way through the house to the stairs. A lift sat in a groove on the left-hand side. A pair of crutches was propped against the wall. Upstairs we found a large fluffy bed and dove inside.

We sat at the breakfast table, sipping coffee and discussing our plans for the day. Now that we were safe, or at least had convinced ourselves that we were, it was time to come clean.

"You're kind of quiet. What's on your mind?" Robbie asked.

In answer, I pulled on a glove and reached into my pocket. Wordlessly, I pulled out the bullet fragment and placed it on the table between us.

The pupils of Robbie's eyes doubled in size as he looked down at the bullet, up at me, and back to the bullet. He couldn't speak.

"It was in his brain."

He continued to stare at the fragment.

"It's kind of beat up, but I was thinking that if we could determine its caliber, you would know whether it was from the prototype XP-100 or something else. You might even be able to trace it to Files directly if there are any prints left."

If I had handed him the keys to a Maserati, his face couldn't have been brighter. "This could link the government to the assassination. Kat, you've given me the smoking gun."

The impact of his words blew through me. I stood in stoned silence, unable to speak.

"Did you hear what I said?" he asked.

I could only nod.

While still staring at the fragment, he began reciting facts as though he had hit "play" on some internal tape recorder. "It was called the triple deuce/triple two/treble two. It was introduced in 1950 and had 50 percent more power than other bullets at the time. The whole bullet was 2.13 inches long so you've got about a fifth of the bullet here, but importantly, you have the base. We can determine the caliber from that."

"But how? We're in the middle of nowhere."

"Did you take a picture of, uh, the brain with this in it?" he asked, disregarding my question.

"I took a lot of pictures, but yes, I think I have it. I didn't see the fragment until I started snapping pictures, so I'm sure I do."

"Then we can make the connection between this and the brain. That's important."

He stood and walked to the window, as though he was steeling himself to ask the next question. I stepped behind him, wrapping my arms around his waist. "Robbie, you don't have to ask. It's yours."

He turned to me and gently caressed my chin with his hands. His kiss was as soft as a feather floating across my face. "Thank you—not just for the bullet, but for finally trusting me."

He told me that he knew a discrete ballistics expert in Virginia who could help him determine the caliber. He promised to keep the fragment safe and untouched. I admitted that I was glad to be rid of it, but regretted that he now bore the weight of its significance. He didn't seem to mind. I guessed after a lifetime of searching for the answer and knowing that it might finally be within reach, the extra weight paled next to that of his quest. Now I was ready for an answer of my own. With this vital link in hand, would Robbie still want me?

The answer evolved over the next week or so. Memories of Washington, the Company, and Ben's assignment faded each time that Robbie hauled wood inside to build a fire, we read by candlelight, or sometimes just held each other close. I fixed breakfasts and lunches, but we both worked side by side on dinners. I found myself whistling *Our House* on more than one occasion. We walked Scout down country roads since the snow made it impossible to run.

Still, every day I checked for new tire tracks or footprints in the snow on the driveway. I repeatedly looked out the window for a strange car or a person on the street who seemed to pause too long when passing the house. When we went to town to purchase food, drink, and newspapers, I scanned the faces of everyone on the street. I checked in with Jermaine regularly, knowing all too well that outside our rustic hideaway, the real world waited, ready to pounce.

After a week, cabin fever set in, so I asked Robbie to take me to Yasgur's Farm—where it had all happened. We drove on 104 and when we turned onto 17B, Robbie pointed to a spot on the side of the road where he and his brother had left their car and walked to the concert. After turning onto Hurd Road, we saw a wood, stone, and glass structure, the Woodstock Museum. We'd catch that some other time, as an unseen force drew us to the field.

First we saw the commemorative marker. At its top was the familiar logo—a dove on the neck of a guitar. Below was the inscription: "This is the original site of the Woodstock Music and Arts Fair held on August 15, 16, and 17, 1969."

We gazed out to the pristine, snow-blanketed expanse surrounded by a wood fence and trees. Robbie pointed out where he and his brother sat, to the left, halfway up the hill. Then he showed me where the stage stood and indicated the site of the performers' pavilion and the bridge they used to reach the stage. Looking to the other side, he showed me where Wavy Gravy ran a food tent. "Breakfast in bed for four hundred thousand people," he laughed.

In a dreamy voice, he continued, "It's hard to imagine what it was like on a day like today, but try to picture this area covered with half a million people," he waved his arm from left to right. "First, the sun beat down and we tried to cool off. Then the rains came. Speakers shorted, guitars didn't work, everything got delayed, and then it rained some more. This entire field was one big mud bath. Mud was everywhere—my clothes, my face, my hair, my food. At some point, I just stopped caring about it and enjoyed the music and everyone around me."

He gazed at the broad meadow and then turned to me saying, "I know that our generation was shaped by many influences—the war, the music, whatever, but for me, Woodstock had the biggest impact. It's funny, but while I was here, I didn't realize how special it was. It didn't hit me until much later." I wasn't sure when he stopped talking to me and was merely reminiscing out loud. "We left thinking that we really could make a difference."

I rubbed his back with my gloved hand and said that I wanted to walk in the field, in hopes that latent spirits would help me feel what it had been like. We plodded through the snow with Scout running ahead, our arms draped over each other's shoulders.

We came to a rock and sat quietly, as though on hallowed ground, as I tried to imagine the event. I was taken aback when Robbie spoke. "That talk we had in Dallas has bothered me a lot. You do whatever you need to do. You are more important to me than anything Ben could have told me." He looked at me with eyes like those of a Huskie—clear, blue, and pure.

Those were the words I needed to hear. "I'm a better person with you, Robbie. You make me care about the world around me; you woke me up." I removed my glove and brushed his face. "I've thought about Dallas a lot, too. I don't know what Ben told you, but there's more than you may know. I've arranged for you to receive everything: physical evidence, photos, Ben's files. You should get a package in a week or two. I'll be retired by then." I bent toward him and kissed him. "I love you. I never stopped loving you, not even when I married Nate. I'm so sorry." There was not a sound—no wind in the trees, no birds in the air, no cars on the road, just us.

He kneeled down, tugged off a glove, and dug into his pocket, pulling out the ring I'd last seen thirty-five years ago. "I don't know what made me keep this all this time, but it's still good, I guess. Kat Hastings, will you marry me?" He slid the ring onto my waiting finger.

I was speechless. We were on the run. People were trying to kill us. We had only been seeing each other for three weeks. It was so unexpected, so impetuous, so Robbie.

But then a whistling sound passed to the right of my head. I felt something rip through my puffy parka and disappear. We heard a muffled splat in the snow and then another and another. Bullets.

Reflexes honed by decades-old training kicked in, and I pulled Robbie behind the rock while I scanned the vacant field, trying to locate our pursuers. A bullet grazed Robbie's cheek, and blood trickled down along his scar. "Follow me!" I yelled as I bolted, zigging and zagging toward the trees, knowing that running in a straight line would make us easy targets. Scout ran ahead, barking as if to say "Hurry up!"

Robbie yelled that he knew a shortcut to the car, and despite the fire now scorching my lungs, I kept up as he turned one way and then another. We slid, we fell, and rose again, leaping over stones, climbing over fences, and ducking under branches. My daily runs had saved me yet again.

Although it seemed to take forever, we found the car, jumped in, and roared out of the parking lot onto Hurd Road, fishtailing on its icy surface and skidding around the corners. I looked back, but could see no one, and hoped that whoever was after us had to backtrack to their own car which would give us some breathing room.

Robbie snatched his cell phone and punched a contact. "They found us. Where should we go?" he hollered as blood dripped from his cheek. While he listened to a voice on the other end, I wondered who knew we were there besides Tom...and how. He spoke again. "Yep, okay. Got it."

Neither of us said a word as Robbie maneuvered down the country roads of Bethel. It was only when we veered into the parking lot of Sullivan County airport that I realized what was happening. The brakes squealed, and the car skidded to a halt. Robbie sprang from the car and ran into the building. By the time Scout and I reached him, he was at the counter, talking to a man who was pointing to a door and looking at his watch. Robbie turned to me and took me by the arms. His eyes said more than his words ever could. "Listen to me, Kat. There's no time for debate. This guy will fly you and Scout to DC. You need to go. Now."

"What about you?" I wiped his bloodied cheek. I didn't want to leave him. Not now, not with so much at stake.

"I'll be a decoy. They'll be looking for my car. Tom will take care of me; he always has." Robbie clutched my arms, locking his eyes onto mine. "You've spent your career trying to make the country safe. Now, make it honest."

He kissed me and was gone.

CHAPTER THIRTY-SIX

I don't remember the flight back, only that I spent most of it imagining the worst and wondering if I would ever see Robbie again. If I hadn't pulled him close, would the bullet have killed him? Had he connected with Tom? Was Tom able to get him to safety? How had they found us? What about the fragment? I never even answered his proposal.

I called Jermaine and endured the usual lecture before telling him what had happened. Robbie told me to leave DC, and he would find me. It was time to follow his and Ben's advice. I called the number Ben gave me. A disembodied, but seemingly familiar voice answered and told me that the earliest he could fly me to Nevis was Monday. It was now Friday. Three days. I had to survive three more days. The voice told me where and when to meet him. I would be there.

I spent a long night reviewing what I needed to do before bidding my current life good-bye. I thought about all the people I wanted to see one last time. Scout's walk was brief and confined to the sidewalk surrounding my building. He seemed to understand. Now for the hard part. Eight a.m. found me on the beltway. Three Dog Night was singing "One is the Loneliest Number." I changed the station.

The serpentine driveway now seemed all too short, the house more imposing, and the air as thin as that on a Himalayan slope. I steeled myself for the conversation ahead, to make the request I'd sworn I'd never make. I needed my father's help.

He opened the door, not Berta. "I was hoping you'd stop by," he said tenderly, as his kissed my forehead.

"Father, I'm in trouble."

"I know, I know." He stepped aside and looked out at the road, checking one way and then the other. "Come in." He gently took my arm and led me into his study. "Some scotch?" It was too early in the day, and I had much to do. There would be no more hypnotics, no dulled brain. I shook my head no. He poured himself a glass and took a swallow, his hands shaking as he raised the glass to his lips. I told him about the men who'd come after me and Jennings's conversation. "Don't say I didn't warn you. You wanted to play with the big boys, and now... "

"Father, I did as I was told."

"Did you?" He looked at me with disdain and disappointment. "My understanding is that you overstepped your bounds." Despite my best attempts, my face betrayed me. "Oh yes, Kat, computer experts know when files have been erased. You were one busy little girl. The question now is, where are those files? What have you done with them? More importantly, what do you plan to do with them? Are you going to give them to O'Toole?"

"Father, I told you I haven't said anything to anyone."

He slammed his glass down, spilling scotch on the table. "Dammit, Kat! I know that you were faking it that night. You were no more hypnotized than I was, but you fooled the one person you needed to and that was all that mattered to me. You even treated me differently, and it felt good—even if you were faking that as well. But no, you couldn't mind your own business. You had to dig deeper. You couldn't accept that there are powers beyond our control. How could you be so naïve?"

"How could you be so willing to play along with them? They don't have to dirty their hands. They have people like you to do it for them."

"In my day, you followed orders. You didn't question things. The good of the country was more important than any individual—even Kennedy. We did everything we could to protect your generation, and what thanks did we get? Rebellion, chaos, thumbing your noses at our most hallowed institutions. The last thing this country needs is to know the truth of what happened that day." His words were hard and hollow, but like the bullets at Woodstock, they missed their mark.

"It's not just that day, Father, and you know it. They got away with it once, so they continued again and again and again. You blindly accepted all of it. You helped them perpetuate their evil, and did everything to eliminate those who could, and would, expose the truth." The pain and fear of the past twenty-four hours took over. I was screaming. Every pore in my body was angry. Every hair on my head was on end.

"Did I?" he turned his back and walked toward the window. "Surely in your investigation, you found some, uh, discrepancies."

"More than a few—the X rays, the autopsy report, the multiple Oswalds." I took a breath to calm myself. This was the moment of truth. "I know that it was you who created the Oswalds. You had them in two places at once. You had an Oswald test-drive a car when the real one didn't drive. You had an Oswald in Mexico City when the real Oswald was at the book depository. You had one Oswald catch a bus while another was jumping in a car after the assassination." He turned to me, his face contorted by some inner pain, as if he wasn't sure how to continue. "You did it on purpose, didn't you?"

"Among other things."

"It was the gun, wasn't it? You planted the gun."

In a limp voice, tired and drained of any affect, he answered, "I thought that no law enforcement agent in his right mind would expect a trained assassin to use a piece of junk like the Mannlicher-Carcano. Kennedy's wounds were from a high-velocity rifle; the Carcano, at best, is a medium-velocity rifle. The shells I placed on the floor were from bullets with full metal jackets. They don't explode on impact like the bullet that entered Kennedy's brain."

"So they might explain Kennedy's neck wound and Connelly's wounds, but not the head shot," I said, thinking out loud.

"Exactly." He took a large gulp of his drink. "No one questioned any of it, or if they did, they were eliminated."

"But why did you do it?"

"I thought those fools on the Warren Commission would figure it out. Problem was, they never saw the information. The Secret Service, the Company, and Hoover kept it from them. Maybe they ignored some evidence intentionally, but they made sure the American people knew about Oswald and Mexico. They made sure that everyone thought Oswald was a communist. It was so easy to blame the reds for everything back then." His shoulders looked like a hanger holding too much weight. His face was gray, and his eyes lifeless. "The only one who knew what I did was Ben Douglas. That's why he put you on the assignment. Maybe he thought I'd understand what he was trying to do."

"If you wanted it all to come out, why didn't you blow the whistle?" The anger I had felt mere moments ago was displaced by confusion. I wanted so badly to understand this man.

"I had a family, Kat. A family I loved very much and wanted to protect. You've seen how many they were willing to kill. I would have been just one more hit." He walked to me and placed his hand on my arm. "I don't expect you to understand; you've hated me for far too long."

"It wasn't hate," I said, wringing my hands and turning away. "It was hurt. Nothing I did was ever good enough. Nothing I wanted was important enough. I'm fifty-nine years old, and you still think of me as a child." I looked down, realizing that we were finally being honest with each other, as time was running out.

"Why did you come here, Kat? For one last jab? To throw one last tantrum?"

"I need your help." He kissed the top of my head and brushed my hair from my face.

"My beautiful daughter. I wish I could take your place." I looked up at him and saw the tears welling in his eyes before he looked away, embarrassed. He walked over to the bar, finished what was left of the scotch in his glass, and poured another. "They're onto you. I can't protect you anymore."

"You *can* help me, Father. Who is after me? Tell me what I should do."

"Stay here. Tell me what you've done with the files. Tell me where O'Toole is. If we give them that information, maybe they'll let you alone." Desperation crept into his voice.

"Who are they, Father?"

"The shadow government. The one that's really in control." He took another swig. "Don't fool yourself, Kat. It's not about ideology. It's about greed, greed for money and power. Always has been; always will be. We're just the chess pieces that they manipulate and knock off at will." He seemed defeated and small.

"Only if you're willing to play their game," I replied. He looked at me impatiently.

"Like it or not, their game is as American as the Founding Fathers, the Declaration of Independence, motherhood and apple pie. You can't have one without the other, and anyone who thinks so is a fool. The irony is that the same greed that allows you to live a life of relative comfort also gives you the luxury to question things, up to a point. It allows protests, up to a point. You and O'Toole are blind to what that point is."

"Freedom with strings attached, is that it?" My sorrow was dissolving in a tide of reemerging anger.

He turned away and gazed out the window. "John Hancock was all for dumping the tea from England into Boston Harbor, and people called him a patriot. Missing from the history books is all the Dutch tea he had, waiting in the wings, from which he would make a fortune. The Kennedys got their money from bootlegging during Prohibition, yet people knighted JFK's presidency 'Camelot.' The Bushes got rich selling arms to Germany before World War II, and still people rallied behind Bush Senior's thousand points of light. We are so desperate for an inspirational leader that we ignore the concessions they make along the way, and then we become indignant when their indiscretions are exposed."

"Your generation handed us the world's most powerful democracy, but you hid the flaws. You made us believe that the United States was always in the right."

"You show me a president, and I'll show you someone who made compromises somewhere along the way. It's built into the system." His voice was growing louder as he tried to reach me. "The difference between you and me, Kat, is that I accepted it. It wasn't perfect, but it was better than what the rest of the world offered. You wanted it all— power *and* integrity. Your generation had the audacity to challenge the system, and when you burnt out trying, you became jaded and dropped out of the process. That's worse. You perpetuated the cynicism."

I touched my father's arm softly. We had come to yet another impasse. "You know I can't stay." He looked at me with vacant eyes and suddenly seemed very old. I called a cab.

"You never did listen to me; why should you start now?" He attempted a chuckle, but it caught in his throat. "You know, you and I, we really aren't that different. We both wanted to serve our country and, in our own ways, tried to keep it on track. The difference is, you're an idealist; I'm a realist," he said.

"Every generation deserves the truth, Father," I said, unwilling to accept that we were similar. I didn't want to be like him.

"Whose truth? Ours? Yours?" He rose with his glass and stole a glance out the window. "The truth isn't all it's cracked up to be, Kat. In fact, it can be downright uncomfortable, and if there's one thing we Americans like, it's our comfort—mental, physical, emotional, psychological—all wrapped up in red, white, and blue." He downed his second drink and hugged me, hard. The cab pulled up in front of the house and honked. I had already turned to go when I heard him say, "Good-bye Kat, I love you."

I climbed in and took one last look at the house, where my father was standing at the window. He gave a brief wave and then walked away. I clutched the locket at my throat, feeling it brand my hand. He'd said he loved me.

CHAPTER THIRTY-SEVEN

Friday night I sat alone in my apartment, dressed in an old pair of PJs, with Scout snoring on one side of me and an untouched glass of wine on the other as I examined the contents of the package Ben left at the Watergate. It was clear that Nixon's plumbers had not been there merely to bug Democratic headquarters. Why would it have taken seven men, many of whom were players in the assassination, to plant surveillance devices? No, their mission was far more complicated.

Also included was a transcript of Nixon's notorious "smoking gun" tape in which he told Haldeman that an investigation of Hunt's involvement in the Watergate break-in would expose too much about the "whole Bay of Pigs thing." What was it Trevor said? Something about Nixon equating the Bay of Pigs with the assassination. Robbie was right; it was all connected, from one presidency to the next. Where did it stop? Did it stop?

In solitary confinement with my fearful thoughts, I jumped at the shrill ring of my cell phone. I sprang to answer it, hoping it was Robbie, but it was Jermaine's voice I heard, sounding unusually alarmed. "There are some men on their way to your apartment. You must leave. Now. Start walking west. I'll get there as soon as I can and will pick you up. You don't have time to pack. Get out of there as fast as you can."

I jammed the papers into a briefcase with the recorder and cassettes, leashed Scout, threw on a coat, and ran out the door. I did as Jermaine ordered, but could not avoid the occasional glance back over my shoulder. Two blocks away, I heard the screech of brakes and slamming of car doors. Ducking behind a tree, I looked back and saw men running into my apartment complex. I began to run, with the package tucked securely under one arm. My other arm was totally extended by Scout, who seemed even more anxious than I to get away. Our breath, made tangible by the cold, punctuated the night air. Our feet barely touched the sidewalk.

Ten minutes later, a Hummer pulled alongside and I climbed in. Jermaine's eyes were like neon lights, darting back and forth continuously. Panting even harder than Scout, I hardly noticed as Jermaine wove his way through the traffic, leaving the lights and sounds of the city behind. As we swerved around the monuments to men of ideals and to those who had sacrificed their lives to preserve those ideals, I felt an emptiness, a longing for innocence lost and for the country I thought I knew.

Jermaine must have sensed my malaise and tried to lighten the mood, "Those are some fancy PJs, ma'am." His smile was a welcome respite. "I'll have us out of here soon, and then maybe you can relax a bit."

"Jermaine, I won't be able to relax until I'm out of this city." I held onto the duffel bag as though it contained the crown jewels.

"Where will you go?"

"I can't say, but Ben made arrangements for me. I'm leaving Monday, but first I have some things to do."

"Do they involve your macho friend?" he asked, with atypical sarcasm. I shook my head. Then, more evenly, he said, "The sooner you leave, the better. If you haven't figured it out by now, these guys want to kill you."

"I know, I know." I pounded the duffel bag. "Just help me make it to Monday. Please." After a few moments, I collected myself. My emotions weren't helping anything. "Can you take me to a hotel?"

"Looking like that?" he laughed. "I'll do you one better. Stay at my place tonight. We need to talk about how we're going to get you out of this mess."

"Jermaine, why are you helping me? You just appeared one day and have been there every time I needed you. How is that?"

"Does it really matter?"

312

I sat quietly, stroking Scout's head, while I pondered his point. It did matter, but I was in no position to debate. We crossed the border into Maryland. He had some sort of gospel music on the radio and occasionally sang along in his deep bass voice.

Thirty minutes later, I heard the sound of tires on gravel as we pulled into a driveway outside of Ellicott City, Maryland. A dense army of trees stood like sentries on either side, their limbs arched overhead like swords at a military wedding, creating a natural tunnel which led to a brick ranch with black shutters, a white door, and evergreen hedges on all sides. A cement slab served as a patio, but it was empty—no chairs, no grill, no toys, or any decoration. Jermaine hit a button to open the garage door and once we parked inside, closed it immediately.

I surveyed the Spartan décor of the kitchen with its plain Formica counters, lightly stained cabinetry, a 1960s stove—totally devoid of the kinds of personal touches that one applies over time. There were no plants, no mail, no magazines, no dishes drying in the dish rack— nothing that would support any notion of home. Instead, there was an intricate bank of machines by the phone, including scanners, computers, speakers, and head sets. This was less a kitchen than a command post.

He brought me a glass of water and suggested that we move to the living room, a slightly more comfortable area that still leaned toward the austere. "I know it's not much, but in all honesty, I spend very little time here—especially since I've been asked to watch you. Scout didn't seem to mind." Jermaine smiled, left the room, and returned with a large bathrobe which he handed to me. "You might be more comfortable in this." I shucked my parka and donned the robe. Its sleeves swallowed my arms and by the time I rolled them up, it looked as if I was wearing two tires.

"Jermaine, what do you think they'll do?"

"Probably trash your apartment, looking for whatever might be there. Do you have anything there that they might be interested in?"

"No, just my things." A sudden tsunami of panic crashed over me. "I need to get some clothes. I need to pack. I need to go to a dinner tomorrow night. All I have are my pajamas!"

"A party? Are you crazy?" his eyes bulged. His voice was like thunder. "That's the least of your problems right now. We need to talk."

Talk we did, for three or four hours. Maybe he just made me feel safe. Maybe some sort of psychological dam had burst and the words came spilling out. I told him about the vault, the threats, the chase, Woodstock—everything. Once I started, I couldn't stop. He sat on an overstuffed sofa, occasionally asking a question for clarification, but mostly, in patient silence, allowing me to unload without judgment. I wore out the neutral-colored, shag carpet as the words tumbled from my mouth. I admitted more to Jermaine than I'd been able or willing to with Ben, my father, or even Robbie. I didn't know why, really.

We covered so much ground that night, and not just because I traversed his living room at least a hundred times. By the time he showed me my room, I had voided every anxiety, fear, and woe from my brain. For the first time in weeks, I slept like an innocent baby, unencumbered by disturbing thoughts and untroubled by macabre dreams.

I woke to the aroma of pancakes, coffee, and sausage. My first thoughts were of how much I had confided in Jermaine and how stupid I had been. I knew nothing about him, who had sent him or why, but he had always been there when I required rescue. I wrapped myself in the folds of his massive robe and found him busy in the kitchen.

"I wasn't sure what you liked for breakfast. Hope this is all right," he said when I appeared. His smile seemed sincere and brightened the room more than the sun. "You sleep okay?"

"Better than I have in ages." I took a sip of the strong, dark coffee and watched him in action. "Jermaine, I don't know how to thank you. About last night..."

"Your secrets are safe with me." As I chowed down on the mountain of food, he added, "Tell me what you need from your place. I've got some tasks to complete and afterward, I'll swing by and pick up some things for you." He moved to the counter where some clothes sat and said, "You can wear these today. "They're a little big, but it's all I've got." I couldn't help but laugh at the thought. "Scout's been out, so you won't need to go outside. You do what you need to do while I'm away. Help yourself to anything you find in the fridge. Just promise me that you won't leave." I promised and smiled with gratitude as he threw the pots and pans into the sink and left.

After cajoling, pleading and making every appeal to reason that I could, Jermaine finally relented and agreed to go to my apartment as well as take me to the party. I felt guilt pangs as he pulled out of the driveway, knowing that his plans for the day placed him in danger. The last thing I could stand right now was for another person to die because of me, but I had to confront Trevor. My father had rattled off his name while I was supposed to be under hypnosis. He was unnerved by my questions about Kennedy and the Cold War, and he was friends with Beau. I wanted to *see* his response to my question as well as hear it. His answer might give me the information that I needed to put it all together. Only then could I be truly safe.

I washed the dishes, cleaned the kitchen, and climbed into the humongous sweats, feeling like a Shar-Pei. Pulling the recorder from my satchel, I began telling my story, hoping that Robbie or someone might hear it. The morning's sustenance carried me through the day, and with no interruptions from Scout, I made it halfway through my account. The garage door rumbled open around four. Jermaine's dark countenance appeared moments later. He carried a duffel bag, a shoe bag, and several hangers bearing clothes.

"They did a number on your place. I'm glad you won't be going back to see it. Sofa's been slashed, chairs overturned, drawers dumped on the rug. You sure you didn't have anything important there?"

"Nothing, Jermaine. I'm sure. My clothes?"

"They were mostly on the floor. They sure were looking for something, and by the looks of it, they were mad as hell that they didn't find it—probably even madder that you weren't there. I just brought the things that weren't ripped apart. I know you want to go to this party, but you shouldn't. I'll give your friends a message, if that's what you want."

"Jermaine, I have to see them." In a halting voice, I added, "It might be the last time."

"If they get you, it will be the last time," he said sternly. "Once you go inside, there's not much I can do to help you."

"Pam and Trevor are my friends. Whoever's after me won't know I'm there. I won't stay long, I promise. There's just one person I need to see." It was stupid, I knew it, but I continued, "He can explain everything that has happened. I'm sure of it."

"I'll drop you off and wait for you outside. You have fifteen minutes—max."

What could happen in fifteen minutes?

It was seven o'clock when I rang the doorbell, and Beau answered, momentarily throwing me off. The house glowed with Christmas lights, and wreaths of all imaginable kinds hung in the windows. A huge tree sparkled in the living room, with piles of presents at its base. I managed to avoid looking back at Jermaine's car. Trevor was making small talk in the parlor, the same parlor where Robbie and I had first seen each other after thirty-five years. While waiting for Trevor to finish, Beau approached me.

"I'm sorry, Beau, but I need to talk to Trevor. Maybe we can catch up later," I gave him a false smile.

"Sure. I'll be waiting." He frowned, but he issued his mock salute and left to chat with some others who were standing nearby. He continued to look my way.

I scurried to the kitchen and found Pam fussing with some appetizers, preparing them for distribution. "Hey there. Glad you could make it. Could you help me pass these around?" She handed me a plate of bacon-wrapped scallops.

"I can't stay. Something's come up." My voice was somber and low. I checked my watch and looked around the room. I was sweating; it felt as though it was a hundred degrees.

"Are you okay, Hon? What's wrong?" She put the plates down and gave me a hug. "Beau said something about Robbie having to leave town for a few days." She pulled me close. "Is something wrong with you two?"

"I wish I could explain, Pam." I could hear the distress in my voice, and I'm sure she could too. "I came to say good-bye. I'm leaving DC—for good. I'm so sorry. I just came by to thank you and Trevor; you've been great." With a quivering voice, I added, "If you see Robbie, please tell him I'm gone." She promised she would, and I could feel her shocked expression follow me as I rushed from the kitchen, passing Beau on my way to find Trevor and ask him a single question.

Beau stepped in front of me. "Hey! You just got here. I was looking forward to catching up."

"Sorry, Beau. I'm not feeling so well. Maybe some other time, okay? I need to find Trevor before I go."

He gripped my arm like a vise. "If you feel that bad, I'll take you home."

"That's not necessary. I've got a ride, but thanks," I responded, trying to extricate my arm.

Beau's grip tightened. His eyes blackened like those of a great white shark moving in on its prey, and his smile was just as menacing.

"Beau, you're hurting me. Please, I need to go."

"Oh, you're going to go, all right." He reached into his pocket, and as he pulled me toward him, I could feel a metallic cylinder pressed into the small of my back. Terror descended as Beau continued in a low, malevolent voice, "Now, you cooperate and none of our fine friends gets hurt." He pushed me out the front door, gestured to two waiting cars, shoved me into the first, and then slid in next to me. I recognized his aftershave. He was the man in the room with my father when I was hypnotized. My father was working with Beau. That didn't bode well.

Two men were in the front seat. The driver floored it and swerved into traffic, as did the car behind us. Engines roared. Wheels squealed. Horns blared. Beau jammed his gun into my ribs, threatening to dissect them. "I think it's time we take a little ride, Kat."

I turned to see if Jermaine had followed. Beau gripped my jaw and jerked it back. "Sit still, bitch. You've caused enough trouble as it is." Then to the driver, "My place, fast. Let Carson deal with her buddy." I thought of Jermaine and hoped he'd be okay, but the numbers were against him. Carson was the man my father was speaking to outside the vault. Maybe Carson was also the man George Jennings was speaking to as I left his office. Or was it Beau? Beau's twinkling eyes and broad smile had become a piercing glare. He was hate personified.

The trip from Alexandria to Mason's Neck went far too quickly. No one said a word. I was glued to my seat, unable to move. Upon reaching the enormous iron gate, now locked, the driver lowered his window, punched some buttons on the keypad, and sped through. The gate closed behind us with a clang, further dampening any hope of rescue. We turned hard into the long drive, propelling stones in every direction. I looked discretely toward Robbie's bungalow as we passed. It was dark, and there was no car outside.

My only thought was of Robbie. Was he alive? If so, would Martha Douglas send the not-quite-complete package and if she did, would he receive it? My own fate looked increasingly dim; I saw no way out.

The car skidded to an abrupt halt outside the stone mansion that now loomed large above us. The driver jumped out and was at my door, flinging it open and grabbing my arm. He leveled a gun at my head. Beau wrenched my arm behind my back and pushed me toward the house. The third man ran ahead, opened the door, and waited for us to pass through. He scanned the area several times before slamming it shut and following us inside.

They shoved me across the giant foyer. I slipped on the parquet floor and nearly knocked over a huge ceramic urn. Beau grasped my arm more tightly, practically separating my shoulder from its socket. The men moved so fast that my knees buckled. One of them yanked my hair to pull me back up, seeming to derive pleasure from the feeble yelp that escaped my throat. "Take her into the den. We'll have a nice cozy fire to warm her up," Beau said, as he pushed me toward one of the men and then left.

Both thugs grabbed an arm, lifting me off my feet and into the den. One lit a fire in the huge fireplace embedded in the far wall. The other pulled the curtains and then moved a ladder-back chair into the middle of the room. He pushed me into it. Beau returned with a rope. They tied my hands behind the chair and then fastened each foot to a chair leg. Without any warning, one of the men slapped my face. "That's for what your dog did to my friend. He's still in the hospital." Then he repeated the slap with the back of his hand, scraping my face with the large gold ring on his finger. "That's for what your dog did to my other friend. Killed him."

I could feel the blood trickling from my lip and a welt forming by my right eye.

Beau slowly circled my chair. I tried to watch him, but he was enjoying my growing fear too much. I lowered my head. It was then he jabbed his index finger under my chin, boring deep into the cleft beneath my jaw. He lifted my face toward his, which was now mere centimeters away. In his thick southern draw, Beau spoke. "Welcome to my little college reunion. I've been looking forward to seeing you again. I was hoping that O'Toole would join us, but it seems that he's disappeared." He smiled in a self-satisfied way and continued. "We had drinks recently, and he told me he'd be at Pam and Trevor's tonight. Looks like he stood both of us up. I don't take too kindly to being stood up."

My arms already ached, and my shoulders felt as if they would pop. He circled my chair again, taking great pleasure in my discomfort. Several minutes later, he spoke again. "Supposedly, you've been playing by the rules and haven't told your sweetie pie anything about what you found." Then he abruptly engulfed my face in his hands, squeezing hard. "But you know what? I don't believe it. I think you and your father staged that hypnosis." He threw my head back, causing the chair to wobble. "It's too coincidental that you're digging through the Kennedy evidence while O'Toole's trying to unearth the conspiracy. You can't really expect me to believe that, while you two are cozied up in bed, no secrets have passed your lips. Tonight my boys are going to get the truth out of you, and for your sake, the sooner you fess up, the better. Now, where is O'Toole?"

"Beau, I don't know where he is, and I've told him nothing. I..."

Another full-palm slap sent me to the floor. I landed on my shoulder with a painful thud, facing the shoe of the man who had hit me first. "This is what I was talking about, Kat. The more you lie, the more it will hurt," Beau said, in a mocking voice. His associates lifted me back to a sitting position, my eyes even with Beau's Pierre Cardin belt buckle.

"Now, I'll ask you a question and you will answer it. You keep lying and that pretty little face of yours won't look so pretty anymore." He removed a riding crop from the mantle and tapped his palm repeatedly with it. "Now, let's try this again. Where's Rob?"

"I don't know. I expected to see him at the party tonight. I was as disappointed as you," I lied.

Beau's eyes blazed brighter than the fireplace. His laugh was sinister, as if he'd caught me in yet another trap. I mentally braced myself for another hit. "You knew he wasn't going to be there. He's running around upstate New York. Isn't that right?"

"I don't know where he is."

"Bullshit!" The riding crop landed hard across my chest, ripping the bodice of my dress and setting my chest aflame.

"It's true. I swear it. I have no idea where he is, and it's worrying me to death."

"Interesting choice of words, Kat. Seems like your worry is well placed, under the circumstances." His evil grin sprouted once again. "Where is Rob, and what did you tell him?"

"I told you, I don't know where he is, and I told him nothing." I didn't even recognize my voice.

"I don't like treating the fairer sex unkindly. It's not gentlemanly." He motioned to one of the men, who smiled before punching me squarely in the jaw, sending me crashing to the floor once again. My head hit the floor—hard. Beau's thug tugged my hair, pulling me and the chair back into an upright position.

"I'm telling you the truth. You can hit me a hundred times, and the answer will be the same. I don't know where he is. He disappears. He finds people who will talk and then interviews them. Some people from California are after him. Maybe they got him, or maybe he's hiding. I don't know. Please believe me."

"While you were supposedly hypnotized, you told your father you followed Ben Douglas's orders to the letter. The computer geeks at the Agency went over your computer, Kat. How do you explain the number of erased files? You did more than just take inventory, didn't you? Where are the files, Kat?"

It was difficult to think clearly with hammers pounding in my battered head, but I had to. "I admit that when I first began the work I created some files, but as things heated up, I knew they'd be trouble. I had second thoughts and destroyed them. There are no files anywhere. The only product from my work was the list I gave Ben. I don't know what he did with that."

I readied myself for another hit, but what happened was worse. One of the men ripped my dress open further, exposing my bare chest. He then seized a poker from the roaring fire and held its red tip above my breast. "I'll give you one more chance. These guys are all too happy to make you talk." Beau crouched over me and pulled my hair until my face looked directly into his. "Let's try this one more time. Where's O'Toole? What did you tell him? Where are the files?"

"And I'll tell you one more time. I don't know. I told him nothing, and there are no files." I knew it wasn't enough as the poker slowly came closer and closer to my breast, its red glowing tip mere inches away.

"I don't get it, Kat. Why are you protecting a loser like O'Toole? He's not worth it."

"He's more a man than you'll ever be."

Beau's eyes glowed with malice. His nostrils flared with anger and hate. He grabbed the poker from the thug's hand and plunged it into my chest.

I screamed. The smell of melting flesh made me nauseated and the pain made me light-headed, but before I could pass out, another blow struck my head and once again I lay writhing on the floor. They left me lying there while they conferred.

My scorched skin continued to burn. I prayed that I would pass out. The room blurred, looking like a Dali painting as oval urns became round and seemed to wobble. Chair legs moved like snakes, and plants crawled across the floor. The chandelier above looked like a large spider spinning a web. Faces sagged in portraits on the wall. I was on my way to a blissful state of unconsciousness when a glass of cold water hit me in the face, reawakening the agony of my wounds, but also my survival instinct.

"You sure are one stubborn bitch, I'll give you that," said the repulsive southern drawl. "I'm going to try this one last time. "Where is..."

Through swollen jaws and puffy lips, I interrupted, "I don't know where he is, but if you give me a day, I might be able to find out." I gasped for air; it felt as if my nose was broken. "I think I could find him. If I do, I promise to tell you. Please, give me a chance." After another shallow breath, I added, "Or kill me now."

"Ah, Kat, still trying to manipulate the situation. Some things never change." He walked in circles around me as I remained on the floor, watching his Guccis, step by step. "They told me that you were like your father, and I guess they were right except for one thing. Your father understands how the world operates." Beau resumed tapping his hand with the riding crop, using it for emphasis as he continued. "You see, I work with some very powerful men. They don't take too kindly to poor performance—either in the market or in the deals they make. If your boyfriend publishes his shit, they might lose some of their, uh, freedom to operate. They won't like that, no sir."

He continued to pace, slapping the riding crop against his palm, contemplating his next words. "Every once in a while, when I see Rob take off, I pop into his office. It's why I offered him the damn apartment—so I could keep an eye on him. I see what he's uncovered and I report back. He's good, I'll give him that, but he's taken it too far. He's getting too close to the truth. We need to stop him." His feet stopped moving, and his words stopped coming. The ticking of the clock was the only sound in the room. I didn't dare look to see what was coming next.

"So, you see, I have a choice. I can let the boys here beat you to a bloody pulp which, from the looks of it, they enjoy immensely, but then I'd still have no Robbie. Or I can give you a chance to deliver the golden boy to me, but risk you pulling a fast one. I need some *insurance*." The riding crop slapped on the first syllable. "So I'm going to let the boys escort you to what's left of your apartment. You have twenty-four hours to find lover boy. If you don't, they will kill you. And let me add, they are very creative when it comes to that."

While Beau whistled *The Yellow Rose of Texas,* the two goons lifted me up and slashed the ropes with knives. My arms fell to my sides, and pain shot from every joint. I pulled my arms forward and linked them across my defiled chest. The large wad of cotton that used to be my head rolled round like a top, spinning erratically before toppling over. If it weren't for the agony of every shaky step, I'd have sworn that I was already dead. "Get her out of here, and use the back entrance at her place. We don't want to scare the residents. Oh, one more thing..." He threw my cell phone at me, hitting me once more in the face. "You may need this. We cut your other line." Beau snickered as he left the room.

They wrapped me in an old coat and pushed me into the back seat of the car. Each bump in the driveway sent another dagger of pain throughout my crumpled frame. At first I was glad; it meant I was still functioning, but after a dozen or so jolts, death seemed preferable. It was somewhere on Route 95 that my survival instinct kicked in. It was now Sunday morning. I had just one day.

CHAPTER THIRTY-EIGHT

There would be no return of my security deposit. My beautiful apartment was in shambles. They threw every bottle from my wine collection against the walls, leaving them blotched with lurid stains. Shattered furniture cluttered the room. Pictures had been torn from the walls and lay shredded on the floor. Ripped drapes hung like shrouds by the windows. I stumbled toward my bedroom only to see the king-size bed, the one where Robbie and I had made love, slashed and defiled. My clothes were in rags; shoes littered the carpet.

"I'd like to wash up," I mumbled though swollen jaws.

"Make it quick. We don't have all day. Neither do you," said one of the men.

I gathered some sweats, the least damaged, and shuffled to the bathroom, hoping that in addition to removing the caked blood from my body, the water would provide some clarity and a moment's respite from my predicament. I looked into what was left of the mirror and gasped, then whimpered. The battered countenance that met my gaze was foreign. There would be scars. I examined the angry, blackened skin on my breast and knew that I was now marked for life, however long that would be. Clumps of hair were missing, having been used like a tether to lift me up or drag me around. I would not cry. I would not give them the satisfaction.

The water stung every cut, every bruise, and every welt. I could not lift my arms. I shielded the hole in my chest, wondering if I would dare let anyone see its ugliness—and then realized that if I didn't come up with something, some way out, this would all be moot. I was thankful that I had committed Robbie's number to memory and deleted it from my phone. If they had checked my contacts, they wouldn't find him. That's why they needed me.

I dressed as quickly as my wounds would allow, trying not to scream as I raised my arms into the sleeves of my jacket, fumbled with misshapen fingers to zip it up, and pulled my sweatpants over throbbing joints. When I limped into the room, the two bulky figures were peering out the windows, watching the street below. They turned and cackled upon seeing me. "Well, if it isn't the beauty queen," one said. "I almost hope that shit, O'Toole, gets to see you like this. I want to see his reaction before we do the same to him. You'll be a matched set."

The other man chimed in, "No one will care when they become crab chum at the bottom of the bay."

"I'd like my phone," I said, my steadiness made easier by a hatred that I never felt before.

"Here," one of them said as he tossed it to me. With useless arms, I couldn't reach to catch it. I could not stifle a yelp as I stooped to the carpet to retrieve it. "Don't get smart; we don't like smart."

I nodded and turned toward my room.

"Uh-uh. You call him here where we can listen." He jerked my arm roughly and threw me toward the shredded couch. I groaned from deep within my tortured chest.

I punched Jermaine's number, hoping he would answer. One ring, two rings, then three. I looked at the men. They were getting impatient. One stood up and started walking toward me. *Answer, dammit.* He finally did. I began talking immediately. "Oh *Robbie*, I'm so glad you're alive."

In a confused voice, he said, "I think you have the wrong number, ma'am. It's me, Jermaine."

"Oh, I know! I was so worried. *Robbie*, I must see you. I must. Can we meet somewhere, anywhere?"

"Are you alone?"

"No. I'll come anywhere. Just tell me how to get to you. I want to see you so badly."

"I get it. Okay, let's do it this way. Can you remember how to get to my house? The end of the street on VFW Lane? I assume they'll be coming with you. How many are there?"

"Right now? Just the two of us?" I paused, as though listening to a reply. "Yes, I understand why you can't come to me." I looked at the two men who were hanging on every word. "I'll be there as soon as I can, and Robbie, no matter what happens, I love you." I hit "end" and turned to the two men. "He's in Ellicott City, Maryland. I know the way."

"Amazing what a little rough stuff can do to a broad, eh?" said the taller of the two men. "I'm glad you're not my bitch, turning on your boyfriend like that."

"What choice do I have?" I asked bitterly.

"You got a point there. By the way, what's his number? We may need it for, uh, future reference." I paused, not sure what to do. He started toward me and yelled, "I said, what's his number? Or didn't you get enough of our southern hospitality?" He raised his arm above his head, ready to deliver another blow.

Through a possibly broken jaw, I mumbled Jermaine's number. I would never give them Robbie's, no matter how many times they hit me.

"Some agent you are—you'd turn on your own mother after a few whacks. All those fancy clothes and fancy wine—you're just a cheap little whore." He yanked my arm. It hurt. A lot. "Let's pay Romeo a visit. You wanted to see him one last time? You're going to get your wish."

The other guy eyed me. It made me nervous. "I don't trust her. It almost seems too easy. I say we beat the address out of her, kill her, and get him ourselves. She's just extra baggage at this point." I knew they'd be all too happy to do so.

"Nah, what if O'Toole won't talk? If he sees us beating on her, he'll give us everything."

"I guess you're right. Let's get out of here before O'Toole changes his mind and disappears again."

The two men sat in the front; I was in the back seat. When we were halfway down the Baltimore-Washington expressway, my phone rang. I looked at the display. It was Robbie. He was alive.

"Don't answer it, or I'll find a home for this bullet right in the middle of your forehead," said the driver. The ring taunted me, daring me to answer. I hit the "end" button, regret brutalizing me more than these goons ever could. "Who called you?" the driver asked.

"My father," I replied meekly.

"Hastings, hah! That worthless sack of shit. Turned soft on us. He'll get his, right after we kill the two of you."

"What has my father done? Leave him alone." Though muted, my voice was harsh.

"It's what he wouldn't do, missy. Tough guy that he is, he wouldn't cooperate when it came to you. Just wanted to scare you off but no, you had to be a hero. You know what happens to heroes? They have a very short life expectancy." The passenger hooted. "Used to be that we could count on the Agency, but not anymore."

"So who do you work for?" I asked.

The passenger answered, "Let's just say we're private contractors." His companion snorted again. "Freelancers."

"You're a regular riot today," the driver responded. Then, looking at me in the rearview mirror, he asked, "Where do I turn?" I told him, and about ten minutes later, we took a left onto VFW Lane, a road lined with small brick homes which curved to the right and led to the VFW Hall at its end. Jermaine's house sat on the right. There was no car in the driveway. The shades were closed. "I hope for your sake, he didn't bolt."

"This is how it's going to go," the man in the passenger seat said. "You and me, we're going to walk up to the door. Bennie will stay in the car and watch for a trap. Anything funny happens, I'll kill you on the spot, got it?" I nodded. "You ring the doorbell. I'll be out of view. When O'Toole answers, my gun will be at your head. I'm sure I can persuade him to let us inside. Once Bennie here is convinced that nothing's wrong, he'll join us, and the four of us will have a nice chat. Once we get what we need from O'Toole, we'll all go for a little ride to the beach."

"He'll never tell you anything," I said.

"Then he'll have a ringside seat while we slice you to pieces," the driver said, snickering.

He brought the car to a halt under the arch of trees and pulled his gun from under the seat. The other man hauled me from the back seat and pushed me toward the door, his gun burrowed into the small of my back. I rang the doorbell; no answer. I rang again. I knocked and knocked, wondering where Jermaine could be. Next, I pounded as hard as my throbbing arm would allow. I could hear the goon's whispered curses in my ear and feel his rapid breathing on my neck. He was staring at the door, which is why he didn't hear the ping of the bullet that penetrated the windshield and found its mark in the side of the driver's head. Nor was he ready for the assault from Scout which leveled him, sending an errant shot into the air. Jermaine finished the job with a single shot through his heart, or at least the place his heart was supposed to be.

I crumpled in a heap on the stoop. I mumbled thanks to Jermaine and stared at the two bodies before me. Although relieved that they were dead, I felt total revulsion. They'd violated my body. I was now scarred for life. But at least the ordeal was over, for now.

"Let's get you inside, ma'am. I'll take care of these two." Jermaine gently ushered me into his living room and helped me to the couch. Scout rested his head on my thigh. Although lifting my arm to pet him was an effort, it was necessary. "They're in the garage and won't be going anywhere. I'll get rid of them later. Now, tell me what happened while I take care of your injuries."

As Jermaine adroitly applied antiseptic creams and covered my wounds with bandages, I recounted the events of the evening. He asked a few questions in between, immobilizing one battered arm by wrapping it against my torso. I was grateful for his professional bearing, which allayed my embarrassment when he tended to my chest. He iced my eye, my cheek, my nose, and any other swollen spots he could find, but I was most grateful for the painkillers he administered. "I know it looks bad now, and you may have a few permanent mementos of the occasion, but you'll be just fine before you know it." He flashed that welcome grin, and somehow I believed him.

"Where did you learn how to do all this?" I asked in my muffled voice.

He merely smiled and left me alone, saying that he had to go out, but would be back soon. There were eighteen hours left before my twenty-four hours were up. First, I returned Robbie's call. He had left no message, and now there was no answer. Frustrated, scared, and alone, the only thing I could do was hobble to the tape recorder and finish my tale, praying that Robbie would live to hear it.

CHAPTER THIRTY-NINE

"I assume you completed your work, ma'am." Jermaine said, as he entered the room eight hours later.

I was relieved to see him, even though he seemed more distant. I assumed that it was because of the gravity of our situation. The catharsis of recording the events of the last three weeks left me emotionally spent. I relaxed by applying nails to my injured fingers. I answered, "Yes, it's finally done, but there's one more trip I need to make. Can you take me to the Douglas residence? I need to drop off some items with Ben's wife and say farewell."

"No offense, ma'am, but your nails are the least of your concerns. If you insist on seeing Mrs. Douglas, we have to move now."

I rose with difficulty, hobbling toward the door. He helped me into my coat and escorted me to his Hummer. Although his medicinal efforts had clearly improved my state, he had to practically lift me into the front seat. Scout jumped in, claiming the back seat as his own.

"I just wish I knew where Robbie is."

"All I can tell you is, he's safe, but he's hiding. He has to. If they find him, he's a dead man."

"You know where he is?" I asked. I felt a flicker of hope inside.

"Yes, but as you found out the hard way, if you don't know something, no one can force it out of you. That's why I can't tell you."

"If only I can make it til tomorrow...Oh, Jermaine, I'm going to miss it all."

Jermaine looked at me with compassion, but I could tell he was contemplating his next steps. It would not be easy on many fronts. Neither of us spoke until we were about five minutes from Falls Church, when

Jermaine said, "You need to say your good-byes quickly. We need to be out of here by 1400 hours, two o'clock."

We pulled into the driveway, where a moving van was parked—its back door opened wide as men walked to and from the house and deposited furniture and boxes in the almost full truck. "Do you need help?" Jermaine asked me. I shook my head no and plodded toward the forlorn-looking home. Martha Douglas greeted me at the door—a tiny scream escaped her mouth.

"Oh, my dear. What have they done to you?" A well-meant hug elicited a stifled moan but was welcome nonetheless. Martha quickly pulled away. "Come inside."

Jermaine helped me with my satchel, which contained the Watergate papers and my taped account of the events of the past three weeks. I placed the items in the lonely box still sitting on the cement floor. After taping it shut, I brushed the letters of Robbie's name, while trying to keep my tears dammed within my swollen, black eyes.

"I'll make sure this gets mailed. Don't you worry," said Martha, trying to be encouraging.

Just then, Jermaine leaped forward and grabbed the box.

"What are you doing?" I asked.

Seeing my startled look, he said, "Don't worry. I'll make sure he gets it. After all you've been through, we can't take any chances."

"That wasn't part of the plan. Put it back." I said.

"You can't mail this. They'll be watching his mail and will intercept any package he receives. Do you want him to get it or not?"

I couldn't stop him. I was at his mercy. Once again, I could only hope that he was really on my side.

Seeing the worry on my face, Martha said, "It's okay, dear. You've done everything you could. Now it's time to take care of yourself. Ben would be very proud." I smiled as much as my abused jaw would allow, and murmured my thanks.

I slowly returned to Jermaine's car, never looking back to the frail woman. I gingerly climbed into the seat with Jermaine's assistance. A few minutes later, we were on the highway when my cell phone rang; it was my father. "Kat, where the hell are you?"

"Father, Beau's henchmen beat me up pretty badly. I'm a mess."

"Kat, you need to come to the house. Now." The urgency of his voice was frightening.

"I can hardly move, Father." I was worried, for him and for myself. He sounded terrified.

"Call a cab. Do whatever it takes—just get here." Then, practically whispering, he added, "You wanted my help, so I called some men. They can get you out of this mess. I'm sure of it."

It was so sudden. I didn't know what to do. After hanging up, I said to Jermaine, "My father says he can help me. Do you think I should go?"

"Yes."

"But do you think it's a good idea?"

"Only choice you've got." His eyes were on the road. He didn't even glance at me.

"What do you mean? You've been protecting me for almost a month." I could hear the growing trepidation in my voice. Jermaine's demeanor had changed completely, and I didn't know why. "Can't I stay with you?"

"My work is done, Agent Hastings. Your father can take care of you now."

"How do I know what I'll find at my father's? You can't leave now. I need you."

"That's a negative. I have my orders."

"Whose orders?" I asked. His face was like stone. "Please, Jermaine. I don't want to go to my father's. Take me with you. Take me to Robbie."

"Can't do that. I have a job to do."

"But you said you were assigned to protect *me*."

"I did. Now I have to get that box to O'Toole. That's Job One. I'll take you to a taxi stand. You can get a ride to your father's."

"Wait a second. You've been working for Robbie this whole time? It can't be. Robbie wouldn't let you abandon me."

He looked at me as though I was a simpleton. "You underestimate how much he wants that box." His eyes were cold, but his manner colder. "If you don't go to your father's, you're on your own."

"I can't do anything on my own—not like this." He said nothing, so I tried again. "Robbie will protect me if you won't. Just take me to him."

Jermaine snorted. "Why do you think he sent you away from Bethel? He had to get rid of you."

I sat back in my seat, totally disillusioned as reality dawned. "So all that macho posturing between the two of you was just an act?"

His wicked smile told me that I'd been a fool.

We didn't speak during the remainder of the ride. My dismal odds of survival left me feeling resigned to my fate. How could I trust my father? He worked with Beau. I began to play with my locket. Until yesterday, I had never heard my father say that he loved me. Would he really protect me? Could a simple "I love you" erase all the years of criticism and detachment? It had to.

I fumbled with the ring that Robbie gave me. My fingers were too swollen to pull it off. Part of me wanted to throw it out the window, but another part was sure that Jermaine was lying. I refused to accept that Robbie would abandon me. He loved me; I knew it. Why did I trust Robbie's love and not my father's?

I had to stop torturing myself. Nothing mattered now. Jermaine had taken the evidence, and with it, my last trump card. We pulled up to the taxi stand in front of Reagan airport. I pulled my crumpled body from the front seat and opened the back door, calling for Scout to come and join me outside. I hoped the cab driver would allow him to ride with me.

Jermaine sprang to the back door. "The dog stays," Jermaine said firmly. He slammed the back door shut. I was helpless to resist him. He was a stranger now. The compassion he had once shown was gone; only disinterest, maybe contempt, remained. Not only had he betrayed me in the worst way, he was stealing the one being that I could count on for unconditional love.

"You monster! How could you?" I shrieked. He was unmoved, folding his arms across his chest and blocking my way to the back door of the car, and Scout. I couldn't fight him. My situation was futile. In a cracked and broken voice, I added, "Please Jermaine. He's all that I have left. Please let him come with me."

He said nothing as he climbed back into the Hummer and roared away from the taxi stand. I stared at his car until it disappeared, unable to fathom how someone could be so heartless and praying that he would treat Scout better than me. I sat on the curb and lowered my head into my hands.

A yellow cab pulled up and idled next to me. The driver made no attempt to call out or assist. With great effort, I pulled myself up and issued a feeble wave. I had nothing to lose by listening to my father's plan. The driver looked over and motioned me in. Slowly, I climbed inside. "Glen Road, Gaithersburg," I mumbled.

Hip-hop played on the radio while the driver talked into a cell-phone earpiece. I was grateful that he was uninterested in conversation, although I did catch him check me out periodically in the mirror. At one point our eyes met, and I said, "Car accident." Lying had become so easy.

The pain of Robbie and Jermaine's conspiracy hurt more than any of my physical wounds. At least history would be served, unless Robbie was labeled a fraud, just like so many others whose reputations were ruined by the Agency. Why should I care now?

I almost hoped that the cab would break down. Even more, I hoped we would get in an accident and I would die, blissfully ignorant of others who betrayed me. *Stop it!* Maybe my father did know people who could help. Didn't Jennings say that my father still had influence?

The torment of my thoughts ceased the moment I saw several cars parked outside my father's house. Most looked like standard government sedans with official license plates. They were black and shiny, like gun barrels. Did they belong to the people my father had enlisted to help? I thought about fleeing, but my father was instantly by the cab door and paid the fare. With his help, I rallied my tender muscles and recalcitrant joints and climbed from the car. The cab roared off as though the driver knew it was best to leave. I noticed the Christmas decorations, now lit as evening descended. Oh, unholy night.

The distress on my father's face spoke far more than words could ever say. "Oh my God. What have they done to you?" His eyes glistened as he guided me inside. "My poor child. I'm so sorry you had to go through this. If only you had listened to me." His voice was breaking. "Come inside. I'll get you a drink."

"No, thank you," I said quietly. He ushered me inside to the den, a place of once-happy memories, where I'd played with my sisters, where my mother sang us songs, where my father watched his sports. Now, half a dozen somber men watched my every move. Jennings and Carson stood in the corner. Beau was near the door. And there stood Trevor, my supposed friend, who couldn't even look me in the eye.

"Have a seat, Hastings," Jennings ordered. "It seems we have a problem. No, let me rephrase that. It seems as though you have a problem." I sat immobile, frightened, and wondering what my father's role was in this gathering. Had he delivered me to them to save himself? Did he know they were coming when he called me? Or was he as helpless as I?

Beau jumped up and was instantly at my side. "Where are my guys?" I didn't answer. He was ready to strike me when my father yelled, "Enough! She's had enough." Beau reeled around to face him. "Shut up, H2. We tried it your way, and she fucked it up." He turned back to me and pulled out his gun. "Don't think I won't use this, Kat. Nothing would give me more pleasure than drilling a hole in what was once your pretty head. You're nothing but a royal pain in the ass. I'm giving you one last chance. Where's O'Toole? Where are the files you copied?'

I swallowed hard. "I told you, I don't know." He hit me with the butt of the gun, opening the gash on my lip. My father jumped to help me, and Beau shoved him away. Trevor winced. I wiped my mouth with my hand and glared at Beau. "Just kill me and get it over with. My answer won't change."

My father knelt in front of me. "Kat, please cooperate. If you give them O'Toole, they'll leave you alone. He's not worth it."

I took hold of his hands and saw the sorrow in his eyes. "Father, don't you see? They'll kill me whether I tell them or not."

Beau pushed my father to the floor and then squeezed my aching jaw. "Okay, have it your way." He pressed the gun barrel to my head.

Suddenly my father kicked Beau's legs, sending him crashing to the floor. Beau's gun fired, hitting the light atop the Christmas tree in the corner. Carson drew his gun and aimed at me. My father pulled his own gun from inside his vest pocket and shot Carson, who fell to the floor.

Trevor kicked the gun from Beau's hand and then stomped on his fingers. Beau's bones cracked like kindling, eliciting a dull groan as he clutched his hand, rolling over in pain. Jennings pulled a gun as well and aimed it at me. "Drop your weapons or she dies," he yelled. Trevor and my father let their guns fall helplessly to the floor. Jennings jerked me back, his arm around my neck. I had one more chance. With my one working arm, I reached up and dug my nails deep into his skin. He screamed and fell to the floor, convulsing in brutal spasms. In seconds, he was completely immobile and silent. Greg's sarin had done its job.

A man I didn't recognize wrenched my arms behind my back; I screamed in pain. He held a gun to my head. It was over.

From out of nowhere, Scout bounded into the room and lunged at the man, sending his gun rattling across the floor. His teeth sank into the man's throat, eliciting a crimson spray and a hideous gurgling sound.

Jermaine appeared milliseconds later, with a gun drawn. "Sorry, Beau, I got here as soon as I could." A new ache emerged as I appraised Jermaine. Gone were the cavernous grin and twinkling eyes. His lips were tight; his ink-dark eyes narrowed. I groaned. Jermaine had all the evidence, had lied to me, and now, it seemed, worked for Beau, not Robbie.

"You ass," Beau thundered. "We lost Jennings, Carson, and now Hoyt. He was rubbing his cracked fingers, glaring at Trevor as he did so. "Did you find O'Toole?"

"You don't have to worry about him anymore," Jermaine assured him.

My bruised, swollen eyes raged from their shattered sockets. I slowly stood, driven by the intensity of my anger and hatred. I charged, my fingernails aimed at his throat.

Jermaine laughed viciously as he pushed me away. "You fell for it. Now it's your turn. You and your father know too much."

"If you have to kill someone, kill me! Leave her alone," begged my father. Jermaine turned toward him and with an evil smirk said, "Glad

337

to oblige," and shot him in the chest. My father's hand went to his heart and he bent slightly, taking a couple of steps toward me before he fell to the floor.

"No. No!" I screamed. I fell to my father's side, holding his head to my breast.

As the light faded from his eyes, his gaze fell upon me. "I failed you, Kat. I'm so sorry. For everything." His eyes closed for the last time. My tears flowed. Nothing mattered now.

Jermaine looked down at me and pointed his gun at my chest. "It's been real nice knowing you." He fired, hitting me right above the hole in my breast. Scout bounded toward him and met the same fate. The gunshot elicited a mournful howl as Scout landed in a heap, his head falling upon me. As I lay on the floor, an odd feeling of peace replaced my despair. The last thing I heard before the darkness descended was Beau saying to Jermaine, "Nice work, bud. I owe you."

It had all been for nothing.

CHAPTER FOURTY

U nder the periwinkle sky of early Monday morning, a Hummer cruised along the deserted northern Maryland road, heading for the Cecil County airstrip, a thin cement slab that looked far too short to land a plane. Its remote location off Route 95 made it a favorite of those trying to avoid larger commercial jets. The airstrip had seen its share of wing stalls by inexperienced pilots who'd overshot its meager length and crashed in the woods beyond, but that was where he was told to go.

He drove with purpose, carrying precious cargo that had to be delivered by seven a.m. It was now six, but he didn't dare exceed the speed limit and invite the scrutiny of a bored cop who might welcome some action. He hoped to be long gone before the police could catch up with him. There was still a definite risk looming, but he was used to risk; it was his life.

WBAL was broadcasting the day's news, and he turned the volume up a bit. Nothing about the incident made the headlines—that was good. No need to incur any additional complications at this point, especially when H2's friends discovered what had happened. He'd made sure they were delayed—all except for Trevor, but they would figure things out soon enough. He hadn't expected that Hoyt would die. No matter how well he'd trained Scout, he couldn't break the dog of his devotion to the woman. He was a good dog though; he'd miss him, just as he missed Shaft all those years ago.

As he replayed the events of the previous night, he was certain that it had to go down this way. There was no choice. Sometimes drastic measures were necessary, and this was one of those times. He had killed people in the service of his country before, and would most likely do so again. He could live with it.

He heard a rustling in the back seat. He looked in the rearview mirror and saw some movement, then heard a moan as she shifted, trying unsuccessfully to sit up due to the weight of the sleeping giant of a dog sprawled across her. "Where am I? Where are you taking me?" Her voice quivered with fear and alarm.

"I believe you have a plane to catch." He tried not to grimace when his eyes connected with the battleground of her face. Still, he saw a look of joy and relief beneath the cuts and bruises, as it dawned on her that the crisis was over and that she would live. He hated to tell her the rest. In a solemn voice, he added, "Ma'am, I have some bad news. I shot your father with the same sedative I used on you and Scout, but he never woke up."

He saw the tears leak from her grotesque black eyes and tumble down her swollen cheeks. She hugged the sleeping Scout for solace. It took a moment for her to grasp the situation.

"You staged the whole thing?"

"Your father and I set it up. Sorry for the way I treated you, but I had to make sure that you were desperate enough to go to his house or the plan wouldn't have worked. Your father knew that the only way you'd ever be safe was if everyone thought you were dead. He knew about your assignment from the beginning. He wrote that memo mentioning the room almost fifty years ago, hoping the vault would be discovered. When he found out about your increased security clearance, he knew Douglas assigned you to find it."

"Why didn't he tell me?" she asked.

"He thought that might make you even more motivated to prove yourself, and spite him." He watched her in the rearview mirror. "He was working with us. He tipped us off to Carson, Jennings, and Hoyt. He kept track of you through Trevor. Trevor was his eyes and ears."

Though her face was disfigured, he could discern a quizzical expression. "Trevor is a CIA contact, has been for more than twenty years," he explained. "Your father told him about your assignment. When you started asking Trevor all those questions, Trevor realized that you were in deep and told your father. That's why H2 didn't want you dating O'Toole. He knew you'd be in even more trouble." Jermaine hesitated, checking the mirror once more as what he said sank in. "Your father was a good man put in an untenable situation. He was trying to set things right."

She had suspected that Trevor was saying something to someone. That's why she had gone to the party—to confront him and find out who.

"Still, my father was willing to sacrifice Robbie."

"Only because he wanted to save you."

She gently fingered the locket at her neck. How could she have been so wrong about her father? So much animosity, so much bad blood spilled, and now she'd never be able to tell him how she felt.

The sun was rising in the east. Shards of light punctured leftover clouds, promising a clear day, perfect for flying. More cars were on the road now, commuters pursuing their daily routine, oblivious to the world in which Jermaine lived and she had briefly visited. She pulled a mirror from her purse and a moment later threw it back.

Jermaine watched her for a moment and then said, "It will heal, don't worry." He drove for a bit and then asked, "Did you ever tell O'Toole what you knew?"

"Not until Dallas, after we found out about Ben. I didn't know about the files Ben had embedded at that point, but it was all in the package. Doesn't really matter now, does it?" Her voice was devoid of affect. She could only stare down at Scout in despair.

"He's alive, ma'am."

"Alive? He's alive?" Suddenly, she was alert and leaning forward. "You said he wouldn't be a problem. I thought he was dead."

"I was just trying to throw Beau off and buy O'Toole some time. That's why I was delayed. If you hadn't used your fancy fingernails on Jennings, I would have been too late, but O'Toole needed the box before he skipped town. His place was torched though. Everything inside is gone. All he has is whatever was in the box I gave him."

"So you *were* working with him."

"No, he didn't know anything about me. Like I said, I made that story up to make you feel hopeless enough to go to your father's."

Relief showered over her, but as quickly as it descended, it disappeared. "I'll never see him again, will I?" She touched the ring on her swollen finger. Her chest heaved as the full understanding of her new life dawned on her. More to herself than Jermaine, she said, "Maybe I should have trusted him more, but I didn't want to make things worse for him. And now, I'll never see him again."

He could see her distress. It made him sad. "You know, when I first met you, I thought you were too, I don't know, lightweight for the job. I thought you'd cave." He smiled broadly. "You had me fooled. I always thought I was a good judge of character, but your father knew."

"What do you mean?" Despite the agony of doing so, she drew herself up in the seat, wanting to hear more.

"He knew you'd honor your oath, but he also knew that you wouldn't be able to avoid digging deeper. That's why he was angry at Ben Douglas. He didn't want you to get hurt." Jermaine caught her eye in the mirror. "He admired you, Kat. He told me so."

"I wished I'd heard it from him."

"Yeah, and I wish Scout could sing the national anthem." He laughed at the thought.

She asked about the others, and Jermaine told her that her father had killed Carson and she'd killed Jennings. Scout took care of Hoyt. Trevor was fine, and the FBI had enough on Beau to keep him locked up for the rest of his life.

"Just curious, Jermaine. Why didn't you kill Beau as well?"

"There are more like him. Even from prison, he can get the word out. If Beau tells his buddies that you're dead, they won't come looking for you."

He saw her gaze wearily out the window as she stroked Scout's back. He knew that her life would never be the same again. Her love, her family, her friends, her job—they were all gone.

"What about Robbie? Where is he?" she asked.

"The day I left you at my place, I moved him to a safe house. He's not out of the woods yet. Beau has some powerful associates, so O'Toole will lie low for a while. At least that's what he told me. I don't know who's more stubborn, you or him." He could tell she wanted to hear more. "I'm sorry I couldn't tell you sooner, about O'Toole or me, but if you slipped or if they beat it out of you, it would have blown everything."

"Wait a second. Beau said 'Good work' to you. I heard him just before I passed out."

"Your father told Beau that I was the carrot and Beau was the stick. He convinced Beau that I would gain your confidence and if Beau couldn't get the information from you, I could."

She nodded in understanding. The Hummer passed through Aberdeen, and she tried to rouse Scout. Jermaine handed her a thermos of coffee. Despite her perforated lips and bulging jaws, she took a sip and reflected for a moment. "Jermaine, do you think that what I did was wrong?"

"It's not for me to say, but if O'Toole blows the whistle, I think people will take a long, hard look at the way we do things and who we do them for. It may help us clean out some of the dirt bags who abuse their power. And believe me, Beau's just the tip of the iceberg."

They passed the sign for Elkton, Maryland. Kat finished the last of her coffee and asked, "So you work for JSOC, but who actually sent you to help me? My father?"

"Remember when I told you I was in Iraq and mentioned the reporter who was embedded in my unit? As I told you, he saved my life and lost both legs doing it. I was in his debt and told him if he ever needed my help, to let me know. He called me a few months ago and told me he had this friend named Rob O'Toole, who had to leave California because of some trouble. I've been keeping an eye on O'Toole ever since. This guy, Tom MacGregor is his name, sent O'Toole his driver's license to use for cover. As things turned out, watching O'Toole's back also meant watching yours. Your father found out, and since he couldn't protect you, he asked me to."

"Did Tom ever tell Robbie about you?"

"Not until you two were chased by those guys at Woodstock. When he picked up O'Toole, he told him that I was on your side, just like I tried to tell you a thousand times."

"Maybe if he had told Robbie sooner, I would have believed you."

"Your father advised against it. It would have jeopardized the plan if Beau found out."

Her head throbbed as she tried to process it all. "So I owe my life to you, my father, and Tom MacGregor. I can't think of three more different people."

They pulled into the tiny parking lot abutting the airport. A Cessna was waiting, its wheels immobilized by blocks so the pilot could check the air pressure in the tires. Jermaine hopped out and opened Kat's door. He assisted her, and then lifted Scout's limp body.

"Jermaine, I don't know how to thank you." She looked deep into his eyes. "Will I ever see you again?"

"Never say never, ma'am. It can be a small world, but if our paths do cross, it would be an honor."

Her damaged arms felt like lead as she attempted to hug the tall, dark man. "You know where to find me," she said and then pulled away, mildly embarrassed. She limped to the plane and turned to Jermaine once more. "If you ever do see Robbie again, please tell him the answer would have been yes."

Jermaine greeted the pilot and gently placed Scout on the bench seat in back. She lowered her head and tried to cover her face with the hood of her sweatshirt. "This is Carla Banks," Jermaine said to the pilot. "Take good care of her." Then turning to Kat, he kissed her lightly on a puffy cheek. "You stay out of trouble now, you hear? But if you ever need me, just call."

He helped her into the plane and stood there as the pilot climbed in, engaged the throttle, and taxied to the end of the runway. Jermaine gave a final wave. She saw him walk back to the car, where he remained until the nose lifted and they were airborne.

"Some guy, huh?" said the pilot. "They don't make 'em like that anymore."

"No they don't," she said.

"By the way, my name's Nate."

Small world indeed...

Epilogue

I lay on the beach, with Scout beside me, absorbing the sun's warmth and enjoying the tranquility of the gentle waves tickling the shore. It had been three months since I arrived. Christmas, New Year's Eve, and Valentine's Day all came and went, leaving painful reminders of my loneliness. Nights were long. Only my daily trips to the beach provided some semblance of comfort.

My wounds had mostly healed, but there were scars—emotional and physical. The mean-looking mutilation over my heart was nowhere near as painful as the one within it. I missed Robbie and cried myself to sleep most of the first month. But reality crept in, and I realized that if he hadn't come by now, he probably wasn't going to.

I never told Nate who I really was. No wonder my father liked him; he was a Company man. Maybe that's how Ben knew of him. When we landed, Nate took me to a hospital. While my injuries mended, he stocked my bungalow so I never had to leave for food or other supplies. He told me to call if I needed anything.

As my appearance became more normal, I made a few friends with my island neighbors—all of whom made me feel welcome. I was finally able to run again and explored the trails around Nevis Peak, throughout the botanical gardens and along the beaches. But each run brought back memories of runs with Robbie around Shirlington and Mason's Neck, presenting their own kind of torture.

The sun grew hot, and it was time for a break. I collapsed my chair, rolled up my towel, and packed it in my beach bag with my book and water bottle. With Scout at my heels, I flip-flopped along the sizzling sand back to my new home and imagined what it would have been like for Ben and his wife to live in Nevis. I wondered how Martha Douglas was doing. For that matter, I wondered about many people—Berta, Pam, my sisters, Greg's family...but mostly Robbie. Was he safe? Would he risk his safety further by telling the truth? He had to. Too many had sacrificed too much.

I scolded myself out loud. "This is your life now. Deal with it." The stairs seemed steeper today, the sun less soothing. Maybe someday it would be safe to return, but who was I kidding? I was almost sixty years old. Would I move back at seventy?

I pulled open the sliding door on the deck and threw the bag onto a chair. The familiar whirr of the ceiling fan stirred oven-hot air. Children were laughing in the yard next door. A radio blared reggae across the street, but there was something else, a subtle tick-tick-tick coming from the study. Petrified that someone had found me and entered my apartment, I snatched a sharp knife from the kitchen, holding it above my head as I crept slowly down the hall and opened the door.

I saw his broad shoulders hunched over the desk. His curly hair was black again and longer. I threw the knife down and ran to him, draping my arms around his neck and kissing his face. At first he jumped, startled by my presence, but then he turned toward me and flashed his crooked grin. He pulled a sheet off the top of a large stack of papers. It was a cover page with the title: *Truth, Justice, and the American Way.*

The End

Afterword

In Paul Simon's song, *American Tune,* there is a line, "Still when I think of the road we're traveling on, I wonder what went wrong." For a full-fledged baby boomer like me, that road began in Dallas. Think about it. If Kennedy had lived and been re-elected in 1964 (a good possibility since Goldwater was beaten soundly by Johnson), we would probably have withdrawn from Vietnam. There would have been no war to protest and fifty-eight thousand troops would not have died. It is quite likely that Johnson would have gone to jail for his associations with Bobby Baker and Billy Sol Estes. There would have been no "peace with honor" platform for Nixon to endorse and without Nixon, there would have been no Watergate. The shame of Johnson's and Nixon's presidencies would have never stained our history.

But it did. It shaped the psyche of an entire generation which we, knowingly or not, passed along to our children and grandchildren. Some of us, upon seeing the actions of government, sigh and shake our heads. Others feel the same anger that percolated in the sixties and respond. Democracy was never meant to be a spectator sport.

This book is my response. Although a work of fiction, I have incorporated much of the current research conducted by some courageous and dedicated individuals whose quest for the truth is strong and ongoing. I have listed those books that were most influential to me in the Bibliography.

If you question the relevancy of this topic to the present, just read or listen to the news. Patrick Henry once wrote, "The liberties of a people never were, or ever will be, secure when the transactions of their rulers may be concealed from them."

It's been fifty years. It's time for the truth.

Claudia Turner

November, 2013

Bibliography

Baker, Judyth Vary. "Me & Lee: How I Came to Know, Love and Lose Lee Harvey Oswald." Walterville, OR: Trine Day, LLC, 2010.

Belzer, Richard and Wayne, David. "Dead Wrong: Straight Facts on the Country's Most Controversial Cover-Ups." New York: Skyhorse Publishing, 2012.

Benson, Michael. "Who's Who in the Kennedy Assassination." New York: Carol Publishing Group, 1993.

Brown, Madeline Duncan. Texas in the Morning: The Love Story of Madeleine Brown and President Lyndon Baines Johnson. Conservatory Pr., (1st ed.), 1997.

Crenshaw, Charles A, Hensen, Jens, and Shaw, J. Gary. "JFK Conspiracy of Silence." New York: Penguin Books USA, Inc., 1992.

Crenshaw, Charles A. Hansen, Jens, Shaw, J. Gary. "JFK Has Been Shot." New York: Kensington Publishing Corporation, 2013

Dankbaar, Wim. "Files on JFK: Interviews with Confessed Assassin James R. Files and More Evidence of the Conspiracy that Killed JFK." Independent Publishing Group, 2008.

Davis, John H. "Mafia Kingfish: Carlos Marcello and the Assassination of John F. Kennedy." New York: Signet, 1989

Douglass, James W. "JFK and the Unspeakable: Why He Died and Why It Matters." New York: Simon and Schuster, 2008.

Ernest, Barry and Lifton, David. "The Girl on the Stairs: The Search for a Missing Witness to the JFK Assassination." Gretna, LA: Pelican Publishing Company, Inc., 2013.

Garrison, Jim. "On the Trail of the Assassins." New York: St. Martin's Press, 1991.

Groden, Robert J. "The Killing of a President." New York: Viking Penguin, 1993.

Hancock, Larry. "Someone Would Have Talked." JFK Lancer Productions & Publications, 2010.

Haslam, Edward T. "Dr. Mary's Monkey." Walterville, OR: TrineDay, 2007.

Home, Douglas R. "Inside the Assassination Records Review Board: The U.S. Government's Final Attempt to Reconcile the Conflicting Medical Evidence in the Assassination of JFK." 2009.

Janney, Peter. "Mary's Mosaic. New York: Skyhorse Publishing, 2012.

Lane, Mark. "Plausible Denial." New York: Thunder's Mouth Press, 1991.

Lane, Mark. "Last Word: My Indictment of the CIA in the Murder of JFK." New York: Skyhorse Publishing, 2011

Mailer, Norman. "Oswald's Tale." New York: Random House, 1995.

Marrs, Jim. "Crossfire: The Plot that Killed Kennedy." New York: Carroll & Graf Publishers, Inc., 1989.

McClellan, Barr. "Blood, Money and Power: How LBJ Killed JFK." New York: Hanover House, 2003

Menninger, Bonar. Mortal Error: The Shot That Killed JFK, A ballistics expert's astonishing discovery of the fatal bullet that Oswald did not fire (1st edition). New York: St. Martin's Press, 1992.

Milan, Michael. "The Squad." New York: Berkley Books, 1992.

North, Mark. "Act of Treason." New York: Carroll & Graf Publishers, Inc., 1991

Prouty, L. Fletcher. "JFK: The CIA, Vietnam and the Plot to Assassinate John F. Kennedy." New York: Skyhorse Publishing, 2011.

Russell, Dick. "The Man Who Knew Too Much (2nd ed.)." New York: Carroll & Graf Publishers, Inc., 2003

Sample, Glen and Collom, Mark. "The Men on the Sixth Floor." Grove, CA: Sample Graphics, 2011.

Sloan, Bill. "JFK: Breaking the Silence." Dallas, TX: Taylor Publishing Co., 1993.

Summers, Anthony. "Not in Your Lifetime: The Defining Book on the JFK Assassination." New York: Open Road Media, 2013.

Thompson, Josiah. "Six Seconds in Dallas." New York: Random House, 1967.

Waldron, Lamar and Hartmann, Thom. "Legacy of Secrecy: The Long Shadow of the JFK Assassination." Berkeley, CA: Counterpoint Press, 2008.

Made in the USA
Middletown, DE
16 October 2018